Second-Chance Cowboy

Carolyne Aarsen

&

The Texan's Twins

Jolene Navarro

HARLEQUIN® LOVE INSPIRED®

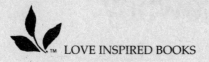 LOVE INSPIRED BOOKS

Recycling programs for this product may not exist in your area.

ISBN-13: 978-1-335-14611-3

Second-Chance Cowboy & The Texan's Twins

Copyright © 2019 by Harlequin Books S.A.

Second-Chance Cowboy
First published in 2017. This edition published in 2019.
Copyright © 2017 by Carolyne Aarsen

The Texan's Twins
First published in 2017. This edition published in 2019.
Copyright © 2017 by Jolene Navarro

www.Harlequin.com

Printed in U.S.A.

Tabitha laid a gentle hand on Morgan's shoulder.

It was only supposed to be a show of comfort. But then he looked over at her, and as his eyes met hers, a quiver of attraction grew deep in her soul.

She didn't want to break the connection. In fact, she wanted to put her other hand on his other shoulder, like she used to. Tease him. Like she used to.

Her breath caught and it wasn't until they were jostled by someone wanting to get past them that the moment was over.

He looked momentarily taken aback as he broke her hold. Then he strode away.

Tabitha struggled with the confusion of her emotions. What was she doing? She had to stay in charge. It wasn't fair to Morgan.

She'd had her chance with him and she'd made her choice.

What if you told him what actually happened and why?

She held that thought as she made her way out the door.

Morgan was gone, and Tabitha knew there was no way she would be able to tell him what really happened. She was on her own.

Carolyne Aarsen and her husband, Richard, live on a small ranch in northern Alberta, where they have raised four children and numerous foster children and are still raising cattle. Carolyne crafts her stories in an office with a large west-facing window, through which she can watch the changing seasons while struggling to make her words obey. Visit her website at carolyneaarsen.com.

A seventh-generation Texan, **Jolene Navarro** fills her life with family, faith and life's beautiful messiness. She knows that as much as the world changes, people stay the same: vow-keepers and heartbreakers. Jolene married a vow-keeper who shows her holding hands never gets old. When not writing, Jolene teaches art to inner-city teens and hangs out with her own four almost-grown kids. Find Jolene on Facebook or her blog, jolenenavarrowriter.com.

CONTENTS

SECOND-CHANCE COWBOY

Carolyne Aarsen

To my nieces, Amber and Chelsey, who inspire me with their loving devotion to their parents.

And with thanks to my nephew, Daniel Aarsen, who helped me with the vet stuff.

Family is everything!

So don't be afraid;
you are worth more than many sparrows.
—*Matthew* 10:31

Chapter One

She was late for work. And not a *sorry I'm late* apology she could toss off while breezing into the café, flashing a contrite smile to her boss as the clock showed a few minutes past.

No, this was a serious, half an hour, *Sepp is going to fire me* late. She knew explaining to him that she was busy laying down flooring in her house until midnight wouldn't cut it. Nor would it help her case to tell him that she had to make a trip to return the nailer she had borrowed from Owen Herne.

Tabitha eased off on her truck's accelerator to make the turn, gearing down as the dust cloud following her seeped into the cab. The engine protested the sudden shift.

Please, Lord, don't let it break down, she prayed, as she shifted down again.

Her phone dinged, signaling an incoming call, then slid out of her purse and onto the floor.

Tabitha glared at the phone, then dragged her attention back to the road. No way was she hitting the ditch for the sake of a phone call.

In spite of being late, Tabitha eased off the accelerator as she turned the corner heading past the old Henry place. No one had lived in that house since Boyce and Cord Walsh bought it three years ago, but she always slowed when she drove by.

She used to dream of living there, pretending the top bedroom with its bay windows was hers and she could look out over the valley to the mountains. She had often imagined herself wandering through the many flower beds, picking lilies, daisies, lupines or lilacs to put in vases in the house. The flower beds were overgrown now, but she could still see the potential.

She preferred that dream to the reality of her place close to town. Work on the house she inherited from her father had taken up every spare moment of her time the past couple of years, and the yard was so messy and filled with junk that even thinking about it was too overwhelming.

Suddenly a large dog bounded across the road in front of her and right behind it ran a little boy.

Her foot slammed on the brakes. She wrenched on the wheel to turn the truck, her backpack falling off the seat. Her phone slid over the floor as her truck crashed into the ditch.

Her ribs hit the steering wheel with a sickening thud and her neck snapped forward. Dazed, she sat a moment, pain shooting through her ribs, radiating up her back.

She sat back, massaging her chest to make sure she hadn't broken anything. All seemed okay.

Then panic clutched her as she looked around to see what happened to the boy or the dog.

Where had they come from? She didn't know people had moved into the house.

Relief surged through her when she saw the boy

standing in the middle of the road, eyes wide, staring at her as her own heart pounded in reaction to the close call.

Then the dog jumped out of the trees and joined the boy, its tail waving joyfully as he ran in a circle around him.

Okay. Boy was fine. Dog was fine.

Tabitha took a few seconds to gather herself, then got out, pain stabbing her chest as she did.

"You okay?" she called out to the kid.

"Yeah," he said, his voice a feeble sound that showed her how afraid he was.

Then the door of the house opened and a man charged out.

"Nathan. What are you doing on the road?" he called, sounding panicked.

Then Tabitha's heart pounded in earnest as she recognized the man dropping to his knees in front of the little boy, running his hands over his face, his shoulders.

Morgan Walsh.

Her ex-fiancé, and the man who still held a large portion of her heart.

As soon as Dr. Waters told her Morgan would be working at the vet clinic, where Tabitha worked part-time as well, she had prepared herself. Had a speech all figured out.

Nice to see you. Hope you enjoy working here.

She'd even decided how she'd look. She'd be wearing her lab coat, making her look all professional and educated, her hair pulled back in a tight ponytail, her makeup perfectly done.

But at the last minute she had chickened out, telling Dr. Waters that she needed the morning off. Truth was she needed a couple more days to adjust to the idea of working with her ex-fiancé.

Morgan was part of her most painful memories. Walking away from him all those years ago was the hardest thing she had ever done. But she had broken up with him for his sake. Now here he was. A veterinarian.

So the sacrifice was worth it. And though she knew she would come face-to-face with him sometime soon, she hadn't figured on it being like this.

With her at the wheel of a truck in the ditch, her hair a tumbled disaster, her ribs aching with every quickened breath.

She gathered her wits, bending over to pick up her phone that, of course, started ringing again. She glanced at the call display. Her sister.

Tabitha tucked it in her pocket, letting it ring as she gingerly made her way through the thick grass of the ditch around the back of the truck, grimacing in pain.

Taking another deep breath, she lifted her chin and walked over to where Morgan still knelt by his son, talking to him.

"You sure you're okay?" Morgan asked again, his hands resting on the boy's thin shoulders.

"I'm fine." The boy wasn't looking at Morgan; instead he was watching Tabitha as she joined them.

Yeah, I know. I probably look like the bad side of a train wreck, she thought, delicately testing her cheekbone to see if there was any blood.

Then Morgan sensed her presence and turned, his hand resting on his son's shoulder in a protective motion. Stubble shaded his cheeks. His brown hair, as thick as ever, curled over his forehead. His blue T-shirt stretched over broad shoulders tucked into blue jeans hanging low on his hips.

He still wore cowboy boots, but the deep furrow between his eyebrows was new as was the length of his hair. He used to wear it military short. But now it hung over his collar.

He had grown more handsome over time, and in spite of her steady self-talk, Tabitha's heart twisted at the sight of his familiar, and once-loved, face.

She knew the second he recognized her. His steel-gray eyes grew cold as ice and he clenched his jaw.

"Hey, Tabitha." His voice was curt. Harsh.

The anger in his expression hurt her more than she thought it could.

"Hey, Morgan." She didn't add "good to see you" because it wasn't that good to see him.

"You almost hit my son."

He ground out the words, his voice gruff. Well, nothing like getting directly to the point, which shouldn't surprise her. She knew seeing him again wouldn't be a happy reunion of old high school friends.

The last time she'd talked to him was on the phone when she told him she was breaking up with him. He'd asked for a reason. All she would tell him was that she was over him, even as her heart and soul cried out a protest at the lies she spun.

Sure, their relationship had been a high school romance, but their feelings for each other had been deep and strong enough that they'd made plans for their wedding.

But on that horrible day she had to push all that aside. Had to prove to him that she wasn't the girl for him and that she had changed her mind about the two of them.

He tried reasoning with her but she wouldn't budge.

And she couldn't tell him why. It was for his sake, she had told herself. She was doing it for him.

Then packed up and left town.

They hadn't spoken to or seen each other since.

Tabitha's phone rang again. She pulled it out and hit Decline. She'd have to call Leanne once she got to town to find out what her sister needed so badly.

"Were you talking on your phone while you were driving?" His words held the sting of accusation.

Tabitha shook her head. Mistake. Her cheek throbbed and she lifted her hand to touch it. It felt warm. It was probably already changing color.

"No." She left it at that. She'd learned too many times in her life that the more she talked, the more trouble she got into.

Case in point: Morgan's mother, who had been her high school teacher and who thought Tabitha was an unsuitable match for her vet-school-headed son. Who had warned lowly Tabitha Rennie, high school dropout, away from Morgan Walsh. He was too good for her, Mrs. Walsh had told her, and Tabitha knew it was true.

Tabitha held Morgan's gaze, then shifted her scrutiny to his son, who watched her with interest.

"You sure you're okay?" she asked Nathan.

He nodded, staring at her as if trying to figure out who she was.

"Good. And your dog is okay?"

Nathan nodded.

"Also good. Glad we don't have to bring you to the hospital or the dog to the vet. Though your dad is a vet, so maybe he could fix it himself. I usually work at the vet clinic, but not today." She caught herself, blaming her chatter on nerves. She was tempted to ask Morgan why he hadn't started work today, like she had been told, but figured that was none of her business.

So she gave the boy a semblance of a smile, then took a step back.

"Do you need a hand getting your truck out?" he asked.

Frankly, given his attitude toward her, she was surprised he offered. But country manners always took precedence over personal feelings when you lived in the ranching country of Southern Alberta. Houses were far apart and people depended on each other for help.

"No. I should be okay," she said with more bravado than she felt.

She got into her truck and waited until Morgan and his son walked away from the road, but they didn't go directly into the house. Instead Morgan stayed by the driveway, watching.

Please, Lord, let me get out of here in one go.

Then she twisted the key in the ignition.

Her truck wasn't its usual temperamental self and the engine turned over only twice before it caught.

She prayed the whole time she had her foot on the gas, her back tires spinning, tossing mud onto the road and spitting it out beside her. Her pride was on the line and she could use a win.

Finally, her tires caught the gravel, spun again, and then with a lurch she was out. She slammed on the brakes and the truck rocked to a halt.

Thanks for that, Lord, she prayed, feeling foolish that she wasted the Lord's time with such trivial things.

But it was important to her to not look bad in front of Morgan. A man who once held her heart. A man she had been forced to toss aside.

She put the truck into first gear and drove past Morgan and his son at a sedate speed.

Both of them were still watching her. One with interest, the other with a frown.

Life had just become much more complicated, Tabitha thought as she stepped on the gas and shifted into second. Hopefully she wouldn't lose her job at the café.

Again.

So, that was over and done with.

Morgan watched as Tabitha's truck drove down the road, a plume of dust roiling in its wake. Since he decided to come back to Cedar Ridge, he knew meeting Tabitha was inevitable. When Dr. Waters told him that Tabitha worked as a vet assistant in the clinic some mornings, he had almost not taken the job.

It was only when he heard she was planning on selling her place and moving eventually that he agreed. He would only have to put up with her for a short while.

"Why were you so mad at that lady?" Nathan asked, watching Tabitha leave as well.

"I wasn't mad," he said, his voice quiet, controlled as he fought down a beat of disgust at his reaction to Tabitha. Since she broke up with him all those years ago, leaving him with an engagement ring and a broken heart, he had moved on. He'd got married to Gillian. Got a degree and a son, whom his wife had kept away from him.

Three weeks ago he buried his wife and got custody of his estranged son.

A lot of changes in his life that had taken up a lot of emotions.

Yet all it took was one glimpse into those aquamarine eyes, one flip of Tabitha's copper-colored hair, one crooked smile from those soft lips for the old flame to reignite.

He had to keep his guard up if they would be working together at the clinic.

"I was scared for you," he said to Nathan, giving him a lopsided smile. "You shouldn't go running out into the road like that."

"I thought Brandy would get run over." Nathan glanced around, looking for the dog that had disappeared again. "Where did she go?"

As if on cue the dog reappeared, bounding over to Nathan, jumping around him, tongue out, tail wagging with glee.

Nathan tried to pet her but the golden retriever wouldn't stand still. His grandmother had given Brandy to Nathan as a puppy but the dog had never been properly disciplined.

Which had made the long drive here from Arizona, where Nathan's grandmother lived, even more tedious.

"That lady sure was pretty," Nathan said in a matter-of-fact voice as he picked up a stick for Brandy to fetch.

"Yeah. She was." That much he could admit.

He had a ton of things to do and to occupy his mind. Getting his son settled in and dealing with the new complication his mother-in-law had thrown at him this morning.

Gillian's mother, Donna, couldn't keep Gillian's other horse, the one she was training when she died, at her place. Could Morgan please help her out?

He would have preferred that Donna simply sell the horse, but when she asked to talk to Nathan, she'd told him about his mother's horse. And suddenly Nathan insisted that Stormy come to live with them at the ranch.

Now he had to find a way to make that happen.

"So should we start unpacking the boxes we put in your room?" he asked.

Nathan tossed the stick and Brandy took off after it. "I guess so," he said, his voice holding little enthusiasm.

"We can finish decorating your room if you want," Morgan said with a hopeful tone. "Hang up some pictures."

This got him a lackadaisical nod as Nathan watched Brandy return.

"Drop it, Brandy," Nathan commanded, but the dog wouldn't relinquish the stick.

"I think we should tie Brandy up again while we unpack," he suggested as he caught the dog by the collar. The dog immediately sat down.

"She doesn't like being tied up," Nathan protested. In fact, he had untied her a few moments ago, which was the cause of Brandy's sudden flight across the road.

"Probably not, but until she gets used to this place, it might be a good idea. You don't want her to get run over." Brandy tugged at Morgan's restraint, but he was used to handling uncooperative dogs and kept a steady pressure on the collar. "Sit," he said, and once again, she did as she was told.

"Can I untie her when I'm done?"

"If you make sure you stay in the yard with her."

Nathan stared at the dog and heaved out a long-suffering sigh. "My mom never made me tie her up."

This didn't surprise Morgan. Gillian had always prided herself on being free-spirited.

Which was probably why she never told Morgan that Nathan was his son until the boy was two years old.

"I know, but we live on a road and we don't want

anything to happen to her." Morgan kept his tone even as he told Brandy to heel and led her back to the rope attached to the veranda and tied her up.

Nathan didn't reply but followed Morgan into the house. He trudged up the stairs behind him, his footfalls heavy. Morgan knew he shouldn't expect more enthusiasm from the boy over the situation. Thanks to Gillian, the kid barely knew him.

Morgan and Gillian had met during his first year of vet school. She was in town to compete in a rodeo. They fell hard for each other, got married quickly, and then, after a year, she left him, claiming that she didn't want to be tied down.

Gillian moved back to her mother's place in Idaho and returned to the life she'd lived when she and Morgan had met. Driving around the country, pulling her horse trailer behind her, entering any rodeo she could.

Two years after she left Morgan, he found out, via her mother, that he and Gillian had a son. A five-year-long battle for visitation rights followed soon after.

For some reason, Gillian kept Nathan away from him with her constant movement, chasing her dream of being a champion barrel racer. Gillian's mother had no explanation either since she had become as estranged from her daughter and grandson as he was.

Then, this spring, as Gillian was competing in a rodeo up in Grande Prairie, her horse's feet went out from under him around the second barrel. Gillian fell beneath him and, in a freak accident, was crushed and in a coma. Gillian's mother, Donna, had flown in from Idaho to be at her daughter's bedside and was with her when she died hours later. Donna had also arrived with Nathan.

Thus it was at the hospital, at his wife's bedside, for

the first time in the seven years Nathan had been alive, Morgan finally met his son.

They were complete strangers to each other. It was a horrible time. Nathan was withdrawn and grieving and clung to his grandmother, the only other person he was familiar with.

While Morgan was tempted to leave Nathan with Donna, he also knew the sooner he could take care of his son, the sooner they would bond.

And he also knew he needed to come back to a place where he had family and community.

Cedar Ridge.

So he contacted Dr. Waters, the local vet, about a job and managed to snag a commitment. He was supposed to start today but he'd asked if he could begin tomorrow instead.

He and Nathan had moved back to Cedar Ridge only yesterday and were barely unpacked. He wanted to spend one more day with Nathan before he went to school. Though it would be a scant three weeks before school was out, Morgan wanted to get Nathan used to the kids he would be attending school with. That way September wouldn't be as much of a shock.

Thankfully Morgan's father lived in Cedar Ridge and was willing to let Nathan come to his place after school. Cord and Ella, his brother and his fiancée, had also offered assistance as needed.

It was a patchwork support system but it would do for now.

He hoped by the time summer vacation began that he would have found a nanny or someone to help out.

"So, it's a good thing that Uncle Cord and Auntie Ella came to help us get the house organized yesterday," Morgan said to Nathan with forced joviality. "I'm sure you'll get to be good friends with your cousins Paul and Suzy."

"I never met them before." Nathan's tone indicated that he didn't care if he ever met them again. He flopped on his back on the bed, staring up at the ceiling as if the conversation was now over.

"But you'll get to know them better," Morgan replied, struggling once again with a sense of sorrow. Ever since he met Nathan, the boy had been prickly and angry and rejected every advance Morgan made.

He knew Nathan was grieving and confused and upset, and that it would take time. Morgan tried hard to understand but each rebuff was like a blow.

"When do I get to see Gramma again?" Nathan asked.

"In a couple of weeks." Donna had asked if Morgan would be willing to drive down to Idaho for her fiftieth birthday and he had agreed. The counselor he talked to had underlined the importance of maintaining contact with the one constant in Nathan's life. "But for now, let's see about making this room cozier." Morgan pulled out his jackknife to cut the tape on one of the few boxes of personal items Nathan had.

Nathan charged to life and yanked the box away from Morgan. "Don't touch my stuff," he cried.

"I was trying to help," Morgan said.

"Don't need your help." Nathan pushed the box under his bed, grabbed the other two larger ones and pulled them closer.

Morgan was too taken aback at the fury in his son's voice to reprimand him.

"Okay. You can put what you want in the dresser.

There are hangers in the closet for your other clothes. Any toys you have can go in the toy box."

"Toys are for babies" was all Nathan said, shoving his hands in his pockets as he turned away from him.

His rejection was like a hit to the stomach. Morgan waited but Nathan didn't turn around.

So he left, closing the door behind him. He leaned against the wall, dragged his hand over his face and uttered a prayer for strength and patience. He simply had to give him time.

For now, Morgan had his own unpacking to do.

He was fortunate that his father owned this house, giving Morgan a place to stay. The house had been part of a ranch that Boyce and Cord had purchased a few years ago and his father was willing to subdivide the acreage and sell it to him.

And thanks to his share of Gillian's life insurance policy and his own savings, he had a down payment to put on the place. The irony of it all hadn't escaped him. Gillian had given him more in death than she had in life.

Morgan pushed away from the wall and headed down the hall to finish setting up his bedroom. The bed, dresser and the bedside table his father and Cord had picked up at a yard sale were the only pieces of furniture in a room that looked like it could house a small family.

While he worked, Morgan listened for any sounds coming from Nathan's room.

Nothing

He was finished putting his own clothes away when his cell phone rang. It was his father.

"So, does the place feel like home yet?" Boyce Walsh asked.

Morgan looked around the bare room and chuckled. "Let's just say I'm unpacked."

"It's a start. Do you want to go out for supper?" his father asked. "I don't feel like cooking and I'm sure you don't either. We could meet at the Brand and Grill."

He hesitated. "What about the pizza place?" He wasn't so sure he wanted to meet in the same place he knew Tabitha worked.

"I hate pizza. Ate too much of that in my bull-riding days."

Morgan had to smile. His father often used his bull-riding days as a convenient excuse.

"Isn't there another place we could go?" Morgan said.

"We could do Angelo's but it's too quiet."

"Guess it's the Brand and Grill, then."

His father was quiet as if acknowledging how difficult going there could be for him.

"May as well get it over with," Boyce said. "You're going to run into Tabitha sooner or later."

"I suppose."

"Good. I'll see you and Nathan then." His father hung up and Morgan tucked his phone into his pocket, blowing out a sigh.

He certainly hadn't figured on seeing Tabitha twice in one day.

He would see her at the clinic tomorrow as well. Maybe the more often he saw her, the quicker he would get used to seeing her around.

And the quicker he could relegate any feelings he still had for her to the past, where they belonged.

Chapter Two

There they were again.

Tabitha hung back, hiding behind the wall of the kitchen as she watched Boyce, Morgan and Morgan's son, Nathan, walk into the café.

Seriously? Twice in one day?

She rolled her eyes heavenward as if asking God what He was trying to tell her.

"You going to just stand here daydreaming?" Sepp Muraski growled at her. "We got customers and supper rush is starting."

Tabitha gave her boss a forced smile. Sepp glared back at her, his dark eyebrows pulled tight together, a few curls of brown hair slipping out from under the chef's hat he wore over his hairnet.

Some might consider him good-looking. Tabitha didn't, and she suspected that was the reason he was always so grouchy with her. She had turned him down twice and he hadn't seemed to have forgiven her.

"On it," she said, straightening her shoulders and sending up a quick prayer for strength, the right words and attitude.

She would need all that and more after her encounter with Morgan and his son this afternoon.

The Walsh men were already seated when she approached them, coffeepot in one hand, menus in the other.

"Coffee?" she asked as she set the menus down in front of them.

"I'd love a cup," Boyce said with a grin, pushing his cup her way. "Pretty quiet in here," he said, making casual conversation.

Boyce stopped in at the Brand and Grill from time to time, as did Cord, Morgan's brother, so Tabitha was accustomed to seeing Walshes around. But she still had to fight a sense of shame every time she saw Boyce. She felt like she had a huge *L* written on her forehead because of the money her father had cheated Boyce out of.

I'm working on repaying it, she reminded herself, thinking of the renovations she was doing to the house she'd inherited from her father. Each new cabinet, each piece of flooring, each lick of paint made the house more sellable, which would mean more money to give to Boyce to repay him for what her father had done.

Then she could tackle the yard, a job that seemed so daunting she avoided thinking of it most of the time.

"It will get busier," Tabitha said as she turned to Morgan. "Coffee?"

He just nodded, looking at the menu.

Okay. She could do the avoiding thing too. She glanced over at Nathan, who was looking at her. "Can I get you anything?" she asked him.

"You're the lady that almost ran over Brandy," Nathan said, his tone faintly accusing.

"Not quite," she said, her ribs still sore from hitting

the steering wheel of her truck. "How is your dog?" she asked.

"She's fine." Nathan just held her gaze. "I got the dog from my gramma and soon I'm getting a horse too." His eyes brightened for a moment.

That was some generous gramma, Tabitha thought.

"What horse is this?" Boyce asked as Tabitha poured Morgan his coffee.

"Gillian's horse," Morgan put in. "She was training it before…" He paused, glancing over at Nathan.

She quickly spoke up with forced cheer. "So, Nathan, we have chocolate milk, orange juice and pop. What can I get you to drink?"

"Chocolate milk," he said, looking down at the menu again.

"Be right back." She scurried off to take care of that. She snagged a coloring book and a pack of crayons, wondering if he was too old for that, but she figured it was worth a try.

When she came back, Boyce and Morgan appeared to still be talking about the horse Nathan was expecting.

"You could get the horse trained?" Boyce said.

"But who could do it?" Morgan asked.

"My mommy was training it already." As he spoke Nathan looked more animated than he had in the past few minutes. "She loved that horse. Said it would be a real goer."

"Here's your chocolate milk," Tabitha said to Nathan. "And I thought you might enjoy this."

She set the crayons and coloring book in front of him. To her surprise, he grabbed them and opened up the book.

"Tabitha knows about horses and horse training,"

Boyce said suddenly, looking up at her. "She could help you out."

Tabitha shot him a horrified look. What was he trying to do? Surely he knew the history between her and his son?

"Would you be able to train my mom's horse?" Nathan chimed in, looking suddenly eager as he leaned past his father. "I so want to be able to ride Stormy."

Tabitha felt distinctly put on the spot. And from the glower on Morgan's face, she suspected he felt the same.

"I'm pretty busy," Tabitha said, and that wasn't too much of a stretch to say. "Two jobs, and I'm renovating the house."

"We can find someone else," Morgan said, giving his father a knowing look.

"Tabitha is capable."

"She said she was busy."

Morgan's dismissive tone shouldn't bother her. It was better for everyone if they kept their distance. Though his mother, with her relentless disapproval of Tabitha, had passed away many years ago, the shame of what her father had done to his hadn't.

When Floyd Rennie left town three years ago, he had also left a number of citizens of Cedar Ridge high and dry when he decamped with money they had invested with him for the building of a new arena. It was all part of Cedar Ridge's great hope to become part of the Milk River Rodeo Association circuit, thereby raising the profile of their local rodeo.

The arena was only half completed when her father left, taking the investors' money with him.

The most prominent of whom was Boyce Walsh. Morgan's father.

Her father died a year later, leaving Tabitha the house she was working on now. She had hoped to sell it but the real-estate agent said she could get double for it if she fixed it up.

So she began working on it in her off-hours. But it was taking much longer than she'd hoped.

"There's not many people close by who can do horse training," Boyce put in, clearly unwilling to let either Morgan or Tabitha off the hook.

"Amber could," Morgan said.

"And you know your twin sister is busy with her own life," Boyce said. "Nor is she living in Cedar Ridge."

"So, are you ready to order?" Tabitha said, pulling a pad of paper and pen out of her apron. She really needed to change the topic of conversation. Morgan clearly didn't want her around and she had no intention of spending more time with any member of the Walsh family than she needed to.

They gave her their orders and she hurried off to give them to Sepp.

"You sure were hanging around that table a long time," he grumbled. "We got other customers, you know."

She ignored him as she set up the coffeemaker to make a fresh pot of coffee. She knew well enough not to engage with Sepp.

"I don't pay you to hang around and bug the customers." He had to get one more jab in before she left.

She wished she could quit, she thought as she cleared a table, trying not to take her anger out on the hapless dishes. She wished she could walk away from Cedar Ridge. Leave it and everything it represented behind her.

But she needed the job to pay for her house renovations. She was going to finish what she had started, and she knew she couldn't leave town with her father's debt hanging over her head.

She shot a glance over at the Walsh table just as she caught Morgan looking at her. She flushed and spun away carrying the dirty dishes back to the kitchen. Adana had finally shown up and she was flirting with Sepp, who didn't seem to be in any rush to get the Walshes' orders done.

"My last order ready yet?" she asked.

"It's ready when it's ready" was all he said. "Scared I'm going to make you look bad in front of your old boyfriend?"

She knew not to say anything more. Sepp was the most passive-aggressive person she knew and the more she pushed him, the worse he would get.

A few more customers came in and Adana took their orders. Finally Sepp was done with Boyce and Morgan and Nathan's food.

"Service is getting kind of slow around here," Boyce said as she set their food on the table.

"I'm so sorry," she said, knowing she couldn't shift the blame.

"I'd say Sepp needs to hire more waitresses but I know he already has enough," Boyce continued.

Again, she could only nod as she put Nathan's burger and fries in front of him.

"Is there anything else I can get you? More coffee? Chocolate milk?"

She looked over at Nathan, who was staring at her. "Grandpa Boyce says that there's not too many people who can train horses here and that you can. Are you sure you can't?"

Were they still on that topic?

Tabitha's resolve wavered as the boy's eyes pleaded silently with her.

"Miss Rennie has other things she's busy with," Morgan said, looking at Nathan, his voice gentle. But she heard a warning in the words.

Stay away from my son.

"I'm sorry, honey," she said, giving him a look of regret. "Working here and at the clinic and fixing up my house keeps me very busy."

Then she walked away. She couldn't get involved though she felt very sorry for the little boy. She only knew snippets of the boy's story. His mother spent most of her time chasing her rodeo dreams and dragged him along. He didn't seem connected to Morgan, which made her wonder what had happened between Morgan and his wife.

Not that it mattered to her. Morgan was part of her past. She had her own plans for the future. And they didn't include sticking around a town that was such a source of pain and humiliation to her.

She couldn't afford any distractions and Morgan and his son were a huge one.

"Will you be okay?" Morgan knelt in front of Nathan on the floor of the school's hallway, handing him the backpack he had painstakingly packed this morning. Young kids ran past them, calling out to each other, their voices echoing in the busy hallway, bumping them in their rush to get to their own classes.

Yesterday morning he and Nathan had visited the school to see about enrolling him for the last few weeks of Grade Two. Though he still had his concerns, he had to think of what the counselor had told them after Gillian's death. That it was important that Morgan and Nathan find their new normal as soon as possible.

Thankfully Nathan hadn't objected to going to school, and if Morgan was honest with himself, it gave both of them a break from each other. Taking care of a seven-year-old was way out of his comfort zone. Especially a sullen young boy who rejected any advances Morgan made to him.

"This is a good school," Morgan said, injecting a bright note of enthusiasm in his voice. "I used to go here when I was a kid."

Nathan took the backpack without looking at Morgan, saying nothing.

Morgan reached out to lay his hand on his son's shoulder but Nathan pulled away, then walked into the schoolroom and went directly to his designated locker.

"You can come in with him, if you like," the perky young woman encouraged with a bright smile. "I know it's his first day here."

Just then Morgan caught Nathan looking at him, eyes wide, shaking his head a vehement "No."

Really? He couldn't even do this for his son?

He wished it didn't hurt so much.

"I think I'll stay here to see him settle in," Morgan said.

"Of course." He could tell the teacher was puzzled, but he was fairly sure she dealt with a variety of parents, so he tried not to take Nathan's clear-cut rejection to heart.

He watched a few more moments as Nathan trudged to his desk, then sat down, holding his pencil case that they had bought yesterday, looking down.

Morgan's heart broke at the sight but he felt stuck. Nathan didn't want to spend time with him, and Morgan wanted to get started at the vet clinic as soon as possible.

Wednesday, at the Brand and Grill, was the last time he'd seen Nathan act with any kind of animation when he was talking to Tabitha. Which made him nervous, especially because ever since then, the only thing Nathan would actually talk with him about was training his mother's horse so he could ride it.

And getting Tabitha to do it.

There was no way he could allow that. He didn't think he could be around Tabitha that much and, more important for his son, he didn't want him to build a connection to someone who was leaving soon.

As he drove to the clinic he found himself praying. Again. Something he'd been doing a lot lately.

Gillian's death, gaining custody of Nathan, moving back here had all taken a toll on him. Never mind working with his ex-girlfriend, whom he would be seeing again in a few minutes.

Help me to stay focused on what I need to, he prayed. *I need to be emotionally available for Nathan and protect him.*

As for his own heart, he could take care of that. The grief he had felt after Tabitha broke up with him had morphed into fury, which had settled into a dull resignation. Then Gillian came into his life and things took an entirely different twist.

His heart would be okay, he told himself. It had to be.

He checked his watch, once again thankful that Dr. Waters kept such strange hours. 9:30 seemed late to open a vet clinic but he wasn't complaining. It meant he could bring Nathan to school and still arrive on time at work. And maybe cover the occasional emergency that came up before opening hours.

He turned the corner to the vet clinic and saw Tabitha's truck parked out front.

When Dr. Waters gave him the key to the clinic yesterday, he had planned to come early. Though Dr. Waters had assured him that Tabitha, Cass and Jenny mostly manned the front desk and took care of dispensing, Morgan preferred to know where everything was himself.

He had also planned to establish his territory, so to speak, before Tabitha came in. Make the clinic his.

And now here she was already.

He sighed, sent up another prayer and headed to the back door. It was locked, so he used the key Dr. Waters had given him. He stepped inside the large open room where they worked on horses and cows. It smelled like disinfectant, and though the metal dividers for the various pens were rusted, he could see they were clean.

The rubber floor matting was also hosed down, water still trickling into the floor drain.

His footsteps echoed in the large empty space as he made his way down the concrete hallway and then through another door into the clinic proper.

He paused in the hallway, getting his bearings, then heard humming coming from one of the rooms farther down.

Tabitha, he guessed, feeling an unwelcome tightening in his chest.

He was surprised at the flicker of annoyance her obvious good mood created. Clearly she was in a good place in her life. Why that bothered him he didn't want to analyze.

She was the one who walked away from you, he reminded himself. *Of course she wouldn't pine after me.*

Like you are for her?

Not likely. She had taught him a hard lesson. He had to take care of himself and those who belonged to him.

Like Nathan.

The thought of his son was a good reminder of where his priorities now lay. And sending up another prayer for strength, he strode down the hallway.

Tabitha was working in the supply room, her hair pulled back in a loose ponytail, the early-morning sun from the window behind it creating a halo of light around her head. She was making notes on a clipboard, her lips pursed, her forehead wrinkled in a frown.

He wanted to make a joke but found himself momentarily tongue-tied, which, in turn, created a low-level frustration. Even after all these years and after all his tough self-talk, why did she still have this effect on him?

She turned around and saw him. The humming stopped as her mouth fell open and her hand clutched her chest.

"My goodness. You scared me," she gasped. "I wasn't expecting anyone this early."

"I thought…" His voice faltered and he cleared his throat. "I thought I would come in early. Get myself acquainted with the place."

"Sure. Of course. I understand." She tucked her hair behind her ear. "I'm doing some inventory."

"Okay. That's good." He wanted to say "carry on," but that would sound patronizing.

"Would you like me to show you around?" she asked, her gaze flicking from her clipboard to him.

"I guess that would be helpful."

"I can bring you up to speed on some of the animals we have staying here. Let you know what kind of work we do. In case some of it might be new to you." She stopped there, flushing.

"Sure."

She nodded and he waited, an awkward silence falling over them. "Right. I should do that now," she finally said, dropping her clipboard onto the counter in front of her. It fell and she bent over to pick it up exactly the same time he did. Their heads hit and pain jolted through him.

"Sorry," she muttered, rubbing her head just as he rubbed his.

Morgan sighed as she carefully set the clipboard on the shelf. This was getting more and more awkward. He was about to say something but she was already swishing past him, her lab coat flaring out behind her.

"The treatment rooms are here and here," she said, pointing left and right, like a flight attendant indicating escape routes, as she scurried down the hall ahead of him. "There's only two. We should have more but Dr. Waters is thrifty. Supply room you've already seen. And here's where we house the animals we've treated." Tabitha opened the door to the large back room and stepped back.

Morgan frowned as he stepped inside the dark room with its crates stacked one on top of the other.

"Looks kind of depressing." Morgan couldn't believe that there wasn't even a window or a skylight.

And it didn't smell very good.

"Do the cages get cleaned?" he asked, stopping by one of the crates, which held a Labrador pup with a plastic cone on its head. The puppy was asleep and Morgan reached between the bars and laid his hand on the dog's stomach. It was not overly warm and breathing properly.

"Of course they do. Every day."

From the defensive tone of Tabitha's voice, Morgan guessed she was the one who did the cleaning.

"The building is old and the smell tends to linger," she continued.

"Sorry. I didn't mean to imply that you're neglectful." He looked back at Tabitha, who stood in the doorway, her arms folded over her chest, her chin up, gaze challenging.

"So what's with this little guy?" he asked, pointing to the Lab.

"Hernia operation. He's due to go back today."

"And this one?" He pointed to a cat who lay on its side, one leg extended out in front of it, bandaged.

"Severed tendon on his foreleg. Got on the wrong side of a grain auger. He's lucky to be alive."

"How much small-animal work does Dr. Waters do?" Morgan glanced around the rest of the crates but they were all empty.

"Not as much as he'd like. He prefers the small animals to the large ones. I guess that's why he hired you."

Morgan nodded, remembering the conversation he and Dr. Waters had had. "And what's the large-animal patients consist of?"

"It used to be mainly cattle, but with more people moving in and more acreages sprouting up around town and people getting horses, he's doing more equine. That's my specialty but he prefers to do that on his own."

Her comment puzzled him as did the faintly bitter tone in her voice. "What do you mean, your specialty?"

"Doesn't matter. I'm just the vet assistant," she said, with a bright smile as if trying to show him she was making a joke. "We don't have specialties."

"But clearly you do," he said. He found himself suddenly curious. The last he'd heard, she had quit high school. When he found out she was working at the clinic, he had assumed it was only as a general helper.

"I went back to school a few years after I dropped out of high school. Got my high school diploma, then went to college and graduated as a veterinary assistant and equine specialist. I'm not such a dummy." She flashed a bright smile, but behind it he sensed an air of defensiveness.

"I never said you were," he returned, holding his hands up.

"Not all of us can get into vet school, but some of us can make something of ourselves."

Her tone puzzled him and he found himself wanting to ask why she'd quit school.

What he really wanted was to ask her why she'd dumped him so casually.

He pushed that last thought back into the dusty recesses of his mind. Clearly he had to do more work to let go of the past and the hurt Tabitha had caused him. *One step at a time*, he told himself.

"Well, I'm glad you did. Never could figure out why you dropped out in the first place."

She looked like she was about to say something. But then the back door opened and Dr. Waters's and Jenny's voices broke into the conversation and signaled the beginning of the workday.

Tabitha spun around, striding back down the hallway, leaving Morgan confused and upset. How was he supposed to make a new start in this town when the harshest memories of his past were right here in the form of Tabitha Rennie?

Okay, Lord, You brought me here. You'll have to help me out.

His prayer was raw and rough. But it came directly from his heart. Because without God's help, he didn't think he would be able to do what he needed to do.

And that was keeping his focus on his son. He had been given a second chance with Nathan and he wasn't going to mess it up.

Not even for Tabitha.

Chapter Three

"C'mon, Tony. Since when did you need money up front from me?" Tabitha leaned on the counter, flashing a teasing grin at the young man behind the counter of Walsh's Hardware Store. "You know I'm good for it."

It was Monday morning and Tabitha had sneaked out on her coffee break to order her kitchen sink.

Morgan hadn't looked pleased at her departure, but since he'd started working at the clinic, that seemed to be his default emotion.

She knew he was stressed. Moving back home, trying to deal with a kid he barely knew. That had to be hard.

Plus, he didn't seem too happy with the fact that they had to work together. Until her house was finished, there was nothing she could do about it either.

She had kept herself busy on Saturday after working in the clinic, putting the final coat of paint on the spare room of the house, which had been her father's old room. On Sunday she stifled her guilt and put in some of the casings and baseboards, electing to stay busy and away from church. That was the trouble with a small community like Cedar Ridge. There were too many opportunities to run into people you wanted to avoid, and right now she wanted to avoid Morgan.

Besides, the sooner she got this house done, the sooner she could sell it and move on. Being around Morgan was harder than she'd thought it would be and she didn't need that extra stress in her life.

Tony nervously rearranged the ball cap he perpetually wore on his head, looking over his shoulder as if to see if the owner, George Walsh, might have made a surprise visit.

"Yeah. I know. It's just…well…your last check bounced."

"I told you why. Sepp didn't pay me on time. That's hardly my fault and I need this sink to finish the renovations on my kitchen." It had taken her a few late nights on Pinterest and home reno sites to figure out exactly which sink would fit in her kitchen. All she needed now was to order it, but Tony was being troublesome and she couldn't charm him out of it.

"I know." Tony tugged on the bill of his cap again. "Trouble is, the owner found out about the check and told my boss, Mrs. Fisher, that any more orders from you need to be prepaid."

"How did George find out?"

"He was going over the books with Mrs. Fisher and saw it. That's when he told her and she told me."

And there it was again. The ever-present Walsh influence pushing, once again, at the Rennie fecklessness.

I'm not my father, she reminded herself, stifling a far-too-familiar flush of shame. *And I'm trying desperately to fix what he broke.*

She knew it would take more than the sale of the

land and the house to make up for the thousands of dollars her father had stolen from people. But it was all she could do at this moment. And she was determined to do it right.

But if she didn't get the sink ordered, she couldn't finish her kitchen, which meant she couldn't sell the house.

Despair threatened to wash over her, and she struggled to push it back. One step at a time. And the way things were going, she wasn't sure when she could get more money. Sepp kept cutting back her hours because he claimed Adana needed them more.

She wanted to yell at him but she had no other options. Dr. Waters had made it very clear that now that Morgan was working at the clinic, the possibility of full-time work was gone.

No one seemed to need her.

"Well, I guess when you own the store, you can do what you want," Tabitha said with forced humor.

Tony shrugged.

"I'd still like to put in the order for the sink, and when I get enough together to pay for it, I'd like you to put it through," she said with more confidence than she felt.

"You don't have to pay it all," Tony said. "Just half."

Which she didn't have either.

"Just give me the total amount so I know how much I'll need." Brave talk, she thought as she gave him a cautious smile, then left. She knew exactly how much the sink, tiles and countertop would cost and how many shifts it would take her to earn that.

Too many. And now that Sepp had cut her hours back, she wasn't sure how she was going to ever catch up. Her wages at the Brand and Grill and the vet clinic covered her daily expenses. She depended heavily on her tips for the extras.

As she walked down the street to her truck, she fought down her anger at Sepp's unreasoning dislike of her, and at a father who had let her and her sister down so badly.

She checked the time and hurried her steps. She made quick work of getting to the clinic and slipping inside.

"Anything happen while I was gone?" she called out to Jenny as she pulled on her lab coat.

"Nope. Pretty quiet. Morgan went out. He got a call from the school about Nathan acting up," Jenny said as Tabitha joined her in the front office. "Asked me not to tell Dr. Waters, so I'm hoping he stays away on his call long enough for Morgan to come back." She tut-tutted her disapproval. "Dr. Waters has already made a lot of concessions for him. Only the second day on the job and already—"

She stopped talking as the front door opened and Morgan stepped inside, looking harried.

"Everything okay?" Tabitha asked.

His eyes looked at her, then looked away. "Yeah. Fine."

The curt tone in his voice told her that, clearly, everything was not fine. So did the frown on his face.

Don't engage, she told herself, *He clearly doesn't want my help.*

"You don't look fine," Jenny pressed. "Everything go okay with Nathan?"

Morgan shook his head, the look of concern on his face making Tabitha feel bad for him. "He's been having a hard time at school," he said. "I knew it would be a difficult transition for him, but he seemed excited about it at the time. He's just having trouble settling in."

"Moving to a new school is tough," Tabitha added. "I feel sorry for the little guy."

"I'm sure you would know what he's dealing with," Morgan said.

His admission and the faint smile accompanying it startled her. It was the first hint of softness she'd received from him. For a moment she longed to explain to him what had happened all those years ago, but she quashed that. It was so long ago it hardly mattered anymore. Besides, even if she did tell him, that didn't change the fact of what her father had done to his father. That couldn't be explained away. She could only fix things by staying on the course she had set for herself.

Then his cell phone rang and Morgan looked at the call display. "Sorry, gotta take this." He answered the phone as he walked away.

Jenny watched him go, then sighed. "That poor man. He's got a lot to deal with. Must be rough being a single parent. Too bad there's not some single girl for him." She looked over at Tabitha. "Actually, I heard a rumor the other day that you two used to date."

Date was hardly the word for the deep and abiding feelings she had felt for Morgan, she thought with a touch of melancholy.

They had made plans to get married. Move away from Cedar Ridge. Start a new life away from the expectations of his mother and the reputation of her father.

"That was a long time ago," Tabitha said. "It was just a high school fling."

No sooner had she spoken the words than Morgan

stepped into the room. From his expression, she guessed he had heard her.

Then the door flew open and a woman rushed in. "My cat got attacked by a dog." Tabitha recognized Selena Rodriguez, an older woman who owned the Shop Easy. She looked around, eyes wide, her long graying hair damp but pulled up in a clip.

Morgan hurried over, pulling a pair of latex gloves out of his pocket, and did a cursory exam of the cat. "I'll take him," he said and glanced over at Tabitha. Cass, the other vet assistant, had left on a job with Dr. Waters, so it was on her to help.

She knew it would happen sooner or later that she would have to work closely with Morgan, and she thought she was prepared for it.

But when she stood across from him at the exam table, their faces covered with masks with only their eyes visible, she felt a momentary discomfort. She was close enough to see the fan of wrinkles at the corner of his eyes. Smell his aftershave. He smelled different, took up space in a different way. His shoulders were broader, his hair longer.

Regret washed through her. What if she hadn't listened to his mother all those years ago? What if she'd had enough confidence in her feelings for Morgan?

But she hadn't and she didn't, and she couldn't spend her life living with regret over might-have-beens.

Then her training took over and she pushed her own emotions aside. *He's not for you. There's too much between you*, she told herself.

Then together they started an IV to anesthetize the cat, then intubated him. As they fell into a routine, and she began prepping the sites, she looked at him as just another vet stitching up some cuts on a cat.

"Looks like we got done on time." Cord dropped his hammer into the hook on his pouch as a dually pickup pulling a stock trailer roared onto the yard. "Here comes your horse."

It was Tuesday evening, and Morgan and his brother had just finished fixing up a makeshift corral to hold Gillian's horse, Stormy, until Morgan could figure out what to do with it. Cord had offered to board it at the ranch, but Nathan had protested loudly. He wanted Stormy on the yard.

So for now, he would keep it here and feed it hay. Not the best solution, but his bigger concern was for Nathan more than the horse.

"I sure hope those old posts hold," Cord said as they watched as Ernest, who drove the truck, turned and backed up to the gate.

Morgan gave his brother a look. "You were the one who assured me they would be strong enough."

Cord punched him lightly on the arm with one gloved fist. "I'm just bugging you. Relax."

"Don't know how to do that anymore," Morgan muttered, looking over at his son, who stood by the fence fairly vibrating with excitement. It was the happiest Morgan had seen him since he got here.

"How are you two getting along?" Cord questioned.

Morgan thought of the boxes the boy still hadn't unpacked. The phone calls with the teachers this afternoon. They had found Nathan in the bathroom, huddled in a stall, crying.

Morgan had been in the middle of a C-section on a

cow and couldn't come to school, and Nathan wouldn't talk to him on the phone. So Morgan had called his father, who lived in town. After Boyce picked him up, he called to tell him that everything was okay. He and Nathan were having cookies and milk, and another crisis had been averted.

"Step by step" was all he could say, something that applied to his job, it seemed, as well as to his relationship with his son. "I don't suppose you know anyone who could work as a nanny."

Cord just laughed. "I had my own struggles and then Ella came into our lives." He grinned at him. "So that's your solution. You need to find a wife."

"No, thanks. Already had one and you saw how well that worked out. Besides, Nathan is my priority and I'm having a hard enough time connecting with him."

Cord looked at the boy leaning against the fence, watching everything with interest. "Give it time. He's been through a lot and he's probably confused. Plus he's still grieving for his mother."

Morgan nodded. But there was no more time for conversation. The trailer had backed up and the truck engine turned off.

Ernest came around to the back of the trailer, hitching up his baggy pants, his eyes bright under unkempt eyebrows. "Well, she's a feisty one," he said with a grin. "Took two guys to get her haltered and loaded. Watch out for her hooves when you go inside."

"Maybe let me unload her," Cord said, holding up his hand to stop Morgan.

Morgan looked at Nathan, who was intently watching the proceedings.

"No. I need to do this," he said, yanking on the door's

latch, slipping it up and pulling open the sliding door. Nathan needed to see him leading the horse.

As soon as he stepped inside, Stormy whinnied, her eyes wide, ears pinned back, her back foot striking hard at the wall of the trailer.

"Easy, girl," Morgan said, walking slowly toward her, pushing down his own trepidation. A horse like this could be unpredictable and therefore dangerous in such a small space.

Stormy stepped back, trembling now, head up and ears still back as he came closer.

He saw Cord peering in the side of the trailer and, in spite of his concern, he had to grin. Big brother watching out for him.

"It's okay, girl. I'm going to untie you and lead you out of this trailer." He pitched his voice low. Quiet. Hoping it would settle the horse down.

He carefully untied the rope. She jerked back, the rope slipped in his hands, and then, before he knew what was happening, she landed on her front feet and hit his shoulder as she shot past him out of the trailer and into the corral.

"You okay?" he heard Cord call out.

"Yeah. I'm fine." His pride was hurt more than his shoulder.

He stepped out in time to see Stormy charging around the corral, rope trailing behind her as Cord rushed to close the gate. Appropriate name, Morgan thought, rubbing his shoulder. Before anyone could stop him, Ernest jumped over the corral fence and snagged the halter rope. Stormy pulled away, Ernest pulled back, and then the horse was suddenly still.

Nathan, unaware of what was going on, laughed,

clapping his hands at the sight as he watched through the railing.

"Looks like this horse will need some training," Cord said.

"Grandpa Boyce said that Miss Tabitha knows how to train horses," Nathan put in. "He said my dad should ask her but she said she was busy and my dad said we would find someone else."

Morgan had to stifle a beat of frustration with his father. He knew about his previous relationship with Tabitha. Why did he keep pushing?

Then Ernest joined them, leaning one elbow on the rail, tugging on his mustache. "She's a good horse. Good feet. Good conformation. She's jumpy, though."

"I want to ride her," Nathan said, watching Stormy as she now stood, her sides heaving with exertion.

"You won't be riding her for a while," Ernest warned, shaking his head. "That horse needs a firm but gentle hand and a lot of training."

"And you can't do it?" Morgan asked. Ernest had trained a number of horses. Though he hadn't for some time, Morgan thought it was worth asking.

Ernest pulled in a breath, then gave Morgan a look tinged with regret. "No. That's a young man's game and I don't have it in me anymore. Have you asked Tabitha? I helped train her. She's a natural, though she hasn't done much of it since she moved back here."

Again with Tabitha?

"Not an option" was all Morgan would say.

"Will I never be able to ride my mom's horse?" Nathan said, his chin now trembling. He looked up at Morgan, who was disconcerted by the tears in the boy's eyes.

"We'll figure something out, Nathan," Morgan

said, kneeling down and catching his son by his narrow shoulders. "Don't worry. You'll be able to ride her. Just not right away."

"So Miss Tabitha will train her?" Nathan asked, wiping his tears away with the back of one dusty hand.

"I said we'll figure something out" was all he said. Though he didn't like the way the conversation was going, at least Nathan was talking to him. That was a plus.

Nathan nodded, seemingly satisfied with this answer.

"I better clean out that trailer and get on my way," Ernest said, pushing away from the fence. "Nathan, you want to help me?"

"Sure." Nathan scooted past Morgan looking happier than he had in a while.

Morgan waited until he was out of earshot, then turned to his brother.

"So what do you think I should do?" he asked. "That horse isn't rideable and Nathan seems to think it might happen."

"A horse you can't ride is taking up space and eating valuable hay," Cord said, ever the practical rancher.

"But Nathan seems attached to the beast because it belonged to Gillian." Morgan sighed, resting his arms on the rail, watching the horse going round and round the pen. "He's the most enthusiastic when he talks about that horse. Nice change from the slightly depressed kid I usually see. But I can't find anyone to train it except, it seems, for Tabitha." He sighed again. "And I'm not sure I want to go down that road. Bad enough I have to work with her. At least at the clinic there are boundaries."

"If she is training this horse, she'll need to be working with Nathan."

Morgan sighed. "I know, but truth is, I don't think she has the time. She's working two jobs and renovating her house."

"Probably just as well." Cord held his brother's gaze as he released a hard breath. "She broke your heart once before. Word on the street is that she's only in town long enough to fix up that place her dad left to her and sell it. She'll take the money and move on, just like her dad. You've got a kid now. He's what you have to think about. Keep Tabitha in the past, where she belongs."

"I think I can handle myself with Tabitha," Morgan returned, feeling a surge of frustration that his brother seemed to think one look into those blue-green eyes would turn him into a mindless lunatic.

Cord nodded, as if he didn't believe his brother's protests.

"I'll get the rest of the fencing stuff" was all Cord said.

But as his brother walked away, Morgan pondered Cord's words. Worst of it was, even in spite of his tough talk, he knew his brother was right.

Fool me once, he thought, heading over to where his son was chatting with Ernest.

He couldn't afford to trust so blindly again.

Chapter Four

Sepp looked up from scraping the deep fryer, glowering at Tabitha as she dropped a couple of mugs by the dishwasher. "Kind of dead this afternoon." His voice was accusatory. As if it was her fault.

"For a Wednesday afternoon it sure is," Tabitha agreed, reminding herself to stay pleasant.

"You may as well go home." Sepp looked back at what he was doing. "No sense paying you to hang around if there's so few customers."

"Things might pick up," she said, trying not to sound too desperate. Any tip she might get, any dollar she made, brought her that much closer to getting her kitchen finished.

"If they haven't by now, they won't in half an hour," he snapped. She wanted to argue but she knew better than to contradict Sepp and cross him when he was in an ornery mood.

Instead she pulled off her apron and set it in the laundry bin, then took her backpack off the hook at the back of the kitchen. "I'll see you tomorrow morning, then."

Sepp stood back from the fryer. "You don't need to sound so testy."

Tabitha pulled in a slow breath, seeing the banked anger in Sepp's eyes. The past few days he'd been sniping and griping at her even more than usual.

"I'm sorry. I'm just tired." She worked on the house until late last night again, putting in the last of the casings and baseboards to finish up the bedroom.

"Tired from hanging around with Morgan Walsh?"

She tried not to roll her eyes, but as she looked at him, she realized maybe that was his problem. He was jealous of Morgan.

"Morgan is the last person I want to be with on purpose." That wasn't entirely true. She had already spent a week working with Morgan, and each time she saw him it became harder to maintain her distance.

"So, you're not seeing him?"

Tabitha blew out a sigh. "No. I'm not."

He nodded. "So then, are you free Friday night?"

Tabitha could only stare, not sure which of his questions disturbed her more. The one about Morgan or the one asking her out.

"I'm busy. I'll always be busy for you." Too late she realized that she had overstepped a boundary she kept scrupulously in place. She had always been evasive with Sepp, cautiously refusing his advances. But she had never been this rude with him.

"Okay. Well, then maybe you don't need to bother coming in for a while."

Tabitha stared at him, suddenly tired of his machinations, his threats and his borderline obsession with her. As long as she kept turning him down it would never end. He would cut her hours back and back. And she was sick of it.

"Well, I won't bother coming in at all, then. I quit." She wished she hadn't already taken her apron off. It would have given her the perfect dramatic exit. Pull off apron. Toss it aside. Turn and storm away without a backward glance.

Instead she shifted her backpack on her shoulder and strode away.

But as soon as the back door of the café slapped shut behind her, dread flooded through her. What had she just done? Quit the job that paid her the most money?

How was she supposed to pay for the rest of her house renovations now?

She leaned against the exterior of the café, the stucco digging into her skin through her shirt. Now what was she going to do?

"I'm sorry, but I'm wondering if it's in Nathan's best interests to be in school right now. It's almost the end of the school year, so he won't miss much." The Grade Two teacher, Miss Abrams, gave Morgan a gentle smile, as if to soften her words. She glanced over at Nathan, who sat hunched on the cot in the school nurse's office, his arms wrapped around his legs, staring out the window. "He's had a lot to deal with the past few months. He's a smart boy. In my opinion he might be better off to spend time with you at home."

She sounded so reasonable and Morgan could hardly fault her for her advice. But how was he supposed to do that?

Morgan looked over at Nathan, who wasn't looking at him. He wasn't crying now but had been an hour ago. Morgan had been out of cell range, working in a farmer's back field on a sow that had farrowed, and she and her newborn piglets had been attacked by a coyote.

By the time they got the sow fixed up and carted on a trailer with her piglets back to the farmer's yard, he was back in service. Then his cell phone dinged steadily with messages from the school. He tried to call his father but he wasn't around. Neither were Cord or Ella. So he told Dr. Waters he had to go to the elementary school, earning him a scowl and a slight reprimand.

He knew it didn't look good. Barely a week on the job at the vet clinic and things were falling apart for him at home. But what else could he do?

"If that's what you think should happen," Morgan said.

"I do," Miss Abrams said. "I know it's not an easy solution, but Nathan needs some time with you more than he needs school right now."

Morgan stifled another sigh. Part of him knew she was right, but he wasn't sure how this was going to work.

"I'll take him home," Morgan said. He put his hand on his son's shoulder and, to his surprise, the boy didn't flinch away. He looked up at Morgan, looking so bereft Morgan knelt and pulled him into his arms.

Nathan stayed there a moment, resting his head against Morgan's neck. His son, he thought, a rush of pure joy flowing through him.

But then Nathan pulled back, withdrawn again.

"We're going back home," Morgan told him.

"Which one?"

The question hit Morgan like a blow. He knew Gillian had moved around a lot. Had his son no sense of which place was home?

"We're going to the ranch. Where Stormy is."

His face lit up at that. "I really want to see Stormy again. I think she misses me when I'm in school."

"Maybe she does."

He picked up Nathan's backpack and held out his hand, but Nathan jumped off the cot and hurried ahead of him toward the door.

Morgan thanked Miss Abrams and, as they walked back to the truck, Nathan smiled. "I'm excited to ride my mom's horse," he said, looking ahead as if imagining himself doing so.

"I'm sure you are," Morgan said. The school counselor he had spoken to before he picked Nathan up had mentioned that the only time Nathan seemed to show any life was when he talked about his mother's horse. She suggested that Morgan let Nathan fantasize about the horse and riding it. Affirming his comments, she said. Morgan wasn't entirely sure how to go about that, so he figured he would treat Nathan's suggestions like he had his twin sister Amber's when they were growing up. Agree and nod and smile.

"But I can't until Stormy is trained," Nathan said.

"That's true."

Nathan said nothing. Instead he stared out the window.

"I have to stop by at the clinic for a minute," Morgan said. He had forgotten to write down the billable hours for the call he did this morning.

Nathan just nodded. At least he wasn't crying.

Morgan pulled up to the clinic, dismayed to see

Tabitha's truck parked there. What was she doing back here? He thought she worked at the café in the afternoon.

"Isn't that the truck of the lady who almost ran over Brandy?" Nathan asked.

"Yes. It is," Morgan said.

"Her name is Miss Tabitha, isn't it? And she works at the café? She gave me a coloring book and crayons even though I'm not a little boy. But it was nice. And Grandpa Boyce says she's the lady that trains horses."

"Yes. Miss Tabitha does train horses," Morgan answered. "But she's very busy working for Dr. Waters and Mr. Sepp at the café." Morgan hoped he got the hint as he helped him out of the truck.

Nathan walked ahead of Morgan, skipping a little, looking a lot happier than he had in a while. Guess sending him to school hadn't been such a good idea after all. Guess he wasn't much of a father for not knowing that.

Morgan opened the door and, as always, his eyes had to adjust from the bright summer sun to the windowless back room with its pens and gates. He wondered why Dr. Waters hadn't at least put a skylight in here. Or replaced some of the penning. One of these days some animal was going to lose it in here and bust one of the rusted posts.

"Wow. What do you do here?" Nathan asked.

"This is where we work with cows and horses and bigger animals like that."

Nathan nodded as he followed Morgan through another door and down the hall to the front office, checking out the posters of dogs and cats and various other animals lining the walls between rooms.

In the office, Tabitha stood by the desk, talking to

Jenny, her one hand pressed to her cheek, her other clutching her elbow. She looked like she'd been crying.

"I doubt Dr. Waters will give you more hours," Jenny was saying.

"Why should he? He barely gives Morgan enough. Dr. Waters is running around like a fool himself, losing business because he can't keep up. Makes me wonder why he hired Morgan in the first place."

"Are you kidding? Who in Cedar Ridge would ever say no to a Walsh?"

"And who would say yes to a Rennie? We both know what my father's reputation has done for my sister and me. Now that I quit the café, how am I ever going to pay off my bills and finish that wretched house? And I still have a ton of cleaning up to do." She stifled another sob, pressing her hand to her mouth.

Morgan held back, realizing he had stumbled into a very personal but potentially disturbing conversation. He gathered that Tabitha had lost her job at the café. But what surprised him more was his reaction to her tears. He wanted to rush into the room and pull her into his arms. Comfort her like he used to whenever she was upset.

He was about to back away and wait until those impulses passed, but Nathan had finally caught up to him. He saw Tabitha and went running past Morgan into the room.

"Hi! You're Miss Tabitha, aren't you?" he said, smiling up at her.

Tabitha's reddened eyes grew wide as she looked from him to Morgan, who now stood in the doorway. She spun away, swiping at her face.

Morgan shot a warning frown at Jenny, who wasn't

looking at him either. He guessed she wasn't too proud of her "he's a Walsh" comment.

Nor should she be. Morgan liked to think that his high GPA, his stellar reputation at his previous vet clinic and his strict work ethic had been the reason Dr. Waters hired him.

Not his last name.

"Why is Miss Tabitha crying?" Nathan said, turning to Morgan. "Why is she sad?"

"I'm okay." Tabitha sniffed, then turned back to Nathan.

"I was crying too," Nathan said, looking back at Tabitha. "I miss my mommy and I want to ride her horse but I can't."

Tabitha gave him a wavery smile and touched his head lightly. "I'm sorry you can't." Then she looked puzzled. "And why aren't you in school?"

He shrugged, suddenly very interested in the hem of his worn T-shirt. "School makes me sad," he said, twisting it around his hand. He managed to poke a hole in it and wiggled his finger through it, making it bigger. "So my daddy says I don't have to go anymore."

"But who will take care of you?" Tabitha glanced over at Morgan, who simply shrugged. He wished he knew too.

Just then Cass came into the office and dropped a file on the desk. She looked around. "Am I missing something?"

Jenny stood and nodded at the other vet assistant. "Why don't you take Nathan to see the new puppy we're taking care of?"

Cass frowned, and then Jenny raised her eyebrows,

motioned her head down the hall, and suddenly Cass seemed to get whatever hint Jenny seemed to be giving.

"Nathan. Do you want to see an adorable Labradoodle puppy?" Cass said, sounding puzzled but obviously going along with whatever Jenny seemed to be planning.

Nathan grinned. "Labradoodle. That's a funny name." But he willingly trotted along behind Cass.

"So. Tabitha just lost her job at the café." Jenny turned to Morgan. "And now you have your son, who can't go to school and who, in my opinion, probably shouldn't have been going to school. The other day you were asking me for names of a nanny and Tabitha was asking me if there's anyplace that's hiring. Seems to me we have a solution to two problems in one right here."

"Wait a minute—"

"But—"

Both Morgan and Tabitha spoke at once. Jenny held up her hand. "Do you have a nanny for your son? Do you know of anyone who can do it for you? I know you're willing to pay decent money because you told me so."

He realized the sad truth of what she was saying. "No. I don't." He felt like a kid being quizzed in school and sensed where Jenny was going. But he wasn't going to be the first to say anything. Ten years ago Tabitha had roundly rejected him. He wasn't about to allow her to do it again on purpose.

"Tabitha, you just came back from walking around town trying to find a job. With no success." She held one hand out to her and the other out to Morgan. "Morgan here needs a nanny. You need a job." Jenny wove her fingers together, indicating a perfect fit. "Voilà. Both problems solved."

Morgan could see Tabitha was fighting her own reaction to the situation. He wished it didn't bother him that she was so reluctant to help. But at the same time, he knew he was being hypocritical. He wasn't keen on her spending time with his son either.

She glanced over at him, her eyebrows lifted in a question. "What do you think? Do you trust me to take care of your son?"

"Guess I have to," he said.

He knew he could sound more gracious than that, but Jenny was right.

He didn't have a choice.

Chapter Five

"Have you seen my mom's horse?" Nathan asked Tabitha after he was done with his lunch. He was sitting at the kitchen island, head propped in his hands, elbows resting on the high counter as he watched Tabitha clean up the kitchen.

Tabitha had arrived at the house early this morning determined to create a good impression. Morgan was also ready to go and he had given her cursory instructions. It wasn't hard to tell that he was still reluctant to have her in his house, yet they both knew Jenny had been right.

They needed each other.

"No, I haven't," she said, tidying up the papers spread out over the dining room table. She and Nathan had spent the morning going over the assignments the school had emailed to Morgan and that he had printed out. Her heart had sunk when Morgan had informed her that he hoped she would help Nathan with his schoolwork. Just to keep him up to speed.

Tabitha had reluctantly agreed. Thankfully he was only in second grade and she had managed to get him to read all his assignments aloud to her as they worked through them.

Nathan didn't seem to notice any hesitancy on her part. He seemed happy enough to be at home instead of school.

Now he was bouncing his head in time to the country music Tabitha played on the radio in the kitchen, ketchup from the macaroni she had made him streaked on one cheek, his long hair sticking up. He needed a haircut but there was no way she was taking care of that. Morgan seemed hesitant enough to have her watch Nathan. She got it, she really did. Because she felt the same reluctance and it only grew with each minute she spent with Nathan. Being around him all morning had created an unwelcome pang of sorrow. Made her wonder what kind of children she and Morgan would have had.

"I haven't," Tabitha said again, taking his plate from him.

"Can we go see her now? I'm done with all my work."

"Is she here?"

"Mr. Ernest brought her here on Tuesday." He grinned, swiping his sleeve over his mouth, moving the ketchup smear to his shirt. Tabitha made a paper towel wet and walked around the island.

"We can go see her, but first let me wipe the ketchup off your shirt," she said.

He held out his arm and she cleaned it as best as she could. The shirt was worn and thin. So were his pants. Tabitha wondered again why Morgan hadn't purchased any new clothes for him.

She looked around the house again at the sparse furnishings of the spacious, open-plan home. A large leather sectional and a television on a wooden shelf were all that filled the living room. An old worn table and four folding chairs huddled around it in the dining area.

Nothing hung on the walls. There were no curtains at the window. It broke her heart. She had imagined the interior of this home so many times, but never in all her dreams did it look this bare and unwelcoming.

She knew Morgan wasn't short of cash. When he told her what he was willing to pay her, she was surprised. Pleased, but surprised. And she'd had to swallow her pride and thank him for it.

All for the cause, she reminded herself.

"Can you wipe my cheek too?" Nathan asked, holding his face up to her. "I think I have ketchup on it too."

She cupped his chin in her hand and gently wiped the remnants of the smear off his cheek. The smile he gave her created another tremor of sorrow at the thought of might-have-beens with Morgan.

She pulled back with a start. She couldn't let this little guy into her heart.

"Let's go see your horse," she said. Nathan jumped off his chair and ran out the door, leading the way.

She followed him across the cracked sidewalk then down a worn gravel path to the corral. Brandy the dog had jumped up from her place in the sunshine and followed them, her tail waving. Nathan ran ahead, the dog at his heels, and Tabitha smiled at the sight. Life distilled to its essence, she thought, watching as Nathan stopped and petted Brandy, then hurried on.

A large bale of hay with a fork stuck in it sat by the corral where a gray horse stood, head over the fence, looking expectant.

"She's always hungry," Nathan said, walking over

to her. But the horse shied away when he came near. "And I don't think she likes me."

"She doesn't know you yet, that's all," Tabitha said, coming closer to the fence. She leaned her arms on the top rail, warmed by the sun. A delicate summer breeze rustled the leaves of the trees surrounding the corral and teased her hair away from her face. Between working at the veterinary clinic and her job at the café and renovations on the house in the few hours she could carve out, she didn't get to spend much time outdoors. "What's her name?"

"Stormy," Nathan said. "Morgan said I can't ride her yet."

"This is the horse you wanted me to train?" she asked, watching as Stormy trotted around the corral, head up, eyes wide.

"Yes." Nathan grabbed her arm. "You're here now. Why don't you train her?"

"I haven't gotten permission from your father to do that." He hadn't seemed crazy about the idea of her training the horse before.

"But you're here now."

"I know." And if she was honest, the horse made her curious. She had trained horses with Ernest, and each time a new horse came on his yard, she felt a tiny rush of energy. What would this horse be like to work with? What was its personality? Its strengths and weaknesses?

She felt the same questions now as she watched Stormy striding back and forth. She had a lovely gait and would make an excellent riding horse.

"But she's my mom's horse, not my dad's…not Morgan's." His voice took on a petulant tone but Tabitha caught the faint hesitation before he spoke Morgan's name.

"Why don't you call Morgan Dad?" she asked.

Nathan looked down, his mouth forming a hard line. "My mom said he wasn't a good dad. He didn't keep his promises."

She wanted to ask but part of her felt a need to keep a distance.

Don't get involved. You can't fix this.

It broke her heart but she knew she had to maintain some emotional distance. This time she was determined to leave Cedar Ridge with her heart whole. She couldn't do that if she got too close.

"I can have a look at her, I guess," Tabitha said, climbing over the fence, watching her to see how Stormy would react. The horse immediately jumped to one side, trembling as she stood.

She turned to the dog, who sat beside Nathan. "Brandy, you stay." The dog looked at her, then lay down. "Make sure that the dog doesn't come into the pen, okay?" she said to Nathan.

He nodded and squatted down beside Brandy, holding her by the collar. Tabitha waited but it looked like the dog understood her command.

Tabitha turned back to Stormy as she walked to one side of the pen, her eyes on the horse, keeping her distance for now. Stormy shied again. Tabitha spent a few minutes observing and she could see the horse relax.

She waved her arms and Stormy ran to one corner, but Tabitha kept pushing her and Stormy started moving. Tabitha had never worked with a horse in a square pen before and was unsure, but when Stormy moved into the corner, Tabitha waved her arms at her again and thankfully Stormy kept moving.

"Why are you scaring her?" Nathan called out.

"This is what horses do in a herd," she said, keeping the horse going, wishing she had a stick to wave around as well to help guide her. "They chase the horse away so the horse understands who's in charge, and that's what I'm doing here." She kept the horse moving, watching for cues that the horse was ready to "talk" to her. "See, when horses are in a herd they have to work together, but to work together, they have to listen and obey the boss horse. Stormy needs to know I'm the boss."

"But don't you want her to be your friend?" Nathan asked, sounding concerned.

Tabitha chuckled at that. "See, that's the difference between Brandy and Stormy. Brandy is looking for a friend. Stormy is looking for a leader. Two different animals, two different things."

Stormy went around a few more times and Tabitha felt distracted, watching to make sure Nathan and Brandy stayed, that the horse didn't push the fence, and yet keeping up her momentum.

But Nathan seemed content to stay beside his dog. Then, after a few more go-rounds, Tabitha saw Stormy slow, drop her head and start the chewing motion that signaled her willingness to now "talk" to Tabitha.

Tabitha stopped in the middle of the pen and Stormy turned to her. Perfect. Just what she wanted. Tabitha waited where she was, talking to Stormy, and then, to her surprise, the horse walked directly to her. Tabitha reached out and laid her hand on Stormy's neck. She felt a tiny tremor, a little rejection, but Stormy stayed where she was. Clearly someone had done some work with her already.

"Good girl," Tabitha cooed, slipping her hand over her neck, then down her back. "Good girl."

She turned to show Nathan, and her heart jumped. Morgan was walking down the trail toward the pen. And he didn't look pleased.

"Tabitha, what are you doing?" Morgan kept his voice low when he saw that Tabitha was looking at him.

"Working with Stormy." She held her chin up, holding his gaze, but she sounded defensive.

He was about to ask her if she knew what she was doing, but with that crazy horse standing quietly beside her as Tabitha turned back to her, stroking her, the question was useless.

Clearly she did.

After Cord and Ernest had dropped Stormy off, the horse had kicked at the fence, bared her teeth at Morgan when he tried to come close and, in general, acted like a horse who was asking for a one-way ticket to the auction market.

It was because Nathan saw this horse as a tangible connection to his mother that Morgan knew he would never get rid of the animal.

"Well, I'm impressed," he said.

His words seemed to surprise her. He suspected she assumed he would say something entirely different. And he might have but for the evidence in front of him.

"This is only a small step," she said. "But an important one."

"Do you think she's trainable?" Morgan asked, glancing down at Nathan. But his son's eyes were fixed on Tabitha and Stormy and didn't even look at him.

His rejection, as it always did, cut him deeply.

"I believe she is," Tabitha said. "She's a beautiful animal with a lot of potential."

Nathan jumped up and, to Morgan's surprise, grabbed his hand, getting his attention. "I want Miss Tabitha to train Stormy so I can ride my mom's horse."

He looked down at Nathan and curled his fingers around his hand, thankful for this tiny connection. As he held Nathan's pleading gaze, he knew he couldn't say no. Initially he'd had his concerns about Tabitha training Stormy because it would mean her spending more time with Nathan.

Well, that was a moot point now that she was taking care of him.

"Do you think you can get her close to rideable before you leave?" he asked, flicking his gaze to her.

Tabitha looked back at Stormy, whom she was still petting, then back at him and gave him a curt nod. "I can make her rideable for an adult. But before a kid can mount her, we're looking at time and miles by an adult."

"I can take care of that," he said. He'd spent enough time on the back of a horse to know what was required.

"Then I can do this." She petted the horse, looking around at his yard. "There is one problem, though. This corral doesn't look very strong and I'm wondering about pasture."

He was well aware of both problems. "This was strictly temporary," he said. "Until I could find someone to train her."

"Well, now you have. But I was wondering if you would be willing to move her to my place. I can work with her better there in my round pen, and I have a decent fenced-in pasture."

"But I won't be able to see her if you take Stormy to your place," Nathan cried out.

"I could take Nathan with me in the afternoons I'm working with him," Tabitha suggested.

"Yay! That would be so cool," Nathan said, still clinging to Morgan's hand. "Can we do that? I really want to go to Miss Tabitha's place."

"You've never been there," Morgan said with a gentle smile.

"But I think it would be cool. And Miss Tabitha is fun to be with."

Morgan knew he didn't have a lot of choice. Nathan's life had already been tossed around enough and he seemed to have formed an attachment to Tabitha.

Which was exactly what he was afraid would happen.

He looked over at Tabitha, surprised to see a tender smile on her face as she looked from him to Nathan. Then Brandy jumped up, barking at who knew what as she ran toward the house, and Nathan ran to follow her.

Tabitha petted the horse one more time then walked to where Morgan stood. "I understand your concerns," she said. "I know you're scared he'll connect with me and I'll leave him in the lurch when I leave. I get that. But I promise you I'll be careful with him. I won't hurt him."

Morgan held her earnest gaze, and in spite of what had happened and what she had done, he felt a softening of the barrier he had placed around his heart.

Her green eyes, the way the sun shone on her copper hair, making it glint like a precious coin, brought back memories of happier times. For a moment they were younger, breathless, blissfully happy simply being together.

"I'd like to believe you." He meant to speak the words

in anger. Push her away. But to his disappointment they came out like a request.

"You can," she said, a shadow of pain flitting across her features. "I know you have every reason not to trust me, but on this you can believe me. I'll be careful with your son."

He held her gaze a split second longer than he should. Allowed himself a moment of remembrance, and then he pulled back and nodded. "Okay. I believe you."

"Thanks." She released a shaky breath that made him wonder if she was as unsettled around him as he was around her. "So now we need to make arrangements to move Stormy to my place," she said.

"I'll give Ernest a call. See if he can do it sometime this week."

Tabitha looked back at Stormy, who still stood, watching, as if gauging what she was up against. Then Tabitha climbed over the fence. Morgan had to clench his fists to stop himself from helping her over. Given his current state of mind, he was afraid he would hold on to her too long.

But she was up and over and walking ahead of him before he could give in to the temptation. "So why aren't you working now?" she asked, glancing at him over her shoulder as he easily caught up to her.

"Dr. Waters told me he would take care of the calls for the afternoon."

She rolled her eyes in response. "He is such a funny little man. Why would he do that? He often has to turn down calls."

"It makes me nervous that I'm on the job barely a week and he's already cutting back my hours."

"I think he needs to know he can trust you with his

clients," Tabitha said. "He's often bragged how he built up this practice one customer at a time. Often berated me and Jenny and Cass for not taking good enough care of them."

"I suppose," he said, though he wasn't entirely convinced that was true.

"Or he could see you as a threat." Tabitha smiled as she said the words, but Morgan wondered if that wasn't closer to the truth. But he wasn't sure what he could do about that. Some of the clients he worked with had made veiled comments about Dr. Waters and his abilities, but he had ignored it, considering it the usual gossip that happened in a community.

"Well, I'll just have to keep plugging," he said. "I'm sure he'll come around. I may be a Walsh, but I still need the job."

She shot him a quick look. "I'm guessing you overheard my comment and I'm sorry. Just feeling…bitter, I guess."

"I understand. I know some of the Walshes haven't always treated you that well."

"Given what my dad did, you can hardly blame them."

Morgan was about to tell her that wasn't what he was referring to but just then Nathan came running toward him, Brandy at his heels. His blue jeans were torn at the knees and the laces of one of his running shoes had come loose. But he was smiling for the first time in a while.

"Hey, son, your shoelace came undone," Morgan said.

Nathan looked down and stopped. Morgan walked over, knelt and tied it up for him. "There. All fixed."

Nathan frowned as he looked over at Morgan's feet then Tabitha's. "How come you both wear cowboy boots and I have to wear sneakers?"

"You don't have to wear sneakers," Morgan said, settling back on his one leg.

"But I don't have any cowboy boots."

"Well, we'll have to buy you some," Morgan said.

"Can we go now?"

"Right now?"

Nathan nodded, his eyes bright with anticipation. "I'm done with my work and you're done with your work and Miss Tabitha is here and we can go together to town."

"I don't think Miss Tabitha will want to come," Morgan protested.

"But I want her to. She can help me pick out boots."

Tabitha lifted one shoulder in a questioning shrug. Morgan had managed to find a tiny place of peace with Nathan. A moment of happiness. It seemed like his son wanted Tabitha along.

Well, if that was what it took to keep a smile on his son's face, so be it.

"Okay. If Miss Tabitha doesn't mind…" He looked her way, surprised to see her nodding.

"I'll follow you in my truck."

"No. You ride with us," Nathan insisted.

The uncertainty on Tabitha's face mirrored his own. But taking two vehicles to town would be wasteful. "Just come with us," he said. "It'll make things easier."

For another second she hesitated, and then, seeming to see the wisdom in that, she nodded. "I'll just get my backpack and we can go." She walked into the house and returned a few moments later.

"Still no purse?" he asked as she slung the knapsack over her shoulder and walked toward his truck. He was fairly sure it was the same one she used to carry to school every day in high school.

"I like the freedom of packing whatever I need for the day on my back."

"You figuring on running away?" He hadn't meant to tease her. He blamed it on spending so much time with Tabitha. It was as if he was slipping back into his old habits.

"No. I've always liked to know that whatever I need I have with me. Survival technique from my days with my dad, I guess." She tossed the words out so casually but it reminded him of snippets of things she had told him about growing up. How often they moved. How quickly she had to be ready to leave.

She looked away and quickly got into the truck before he asked more questions or opened the door for her. Like he used to do.

Instead he opened the back door of the truck cab for his son and he clambered into his booster seat.

"I'm so excited to get some boots," he said as he tugged on the strap and buckled himself in. "I want some like Miss Tabitha. Or maybe some red ones." He grinned, and Morgan felt a delightful warmth sift through him. Nathan seemed a lot more relaxed than he had yesterday.

Then Nathan looked at him, his smile still in place. "I'm happy Miss Tabitha is coming with us."

Morgan nodded, his good mood cooling a little.

"Me too," he said with a forced grin.

But then, as he walked around the truck and got in, he glanced over at Tabitha, who was looking down.

Her hair had slid over her face, as she rifled through her backpack and pulled out her phone and studied the screen, as if avoiding looking at him.

He thought of what she'd said earlier. About her father.

"You know, I apologize for not saying anything sooner, but I was sorry to hear about your dad's passing."

Her hands stopped flicking over the screen and she looked over at him. "Thanks."

"I know it was a few years ago, but it still must be difficult at times."

"It can be. But sometimes I wish my dad looked out for me and Leanne the way your parents did for you. Especially your mother."

"What do you mean?" he asked.

"Nothing."

She turned away but Morgan sensed there was more to her comment than she let on.

But he knew he would get nothing from her now, even though the faint bitterness in her voice made him wonder what she referred to.

Chapter Six

"I like *these*." Nathan grabbed a pair of blue boots with a gray shaft and held them up to Tabitha for her inspection.

"You should ask your father," Tabitha said, pointing her chin to Morgan.

"I don't know if they have those in your size," Morgan said, hating to take the smile off his son's face.

"Can you see if they do?" Nathan handed him the boot, and for a fleeting moment Morgan caught a glimpse of yearning in his face. But it disappeared so quickly, he thought he might have imagined it.

"Is there anything I can help you with?"

Lorn Talbot's voice broke into the moment and Morgan spun around, still holding the boot Nathan had given him. The middle-aged man wore metal-rimmed glasses, his hair brushed neatly back, his shirt cinched with a narrow tie. When he smiled he showed the crooked teeth that gave him a faint lisp.

"If you could find a pair of these boots in my son's size, that would be great," Morgan said, holding out the boot.

Lorn looked momentarily taken aback. Then his polite smile reappeared. "Oh yes, I had heard that you came back with a son."

As if Morgan had picked Nathan up from the side of the road. Or at a souvenir shop.

"Let's first see what size he is." Lorn moved past Morgan and snagged a large metal plate he remembered Mr. Talbot using on him whenever he was due for new boots or shoes.

He got Nathan to stand on it, measured his foot then sat back, his arm resting on one knee. "You're in luck, boyo. I think we might have a pair left like that in your size."

Tabitha stood to one side, and as Lorn got to his feet, he glanced her way. "Ah, Miss Rennie. Did you come to pay your dad's bill?"

Lorn turned to Morgan, still grinning. "Floyd, Tabitha's father, ordered three pairs of boots before he did his own boot-scooting-boogie out of town. Guess his boots really were made for walking, except he didn't pay for them."

Morgan stifled a groan at Lorn's bad jokes. Then he saw Tabitha's features harden.

"I'm sorry my father did that to you," Tabitha said, her voice stiff, her hands clenched at her sides.

"All part of running a business, hon," Lorn said with a grin, clearly showing that there were no hard feelings. "Sometimes you're the windshield, sometimes you're the bug." Then he sauntered off to get Nathan's boots.

Tabitha gave a tight grin but it wasn't hard to see her discomfort.

Morgan wasn't sure what to say but it bothered him to see her so upset and clearly embarrassed.

"What your dad did is no reflection on you," he said, giving in to an impulse and laying a hand on her shoulder. "You can't take all his mistakes on."

Tabitha took a breath and he felt her relax under his hand. "It's hard not to feel the humiliation of it."

"I can understand that," he said, not moving his hand. "But you have nothing to be ashamed of."

"Thanks," she said, her voice quiet as her eyes locked on his. "That means a lot."

Their gaze held for a few heartbeats longer.

Morgan tightened his grip on her shoulder, and as he lost himself in her eyes, he felt an inexpressible compulsion to kiss her.

Whoa. He was approaching dangerous territory.

Then Lorn returned and thankfully the moment was broken.

"Look at my boots." Nathan held one foot out for their inspection.

"They look great," Tabitha said, stepping away from Morgan. "How do they feel?"

Nathan strutted back and forth in the store, and when he returned, he dropped on the chair, tapping his toes together, looking proud of himself. "I'm so excited to wear these when I go riding."

"It will be a lot of fun when that happens," Tabitha said, affirming his comment.

"Thanks for your business," Lorn said as Morgan tucked his wallet back in his pocket. Then he turned to Tabitha. "And I'm sorry for what I said about your father. Was trying to make a joke and it fell kind of flat."

"Of course, Mr. Talbot. I understand," Tabitha said, giving him a kind smile.

They walked out of the store, Nathan looking down at his boots.

"That was very gracious of you," Morgan said as he held the door open for her. "It bothered me, what he said about your father."

Tabitha shrugged. "He apologized. I have to accept that."

"That's quite something to say," he said.

The flush on her cheeks surprised him. She didn't strike him as the blushing sort.

Nathan stopped in front of another store, looking at the mannequin in the window. "That lady has funny lips," he announced.

Tabitha stopped to look and chuckled with him. "Maybe she's pouting because she doesn't like the clothes she's wearing."

"Do you think that little boy likes his pants?" Nathan asked, pointing to the other mannequin standing beside the female one. "He's smiling."

"I think he does and I think they look nice."

Nathan looked down at his pants, and Morgan, once again, felt a flush of shame at the raggedness of them. But what could he do? Nathan had insisted on wearing them and not the ones he bought for him. "Mine have holes in the knees," he said.

"Well, maybe we can buy you a new pair," she said, glancing up at Morgan as if it was his fault his son looked so shabby.

"Will you help me pick them out?" Nathan looked up at Tabitha with that adoring expression he always seemed to have around her. It bothered Morgan to see the boy so attached, but he understood far too well the hold this woman could have on a guy.

"I guess I can." To her credit, Tabitha tossed a look at him as if seeking permission. All Morgan could do was nod his acquiescence.

Nathan fist pumped, then yanked on the shop's door to go inside.

"I hope you don't mind," Tabitha said, lowering her voice as Morgan held the door open for her.

"Not at all. Maybe if you help us pick out some new clothes, he might actually wear them," he muttered.

Tabitha frowned her puzzlement as they followed Nathan into the store.

"I bought him new clothes when I picked him up from his grandmother's place," he explained. "But he won't wear them."

"Well, that makes a lot more sense," Tabitha said with a gentle smile.

"What does?"

"Why he's dressed the way he is."

"What? You thought I preferred that my son go around looking like a little homeless boy?" Morgan couldn't keep the offended tone out of his voice.

"Actually, I thought you might not notice. Which surprised me. Considering how you always dressed so nicely."

"Past tense?" he teased as they walked to the back of the store where the kids' clothing was located and Nathan stood waiting for them.

She flicked her gaze over his cowboy hat, twill shirt and worn jeans. "I like this look better." Then their eyes met and Morgan felt it again.

That faint quiver of renewed attraction. A gentle back and forth of flirtation.

"I like these pants," Nathan said, pointing to a pair of blue jeans.

To Morgan, the pants with their pre-ripped holes didn't look much different than the ones Nathan already wore. But at least these weren't as faded.

"I think they are cool, but what do you think about these?" Tabitha suggested, steering him toward another pair without rips or holes. "You probably want something different than what you already have," she said. "That way you have some choices of what to wear."

"Okay."

And that was that. Though if Morgan had his way, he would get rid of the worn and ripped blue jeans Nathan wore as soon as they got home.

"Does Dad have a budget?" Tabitha asked, shooting him a teasing glance. "Just wondering how much we can load onto the credit card."

"No budget," he said with a dismissive wave of his hand, adding a grin. "But remember, these days I seem to be only a part-time veterinarian."

Tabitha made a sympathetic face. "We'll try not to bankrupt you."

"Your generosity astounds me."

She just grinned, then turned to his son. He stood back as Nathan and Tabitha picked out two more pairs of blue jeans, a couple of pairs of cargo shorts, some T-shirts and, after some long deliberation, a cowboy hat. It was only straw but Nathan was thrilled with it.

"Thought you weren't going to bankrupt me," Morgan laughed as he pulled out his wallet again.

"Nothing a couple more hours at the vet clinic won't cover." Tabitha looked over at Nathan, who was clutching one of the crinkly bags and grinning from ear to ear as he led the way back out of the store. "I'm sure Dr. Waters will come around sooner rather than later and you'll be able to pay off your credit card."

"Hope so. But I guess I can be thankful I can spend more time with Nathan for now."

"He seems…distant with you, if you don't mind my saying," Tabitha said.

"We're struggling."

Nathan looked so happy, however, that Morgan felt a tiny flicker of hope. Maybe, in time, they would become more connected.

"Time and miles, Ernest always says," Tabitha said as if she had read his mind. "That's the best way to connect with a horse and, I suspect, with a son you barely know."

Morgan held her gaze, recognizing the wisdom in her words. "Thanks."

She returned his look, and again, he found himself unable to look away. Unable to break the growing connection between them.

She was the first to turn her eyes away, which made him realize how she was getting under his skin. He couldn't let it happen but he wasn't sure how to stop it.

The hum of the engine was the only sound in the truck on the drive back to Morgan's place. Nathan had fallen asleep, clutching his bag of clothes, his head tipped to one side. Morgan kept his eyes on the road but occasionally she caught him looking at her as if not sure what to do about her.

Tabitha kept reliving the few moments of connection they had shared, wishing she could be stronger. Wishing Morgan didn't still have such a hold on her heart.

She had to keep her focus on what was important, she reminded herself. Not indulge in past fantasies that she had no right to.

But in spite of her self-talk, she still stole a glance over at Morgan, disconcerted to see him watching her instead of the road.

She gave him a tight smile, determined to stay in charge.

"So, Dr. Waters. He's being difficult?" she asked, latching on to a neutral topic, pleased at the conversational tone of her voice.

He shot her a puzzled glance but seemed willing to go along.

"Yeah. I thought he would be easy to work with but he's turning into a problem."

"He's losing business, so I don't see why he's cutting your hours." Tabitha let some of her own frustration with Dr. Waters show. "I know when I first applied, Cass told me that Dr. Waters needed the help. But I guess he figured my equine specialist degree and my vet assistant program wasn't enough."

"In ranching country, with all these horses around, you'd think it would give you full-time work."

"You'd think. I sometimes wonder—" She stopped there, knowing she was veering into self-pity territory. She never knew how much was Dr. Waters just being Dr. Waters or how much was her father's reputation.

"You wonder what?"

She brushed off his question. "Would you ever consider going on your own?"

"You mean, starting my own business?" Morgan slowly shook his head. "I don't know. I'm not much of a risk taker. Don't like stepping outside of my comfort zone."

"That's what comes from growing up with money," Tabitha said, unable to resist the urge to tease him. "All your problems get swept away."

He held her gaze and she knew he was thinking of their past. "Not all of them can be fixed with money," he said.

She was silent, feeling the emotions, older and dangerous, trembling between them. Part of her so badly wanted to give in. The only time she'd ever felt like she was worth anything in her life was when she was with Morgan.

But she had to find her own way and so did he. They weren't young kids with no responsibilities anymore. Life had beaten the optimism out of both of them.

"I've had to quickly learn how to adapt," she continued. "I've been in too many situations where I'm not in charge, which made me want to find a way to change that. I don't want to be working for someone else all my life, letting them determine how many hours I work or whether I have a job at all."

"Sepp was an idiot to let you go," he said.

His defense of her gave her a small shiver of happiness. "I like to think so, though he wouldn't agree. But that's a prime example of having other people in control of my life. My father did the same thing, dragging me and my sister hither and yon, and if you're going to ask me where yon is, I can tell you. It's in the northwest corner of Saskatchewan."

"Good to know," he said, grinning. "So you want to be in control of your life. What would that life look like?"

"I want to save up enough money to build a training facility. To train horses full-time. It'll take years, though, to build up my reputation, I'm aware of that, but it's the only way I can feel like I'm in charge."

"That would require taking a risk, wouldn't it?"

"Of course it would. If there's one positive thing I learned from my father, it's that if you don't take risks, you don't get anywhere. The trick is not to take risks with other people's money." She heard the usual angry note enter her voice and she stopped herself. She had to get past all that sometime, but she knew the sooner she could pay Morgan's father his money back, the sooner that would happen.

"That's admirable. That you're willing to do that."

"You wouldn't?"

"I don't know how. Your comment about money was kind of dead-on, hard as it is to hear. My dad was harder on us but my mother spoiled us rotten. I know that now that I have a son myself. She would move mountains to make sure my twin sister, Amber, got the barrel-racing horse she wanted, no matter the cost. She pushed Dad to pay for vet school so that I could graduate without debt. I never learned to take a chance. There was always a fallback. A safety net."

His confession surprised her. As did what he said about his mother.

"But working with Dr. Waters frustrates me. He keeps pushing me away. Taking cases from me." He released a harsh laugh. "I sound like a pouting child, don't I?"

"So start something of your own," she said.

"I've thought of it."

"But it's a risk."

"Yeah. I'm not going to ask my dad for help. I would need to do it on my own."

"So do it."

He gave her an odd look. "You really are fearless, aren't you?"

"No. Just want to be in control, that's all."

He frowned, holding her gaze as if trying to delve behind her comment.

But she forced herself to look away.

Control, she reminded herself, grasping the very thing she had just said. She needed to be in control. And if she let herself weave too many daydreams around this man, she would lose that control.

Because no matter what she thought or dreamed, until her debt to his father was paid, she would feel as if that had control of her life and would determine her value and worth.

She wouldn't let that happen.

Chapter Seven

It had been a busy Saturday, Morgan thought with a feeling of satisfaction. Dr. Waters had been sick, so Morgan had taken over most of the cases at the clinic today. Now that the day was over, he was on his way to Tabitha's. She had given him instructions to her place, but Morgan knew the way. Back when they were dating, he had brought her home once. It was the only time.

Usually she would take her car, or whatever vehicle her father had bought for her to drive, and meet him wherever they were going. Though it was at the end of a long, narrow road, it was close enough to town that sometimes she walked to the highway and met him in town.

He didn't like it but she'd always been insistent.

The road made another bend and he saw a driveway ahead of him. It looked like the main road but Tabitha had been adamant that he take the second driveway. So he drove past the clearly marked one, turned another bend and saw a pair of white reflective posts marking the second driveway. It was narrower and didn't look very well maintained, but he turned down it anyway.

Then he came around a tight corner and saw the house. A grove of trees sat between it and the rest of the yard. The area around the house was tidy and neat with clipped grass and edged with brick and heavy rocks. Flower beds flanked a house that gleamed a pale yellow in the sun, trimmed with white around the windows and eaves. It looked like a fairy cottage tucked into the hillside.

He could hardly believe this was the house that Tabitha, Leanne and their father moved into when they first came here. Back then it was a dingy brown with peeling paint and a porch that looked like it was falling apart.

Now it looked sturdy and welcoming. Bright and fresh.

He got out of the truck and caught a glimpse of the barn just beyond the house. Tabitha had said she would be working in the pen, and he should go around the right side of the house to get there.

Again, she'd been very insistent.

But he ignored her orders and went around the left side. He walked past the trees, up the hill, and his heart sank. Below him lay a graveyard of cars, stacks of wood and endless boxes of unidentifiable junk. The old driveway wound through it all and he understood why Tabitha had been so adamant he take the other way in to the house.

He was dismayed at the sight. It would take weeks to clean all this up. He shook his head, wondering again at Tabitha's father and how he could have done this to his daughter.

He heard Nathan's excited voice coming from close to the barn. He knew he could get there from here but he chose to follow Tabitha's orders and walked on the opposite side of the house. He walked down a path, through the same grove of trees hiding the house from the other side of the yard, and there they were.

Nathan hung over the edge of the round pen and Tabitha stood with Stormy, flicking a tarp over her backside, holding her still with the halter rope.

To his surprise, the horse didn't even flinch.

"You've come a long ways," Morgan called out as he came near.

"It's coming."

Nathan glanced over at him, grinning, and then looked back at Tabitha.

"But I think that's all for today," Tabitha said, hanging the tarp on the fence. She led Stormy to the gate leading to the pasture, took off the halter and let her go.

Morgan was disappointed he didn't have a chance to see her in action. He would like to see what her technique was, how she worked with the horse.

Tabitha carefully climbed over the railing instead of going through the gate. The panel wobbled as she stepped over and Morgan caught her as she faltered.

For a split second she was suspended, leaning on him, her shocked glance holding his as time wheeled backward. She was seventeen and he was helping her over a fence at his parents' place after they had gone for a long walk along the pasture, up into the hills.

Just for a moment he remembered how much she had meant to him then. The dreams he had spun around her and the future he had planned for them.

Then she regained her balance and tugged her arm free, and they were both firmly back in the present again.

"Thanks," she murmured, to his surprise.

He thought she would be upset with him.

Tabitha looked over at Nathan as she slipped the halter and rope over her shoulder. "So, what do you think, buddy?"

"I think I really like Stormy," he said. "And I'm excited to ride her."

"You know it won't be for a while, though," Morgan put in.

But Nathan ignored him, looking instead at Tabitha as if the sun rose and set on her. "I'm thirsty," he said, suddenly. "Can I have a drink at your house?"

"Well… I suppose…" Tabitha hesitated, glancing at Morgan.

"Maybe Miss Tabitha wants to get to her work," Morgan advised, sensing Tabitha's uncertainty. "You've been with her all day."

"I can't wait until we get to our house," Nathan said, his gaze firmly fixed on Tabitha. "I'm thirsty now."

"That's no way to ask," Morgan reprimanded him.

"Can I *please* have a drink?" Nathan asked, correcting himself.

Tabitha looked from Morgan to Nathan, then gave in. "Sure you can."

Tabitha gave Nathan a smile and he beamed back at her. Morgan felt a surprising twinge of jealousy. His son seemed more connected to Tabitha than to him.

"I need to put this halter away and then we'll go to the house," Tabitha said.

"I'll come with you," Nathan said.

"No, that's okay—" But Nathan was already running ahead.

Morgan guessed why she had protested, but now they were all together, walking to the barn.

As they did, they skirted the bodies of a couple of old cars. The windows of the vehicles were broken and the tires flat. They weren't going anywhere soon.

"Where did those cars come from?" Nathan asked as Tabitha pulled open the door of the old hip roof barn and stepped inside.

"My dad got them from a friend," Tabitha called out from the dim interior. She came back out and closed the door, the hinges creaking out a protest.

"Do they work?"

"Nope. And they didn't when he purchased them, either."

"Then why did he buy them?"

Tabitha shoved her hands in her pockets, her steps more hurried as they walked around a couple of old farm implements and a stack of metal and wood leaning precariously against a weathered shed. "Same reason he bought all the other stuff in the yard. Thought he would use it someday for something."

Tabitha's voice held a defensive edge, and Morgan knew they weren't supposed to see this side of the place.

"Your dad bought this place when your family moved here, didn't he?"

"Yes, he did."

"I remember my father being upset because he was hoping to buy it."

"Probably one of many times that would happen, I'm sure."

He was about to ask her more but then they came near the house. "I have to say, you did an amazing job on the house and the yard."

She smiled, her shoulders lowering, her posture less defensive.

"This place has been a huge work in progress for me," Tabitha said with a faint note of pride in her voice. "Every minute I can spare, I've been fixing it up."

"You can be proud of what you've done."

"It's all about resale value," Tabitha said as she bent over to pick up a stray plastic bag that had blown into the yard and tuck it in her pocket.

"And what will you do once you sell?" He wished he could sound more casual about it, and it bothered him that he couldn't.

Tabitha paused, her eyes grazing the hills beyond the house, and for the briefest moment Morgan caught a look of yearning on her face. As if she wished things were different. But then her features straightened and she looked directly at him.

"Then I walk away from Cedar Ridge and never look back."

That hit him like a physical blow.

Did he think Tabitha would change her mind because he shared a few happy experiences?

Would he never learn?

"Are not two sparrows sold for a penny? Yet not one of them will fall to the ground outside your Father's care. And even the very hairs of your head are all numbered. So don't be afraid—you are worth more than many sparrows."

Pastor Blakely looked up as he closed the Bible, a gentle smile on his face as he looked out over the congregation. "I always get such comfort from this piece of Scripture," he said. "Sparrows have never held much value, and yet God is telling us that He watches over them too. And that if He watches over them, how much more does He watch over us? How valuable does that make each of us?"

Tabitha clung to her open Bible, the pastor's words resonating with her.

She looked down at the Bible in her lap, shaking her head at the sight of the scrambled letters in front of her. Most of her life had been spent making connections between the squiggles she saw on the paper and the words they represented. Her memory and recall were amazing but they had all been coping skills she'd perfected in her lifelong struggle with dyslexia. Something that was only diagnosed when she was in junior high, a couple of years before she had come to Cedar Ridge.

A caring teacher had finally explained to her why reading was so difficult for her compared to her classmates. Tabitha had found out that there were various levels and kinds of dyslexia, and while hers wasn't as extreme as some, it was still a tremendous amount of work for her to read. Her dyslexia was exacerbated by the constant moving. So when Tabitha, her sister, Leanne, and their father had moved to Cedar Ridge, it was simply one more barrier, one more mountain to climb. She'd struggled along as much as she could, hiding her difficulties from everyone, including Morgan. For the most part she managed, and she and Morgan had never shared any classes.

Then she got Morgan's mother as an English teacher in the first term of Grade Twelve and things went downhill from there. Mrs. Walsh never approved of Tabitha as Morgan's girlfriend, and Tabitha resorted to her usual antics in class to hide her disability and her frustration with Mrs. Walsh's assessment of her. A month later, in utter frustration, she'd quit school. Six months later Mrs. Walsh had confronted her.

"We are valuable. Precious. Loved," the pastor preached, underlining what the passage said.

Tabitha heard the words and, once again, fought to make them her own. To weave them into her life. Even in church, around people who were followers of God, she battled feelings of inferiority.

When Morgan came to pick Nathan up at her house yesterday, she had tried, in vain, to keep the mess of the rest of the yard away from him. She could still feel the shame as she saw the mess through Morgan's eyes.

Yes, she felt like saying, *this is what my life with my father was like. Looks good on the one hand, but there is a darker, messier side.*

And that's why I need to leave here, she thought. *I don't need to be reminded every time I turn around of who I am and where I come from.*

Despite those thoughts, her eyes sought out Morgan and Nathan sitting with Morgan's father. They sat one pew ahead and across the aisle, and she could watch them without them knowing. Nathan was looking down, probably staring at his new cowboy boots, rocking slightly. Morgan's attention seemed to be split between the pastor and his son, and every time he looked at Nathan, Tabitha saw the sorrow on his face.

Tabitha wanted to assure him that it would take time for Nathan to get to know and trust him.

The sight of Morgan wanting to connect with his boy also brought back memories of when they were dating. He could be so kind and protective.

She swallowed down an unexpected and unwelcome

ache at what she had lost and forced her attention back
to the pastor. Morgan was part of her past and he was
settling here in Cedar Ridge.

Her future meant putting Cedar Ridge and all it represented behind her.

The rest of the service flowed along, but as the congregation stood for the last song, Tabitha felt her heart
drop.

It was her favorite song. One that Morgan used to
hum when he was in a good mood.

*"You are worth, more than all gold, My dearest trea-
sure of wealth untold. I see you child, as I want you to
be, Perfect and lovely, whole and free."*

To her shame Tabitha felt her throat thicken at the
familiar words.

My dearest treasure of wealth untold.

She held on to the words as the old weariness washed
over her. She was so tired of the stress of living with
her father's shadow, and her own lack of abilities. She
was tired of always feeling unworthy.

And now, with Morgan around, she was reminded of
a life that had been within her grasp. A good life with
a man who had roots and family.

Perfect and lovely, whole and free.

She drew in a trembling breath, and as the last notes
of the song resonated through the building, she tried to
find a quick escape. She didn't want to run into Morgan
while she felt so emotionally shaky.

Trouble was, she wasn't sitting in her usual spot because she had waited for Leanne, who had told her at
the last minute that she couldn't come. So she had to
sit farther ahead. Now she was caught between two el-

derly women who weren't in any rush to finish their conversation with the people in the pew in front of them.

Which put her in the awkward position of ending up right beside Morgan and Nathan when she finally managed to step into the aisle.

"Miss Tabitha," Nathan cried out, grabbing her hand. "I'm wearing my new boots. See?" He held out his foot for her inspection. "And my new pants and shirt."

"You look very spiffy," she said, still gathering her composure.

"We're going to my uncle Cord's house for lunch. Grandpa is coming. You should come too."

Tabitha was at a momentary loss for words. There was no way she could face Boyce Walsh across a dinner table when she had spent so much time trying to stay off his radar.

"Maybe Miss Tabitha has other plans, Nathan," Morgan jumped in, giving Tabitha an out.

She didn't know whether to feel hurt or relieved, which in turn exasperated her. She didn't like how being around Morgan confused her so much.

"I want you to come," Nathan said, his voice rising and falling in a classic put-out child's whine as he grabbed Tabitha's hand. "Please. You can tell Grandpa Boyce about my horse."

"Yes, I'd love to hear about this horse."

And there was Boyce Walsh. His eyes holding nothing but a sparkle, a grin lighting up his face.

"I think you should join us, Tabitha," Boyce continued. "You can tell us how the training is going with Stormy. I know Cord and Ella won't mind."

"What won't we mind?" Ella joined them, her soft

brown eyes flicking from Nathan, still holding Tabitha's hand, to Boyce.

"We just invited Tabitha for lunch."

"I think that's a great idea," Ella said, smiling at Tabitha, her expression welcoming. "We can serve you for a change instead of you waiting on us."

Tabitha knew Ella meant it as a gentle joke but somehow it underlined the differences between them. Ella, a renowned artist who had reinvented herself and was gaining praise for her new work. And Tabitha. Ex-waitress and daughter of the local loser.

"Please come," Nathan said, still holding her hand. "You can meet my new cousins. Paul, Suzy and Oliver. Suzy teases me but Paul says she teases everyone."

Tabitha was even more torn. She knew Nathan was growing attached to her, but to refuse his, Boyce's and Ella's invitations seemed rude.

"You know how to get to the ranch," Morgan said, taking the decision out of her hands. "We'll see you there." He held his hand out to Nathan. "Why don't we go ahead and get lunch ready for Miss Tabitha?"

But Nathan simply walked away, spurning Morgan's gesture.

Tabitha saw the hurt on Morgan's face and she laid a gentle hand on his shoulder. It was only supposed to be a show of comfort. But when he looked at her and their eyes met, a quiver of attraction grew deep in her soul.

She didn't want to break the connection. In fact, she wanted to put her other hand on his other shoulder, like she used to. Tease him. Like she used to.

Her breath caught and it wasn't until they were jostled by someone wanting to get past them that the moment was broken.

He looked momentarily taken aback and then, to her dismay, he stepped back, his expression hardening. Then he strode away.

Tabitha struggled with her roiling emotions. What was she doing? Whatever it was, it definitely wasn't fair to Morgan.

She'd had her chance with him and she'd made her choice.

What if I told him what actually happened and why?

She held that thought as she made her way through the crowd of people on the way to the door, taking her time.

Then she stepped outside, heading toward her truck, which was parked right beside the church. That was when she saw him.

Morgan stood by his mother's grave. His hand rested on the stone, his head down. He swiped at his cheeks, as if he was crying, and the sight cut into her soul. He missed his mother.

Then someone stopped her to ask a question about her cat. Tabitha obliged, thankful for the chance to pull herself back to ordinary.

By the time she was done, Morgan and Nathan were gone.

And Tabitha knew there was no way she would be able to tell him what had really happened.

Not ever.

Chapter Eight

Tabitha slowed her truck down as she approached the driveway leading to the Walsh ranch house. She still had a chance to change her mind and go back home.

But the thought of letting Nathan down kept her going. He had asked her to come. She knew better than to disappoint a young child.

She turned into the driveway. She had been to the Walsh house a couple of times before, so she knew what to expect. The driveway split after passing the small house to her right that she guessed Ella lived in until she and Cord were married.

Tabitha drove on past a copse of trees, turned a corner and there it was. The Walsh home.

Except it looked different. The lower half of the house was now covered in rough stone, which also framed the doorway. The house had wooden siding instead of dusky blue vinyl siding and it looked like the windows had changed.

The wraparound veranda was also different. Tabitha suspected Cord's now-deceased wife, Lisa, had been responsible for the updates.

But while the house had been redone, the amazing view was as timeless as she remembered.

The ranch house sat on a rise that overlooked a valley. Beyond the valley rose the Rocky Mountains, majestic and imposing. Tabitha knew the house overlooked only a portion of the Walsh ranch. But it was an impressive portion.

She parked her truck beside Morgan's and the other two vehicles. She suspected one belonged to Boyce, the other to Cord.

She wondered what Cord thought of her coming for dinner. While she and Morgan were dating, his brother had kept his distance. Tabitha knew Cord wasn't crazy about her. In fact, shortly after she broke up with Morgan, she had seen Cord in town. He hadn't said anything, but the look of fury on his face toward her was enough. Tabitha left town shortly after that so she didn't have to face him again.

Since she came back, she'd seen Cord in town now and again, and he was always unfailingly polite, but she'd never been able to erase that look from her memory.

Maybe she should go.

She reached for her keys still dangling in the ignition when the door burst open and three children came running out. A large dog she hadn't seen before came bounding down from the veranda to join them.

She saw Nathan waving at her, his face full of joy as he ran to her truck.

Paul and Suzy came down the stairs too, but they held back, as if unsure what to do with the woman who usually served them French fries and ice cream and now stood in their yard.

"You came," Nathan said as she closed the door of her truck and slipped her bag over her shoulder. "My... my... Morgan said you might not and not to be disappointed."

That was the second time she'd heard him make that slip. Saying "my" and then switching to "Morgan," as if he was about to say "my dad" but didn't dare.

Tabitha looked at Paul and Suzy and waved at them. "Hey, you two."

"I wish you could paint my face like a cat again," Suzy said, bouncing up to her, her pigtails bouncing. "Like you did at the fair."

"I don't have the paints with me, otherwise I could." Tabitha had manned the booth for the Brand and Grill at the spring fair in the park.

Then Suzy grabbed her hand and pulled. "We were waiting for you and I'm hungry."

"I see that," Tabitha said, allowing the girl to drag her onto the veranda.

"What took you so long?" Suzy demanded as Paul opened the door for both of them.

"Temperamental truck" was all she said. She hadn't been able to start her truck after church and had needed a boost. Tony Schlegal had been more helpful boosting her car than he'd been at the hardware store. Hopefully it would start again when it was time to leave.

She heard voices and laughter when she came into the house. As she tugged her sandals off, she glanced around the hallway. It too had been renovated. The floor was done in tile with an inlaid compass. The colors were now fresh aqua and white.

"Miss Tabitha is finally here," Suzy called out as

she flounced into the kitchen, Paul and Nathan trailing behind her.

Ella stood at the quartz kitchen counter mixing something up in a bowl. Her hair was pulled back in a loose ponytail and she wore a gauzy white blouse with intricate pleats at the yoke and top of the sleeves. Very artsy, Tabitha thought.

She looked up when Tabitha arrived. "Hey. Glad you came," she said, her voice friendly and welcoming.

"Thanks for the invite. Can I help you with anything?"

"I'm just putting the finishing touches on this potato salad and then we can eat." She nodded toward the large table beside the kitchen where Morgan, Cord and Boyce sat. "Why don't you join the men?"

"And talk about cows and tractors and rodeo?"

Ella chuckled at that. "I think it's mostly rodeo talk these days. Something about getting the arena looked at by their cousin Reuben. They want to see if it's worth finishing."

Ah, the unfinished arena. The dark cloud over Tabitha's life.

"I'll stay here until you're done," Tabitha said, leaning her elbows on the kitchen island.

The kids were playing a game in the family room located just off the dining area. Toys were scattered over the floor and music played softly in the background. Quite a change from when Mrs. Walsh lived here, Tabitha thought.

Pictures and wooden plaques with inspirational sayings hung on previously stark and bare walls. A rough bouquet of wildflowers, shoved in an antique watering can on the counter, was parked beside a bright striped bowl of fruit and a matching tray that held odds and ends.

Mrs. Walsh kept everything achingly neat and tidy. The house was always immaculate and beautifully decorated.

But this house looked like a home.

"The kids were excited to see you again," Ella said, setting the bowl aside and washing her hands. "Suzy was hoping you would bring the face paints along."

"As if I could compete with you," Tabitha returned. "How is the art coming? I heard you were getting ready for a new show."

"You heard correctly."

Tabitha could hear the question in Ella's voice and smiled. "I used to work at the Brand and Grill. Where there are no secrets."

Ella chuckled. "And I imagine you heard most of them."

"I try to be discreet. Though I have thought of starting a gossip column for the local paper."

"I'd read it," Ella said, drying her hands on a towel. "Be a great way to find out more about my new home and community."

"You like it here?" she asked, curious as to Ella's reaction.

"I do. The people are welcoming, the town is just the right size and it's a great place to raise kids." Ella grinned. "You know, the usual sales pitches real-estate agents use to sell homes In places people are reluctant to move to. Make it about the kids." Then Ella shot her a curious glance. "I understand you're not originally from around here either?"

"Nope. No grandparents buried in the cemetery."

Ella looked puzzled as she picked up the bowl of potato salad.

"That's the usual cliché when talking about whether you were born and raised here or are from somewhere else," Tabitha explained.

"So when did you move here?" Ella walked over to the table where the men were sitting and set the bowl beside plates that held buns, cold cuts and another that held cookies and bars.

"I was in junior high when we came to town."

"Whoa, that must have been rough."

Tabitha shot a glance at Morgan, who had been talking to his brother but now looked up.

"It was hard on her," Morgan added, getting up to pull a chair out for Tabitha. "No thanks to me and Amber."

"What do you mean?" Ella asked her future brother-in-law.

"Let's say we didn't make it the easiest on her."

"That's because you had the biggest crush on her," Boyce put in. Then he gave Tabitha a gentle smile. "Sorry, but it was true."

Tabitha could hardly speak. She was so surprised to hear Boyce speak so openly about his son's relationship with her.

"He was definitely smitten," Cord chimed in, giving Tabitha a careful look.

She wasn't sure how to interpret all of this.

"I wish Amber was easier on you, is all," Boyce continued. "I always felt like I should apologize for her behavior."

"Amber had her own stuff," Morgan put in.

"Well, if your mother hadn't spoiled the two of you rotten, she might not have had *stuff*," Boyce grumbled.

"Oversharing, guys," Cord said, shooting a warning glance around the table. "I don't think Tabitha needs to hear all the Walsh family dysfunctions."

Tabitha was amazed at the completely unexpected comments. Boyce apologizing for his daughter? Mentioning dysfunction in the Walsh family?

"I think we can eat now," Ella called out. "Kids! Time to come to the table."

They scrambled to their feet and hurried over.

"Is Oliver napping?" Morgan asked, looking around as Suzy and Paul found their places.

"Yeah, he's always so tired after church." Cord pulled a chair out for Ella and settled Suzy in another one. "And grumpy."

"Like his dad," Ella teased. Cord tugged her ponytail in reply and sat down.

"I want to sit by Miss Tabitha," Nathan announced as he dragged a chair away from the table. "You sit here," he said, pointing to an empty chair beside him.

Which would put her right beside Morgan.

"Don't you want to sit between your dad and me?" she suggested.

Nathan glanced over at Morgan, looking as if he was considering the idea. Then he shook his head. "No. I want to sit with you."

Again embarrassment washed over Tabitha, but as she sat beside Morgan, another feeling superseded that emotion.

Here she was again. Sitting beside Morgan at the table in the Walsh house with members of his family.

She remembered all too well how much she enjoyed

being here once Morgan dared tell his family they were dating. For a few months, before she dropped out of school and before things fell apart, she felt a part of a family that had roots and belonged to a community.

Things she had always longed to be a part of.

But thanks to his mother, her father and her own past with Morgan, it was not to be.

"Let's pray," Boyce said, looking around the table, his gaze resting for a few seconds on Tabitha.

Then everyone reached out their hands. She took Nathan's and then, after a moment's hesitation, Morgan's. His hand was warm. Rougher than it used to be. The hands of a man, not a young boy.

And as his fingers curled around hers, she couldn't stop from seeking out his face.

Only to find him looking at her as his features softened.

And when his hand tightened around hers, Tabitha thought her heart would burst.

Morgan sat back in the wooden chair on the deck, a feeling of satisfaction washing over him as he looked out over the view. Good lunch. Good company.

Tabitha sat upright in her chair beside him, her hands clasped tightly on her lap. She looked tense. Did being around his family do that to her?

Or did his presence cause it?

Cord had settled on a rattan sofa beside Tabitha's chair. Boyce had gone back to his house in town, claiming that he needed a nap. The kids were playing on the swings and play center that Cord had set up a month or so ago. Nathan seemed happy enough to join them. Another small victory.

Though he'd been back to the family home since he left, it still shook him to see the changes that Lisa had made when she and Cord got married.

"If you have the time, Morgan, I'd like you to check out a cow that's having some trouble," Cord said, clasping his hands behind his head, his one foot resting on his knee.

"Surely you're not going to make the poor guy work on his day off," Ella teased as she sat down beside Cord, cuddling up against him.

"He doesn't work that hard," Cord returned, giving Ella a gentle smile as he fingered a strand of hair away from her face. "He can help his big brother out."

Morgan felt a flicker of jealousy at the sight. He knew his brother had traveled his own dark road to get to this place. Losing his wife in childbirth, trying to raise three kids on his own.

Ella coming into his life was an answer to many prayers sent up by his father.

"I don't mind," Morgan said, leaning back. He looked over to where Nathan was playing with Suzy and Paul. The sound of his laughter floated back to him and it made him smile to see his son happy for a change.

"And how is the horse training with Stormy coming along, Tabitha?" Cord asked.

"She's headstrong but we're working on that." Tabitha's voice sounded strained.

"Do you seriously think you'll get her to the point that Nathan can ride her?"

The incredulity in his brother's voice annoyed Morgan.

"Tabitha knows what she's doing," he snapped.

Cord shot him a surprised look. "I'm sure she does. Ernest taught her, after all."

Tabitha spoke up. "A horse like Stormy might not be the best mount for a child now, but in time—"

"She sure looked explosive to me when Ernest brought her over," Cord said, shaking his head. "I think it'll take way too much work to turn her into a kid's horse. Waste of time, if you ask me."

"We didn't ask you." Morgan shot a warning look at his brother.

"We'll have to see how it goes," Tabitha said, her voice tight.

Morgan wanted to reassure her that he thought she was capable.

But before he could say or do anything, she stood. "I should go," she said, turning to Ella and Cord. "Thanks for a wonderful lunch. I enjoyed it."

"You don't have to leave yet, do you?" Ella protested.

"I should. Thanks again for lunch. It was delicious." She gave Ella and Cord a tight smile, then walked past them all around the corner.

Morgan waited until she was gone then turned on his brother.

"You could have said that more tactfully." Morgan blew out a sigh, shaking his head at his brother's disappointing insensitivity. "I'll be back."

Cord held his angry gaze, his own expression impassive. But Morgan saw the warning in his eyes and knew that his brother still had his concerns about Tabitha.

Tabitha was still in her truck, grimacing as she turned the key. The engine turned over once. Then again.

"Won't it start?" he asked as he came to stand by the truck's open window.

She wouldn't look at him as she shook her head. "Nope. Might need a boost."

Morgan tapped his hand on the door of his truck, trying to find the right words. "I'm sorry about Cord. I don't know what's gotten into him."

"I think I do."

"What do you mean?"

"Nothing. It's just…nothing." She opened the door of her truck and he stepped back. "I have a set of booster cables if you don't mind helping me out."

He wanted to ask her more but he sensed she wasn't going to tell him.

So he opened the hood, then went to move his truck closer. She was ready with the booster cables when he turned his truck off and got out.

"You put the red cable on the positive?" she asked.

"Make sure you keep the clamps far away from each other" was all he said as he got ready to hook up the negative post.

She nodded, keeping the black cord well away from the red. She had that snappy look on her face that he remembered all too well. It was her habitual expression the first year she was in school.

He sighed as she got in and started her truck. It turned over once, twice, and then the engine roared to life.

He made quick work of unhooking the cables before she got out, rolled them up and handed them to her. She avoided his gaze, which annoyed him and frustrated him simultaneously. He thought they had been getting somewhere. When she agreed to come here after church, he'd taken that as a positive sign.

But now she was reserved, withdrawn and angry.

"Maybe let it keep running for a while when you get home," Morgan said. "Make sure the battery is charged up good and proper."

"I will. Thanks." Again, minimal eye contact. "Say goodbye to Nathan for me, please."

She put her truck in gear and he stepped away. She drove off leaving Morgan behind, annoyed and confused. He thought about how Cord had treated her. What his father had said about Amber and him.

Both were a good reminder to him why Tabitha was leaving. He didn't blame her.

And he knew it was for the best. She was starting to get to him and he couldn't let that happen again.

Chapter Nine

Tabitha kept pulling Stormy's halter, keeping her pressure steady.

"What do you want her to do now?" Nathan asked from behind the fence.

"I want her to move her back feet and I won't let go until she does." Tabitha fought down a beat of frustration at the horse's stubbornness, remembering Ernest's constant mantra. *To hurry is to lose control.*

She and Nathan had spent the morning going over his schoolwork. It was exhausting for her, but she wouldn't admit it.

When he was done, they drove to her place to work with Stormy some more. She'd texted Morgan to let him know where she was. To her surprise, he had shown up a few minutes later, saying that Dr. Waters had said he could handle the rest of the calls himself. Again

Tabitha could tell Morgan was frustrated but he also seemed happy to be with Nathan. He had joined them at the corrals. While part of Tabitha was pleased he was there, she also felt very self-conscious suddenly. Ever since Sunday, Cord's questions about Stormy taunted her and made her second-guess what she was doing.

Was she truly wasting everyone's time by working with this horse, as Cord had inferred?

The question haunted her and was all the worse because it only underlined her own concerns.

"She's persistent, isn't she?" Morgan asked.

"I just need to be *more* persistent." Tabitha struggled to keep the snappy tone out of her voice. Yesterday when she came back home, second thoughts and doubts dogged her again, and she wondered if Morgan had the same misgivings about her abilities as his brother.

Then, finally, Stormy moved her back feet away from Tabitha and she immediately released the rope, petting the horse, stroking her side and encouraging her. Then she did the same thing all over again to reinforce the lesson. This time it took only a few minutes.

"She's catching on," Morgan said.

"Morgan found me a saddle, Miss Tabitha," Nathan piped up. "And it fits me."

Tabitha glanced over at Morgan, looking puzzled.

"I found one at the ranch. Used to be Amber's. Cord is fixing it up for Nathan. One of the stirrups needs repairs and it needs to be oiled."

"That's great," Tabitha said, wondering if Morgan wasn't pushing things too quickly.

"I'm excited to use it," Nathan said, adding one more burden to Tabitha. "When can I?"

She could hear his frustration. She knew exactly how badly he wanted to ride his mother's horse.

It won't happen.

She pushed the unhelpful voice aside and concentrated on what she was doing, wishing, as she often did, that she didn't have an audience.

After half an hour of watching little happen, Nathan jumped down off the fence. "I want to go for a walk around the yard," he said. "Can I?"

"Not by yourself, sweetie. Your dad will have to go with you."

"Okay." Nathan turned to Morgan. "Can you come?"

"If it's okay with Tabitha, sure."

It wasn't really, but Morgan had already seen the mess on the yard. It wouldn't be a surprise.

"Just be careful. There's a lot of…stuff." While she wasn't keen on having Morgan and Nathan see the mess that was her yard close-up, she was grateful for the reprieve.

Sunday had created such a maelstrom of emotions in her, she was thankful she didn't have to work in the vet clinic with Morgan this morning. That gave her a chance to breathe.

It had been so difficult to sit beside Morgan at the house that she'd once visited when they'd dated. To hold his hand while his father prayed over the meal. To hear Boyce bring up her and Morgan's old relationship.

And having him standing by the fence, patiently watching her as she second-guessed everything she was doing, only made it harder to concentrate.

They soon left and it was just her and the horse.

Half an hour later, Morgan and Nathan were still gone. And Tabitha was reasonably satisfied with the progress she'd made with Stormy. The horse had a long way to go, but things were moving in the right direction.

She let Stormy go into the pasture, then clambered

over the fence to see where Morgan and Nathan had got to.

A few minutes later she found them by an old car. Nathan was inside the car, pretending to drive it. Morgan was grinning at the sight.

"This is an awesome vehicle," Nathan called out. "Does it still work?"

"No, it doesn't," Tabitha said with a smile at the boy's pleasure.

"I'm thirsty," Nathan announced.

"I've got some lemonade and cookies in the house," Tabitha answered.

Nathan spun the steering wheel of the car one more time, then got out, following Tabitha and Morgan through a maze of boxes and stuff. Once again Tabitha had to resist the urge to explain all the junk. Resist the embarrassment that rose up at the unsightly mess.

"You have a lot of things," Nathan said, pausing to check out an old bathtub full of boxes of belts and rusted-out machinery parts. "It's like a treasure hunt."

"If rust and metal is your treasure," Tabitha said. "I hope to get it cleaned up soon, before I sell the place."

She felt she had to explain. Just in case Morgan thought she didn't see it for herself.

"That will be a lot of work for you," Morgan said.

"I prefer not to worry about it," Tabitha said, glancing around the old truck bodies, pieces of tractors and boxes of junk they passed on their way to her house. "I'll deal with it once I'm finished in the house."

Tabitha followed Nathan into the kitchen, cringing at the sight of the counterless kitchen, the patchy spackling job she'd done on the backsplash.

She pulled open the refrigerator and took out the

lemonade she had made for Nathan and put it on the table. She snagged a couple of glasses from the cupboard and poured the lemonade in. Nathan slurped his down right away.

"Can I go outside?" he asked.

"What do you say to Tabitha first?" Morgan reprimanded.

Nathan frowned at him, but turned to Tabitha. "Thanks. Now can I go?"

"Sure, but be careful," Tabitha said. She turned to Morgan.

"Some lemonade?" she asked, holding up a cup.

"No, thanks," he said, looking around the house. "I like what you did here."

She smiled at his approval. "Thanks. I hope the future buyer sees the potential."

"Right. Well, as for Stormy, what do you think we should do?"

The businesslike tone had returned to Morgan's voice and she suspected it had much to do with her talk of selling the house. She let the thought linger. Could she keep the house? There was no debt or mortgage against it. Her father had life insurance against the loan, which was paid out when he died.

But then she looked over at Morgan and the set of his jaw. She quashed that thought. There was too much between them, and besides, he had Nathan to think of now.

"I think you're going to have to tell him that it will be a while before he can ride Stormy."

"I'm inclined to agree with you." Morgan sighed.

Tabitha heard the sorrow in his voice. She knew how badly Morgan wanted to be able to do this for a son who was so distant from him.

"How about if you take him out riding on a horse you can trust? Get him on another horse and maybe that will be enough of a distraction that he's not thinking about riding Stormy so much."

Morgan nodded slowly as if considering the idea.

"It would be an outing with your son," Tabitha pressed. "A chance to connect on another level."

"I could use the connection."

"I think he's softening to you," Tabitha said. "I don't know if you've noticed, but there were a couple of times where he almost referred to you as 'my dad' but caught himself."

"Well, that's something," Morgan said, giving her a wry smile.

"It's like training a horse. You need to be patient but persistent."

Morgan's smile shifted as he held her eyes. "This matters to you, doesn't it?"

"Yes. Of course. I don't like seeing kids disconnected from their fathers."

"Were you? Disconnected from your father, I mean."

She slid her eyes away from his probing glance. "I loved my dad. He was a lot of fun. But fathers like him are more interesting when they're someone else's. My love for him was worn away one scheme, one lie, one disappointment at a time."

Suddenly, to her surprise and dismay, she felt Morgan's hand on her face. His fingers curled around her cheek as he gently turned her to him.

"You're not your father, you know."

She could only stare at him, a chill slipping down her spine. How did he know that was how she felt?

"You are your own person," he continued. "And

while I'm sure you loved him in your own way, you don't have to take on who he was. You don't have to make up for who he was."

"I don't know if you realize who he was and what he did," Tabitha said, unable to keep the bitter tone out of her voice. "I get reminded enough." She wanted to look away and pull away from his touch, but it felt so good to have his hand holding her. It had been so long since she felt that anyone saw her for herself.

Morgan's fingers caressed her cheek as his eyes traveled over her features. "Is that why you want to leave?"

She held his curious gaze, then gave in to an impulse and lifted her hand, covering his, giving herself a few more seconds of this connection.

"I have to leave" was all she could say. "It's the only way I can live with myself."

"Why?"

She wondered if he would truly understand her reasons.

"Please, tell me."

She thought back to his father. So caring. So considerate.

The difference was too great. So she shook her head and turned away, breaking the moment between them.

"My dad wants to go riding with me tomorrow." Nathan was sitting in Tabitha's truck, looking out the window as they drove down the road to the Walsh ranch Wednesday afternoon. Tabitha had worked at the clinic that morning, then had picked up Nathan from Cord's place. Ella had been watching the kids. Thankfully Cord wasn't there. She didn't want to face his condemnation again.

She and Nathan had spent the afternoon with Stormy and it had gone well.

"I don't think I want to go riding."

"Why not? I think it's a great idea," Tabitha said. "You like riding, and Stormy won't be ready to ride for a while, so you may as well ride another horse."

Nathan was quiet, looking down at his boots. "What if he changes his mind? What if he doesn't take me?"

Tabitha thought of something Nathan had said to her last week about his mother telling him that Morgan didn't keep his promises. At that time she had told herself not to get involved and she still knew that to be true, but it bothered her that Morgan was trying so hard and Nathan couldn't see it.

"Your dad cares about you a lot," she said, looking ahead at the road, struggling to find the right thing to say that could help these two. "He is taking good care of you. He really loves you."

"My mom said he didn't."

"What?" Tabitha shot him a quick glance, surprised to see the little boy's deep scowl.

"My mom said he didn't love me. That's why he didn't come and visit me. Or live with my mom and me and be a family. He didn't want to have me."

The words tumbled out of Nathan's mouth in a rush. It was as if he'd heard them so many times, he could spout them off by heart.

Shock and anger surged through Tabitha. How could a mother say that to her child?

"Your father does love you," Tabitha said, wanting to reassure him. "He wanted so badly to visit you but—" She caught herself there, knowing that her anger with Nathan's mother would cloud her words and her judgment. No matter her opinion, Gillian was still his mother.

"He didn't try," Nathan snapped. "If he did try, why didn't I ever see him? I wanted to, but my mommy said my daddy didn't care." Then, to her dismay, his lower lip trembled and Tabitha caught the glint of tears in his eyes.

The poor kid.

Tabitha pulled over to the side of the road, stopped the truck, unbuckled her seat belt and scooched over. She put her arm around his thin shoulders. Nathan melted against her and started to cry.

Tabitha's heart shifted with pain and she pulled the sobbing boy close.

"He *did* try to see you," Tabitha said, stroking his hair, holding him tight, bewildered at the maternal feelings he raised in her. Surprised how her heart broke at the sound of his tears, at the shake of his shoulders under her arms.

Please, Lord, give me the right words, she prayed. *Help me to help this poor child. And his father.*

"He did try," she repeated. "But your mother was so busy traveling all over the place, going to rodeos. He couldn't always find you."

Nathan sniffed as his sobs slowly eased off.

"He wanted to find you," she insisted. "But it's hard when someone is moving around so much."

He lifted his head, his glance latching on hers as if testing her to see if she was telling the truth. "Is that for real?"

"It is. I know it. Morgan—your dad," she corrected herself, "is a good man and he wants to be a really good father."

Nathan seemed to consider this, and Tabitha pressed the point.

"He wanted to be with you," she continued. "He loves you so much. But every time he thought you were in one place, you moved." She was winging it with what she was saying, but she also knew that Morgan would have moved heaven and earth to find his son. "And when he finally found you, he brought you here. To his home. Where he grew up because he wanted you to have a real home."

"A home here in Cedar Ridge?"

"Yes."

"And he won't move?"

"No. He has family here. A dad, a brother who has kids, and uncles and aunts. He belongs here." As she listed off Morgan's connections to Cedar Ridge, Tabitha couldn't stop the usual glimmer of envy. Morgan was so rooted here. Unlike Nathan's mother, who had always been on the move. Seeming to be avoiding something she preferred not to face.

And what about me? Aren't I doing the same thing?
The words floated through her subconscious.
Aren't I trying to outrun what I should face?
Her heart shifted its rhythm as the words accused her.

No. She wasn't. She had to clean up her father's mess. Give herself a reason to hold her head up, redeem herself and leave.

She needed to finish the house, clean up the yard and sell, then start fresh somewhere else.

The list of reasons seemed to calm and center her.

"So my dad is going to stay here?" Nathan sniffed, swiping the back of his hand over his nose.

Tabitha reached into her backpack and pulled out a package of tissues. "Your dad is staying here," she said, handing him a couple. "I know that for a fact. This is where he grew up and always wanted to live."

Nathan wiped his nose and drew in a shaky breath. "And he loves me?"

"He loves you a lot. Your father is a good man and a good father."

And listen to me. If he's such a good man, why am I leaving? I know things are growing between us.

She shook her head as if to eradicate the memories, put her seat belt back on and put the truck in gear.

Stay focused on the next job, she reminded herself. *Just do what comes next. Don't think too far ahead. Don't plan too far ahead.*

It was how she got through all the disappointments in her life. The false hopes. Staying in control and sticking with her plan.

Morgan and Nathan were only a momentary distraction.

But as she drove away, she couldn't get rid of the idea that they were more than that. Much more.

Chapter Ten

"Not the best weather for riding," Cord said as he helped Morgan saddle up the last horse.

Morgan squinted up at the low-hanging clouds scudding across the sky. "As long as it's not raining, we should be okay."

"I think it's a great idea that you and Nathan go out riding together," Cord said, yanking on the cinch strap to tighten it. "It's a good way to spend some time with him. I'm not so sure it's a good idea to take Tabitha along."

Morgan glanced over his shoulder.

Tabitha had Nathan astride Bronco, a bay gelding, and was leading him around the corral, giving him a chance to get used to the horse. Cord had insisted that she was bombproof and Morgan believed him, but he was still thankful for Tabitha's help.

"Nathan wouldn't come unless she came along too."

Morgan read disapproval in his brother's shrug. He understood Cord's concerns, and while he felt stuck between pleasing his son and guarding his heart, pleasing his son was winning out.

Trouble was, the wall around his heart was slowly

wearing away the more time he and Tabitha spent together.

"Look, I know you don't like her—"

"I like her fine. She's a great girl." Cord leaned one arm against the horse, looking past him to where Tabitha was leading Nathan around on the horse. "She's not been quiet about how glad she'll be to leave this place, so I wouldn't count on changing her mind. I also see how connected Nathan is to her. So I guess I'm just saying, be careful. Again."

"Thanks for the advice," Morgan said. "And I'm trying to be careful. Again. I'm a big boy." He held Cord's warning gaze a beat longer to reinforce the point. While he knew Cord was only being a big brother, he also knew Tabitha better than he did. And somehow, in the past few days, he sensed there was more to their breakup than she was telling him.

"Look at me—I'm riding," Nathan called out, happier than Morgan had seen him in a while.

"Lookin' good, buddy," Morgan called out, turning his attention back to his son.

"He seems happy," Cord said. "Taking him out on the horse will be good for him." Then he handed Morgan the reins of the horse he'd just saddled and Morgan led it over to where the horse Tabitha would be riding stood ready. "So, you're good to go." He grinned up at Nathan astride his horse. "Looking good, cowboy," Cord said.

"I'm not a real cowboy. I'm not allowed to steer the horse myself," Nathan complained.

"You will eventually." Cord checked his stirrups, then took the rope of Nathan's horse from Tabitha. "Why don't you mount up? I'll bring Nathan over to Morgan."

Tabitha did so but Morgan saw how she avoided

looking at him. As if she also sensed his brother's disapproval of her.

She mounted up in one fluid motion, making it look graceful and easy.

Morgan got on, Cord handed him the halter rope of Nathan's horse and they were ready.

"I'll get the gate," Cord said. "You taking the ridge or going down along the creek?"

"I think we'll do the creek," Morgan said. "The terrain is less sketchy."

"See you in an hour or so?"

Morgan nodded, glancing back at Tabitha, who was looking back at his son.

"Let's go." Morgan nudged his horse, adjusting his seat as they moved along, and a peculiar happiness settled on him. The old saying "the best thing for the inside of a man is the outside of a horse" came back to him, and he smiled as they rode through the gate and out into the pasture. Hard to believe it had been years since he rode.

Tabitha came up alongside him, her eyes looking out over the valley. "This view is stunning," she said, a reverent tone in her voice.

"It is. Even more after being away from it for a while." He gave her a quick smile, then looked back at Nathan, who swayed slightly with the horse's movements, his hands planted firmly on the saddle horn. In spite of the fact that he hadn't been allowed to steer the horse himself, he was now grinning from ear to ear. "How are you doing, son?" he asked.

Nathan gave him a wary look and nodded.

"And how about you?" he asked Tabitha.

"I'm doing great." She shifted, as if getting settled in. "This saddle is fantastic."

"Should be. All our saddles were custom-made in Montana by Monty Bannister."

"Really?" Tabitha seemed impressed. "I've heard good things about his workmanship."

"Yeah, his daughter has taken over the business but it's still a going concern."

"Nothing like your own custom-built saddle. Whose was this?"

"Amber's, and before that, my mother's."

Tabitha's face grew tight, and then she looked away.

"Bad memories of my sister?" he asked, sensing her withdrawal.

She shot him a look of surprise, then shook her head. "Amber didn't pay a lot of attention to me."

"So why the tense face?"

She bit her lip, and he could see she was getting her ornery expression on.

"You don't want to talk in front of Nathan. I get it." Morgan eased out a sigh then looked out over the hills, green now from the spring rains, the halter rope from Nathan's horse slack in his hands. "Let's simply enjoy the ride, then."

"I like the sound of that." She seemed to relax and Morgan grinned at her. Their eyes met and she returned his smile. "I know I'm here because of Nathan, but I'm glad to be out riding again."

"I feel bad that we've taken you away from your work on your house." He hadn't even thought that she might have other things to do this evening. Nathan had wanted her to come, so he'd asked.

"I gladly came," she said, looking back at Nathan,

who was still smiling. Still enjoying himself. "Besides, the renovations have come to a grinding halt until I can pay—" She stopped abruptly there, looking ahead again.

"Until you can pay what?"

"Doesn't matter."

He knew she wasn't going to elaborate. But that quickly reminded him of another obligation. "I'll write you a check for your work at the end of the week, if that's okay."

"I wasn't hinting at anything." She looked straight ahead.

"I know, but it reminded me of my own obligations."

"Because I'm not that broke, Morgan," she said.

"Of course you aren't." She sounded upset and he guessed he had hit a nerve.

"When are we getting to the creek?" Nathan called out.

"In a little while." Morgan drew in a long, slow breath, looking around as the setting and the rhythm of the horses' hooves eased away the tension of the past few days. The low-hanging clouds were slowly drifting away, letting beams of sun come through.

"You sound like you're getting rid of some bad vibes," Tabitha said.

A quick look over his shoulder showed him that Nathan was looking around, seeming to be off in his own world again.

"Probably am. Past few weeks have been stressful. I wish I could figure out how to connect with him."

"Taking him out like this is a good start," Tabitha said, giving him a smile. Then she too looked back as if to see if Nathan was listening. She moved her horse closer to his and lowered her voice. "I need to talk to you later. Just the two of us."

"That sounds intriguing," he said, giving her a teasing smile.

She frowned. "It's about your son."

He held her gaze a few heartbeats longer than necessary. Then he nodded, pulling himself back to the matter at hand. He had to keep his focus on his son, not be distracted by an old flame.

"I had such a fun day," Nathan said as he, Morgan and Tabitha walked into the kitchen of Morgan's house. "I liked riding horses."

"I'm glad, Nathan," Morgan said, reaching out his hand as if to ruffle his son's hair, then pulling back at the last minute, a look of pain on his features.

The gesture broke Tabitha's heart and she yearned to tell him what Nathan had said right then and there.

"But it's bedtime now, mister," Morgan said. "You need to wash up and then straight to bed."

When they'd got to the creek, Nathan said he wanted to skip rocks, so they'd ridden until they'd found a place where the creek was wider and quiet. Then the three of them had hunted up and down the creek bed looking for flat skipping stones.

By the time they'd got back on the horses, it had been getting dark. Now it was closer to 9:00 p.m. and Nathan was yawning.

"I want Tabitha to put me to bed," Nathan insisted.

Tabitha exchanged a quick glance with Morgan. While it was touching that the boy was so attached to her, it was also growing more precarious.

What will it be like for him when I go? It's not fair to keep encouraging him.

"I think your daddy should," Tabitha said quietly but firmly.

"Can you both tuck me in?"

Tabitha knew she should go home, but she wanted to talk to Morgan about what Nathan had said to her. So she reluctantly agreed to the compromise.

While Nathan washed up, brushed his teeth and changed into his pajamas, he chattered about the ride. About skipping rocks and about cutting tree branches and floating leaves down the creek. About his horse and how fast he was and how he wanted to do it again tomorrow.

His cheeks were red and his eyes bright and Tabitha wondered if he would settle down to sleep.

"Come and see my room," Nathan said, charging ahead of both of them down the carpeted hall, his footfalls muffled.

As Tabitha stepped inside his room, the first thing she noticed was how bare it was. Nathan's bed sat along the wall under the window with a cute little desk and chair beside it. A dresser hugged the wall to her left and a shaggy rug lay on the floor.

Though a fun animal-print quilt covered the bed, no pillows lay on it. The walls were devoid of any kind of pictures or posters. No knickknacks crowded the dresser or the shelves above. No toys lay scattered on the floor or dumped in the toy box on the other side of the dresser.

She noticed the pile of cardboard boxes with his name scribbled on them stacked in one corner of the room and guessed his personal effects were in there, hidden away.

As if he was afraid to settle down.

Tabitha thought of what Nathan had told her about Morgan and her heart melted for the little boy.

"This is my bed," Nathan announced, jumping on it and bouncing once, as if unable to contain himself.

"Why don't you get under the blankets and we can say your prayers," Morgan suggested.

"Morgan makes me say my prayers every night," Nathan told Tabitha, making it sound like he wasn't crazy about the ritual.

Oh, kiddo, you don't know how blessed you are, Tabitha thought as she stood by the foot of the bed, watching Morgan tuck Nathan in, pulling the sheets and blankets tight around him.

Her father had often been gone at bedtime, so it hadn't been unusual for Tabitha and Leanne to fall asleep in front of the television. Sometimes they'd woken up in their own bed, which meant their father had moved them during the night. Sometimes they'd woken up on the couch or on the floor, which meant he either hadn't come home or couldn't be bothered to bring them to bed.

How often Tabitha had wished her father would be home in the evenings. Just to simply be present in the house so it wouldn't feel so empty and lonely.

"May angels guard me while I close my eyes and keep me safe until I rise. Amen." Morgan finished the prayer that Nathan recited with him, a rare moment of father-son unity.

Morgan brushed his hand over Nathan's forehead and, to Tabitha's surprise, the little boy didn't flinch away this time.

"Good night, Nathan," Tabitha said as Morgan stood.

"Can you kiss me good-night, Miss Tabitha?"

Nathan's request was spoken so quietly, Tabitha might have missed it. But it sent a shock wave through her.

"I don't... I'm not sure..." Her protests were hesitant. She didn't want to hurt his feelings, but at the same time, the boundary she thought she had set in place with this child was slowly getting eroded.

It's only a kiss and he's only a lonely, sad little boy.

It was the thought of the unpacked boxes that tugged at her emotions. So she gave in to his simple request.

But as Tabitha bent over him, inhaling the scent of toothpaste, soap and little boy, and as she brushed a gentle kiss over his forehead, a deep yearning rose up inside her.

Would she ever have a child of her own? A home of her own?

Against her will, her thoughts focused on the man beside her.

She shook them off.

"I hope you have a good sleep, Nathan," she said, brushing his damp hair back from his face with a gentle touch.

He snuggled down in the blankets looking satisfied with himself.

"Leave the door open," he said. "And the hall light on, please."

Morgan nodded, and then he and Tabitha left the room.

"Do you want a cup of coffee?" Morgan asked when they were downstairs.

Tabitha knew it was dangerous to stay. Morgan was too appealing and she was feeling vulnerable. But she needed to tell him what Nathan had said.

"Would you mind making it tea?" she asked. "I don't like to drink coffee this late."

"You're in luck," Morgan said as he plugged the kettle in. "Ella likes to drink tea as well and she gave me some different varieties, plus a teapot to boot." He pulled a large ceramic pot out of one cupboard.

"Excellent. I'm glad Ella is on top of things."

"That and more. She's a great person."

"And I understand she and Cord are engaged?"

"They'll be married in a couple of months. Probably on the ranch."

"It's a beautiful place. And the house looks nice." Tabitha walked over to the bay window of the dining room, watching the sun going down. "I imagine Cord's first wife, Lisa, did the renovations."

"After she and Cord got married. Dad had moved out already. Mom was gone, so he didn't care what Lisa changed in the house."

"That must have been hard for your father. Losing your mother and moving away from their home."

Morgan set the mugs out on the counter. "It was hard for all of us. Especially after Cord started having kids. Mom wanted to be a grandmother so badly. She was already talking about fixing up one of the rooms in the house for a nursery when Cord and Lisa got engaged. Mom was always one for looking to the future and making plans for everyone."

Tabitha knew far too well Morgan's mother's penchant for plans.

"And now you're a veterinarian and living in Cedar Ridge again. I think your mother would have liked that," Tabitha said, choosing to be gracious. "I know you becoming a vet was important to her."

"I wish she could have been around to see it happen. She was encouraging and a support to us kids. She set high standards for us. Pushed us to achieve our potential. I really miss her."

Tabitha heard the obvious love in his voice and thought of him standing by her grave. She thought of her own mother, who, according to the doctors, had died of pneumonia when Tabitha was five. Leanne had often thought it was the constant moving and lack of money that wore her down.

What would hers and her sister Leanne's lives have been like if their mother had lived? Had she made plans for her and Leanne's future? Had she worried about what would happen to them?

Useless questions, she reminded herself.

"I'm sure you do," she said with a forced smile.

Then Morgan frowned at her as if he had just realized something. "How do you know my being a vet was important to her?"

Tabitha quickly realized her mistake and waved off his question. "Everyone knew. She always talked about you and what she wanted for your future." She walked over to the kettle, which was now boiling furiously. "Where are the tea bags?" she asked, changing the topic.

"I'll take care of that," Morgan said, opening another cupboard. As he did, his arm brushed hers, and Tabitha felt a frisson of attraction.

She knew she should leave but couldn't until she had told him about Nathan. That was the only reason she was sticking around.

Morgan made the tea. Then she took the mugs in one hand and the sugar bowl in the other.

"Let's sit in the living room." He walked ahead of her, past the dining room table, which still held some boxes as well. "I'm not completely moved in yet," he said, jerking his chin toward the table.

"Looks like Nathan isn't either." Tabitha set the mugs on the low table in front of the couch and put the sugar beside them. She settled on the couch, and then Morgan set the teapot down and sat down beside her.

"I've tried and tried to get him to unpack, but the only box he would let me open was the one with his clothes."

"It's like he doesn't want to get settled," Tabitha said.

"I wonder if it's because he thinks he might be moving back to his grandmother again. I know he's mentioned her a few times."

"It could be. Or it could be that he's afraid."

"Of what?"

Tabitha held his puzzled gaze, praying she could find the right words.

"He said something that gave me an idea of why he might be holding back from you," she said.

"Please. Tell me. I don't know what to do anymore with him." Morgan grabbed her hands as if hoping to draw out what she was going to say.

Part of her wanted to pull her hands free, but the warmth of his fingers and the way they molded around hers reminded her of better times.

How their lives had changed, she thought, looking down, tightening her fingers on his, the past melding with the present, older emotions blending with new ones.

"What did Nathan say?" Morgan encouraged, bringing her back to the present.

Tabitha hoped what he heard wouldn't be too devastating. "Please remember this was a little boy talking. That he might have gotten things wrong."

"Please," Morgan asked.

Tabitha sent up another prayer then began.

"He said his mother told him that you didn't love him," she said, keeping her voice quiet, as if that might help soften the blow. "That was why you didn't come and visit. She told Nathan that you didn't want him."

Morgan gasped.

"She said that?" His words came out in a hiss, his jaw clenched in anger.

Tabitha felt so sorry for him. To hear of such betrayal from the mother of your child had to hurt deeply. Did his ex-wife even stop to think what power she had over their child? What impact her words had?

Though Tabitha's mother died when she was only five, she still remembered things her mother had said. She still clung to the stories she'd told Tabitha. The encouragement she'd heaped on her whenever Tabitha tried to do anything.

"I'm only going by what Nathan told me," she continued. "I guess it doesn't matter how Gillian said it— what matters is that he believes it."

Morgan withdrew his hands from hers and started massaging his temples with his fingers.

"No wonder he pushes me away from him," he murmured, the devastation on his face like a knife to Tabitha's heart.

"You know it's not true that you don't love him." Tabitha placed a hand on his shoulder, trying to find a way to comfort him. "*I* know it's not true."

"So what do I do?" he asked, the pain in his voice adding to Tabitha's pain for him. "How do I counteract what she said? How can I show him I want to be his father? That I love him."

"I think you're doing it already," Tabitha said. "You're here for him. You're finding ways to show him that every day. I'm sure, in time, he'll understand that too. You're a good father. He's so lucky to have you."

"You think so?"

"I know so. Every child should be so blessed to have a father who cares so much about their child. I wished I did."

The words came tumbling out of her mouth before she could stop them.

She read sympathy in Morgan's eyes. Then, to her surprise, he brushed his fingers gently over her cheek. "I know your father wasn't always around. I'm sure that was hard for you and your sister." His hand came to rest on her shoulder, his fingers gripping it enough to anchor her.

Tabitha's breath felt trapped in her chest as her heart jumped at his touch, the kindness in his voice and the warmth of his hand. She wanted to make a joke to lighten the moment, but her words grew jumbled. She didn't want to sound self-pitying but she wanted Morgan to understand.

"He had his moments," Tabitha said, feeling the innate need of a child to defend their parent. "He could be attentive when he wanted to."

"I remember him as a charming man."

"I'm sure your own father remembers him that way as well." Tabitha couldn't keep the bitter note out of her voice.

Morgan frowned in confusion, shifting closer. She could see the five o'clock shadow on his chin, a faint smudge of dirt on his shirt from where he'd wiped his hands after gathering rocks. Smell the scent of soap from when he'd helped Nathan wash his face. His nearness resurrected memories of times in his truck when they talked, sitting with their arms around each other. The times they spent on the couch in his parents' house when they whispered their love for each other, keeping their voices low but enjoying the delicious thrill of being alone while his family slept upstairs.

"What do you mean by that?" he asked, his voice low, his hand still on her shoulder.

"The arena. How my dad left town with other people's money. Something I'm reminded of almost daily." Tabitha tried to pull away, but Morgan held her fast.

"You're talking about Lorn Talbot? When we bought Nathan's boots?"

"Him…and others."

"Are you talking about the money my dad put into the arena as well? Did your dad take that?"

"Not only took it, but left a number of businesses with unpaid bills."

"I heard bits and pieces about that," Morgan said. "But just from a few things Cord had said. But I never heard it from my father."

Tabitha was surprised and, somehow, was even more ashamed. The brokenness of their past and the emptiness of her future combined to create a bleakness she couldn't fight.

To her dismay, a tear trickled down her cheek. He stroked it away with his thumb.

"I don't think I've ever seen you cry before," he said.

"I'm not crying." She attempted to tamp down the upcoming tears.

To her surprise, he pulled her close, tucking her head in the crook of his neck, and Tabitha couldn't fight her emotions.

She leaned into his embrace, crying silently, promising herself this was momentary. She was lonely and tired and she appreciated his support.

"You are your own person," Morgan said, laying his cheek on her head, holding her tightly against him. "I can't think of anyone who works harder than you do. Fixing up that house, holding down two jobs, taking on extra work. I've always admired you. Even when you lived here, you always worked so hard."

"I had to," she said, resting in the sanctuary he offered.

"Because you needed the money?"

She nodded.

"Is that also why you dropped out of school?"

She was tempted to tell him the truth.

Just tell him. Let him know. Here's a chance to lay bare the secrets of the past.

Except she knew, after the admiring things he had said about his mother, after seeing him standing by her grave, grieving her loss, she just couldn't do it.

"No. That wasn't the reason," she said finally. "Though it helped me and Leanne that I could earn some money. It was always tight."

"So why did you quit school?"

She pulled back so she could look directly at him and gauge his reaction.

"I quit because at the time it was too hard for me and too much work." She saw the incredulity on his face and pushed on. "I've got dyslexia."

Morgan stared at Tabitha, incredulous.

"You're dyslexic?"

"Yeah. You know how some people say life gives

you lemons? Well, it gave me melons." Her words were flippant but he heard the defensive tone in her voice as she drew away from him.

And crowding in behind his surprise was disappointment. Old feelings of lack of trust rose up. "Why didn't you tell me? We were dating. We were going to get married."

"Don't worry. I would have known where to sign my name on the marriage license," she returned, looking away.

Part of him wanted to leave it be. Tabitha was always one for keeping things to herself. Just like Gillian.

But he knew, deep down, that Tabitha wasn't like his deceased ex-wife. That unlike Gillian, she had a strong sense of pride.

She also had a growing connection with his son. Though it bothered him, he couldn't deny that she had been able to discover something he wouldn't on his own, and for that he had to be grateful.

"I didn't mean that as an accusation," he said, keeping his voice quiet.

"It sounded like one to me."

Oh, boy, was he doing this wrong. His sister often accused him of being too much of a guy and not enough of a man. Clearly the guy part of him was in action here.

"I know you don't trust me," she continued, "but that was something that I was deeply ashamed of and not ready to share. With anyone."

Her comment about his lack of trust stung even though it was true. Yes, he hadn't trusted her when he first came back to Cedar Ridge, but he had seen a vulnerable side of Tabitha that showed him she was softer and gentler than she always came across when they were dating.

She's still leaving.

"When would you have been ready to share that with me?" he asked, bringing himself back to the topic at hand.

Tabitha drew away, wrapping her arms around her midsection. "I don't know."

"You say that I haven't trusted you and you're right, but right about now I think it goes the other way as well."

Tabitha released a humorless laugh. "I guess that could be right."

"Please. Just tell me why."

She waited a moment as if trying to decide whether or not he was worthy. He stifled a beat of annoyance but waited.

"I moved from school to school struggling with each new change, trying to adapt in so many ways. Each school was an adjustment socially and academically, which became more difficult each time," she said, looking away from him as if delving into her past. "I was never diagnosed until right before I moved here. I thought the teachers here knew but I'm guessing my records didn't get transferred. At least it seemed to me they didn't. I didn't expect to get special treatment but I thought they might understand. I had found my own coping skills. Lucky for me I had a good memory and I had a friend in Helen Jacobs, who was willing to help me out."

"Did she know?"

Tabitha nodded slowly and Morgan pushed down another beat of annoyance that he had been kept in the dark about this very important issue. "Didn't you think it would matter to me?"

"You have to understand that I was still a teenager. Still overly worried about what people thought of me. You especially. You were always the smart one. The

Walsh who had everything. When you teased me when I first came to town, it hurt more than I wanted it to. And when I found out you did it because you liked me, it meant so much to me. I didn't want you to know because I was so thankful that you cared for me. A Rennie. As for school, I stumbled on as best as I could but then—" She stopped there, chewing her lip.

"Then what?"

"I was tired of fighting and working so hard. Tired of being thought dumb. And the other reality was, quitting school was a good excuse to find a job. My dad had just begun his contracting business. There wasn't a lot of money and I wanted to help out."

"What was the other reason? Was it something I said? Something I did?"

"No. Not at all. Never you." She rested her hand on his arm, her glance holding his as if pleading with him to believe her. "You were the best thing that ever happened to me."

Her words were like a double-edged sword. They confused him even as they created a flurry of hope.

"But I thought I was a waste of your time," he said. "At least that's what you told me when you broke up with me."

The words echoed between them, and as Morgan held her gaze, he saw her determination falter and she glanced away.

"I should go."

This time, however, he wasn't going to let her avoid him. He placed his finger under her chin and turned her face to him. He knew he was taking a chance but he had to know.

"What did you mean when you said just now that I was the best thing that ever happened to you?"

Tabitha chewed her lip, as if considering what to say. "It was something I realized afterward."

"So you admit you made a mistake, breaking up with me?"

She slanted her eyes away, her lips pressed together, and Morgan felt another beat of frustration. She was still holding something back.

"Does it matter if I do? Admit I made a mistake?" she whispered.

Morgan sighed at her evasion. What they'd had was in the past. He had told himself many times that he was over her.

However, the more time he spent with her, the more questions she raised. He now sensed there was more to their breakup than what she had said to him at that time.

Though he was growing more and more determined to find out why, he also knew he had to take his time.

"It doesn't matter," he said, even though it did. "I'm glad that I wasn't simply a distraction for you."

She smiled at that but it held no humor.

"I think part of it was I was tired of feeling like I didn't measure up," she said. "Tired of feeling like I should have been more than I was, instead of less."

"You had lots going on in your life for a teenager," he said. "You had your father, your sister. I think it's amazing that you were able to help her out. It shows what a generous and caring person you are."

She tilted her head to one side, a quizzical expression flitting over her face. "I don't always feel so generous and caring."

"None of us do. But you have other gifts and you

shouldn't sell yourself short. You've done an amazing job of fixing up your house. I can't think of too many women who would be willing and able to tackle such a big job. And I see you with Stormy. I watched you with my brother's horses and I realize that you may have problems reading words but you are amazing at reading horses."

A faint blush tinged her cheeks. "Thanks," she murmured.

"You should do more of it," he said. "Horse training. You have an amazing ability."

"I've thought of it but I need a decent place and time to do it. To do that, I need to spend my time making money so I can fix it up. And round and round we go."

"But you would consider it? If you had somewhere to train?"

"I would love to do more training."

Her simple comment gave him a glimmer of hope. Could she be convinced to stay here in Cedar Ridge?

Then she looked up at him. "Thanks again for what you said. That I have other gifts. That makes me feel better."

Morgan sensed she was getting ready to leave but he wasn't ready to let her go. He took a chance.

Cupping her face in his hands, he leaned in and brushed a gentle kiss over her lips.

He thought she might pull away, but she stayed where she was, her eyes closed, as if savoring the contact.

Then he slipped his arms around her shoulders and kissed her properly. Her gentle response kicked his heart up a notch and created an optimism he hadn't felt in years.

And when her arms went around him and she returned his embrace, when her lips softened and she melted against him, he felt as if he had finally, truly, come home.

Tabitha was the first to break the connection between them. She released a gentle sigh as she got to her feet.

Morgan stood beside her, his hand still on her shoulder. "So what happens now?" he asked.

Tabitha caught her lip between her teeth. She looked confused.

"I don't know."

Her words echoed between them in the silence of the house.

"We can't act like nothing happened because you and I both know that would be untrue."

She said nothing and Morgan was encouraged by her silence. At least she wasn't rejecting him outright.

"Will you be working with Nathan's horse again tomorrow?" he asked.

She nodded.

Morgan brushed another kiss over her cheek.

"Then we'll see you tomorrow," he whispered.

Her faint smile ignited a spark of hope. They would simply have to see how things played out. He wasn't sure how she felt, but he knew that for the first time in a long while he felt as if he had something to look forward to.

Chapter Eleven

Tabitha sat in her bedroom, legs tucked under her, Bible on her lap. She had meant to read it, but for the past hour all she had been doing was reliving that moment in Morgan's house. The kiss they had shared.

It was so familiar and yet so different. They had each dealt with so much since those first innocent moments they'd shared when they were dating.

She traced her lips with her forefinger as if to find Morgan's kiss there, then smiled at her action. She shook her head as if to dislodge the errant thoughts and looked back down at the book on her lap. She'd been reading Philippians. Today it was chapter two.

Do nothing out of selfish ambition or vain conceit. Rather, in humility value others above yourselves, not looking to your own interests but each of you to the interests of others."

She read the words again, trying to match them with what the minister said on Sunday. About having value and worth.

Was allowing herself to think about Morgan selfish? Was she allowing her old feelings to distract her?

She set the Bible aside and looked around her bedroom. This was the first room she had fixed up in the house. It had been her and Leanne's room and they'd always hated the bright orange walls. So they'd covered them with posters they'd scrounged from thrift stores, pictures from magazines and papers from homework, making it their own.

Now the walls were a dusty blue and she used the same white trim she had in the rest of the house. Gauzy white curtains hung at the window and a blue quilt with touches of pink that she had found at a thrift shop covered the bed.

Everything she had done here was with one goal in mind. Sell the place.

But spending time with Morgan was distracting her from that. Could she allow herself that distraction? Was she being selfish?

She was thinking too much. And the cure for that, according to her father, was work.

She got up and went downstairs. And was promptly faced with her ongoing kitchen reno.

She had finally got the money that Sepp had owed her, and, to her surprise, he'd actually given her holiday pay as well. Her bills were paid for the month. When Morgan paid her, she would have enough to pay for half of her hardware-store order. Then she could finally finish the kitchen.

What happened after that?

The question hovered and for a moment she allowed herself a tiny fantasy.

She and Morgan and Nathan living in Cedar Ridge. A family.

No sooner did it form than other thoughts invaded.

Lorn's comments. Cord's reaction to her. The reality of her father's debt.

But if she finished the house and sold it, and if she and Morgan got closer...

Did she dare? Would he?

And what about Nathan? Was it fair to bring someone else into his life right now?

She closed her eyes, leaning against the opening to the kitchen.

Help me make the right decision, Lord, she prayed. *Help me not to decide for myself. Help me to make the best decision for everyone.*

"Did you get off from the clinic early again?" Tabitha asked as Morgan joined her and Nathan by the pen in her yard.

Morgan nodded, releasing a heavy sigh. Dr. Waters told him things were slower today, but he knew that wasn't true.

If it wasn't for the fact that it meant he'd be seeing Tabitha, he'd be completely disheartened.

"And how are things progressing?" he asked.

"Better," Tabitha said. "Stormy is much more willing today."

She seemed a lot more relaxed than he was. Last night he couldn't sleep. He had too much on his mind.

Tabitha's dyslexia. What Gillian had told Nathan about him not loving his own son.

You were the best thing that ever happened to me.

For so many years he had tried to come to terms with Tabitha's reasons for breaking up with him. He couldn't reconcile her telling him that she only went out with him as payback with the real true feelings he knew they had shared. And now he sensed that what she told him last night was more the truth than what she had said that horrible day.

So why did she do it?

"Nathan, Morgan, why don't you come into the pen with me," Tabitha said, her voice breaking into his thoughts. "I'd like Nathan to lead Stormy around and I'd like you to help him, Morgan."

He guessed she was trying to work on their connection as father and son, and while he appreciated it, he had his concerns. This morning, in spite of the brief moment of connection they had shared last night, Nathan had withdrawn again.

"Is that a good idea?" Morgan asked, concerned that Tabitha was pushing things too quickly with both the horse and their relationship.

"I think it is. She leads really well, and if Nathan wants to make this horse his, he has to learn to handle her sooner rather than later."

Morgan held his hands up in a gesture of concession. "Just trying to be a father," he said, trying to justify his actions.

A genuine smile curved Tabitha's lips. "I'm sorry. Just being a teacher."

Her apology and her smile combined to reignite the hope that the kiss they'd shared last night had kindled.

"And I know you're a good one," he said.

He was surprised to see a flush tinge her cheeks "Thanks for that," she said quietly.

He shared her smile for a few beats, expectation growing, and she dragged her gaze away to focus on Nathan. Morgan got into the pen and Nathan gave him a careful smile.

One forward, two back, he told himself.

Tabitha gave Nathan some basic instructions and handed him the halter rope. Then she walked to the opposite part of the pen and brought back a large exercise ball.

"I'm going to work on Stormy's basic curiosity to help you learn to lead her," Tabitha said to Nathan. "What I want you to do is turn your back to her, hold the halter rope and start bouncing this ball. Nice even bounces, not too high."

Nathan did as he was told and Morgan had to smile at how Stormy immediately locked in on the ball.

"Good. She's paying attention," Tabitha said. "Now I want you to walk around the pen while you bounce that ball. Morgan, you need to walk beside the horse. Not enough to distract Stormy but enough to help her know where she should go. Gentle pressure." He wondered if she was talking as much about him and Nathan as she was about him and the horse.

"This seems silly," Nathan objected, glancing at Morgan.

"It might, but wait to see what happens," Tabitha said.

Nathan started walking, bouncing the ball, and to Morgan's surprise, Stormy followed behind him, moving in rhythm with his son.

"That's a fun exercise," Morgan said, following alongside like Tabitha told him to.

"Like I said, it's working with the horse's innate curiosity." Tabitha sat on the fence, watching. Morgan tried not to be distracted by her, focusing on his son. But each time they passed her, his eyes drifted toward her and he caught her looking at him.

But she wasn't smiling.

Morgan stayed with Nathan as he walked and

bounced, Stormy following right behind him, docile. Nathan's grin almost split his face, he looked so pleased with himself.

"Look at me," he said to Morgan. "My horse is following me."

His son's joy, the fact that he actually addressed him personally, added to Morgan's own happiness. "Doing a great job, son," he called out.

When he was done she had both of them do another exercise with the ball, coaxing Nathan, encouraging him. Her patience and gentleness with his son warmed Morgan's heart. And created a faint promise of possibilities.

Him, Nathan and Tabitha? Did he dare think that far?

After half an hour Tabitha got Nathan to take Stormy's halter off and let her go out of the pen into the small pasture attached. The mare pranced around a few times, tossed her head, then came to the fence as if to say goodbye.

"I think she likes me." Nathan scrambled over the fence, joining the horse. He stroked her head, still smiling.

"I think that session went well," Morgan said as Tabitha joined them. She smiled as she looked at Nathan, still stroking Stormy's neck.

"Very well. Though it will take a lot more time before Nathan can ride her on his own, I'm feeling more optimistic."

She grinned at him, and he gave in to an impulse and stroked a loose strand of hair from her face, his fingers lingering on her cheek. To his surprise, she shifted her weight, came in closer.

He wanted to kiss her again, but Nathan was here and he didn't want to confuse his son. Things were still so precarious between him and Nathan. But now that he understood what was happening, he was willing to give him some space but, at the same time, show him that he was part of his life. That he wasn't leaving, as Nathan seemed to suspect.

"So now I have to ask you if you're free Sunday. I'm on call, but knowing Dr. Waters, he might be intercepting some of the calls anyway."

"He's not the easiest boss, is he?"

"Nope." Morgan thought about some of the things Tabitha had said. About starting his own clinic. He wasn't sure he dared to risk it. But if he didn't, he would be stuck with Dr. Waters and lousy hours for who knew how long until Dr. Waters trusted him.

"What are we doing Sunday?" Nathan asked, glancing from Morgan to Tabitha, who had now taken a few steps away, creating a distance Morgan didn't like but couldn't argue with.

"We're not sure yet," Morgan said, wary of making any plans on the fly in front of his son.

"I hope it's something fun." Then Nathan ran on ahead, skipping through the paths between the boxes and piles.

"He seems happy," Tabitha said.

"He is. I feel more relaxed now that I know better why he was so reserved around me. I feel like I can make a plan for how to treat him thanks to you."

"And how is that?"

Morgan shoved his hands in his pockets. "Just love him and be there for him. I have to get him to trust that I'm not going anywhere. Which is why not working so much for the clinic right now is a mixed blessing. It gives me a chance to connect."

"Give Dr. Waters time as well. He hasn't had someone working for him since his other partner died four years ago. He has to learn to trust too."

"I know. He did tell me that the work would be slow at first. I just hope that by the time school starts, I'll be working full-time. That's what I signed up for, after all."

"But this works out good, overall. It means you've got the whole summer to spend with Nathan."

"That's true. I'm planning a few outings with him. The zoo in Calgary. A trip to Drumheller to see the dinosaurs. Maybe a few more horseback rides." He stopped there, holding back on the idea that Tabitha might join them on the outings. He wasn't ready to move that far ahead.

"Sounds like a good plan. He's a lucky little boy."

Tabitha bent over and tugged on a piece of metal that had fallen, shifting it to a pile beside the path. She sighed as she looked over the yard.

Morgan felt again a clench of dismay for Tabitha. "This will take a lot of work to clean up," he said.

"Tell me about it," she returned, wiping her hands on her pants. "I've been tackling what I can, sorting through it, but some of the stuff is too large for me to move on my own." She shook her head at the collection of boxes and junk. "I can't believe how quickly my dad amassed all this stuff."

Morgan felt sorry for her, but as he looked around, a thought occurred to him. "I could help you clean it up."

"How?"

"I know people with trailers and tractors that have front-end loaders. In fact, I even know a guy with a backhoe that has a thumb."

"The backhoe or the owner?" she joked.

"Ha-ha. The backhoe. A thumb is an extra grapple on the bucket that helps grab stuff."

"I know what a thumb is."

Her coy smile and the way she kept looking at him reminded him of how they had acted when they were dating. When they were both crazy about each other.

And he really wanted to kiss her again.

"I could ask them to come out and help clean this up," he said.

"Where would you bring the stuff?"

"I'd have to ask around, but I'm sure we could bring most of it to a scrap iron dealer in Calgary. Maybe one or two of the guys might want some of it."

"What could anyone possibly want?"

Morgan heard a faint note of despair in her voice as she looked around, and he gave her a quick, one-armed hug. "You never know. One man's junk is another man's treasure."

"Well, here's hoping. And thanks so much for the offer. I appreciate it. It's been a long struggle."

"You've done a lot on your own. I can't believe you haven't asked anyone for help."

Tabitha released a faint laugh. "I made a few friends the years I went to school here and since I moved back, but not the kind of friends you ask to help you out with house renovations or junk removal."

They skirted a pile of rotting lumber, following Nathan as he meandered through the stuff to where the truck was parked.

Before he joined his son, Morgan took her hands in his. "You're not on your own with this now. I'll gladly help out."

She shot a glance at Nathan, who was swiping a

stick through the tall grass by the old barn. Then, to
his surprise, she stood on tiptoe and brushed a quick
kiss over his cheek.

"Thanks," she said. "That means a lot to me."

Morgan wanted to grab her and kiss her properly but
Nathan was waving at him now.

"I should go," he said, squeezing her hand. "When
will I see you again?"

"Sunday?"

"Do you want to come to my place for lunch after
church? So you don't have to run the Walsh family
gauntlet again?"

"Sounds good. Tell me what to bring."

"Just yourself. I'll take care of lunch."

"Okay."

"You sound like you don't trust me."

"I guess I'll have to." She grinned and Morgan felt
a calm settle over the part of his soul that had always
felt tense. Chaotic. Restless.

Did he dare take a leap and risk his heart again?

"You have to make sure you don't get it too close
to the fire."

Tabitha knelt beside Nathan, who was trying to roast
a marshmallow to golden perfection over the crackling
fire Morgan had built in his backyard. So far he wasn't
having much luck.

"Just keep turning it," Morgan offered, kneeling
down on his other side.

"I don't know how."

Tabitha was about to show him but pulled back at
the last minute. This was Morgan's job, she reminded
herself. She'd been interfering too much lately and Nathan was turning to her too often.

Morgan carefully put his hands on Nathan's as he held the roasting stick, showing him how to keep the marshmallow slowly turning. Finally they were done and Morgan carefully brought the graham cracker with the piece of chocolate close and together they managed to put the whole gooey business together.

"I did it!" Nathan crowed, holding up the s'more that he and his father had made, toasted golden marshmallow oozing out the sides.

"Your dad helped," Tabitha countered.

Nathan nodded, shooting a quick glance Morgan's way and adding a shy smile. "Thanks."

Morgan patted him on the shoulder and thankfully Nathan didn't flinch away. Morgan and Tabitha exchanged a look, both of them pleased by the small step.

Nathan took a big bite out of his s'more, laughing as melted marshmallow slid all over his fingers and down his chin. Morgan pulled a wet wipe out of a bag sitting close by and handed it to his son.

"Can you wipe my face?" Nathan asked instead, holding out his chin.

Morgan obliged and Tabitha could see that even this tiny acceptance of Morgan's help was another step in the right direction.

"Well, that was a great lunch," Tabitha said, sitting back in her lawn chair and wiping her mouth with the napkin she had stuffed in the cup holder. "I haven't had hot dogs for ages."

"It was Nathan's idea," Morgan said, grinning at his son. "Not your usual Sunday lunch, but it works."

"I like wiener roasts," Nathan mumbled past a mouthful of graham cracker, marshmallow and chocolate. "Me and my mom would have them—" He stopped there, lowering his eyes as if the memory of his mother hurt.

"I imagine those were fun," Morgan said, resting his hand on Nathan's shoulder. "I think you miss having wiener roasts with Mom."

But this time Nathan pulled away. He didn't say anything but swiped the sleeve of his sweatshirt across his face, leaving a smear of chocolate on his new red hoodie.

Then, without a backward glance, he walked over to the swing set that still sat in the backyard. He got on and swung slowly back and forth, the rusty chains squeaking with every movement.

Morgan sighed and sat down on the lawn chair beside Tabitha. "I keep reminding myself that it's step by step. But sometimes those steps seem small."

"As long as he knows you love him, they'll get bigger." Tabitha wove her fingers through his and gave him an encouraging smile. "Don't forget he had a completely different relationship with his mother than you did. In spite of what she was, she was still his mother."

Morgan tightened his grip on Tabitha's hand, his other finger tracing circles over the back of her hand. "Is that how you feel about your father?"

His words ignited a tiny jolt that was a mixture of shame and affection. She wasn't sure which was uppermost.

"He was my father in spite of everything he did. But loving him was…hard at times. He and I fought a lot when I became a teenager."

"About?" Morgan prompted.

"Moving so much. Settling down in one place. Most of the time, I felt like the adult in the relationship. He was so flighty."

"It must have been hard to move here at the age you did."

Tabitha heard the regret in his voice, and before he

could apologize, yet again, for how she was treated when she got here, she answered him.

"It was hard, but I didn't help matters much by being so prickly," she admitted.

"Self-defense mechanism common to self-reliant teenagers," Morgan said, his smile holding a hint of melancholy. "But it was your prickly attitude that caught my attention."

She held his gaze then grew more serious. "And it was your teasing that caught mine."

"I sometimes wonder…" Morgan let the sentence drift away as he looked back at the fire, still holding Tabitha's hand.

She wanted to ask him what he was thinking, but suddenly his cell phone rang and Nathan came over to join them.

Morgan glanced at the phone, then gave Tabitha a look of regret. "Got to take this." He answered with a hearty hello, leaning back in his chair, releasing Tabitha's hand. She guessed that was for Nathan's sake as the boy sat down beside her, swinging his legs.

"I'm not working, so I think tomorrow should work fine," he said. "Let me check." He held one hand over the phone, looking at her. "Are you around tomorrow? Owen is organizing a work crew."

Tabitha was momentarily taken aback. "Already?"

"The sooner it gets done, the better."

She had figured on working on the kitchen tomorrow. She'd planned on heading over to the hardware store to pick up whatever she could get for the money Morgan had paid her for the week.

She had tried to protest at what she saw as an overly generous amount but Morgan waved off her objections, saying that he'd asked Ernest what the going rate was for horse training and paid her accordingly.

"Okay. Monday sounds good," she said, still feeling rather uncomfortable with the idea. She knew she had to pay the people who came to help. She couldn't expect them to do it all for nothing. Owen Herne barely knew her other than the fact that she served him at the café from time to time. The other names Morgan had mentioned were familiar to her but not people she knew well enough to expect a favor from.

While she was thankful for the help, she didn't know where she was going to get the money.

"Can you help me make another s'more?" Nathan asked while Morgan returned to his phone call.

"Sure." Tabitha helped him stick a marshmallow on a stick, set out the graham crackers on the table and set a block of chocolate on it.

All the while she worked, she had half an ear on the arrangements Morgan was making on the phone. Sounded like he was getting a lot of people together.

When he was done he slipped the phone back in his pocket, giving her a self-satisfied grin.

"Why don't you look happy?" he asked.

She caught herself, forcing a smile as she turned her attention back to Nathan, who was engrossed in carefully turning his marshmallow. "I'm thrilled that the yard will get cleaned up. It's a huge job and I'm thankful that I'll be getting all that help."

"But…?"

"No. No buts. It's just…well…how many guys are coming and how much equipment are they bringing? I'm sure they can't all spare time from farming to help someone they barely know. That's a lot to ask and I'm wondering how I can…how I'll…" She faltered, wishing she knew how to say what she wanted to.

Morgan slowly nodded as if he finally understood. "You're wondering how you can pay them."

She pressed her lips together, realizing how that sounded, but then she nodded. "That's exactly what I'm wondering."

"Tabitha. This is a community. We help each other when we can. That's what we do."

"But I can't begin to pay them back," she said. "And I don't know how."

"The books don't have to be balanced."

"In my world they do." She gave Nathan a thumbs-up when he showed her the perfectly cooked marshmallow and helped him get it on the graham cracker. Then she stood, brushing off the grass from her blue jeans, her face warm from the fire.

Morgan stood as well, his expression suddenly serious. "Well, in my world they don't. And right now that's where you are."

His words gave her heart a peculiar lift and a breathlessness she wasn't sure what to do about.

His world? Was she truly a part of his world?

Did she dare allow herself that dream again?

But, as always, then came the specter of the debt she owed. Morgan could talk all he wanted about being a part of a community and not needing books to be balanced.

But he wasn't living with the legacy she was.

A legacy of broken promises and dreams and debt that, no matter how much she wanted, needed to be repaid before she could feel free.

Chapter Twelve

The steady beeping of equipment backing up blended in the afternoon air with the shouts and orders of guys loading stuff onto trailers. A faint breeze sent clouds drifting across a blue sky and, for the first time in a long time, Tabitha felt a sense of peace and order in her life.

This morning she had been woken at 6:00 a.m. by the roar of a tractor. Morgan was driving and he was pulling a large, empty trailer. He was completely unapologetic about waking her up so early. In fact, when she had come to the door, he had dropped a kiss on her lips and called her Sleeping Beauty. Then he grinned and sauntered off to do some heavy lifting, as he called it.

Nathan had a sleepover with his cousins Paul and Suzy, so he was taken care of.

While she was getting dressed, another tractor came as well as the loader with the infamous thumb. As she stepped outside her house, two more trucks and another tractor arrived. She felt completely overwhelmed and had to fight her initial resistance to all the help. But they were here and there was nothing she could do about it now. She had to go to work at the veterinary clinic until noon. She was surprised that Morgan had asked Dr. Waters for the time off, knowing it wouldn't endear him to the man.

In the late afternoon, when she'd returned from the clinic, she was packing stuff around and trying to co-ordinate all the volunteers who had been there all day. She swallowed her pride and made a lunch run to the café. Sepp didn't say anything but thankfully made the sandwiches she needed. Even gave her a discount.

She brought them back and they were wolfed down before everyone got back to work again.

She lifted up another soggy cardboard box, holding it carefully so its contents wouldn't come out, and carried it to a flat-deck trailer that Morgan had designated for odds and ends. As she did, she looked around, still try-ing to absorb how quickly the yard was getting cleaned up and what a transformation it was.

"Hey, Tabitha," a voice called out.

Tabitha set the box down on the half-full trailer and looked around, then saw Owen Herne come striding to-ward her, waving to get her attention. Owen was tall, broad-shouldered and somewhat intimidating with his square jaw, firm lips and direct gaze. Plus he wore his sandy blond hair long, waving over the collar of his shirt, which made him look like a Wild West outlaw. He'd been very helpful today, if a bit terse.

"Was wondering what you plan on doing with all those old cars," he said.

"Which ones?" Tabitha made a face as her eyes skimmed the yard. There were about eight to choose from.

"All of them."

She shrugged. "I don't know. Junk them?"

Owen shot her a look of pure horror, slapping a hand to his chest as if he was having heart problems.

"They're worth a ton to car collectors. Some of these are still in excellent shape. Like this one."

Tabitha looked at the car he was pointing to. Crusted with dirt, it sat up on blocks, its windshield cracked and broken, windows missing on the side.

"Seriously?"

"Dead serious." Owen scratched his chin as if thinking. "Would you consider selling them?"

"Sell them?"

"Well, I know they might mean something to you—"

"They mean nothing to me. My dad collected these from all over. Still amazes me how little time it took for him to accumulate this junk and why he thought he needed seven bathtubs."

Then she realized she was rambling, and Owen wasn't particularly interested.

"You can take them. Please," she said.

Owen slowly shook his head. "I don't like the idea of taking them. I'll bring the cars to my place and talk to my buddies. See what they might be interested in, what they're willing to pay, and take it from there."

Tabitha still couldn't absorb the idea that they might be worth something, but Owen seemed to want a reply.

"Well. Okay, then. If you don't mind taking care of it, help yourself. Please."

"Excellent." And without another word, he headed toward the flat-deck tow truck he had brought.

"So what did Owen want?" Morgan joined her, looking all sweaty and attractive with his messy hair and a streak of grease on his cheek.

"To sell my dad's cars. To his friends."

"I'm sure if anyone can, he will. Why do you look a little stunned?"

"Still surprises me that someone sees them as valuable when I've only ever seen them as junk." Then she grinned. "You're looking a little grubby," she said, lifting a corner of her shirt and wiping off the grease from his face.

He grabbed her and pulled her against him. "Just for that, I think I'm going to kiss you."

She looked around, as if checking to see who was looking.

"Everyone else is busy," he said with a laugh. "No one is paying attention to us."

Tabitha rested her hands on his shoulders, pure happiness flowing through her. "I still can't believe this is happening."

"What? The yard getting cleaned up?"

"That. But mostly this." She leaned in and kissed him, surprising herself with her boldness.

He looked surprised too. And pleased.

"I like that part too." He grew suddenly serious, his hand tucking a strand of hair behind her ear. Her heart trembled at his touch and the sight of his solemn expression, knowing what was behind it. They were cleaning up the yard to make her place more attractive to a future buyer. Hard not to avoid that reality.

Thoughts gathered up within her, confusing and contradictory. For now, she felt as if they were moving from moment to moment and she didn't dare look too far ahead.

Because every time she made plans, something changed. Every time she made a good friend, they moved. Every time something good came, life or her father's decisions or someone else's choices took it away from her.

She hardly dared hang on to this longer than the minutes in front of her.

"I better get back to work," he said, tugging at his gloves and giving her another smile.

He walked away, leaving her both confused and happy. She returned to the pile of stuff she'd been collecting and began filling a box with the glass jars she had set aside. They could go to the recycling depot. The tin cans full of screws and bolts would go in another box.

"Need a hand?"

Tabitha smiled up at Boyce, who had dragged an old metal lawn chair over to join her.

"You can give me moral support," she said, sitting back on her haunches.

"I can sort things out too." He sat on the chair that he set within reach of the pile and pulled the glass jars out, handing them to her.

"Morgan seems awful happy these days," Boyce said.

Nothing like getting directly to the point. She didn't know what to say, so she just nodded, pulling another tin can out of the pile and setting it aside.

"Happier than I've seen him in a long time," Boyce continued.

His comment hung between them, rife with expectation and question.

"I'm happier too," she said finally.

"I can see that and I'm glad," Boyce said. "You deserve some happiness in your life. So does Morgan. He told me what Nathan said to you. About his mother and what she told the boy. It was hard for Morgan to hear but it's helped him understand his son better. He wouldn't have found that out without you."

"Nathan seems to have formed an attachment to me," she said with a wry smile.

"Like father, like son."

Tabitha's face grew warm as she set another jar in the box.

"I always liked you," he added, his words making her flush even more. "Always thought it was too bad that you and Morgan broke up."

What was she supposed to say to that? *We broke up because your wife didn't like me?*

"And now you're back together again." Boyce's voice held a faint question, as if checking in with her.

She didn't reply to his unspoken query. "Together" made it sound like there was a commitment between them.

Wasn't there?

I've kissed him more than once. I'm spending more and more time with him.

Boyce sat back in the chair, giving up all pretense of helping her. "Cedar Ridge is a good place," he said, the subtext in his words not very "sub." "I think you'll find many of the people here quite forgiving."

"Some have long memories," she said, thinking back to her exchange about her father with Lorn Talbot at the shoe store. It showed her that her father's legacy was still alive and well in this town.

"You don't need to take on your dad's burdens and try to fix what he broke."

Tabitha looked down at the old tin can she held, brushing at the rust with one gloved finger. "When something is hanging over your head, it's hard to dismiss it."

"Like the money your father owes me?"

Tabitha gave him a wary look. "What do you mean?"

Boyce held her glance. "You don't have to leave because of it."

Tabitha's heart wouldn't stop pounding in her chest. She glanced toward Morgan and thought of Nathan. Thought of what Boyce had said.

Did she really want to leave?

She wasn't sure how to answer that question anymore.

"Can you turn the tap on?" Morgan asked from his position stretched out under Tabitha's sink. "I want to make sure there aren't any leaks in the water line."

When Morgan had come back from work late this afternoon, he noticed the boxes from the hardware store sitting in the back of her truck. She had picked them up yesterday, when everyone was here.

As soon as he found out they were materials to fix her kitchen, he had made plans to help her finish that. Thankfully Cord and Ella were willing to watch Nathan again.

He saw Tabitha's feet come close, heard her turn on the tap as he bit his lip, hoping, praying the line wouldn't leak.

He released a sigh of relief when all was clear.

"Looks good," he said, wriggling out from under the cabinet, almost bumping his head as he sat up. "I think we're done."

"I can't thank you enough for doing this," Tabitha said, bending down to help him gather up the tools he'd used to install her faucets. "Made things a lot easier."

"I know you probably could have done it yourself," Morgan said, a teasing note in his voice. "But think how much time I saved you."

"I would have had to jump up and down under the

sink like a rabbit, checking and double-checking everything. Would have taken me more than twice as long." She gave him a shy smile. "Thanks again."

He wanted to kiss her, but he felt grubby and wanted to clean everything, then wash up.

"Kitchen looks great," he said as he dropped the plumbing tools into the metal box, then washed his hands. "These cabinets look brand-new now that you've painted them. And the flooring is amazing. You're a woman of many talents."

Tabitha shrugged away his compliments. He knew she wasn't comfortable with them but that didn't stop him from handing them out. He sensed she could do with as much building up as he could give out.

"So, you're almost done in the house. What's next?"

"Talk to Irene Burgess. The real-estate agent. She said she had a lead on someone who might be interested." Tabitha rinsed the sink, her back still to him. "The tap works great. Thanks again for helping."

Morgan stood there a moment, torn between avoiding the topic of Irene or sticking his neck out and bringing up the future.

"So what would that mean? If you sold the place?"

Tabitha stopped moving, still not facing him, then drew in a long, slow breath. "It would mean I can finally get rid of my obligations."

"Your *father's* obligations, you mean," he clarified.

"Maybe so, but I can't act as if they're not there."

Morgan rested his hands on her shoulders, turning her to face him. "And once you get rid of those obligations?"

"I don't know what I would do. I can't work full-time

for Dr. Waters, and there's not many places around here that will hire me."

"Well, what would you have done for work in another place?"

"Work at a vet clinic using my equine sciences degree as well as my vet assistant certificate. Something Dr. Waters never wanted to acknowledge."

Morgan felt a flush of sympathy for her. "Look, I know Dr. Waters is hard to deal with. I'm certainly having my own issues with him—" Morgan stopped there. He wasn't sure he was ready to talk to Tabitha about his plans yet. In spite of how things were moving between them, he still sensed a hesitancy to change her plans.

"I'm sure you could find another way to use your skills here. You could do more horse training. Horse therapy. Working with problem horses."

"I need to establish a name for myself."

"It would take time—"

"I have the wrong last name for Cedar Ridge," she said, a bitter note entering her voice.

"You could change it," he joked, trying to lighten the mood. But as soon as he spoke, he realized how she might interpret what he said.

"I'd still be Floyd Rennie's daughter," she returned. "People's memories aren't that short."

"But you're already changing people's minds. Not everyone thinks you are like your dad."

Tabitha nodded slowly, trying to absorb what he was saying

"You're a hardworking girl," he said, hoping to encourage her. "Very unlike your father. Give Cedar Ridge another chance. It's a good place with good people. I think you can make a home here."

He stopped there. More than anything, he hoped she would take what he said to heart.

Please, Lord, he prayed. *Help her to see her own value.*

Right now, it seemed that praying was all he could do.

"So just one pill a day for the next week, and if things don't change, bring Sparkles in again." Morgan handed Mrs. Fisher the bag holding the medication and petted the calico cat on the head.

"Thanks so much, Dr. Walsh," Carmen Fisher said, scooping up her cat and cuddling her close. "And Sparkles thanks you too."

"I'm sure she does." Morgan tucked his hands into the pockets of his lab coat, smiling as his latest client walked out of the door.

"Busy afternoon." Dr. Waters joined him in the front office, bending over a computer to enter information on his most recent client as well. Then he straightened and checked the clock. "I've got to run over to the Jacobses' ranch. Check out some problems they've been having with calf scours. Mrs. Vriend will be coming in an hour or so with her dog. It needs stitches taken out. Can you deal with it?"

Morgan inwardly sighed. Really? Stitches?

"You know, Dr. Waters, I was thinking. I don't know why you won't give Tabitha full-time work here," he said. "We could use the help."

Dr. Waters frowned and shook his head. "We're managing."

"Actually, we're not," he said, his frustration finally spilling out. "Cass is run ragged and Tabitha could use the work."

As soon as he saw the stubborn look on Dr. Waters's face, Morgan knew he had pushed too far. Maybe even made things worse for Tabitha.

"When you own your own vet clinic, maybe you'll understand what I'm dealing with," Dr. Waters snapped.

"Mrs. Vriend will have to wait," Morgan said, firmly. "I've got to go to Uncle George's place in half an hour. He needs me to see about a stallion he wants to geld and a mare that needs her teeth floated."

"That didn't show up on the roster." Dr. Waters glowered at him. All work had to be routed through Jenny the secretary, who was currently out on a quick errand.

"He called me last week. I said I would do it for him."

"I don't know about this. Can't have you taking on any job you want. We need order here."

Or complete control, Morgan thought.

"I promised Mrs. Vriend you would be available to take care of her dog," Dr. Waters continued.

"I put George's appointment into the computer." Morgan felt petty but he had to show Dr. Waters that he had followed procedure. He opened the screen to the appointments and showed his boss. "Here. I put it in Monday morning."

Dr. Waters harrumphed, then adjusted his glasses. "Okay. But you still should have run it by me."

"I thought that was why we had a secretary. To keep appointments organized."

Dr. Waters shot him another angry look and Morgan knew he had crossed yet another boundary. "I don't like being contradicted," he sputtered. "I'll call Mrs. Vriend and tell her to reschedule."

Morgan would have preferred to do that himself.

Who knew what reason Dr. Waters would give her for not being able to see her dog. But he let it rest.

Dr. Waters left on another call, and when Jenny came back a couple of minutes later, Morgan was finally free to go.

As he drove away, he found himself second-guessing his decision to work for Dr. Waters. The man was getting harder and harder to deal with.

Should he go out on his own? And what about Nathan? Things were slowly, slowly getting better with him. Did he dare risk it? He wasn't much of a risk taker.

The conversation he'd had a while back with Tabitha came back to him. How she'd challenged him.

Well, maybe it was time he took a few risks. Step out on his own. Stop thinking other people had to take care of things for him. Tabitha certainly didn't wait for things to work out exactly right.

He got to Uncle George's place and drove down the hill to the ranch. A truck was racing toward him, dust billowing out from behind it. It stopped as it came alongside him, the back tires slewing sideways on the graveled driveway. Morgan recognized Devin Alexis, one of George's hired hands. The driver's window slid down.

"Didja hear?" Devin said, breathless, his hat sitting crooked on his long, dark hair. "About Tabitha's place?"

"No. What?"

"It's burning. We got the call. I'm on the volunteer fire brigade. I gotta get there. Recognized your truck coming. Thought you should know."

Then Devin spun away, spewing gravel in his haste to leave.

Morgan was frozen in his tracks, staring unseeing

out the windshield of his truck as he absorbed this horrible news.

Then he made a sudden decision, reversed the truck and headed up the road, spinning his wheels as well.

Uncle George and his horses would have to wait. He needed to help Tabitha.

Chapter Thirteen

"Let me go. Please, let me go." Tabitha pushed at Owen Herne as he grabbed her arms again.

"You can't go in there. There's nothing to save," he grunted, pulling her back.

Tabitha could only stare at the flames licking at one side of the house, her heart hammering like thunder in her chest, voices screaming in her head all saying one thing.

No! No!

This couldn't be. All her work. Everything going up in smoke.

She pulled at Owen again, sobs of anger, frustration and sorrow clawing up her throat as she pulled and tugged.

"I got her."

A familiar voice. Familiar arms. Morgan was holding her tight. But she couldn't look away from her house or tear her eyes from the flames now roaring as they grew in intensity, throwing out waves of heat.

"Where's Nathan?" he asked.

"At your father's," she managed to sob. "We were

in town—" She stopped as the flames crackled loudly, growing.

"We need to step back," Morgan murmured.

Tabitha couldn't move. Her legs wouldn't obey. Everything she had done for the past few years was now being eaten up in minutes.

The firemen were finally able to pump water on the fire again, sucking water from a dugout across the road, but it was too late. Nothing could save the house now.

They heard the whinny of a horse.

"Stormy," Tabitha cried out.

"Look, someone is leading her away," Morgan said. "She'll be okay."

Tabitha was torn between the house and the horse, but it seemed that, for now, Stormy was okay.

"Everything is in there," she cried, clutching Morgan's arms, her fingers digging into his shirt. "Everything I own." Her clothes, any mementos left from her mother, the few photographs she had. The hungry flames were devouring the only precious remnants of a gypsy life as they roared and grew. She fought him once again, and then, realizing that nothing could be done or saved, she collapsed against him.

"Oh, sweetie, I'm so sorry." Morgan held her up, supporting her. He stroked her hair, then turned her head into his chest so she couldn't see the destruction of everything she owned.

Despair washed over her and the sobs she'd been holding back finally released. She clung to Morgan, her grief and sorrow washing over her in waves of torment and hopelessness. She couldn't think, couldn't process as the heat almost seared her.

Morgan drew her back, his arms holding her up as

she staggered alongside him. He fitted his arms under her legs and, ignoring her protests, scooped her up. She wrapped her arms around his neck, her face buried in his as she gave way to her grief.

She didn't know what happened after that. It was a wave of noise, bodies bustling about, the hiss of water hitting the fire and the sickening smell of smoke.

"I'm taking you to my place," Morgan said as he set her down by his truck.

"What about Stormy?"

"I'll call Cord. He can take care of her."

"But I need to stay here." Tabitha raised her head, looking past him to the fire that now engulfed her entire home, black clouds of greasy smoke roiling above the hungry flames.

"There's nothing you can do."

"I know that," she said, her hands clutching his shirtfront as she looked into his eyes, his face blurry from the tears filling hers. "But I just… I need to see it to the end."

Morgan shook his head, then gave her a tight hug. "Okay. But I'm staying with you."

"Don't you have to work?" The thought came sideways at her, a random plucking at something, anything other than the destruction of all her worldly goods.

"Doesn't matter. I need to be here. For you."

His words settled and eased some of her pain. With Morgan holding her, she watched the inferno, the heat pushing at her, her emotions drained.

Cord came with a stock trailer and Morgan helped him load the horse, but he was back right away, standing beside her.

An hour later it was over. Remnants of the brick chimney still stood defiantly above the rubble, the hulking mass of the cast-iron woodstove in front of it, but everything else had been reduced to a blackened and smoking rubble.

"Do you think anything survived?" Tabitha asked, her voice sounding far away to her.

Morgan was quiet, which gave Tabitha her answer. No.

The fire chief, someone she didn't recognize, walked over to her. He pulled off his helmet, his face blackened by soot and streaked with sweat, then gave her a tight nod as behind him, acrid and harsh smoke still swirled and eddied, and ash and soot drifted down. "I'm so sorry we couldn't do anything. It was too late by the time we got here."

Tabitha nodded. She'd been in town when she got the desperate text from her sister.

"When did you find out?" Morgan asked, his voice pitched low, his mouth close to her head.

"Leanne texted me," Tabitha said. "She had come to the house to drop off a recipe book I had asked her for. I wanted to make a cake. To celebrate finishing the house," she said, her mind latching on to the basic, simple concept of a shared recipe. "It's a good recipe. Our mom used to make it. I gave Leanne the recipe book when she got married." She released a humorless laugh. "At least we'll still have that."

Morgan tightened his arms around her.

She wished she could tell him how much she appreciated his support. Him being there. But she was still trying to absorb what had happened.

Slowly reality washed over her like a chilly rain.

She had precious little left to sell to pay back the debt. The acreage wouldn't be worth as much without the house. Her truck was worthless and she had no savings. Every penny she had made had been poured into the house.

Closing her eyes, she rested her head against Morgan's chest, trying to shut off the voices in her head.

"We can give you any help you might need when you deal with the insurance adjuster," the fire chief said, turning his helmet around in his hands, his expression so woebegone a bystander might suspect it was his house that had burned to the ground. "Let me know what you need."

She nodded again. Insurance. Of course. She would have to deal with them.

The thought exhausted her.

Then she eased out a heavy sigh and turned back to Morgan. "I need to go get Nathan."

"No. I'll call my dad. He'll be okay."

"Then I want to go to Leanne's place." She fished the keys out of her pocket but Morgan stopped her.

"I'll take you," he said. "You're not in any shape to drive."

"I can go."

Then Morgan gently but firmly extricated the keys from her tight grip. "I'll drive you," he said.

Another sob broke free and again she was leaning against Morgan. "I'm sorry. This is so silly. It's just a house. Just stuff."

Morgan smoothed his hand over her hair, rocking her lightly. "Maybe, but it was yours. It represents a lot of hard work."

Hard work. Work to make the house sellable. Work that had just gone up in flames.

A colossal waste of time.

Morgan talked to Owen about picking him up from the Walsh place and Morgan led Tabitha back to her truck. He helped her into the passenger side and, as he got in, Tabitha saw it through his eyes. Torn seats, knobs missing on the dashboard. Visor tied with hay wire.

A broken-down truck for a broken-down life.

Tabitha closed her eyes, trying to shut off the chattering in her brain.

The drive back to her sister's place was silent. Tabitha didn't know what to say and Morgan was quiet too. But he had his hand on hers all the way there. She clung to him, thankful for his presence and for his strength.

All she wanted to do was crawl into a bed, pull the covers over her head and sink into denial even though she knew the sight of her house burning would be seared into her memory. She knew she would constantly relive it and behind all that would be the growing despair that now she had nothing to use to pay off her father's debts.

Finally they were at Leanne's place.

Leanne was at the front door and coming toward them as soon as Morgan shut the engine off.

She pulled open the truck door and grabbed Tabitha's hand.

"Oh, hon. I'm so sorry." The anguish in her sister's voice was almost her undoing.

"It's not like someone died," she said, trying to put her own wavering emotions in perspective.

"No. But still, it's a huge loss."

And Leanne would know what was at stake.

She let her sister help her out of the truck and then Morgan was beside her on the other side. "I'm not an invalid," she protested.

Morgan said nothing as he slipped his arm around

her shoulders. They walked up the stone sidewalk and then up the wide stone stairs leading to double doors flanked by tall narrow windows, with a large, half-round window arched over the entire entrance.

For the briefest moment Tabitha felt a flash of envy at the impressive house that her sister called home.

Leanne led her through the echoing front foyer with its sweeping staircase to a narrow hall leading to a breakfast nook off the kitchen.

"Sit down, hon. I'll make you a cup of tea. Morgan, can I get you anything?"

Morgan hovered and Tabitha could see he wasn't sure what he should do.

She looked up at him, giving him a careful smile. "I'll be fine. I'm with my sister."

He laid his hand on her shoulder. "Are you sure? I can stay."

"No. I'm sure you have work to do, and the last thing you want is to antagonize Dr. Waters."

"Actually, I'm supposed to be right here, so I'll go find George, get the work done. Then I'll be back."

"There's no need," Tabitha said even though the thought that he would be right on the yard gave her some comfort.

"I'll be back." He bent over and gave her a gentle kiss on her forehead, then left.

Tabitha leaned back in the chair as her sister bustled around the kitchen. "Where's Austin?"

"Sleeping. I put him to bed as soon as I came back from your place." Leanne gave her a look of despair. "I wish I had gone sooner. Maybe—"

"Stop. Don't think that. Maybe you'd have been

caught in the house." She had to stop her mind from going there.

"I just came there and I saw the flames." Leanne sat down beside Tabitha and grabbed her sister's hand. "I didn't know what to do. I called the fire department, then you. Then raced back here to see if the hired hands could help out."

"You did the right thing. You couldn't have done anything more." Tabitha rolled her head to ease the crick of tension in her neck. Then she took a long, slow breath. "Well, I guess I'll have to change my plans now."

Leanne squeezed her hand. "No matter what happens, you know you're not alone. I'm here. I'll be praying for you. And now it looks to me like you've got Morgan beside you."

Tabitha eased out a smile. "Yes. I guess I do."

But even as she held that thought came a harsher reality.

Now she had no way of paying back the people her father owed. Especially Morgan's father.

Morgan finished filing down the horse's teeth, listening halfheartedly to Uncle George's chitchat about the upcoming rodeo this summer, the rest of his mind on Tabitha. He wanted to go see her but also realized that being with her sister was probably exactly what she needed.

"Sad what happened to Tabitha," George was saying now. "Those Rennie girls haven't had an easy life. I know Leanne hasn't."

Morgan didn't know how to respond, so he nodded as he popped off the eye protection he'd been wearing, wrinkling his nose at the smell of filed horse teeth. He'd done this a few times in his previous practice and still wasn't used to the acrid scent.

He removed the speculum and put it in a plastic bag to sterilize at the clinic, then stroked the horse's neck to reassure it. The horse blinked slowly, still under the effects of the mild anesthetic Morgan had given him to keep him calm during the procedure.

"He should be eating much better now that I've gotten rid of those hooks on his teeth," he said to his uncle, picking up the tools he'd been working with and putting them away in the veterinary kit.

"That's good. He'd been spilling his grain and chewing on the fence. Figured something was up." Uncle George untied the halter and cross tie they'd used to keep the animal still. He gave the horse one final pat, then followed Morgan to his truck. "So, is there anything left of Tabitha's house?"

Morgan shook his head. "Just a brick chimney and what looked like a heavy-duty cast-iron woodstove."

"Really? Chimney fire from the woodstove, you think?"

"It's summertime, so I doubt it. Doesn't matter anyway. Everything else is gone." Another wave of sorrow and frustration for Tabitha swept over him. And if he felt like this, he couldn't imagine what she was dealing with.

"In a way, I'm not surprised. If a Rennie is involved it can't be good."

"How can you say that? Your own daughter-in-law is a Rennie."

"I didn't have any choice in that. But she gave me a grandson. Someone to carry on the Walsh name. And for that I'm grateful." George's expression grew serious and Morgan thought of his cousin Dirk, who had been married to Leanne. Dirk had died in a tragic vehicle accident. He knew it was hard on his uncle. "But she's a good girl in spite of her father," George said in a condescending tone.

"Tabitha is a good girl too," Morgan said. "She's a hard worker and she's determined to do right. To make up for what her dad did."

"That won't happen now," Uncle George said with a snort, his eyes narrowing and his fists clenching. "Floyd Rennie was a snake who cheated a lot of people."

Morgan stopped there, knowing that anything he said would only get his uncle riled up. He wanted to see Tabitha, not listen to yet another one of Uncle George's rants.

"So is that everything?" Morgan asked, slamming the tailgate of his truck shut, shifting the conversation.

"In a week or so I'm going to need you to come and look over a couple of my mares. Can't seem to get them bred."

Morgan pulled out his phone and made a quick note. "Seem to be getting more horse work lately," he said as he shoved his phone back in his pocket.

"Yeah. More people getting acreages closer to town too. They all want horses and Dr. Waters can't keep up." George shook his head in disgust and Morgan sensed another rant coming.

"Thanks for the work," he said to his uncle. "I want to see how Tabitha is doing. Then I should push off."

"Sure. And I'll call Doc Waters. Tell him I want you to come to take care of the horses."

Morgan didn't know how that would go over with his prickly boss, but he let it be. That was to deal with at another time.

He drove to the house and parked his truck in the driveway.

He had seen Uncle George's place many times when he and his brother would come to play with their cousins, Reuben and Dirk, but it always made him shake his head. His dad often teased his uncle about his need to impress, and this house, with its soaring roofs, brickwork and timbered entrance, did all that and more.

He rang the doorbell and stepped inside. Leanne came to the front entrance, then stopped when she saw him.

"Is Tabitha okay?" he asked, pulling off his hat and turning it around in his hands.

"She's sleeping, believe it or not." Leanne slowly shook her head as if trying to absorb what had happened. "Poor girl is exhausted."

"I believe it." He gave her a rueful smile. "Tell her I said hi. I'll stop by tonight, when I'm done with work, if that's okay."

"I'll ask her when she wakes up."

Morgan didn't miss the switch in her words and wondered what she meant by it.

"Okay. Can you ask her to call me?"

"I can do that." Leanne crossed her arms over her chest in a defensive gesture, which annoyed him. As if she had to defend Tabitha from the big bad Walsh.

He dropped his hat back on his head and left. Nothing more to do until Tabitha called.

He just hoped she would.

Morgan's phone rang and he yanked it out of his pocket, then frowned at the unfamiliar number on the display. Someone calling from Idaho? He was about to ignore it, thinking it was a telemarketer, when the number registered. Nathan's grandmother.

"Hey, Donna," he said as he tucked the phone under his ear. He dumped a handful of pasta into the water he had boiling on the stove, glancing over at Nathan, who was playing some computer game on the television. When he went to his dad's place, he had offered supper, but Morgan wanted to be available in case Tabitha called.

But she hadn't.

"Is this a bad time?" Donna asked.

"No. Not at all. How are you?"

Donna sighed, and he heard loneliness and sorrow. "I'm okay. Surviving."

Morgan felt a flush of guilt. He should have called sooner to see how she was doing. She had lost her daughter, after all, and was living hundreds of miles away from her grandson.

"I'm sure it's been difficult."

"I'm coping. How is Nathan doing?" she asked. "He must be loving it on the ranch."

"He's coping too," Morgan said. "Did you want to talk to him?"

"In a minute. I wanted to double-check on the arrangements you had made for my birthday. If you were driving down or flying."

Driving? Flying?

Morgan scrambled through his brain, thinking. Then it hit him like a ton of bricks. Of course. He had promised Donna that he would bring Nathan to visit her on her fiftieth birthday. She was throwing a huge party and she wanted Nathan to be there.

"Don't tell me you've forgotten," she said, a hurt tone entering her voice.

"I'm sorry," he admitted. "Things have been haywire since I got here." Seeing Tabitha and getting involved with her had erased Gillian from his mind. "I don't have my calendar handy but is it next week?"

"No. This Friday. I was hoping you could come early. Give me some time to spend with Nathan before things get busy."

That meant he would have to drive, which meant they had to leave tomorrow morning. It was at least nine hours from here to Coeur d'Alene, where she lived. How could he have been so dumb to forget this?

But even worse, it meant leaving Tabitha on her own for a few days right at this horrible time. He stifled a groan at the timing and at his forgetfulness.

"We'll be there tomorrow night," he said with more assurance than he felt. He'd have to ask Dr. Waters for more time off and he was fairly sure how that would go over. Not well.

Suddenly, however, he didn't care. There were bigger things going on in his life right now than dealing with a finicky, unpredictable boss.

"I'm so glad. I'm looking forward to seeing Nathan again."

They chatted about Nathan and Stormy. Morgan had never got to know Donna, so the conversation didn't last that long. They said goodbye, and when she ended the call, Morgan dropped his phone and leaned back on the counter.

What lousy timing.

Then he felt horrible for the resentment he felt. Donna had every right to see her own grandson on such a milestone birthday.

But why did it have to happen now?

Oh, Lord, he prayed. *I want to be here for Tabitha. I want to support her. But I want to do right by my son.*

He knew the prayer wouldn't change anything, but he needed to vent and let go of his frustration.

He grabbed the phone and for the umpteenth time he dialed Tabitha's number.

And for the umpteenth time it went directly to voice mail. She must have shut her phone off. This time, however, he left a message.

"Hey, Tabitha, I forgot about Nathan's grandmother's birthday. We have to leave tomorrow for Idaho. I'll try to call again when we're on the road. Please call me back." He paused, wanting to say so much more, but there was no way he was doing that on a voice mail. "Thinking of you and praying for you," he said instead.

Then he ended the call and did exactly that.

Chapter Fourteen

"We can't say much until the insurance adjuster files his final report," Carl Tkachuk said, his hands folded on the desk, his expression suitably sympathetic. "Lucky for you he's able to come tomorrow, which is lightning quick. I pushed him to get it done."

Tabitha shifted on her seat in the insurance office, struggling to make sense of what Carl was saying. "I appreciate that," Tabitha said, clutching her backpack, the only thing she had left that belonged to her.

"For now, all I can give you is out-of-pocket expenses. To cover a hotel and meals for you."

"I understand." Tabitha was still walking around in a haze, trying to process what had happened.

While Carl talked about the process of filing a claim and what would happen, her mind drifted off.

She'd lost everything. Clothes. Shoes. Groceries. The tiles she needed to install above the new counter she'd put in. The few pictures she had of her mother. A few school mementos, like the notes she and Morgan would shove in each other's lockers in high school. Silly little messages about how much they missed each other.

The thought of Morgan sent another sob creeping up her throat.

Deal with what is right in front of you, she told herself. *Don't think too far ahead.*

Behind that came another desperate prayer. One of many she'd been winging heavenward the past twenty-four hours.

Please, Lord, give me the strength to get through this.

Yesterday, after she had woken up from an exhausted sleep, she had lain in the bed at Leanne's house fighting a myriad of emotions. Grief, anger with God that He had let her down, a very unwelcome jealousy of her sister and the beautiful house she lived in.

But more than that was a deep, unwelcome and all-too-familiar sorrow and shame.

How could she face Morgan now? As long as she could cling to the hope of paying back his father, she dared dream of a future with him. The dirty slate her father had left could be wiped clean. The books balanced.

She had dared to make tentative plans to maybe stay in Cedar Ridge. To see if she could, somehow, somewhere, set up a horse training facility. To allow herself the faintest dreams of a life with Morgan. With Nathan.

But now?

Now Morgan was gone along with her tentative hopes. He had left a message on her phone but she hadn't called him back. She couldn't. Not yet.

Too many things going on in my head. Deal with them one at a time.

"I do have one question, though," Carl was saying.

Tabitha snapped back to the present and gave him a tentative smile.

"Sure," she replied.

He rolled his pen between his fingers. "I was chatting with the fire chief. He told me that all that was left of the house was a brick chimney and what looked like a woodstove."

"Yes. My dad put it in. Said he liked wood heat."

"Were you using it?" He made a quick note on his file. His deepening frown created a tiny foreboding of dread.

"No. It was a hassle. I never used it."

"So you didn't have it going yesterday?" Another note, a pursing of his lips and Tabitha's apprehension grew.

"Of course not. It's summer. No." She felt a niggling suspicion that they might pin the blame for her house burning down on a chimney fire.

Carl tapped his pen on the folder, then flipped through another file, folded papers back, scratched his temple with his pen, whistling through his teeth while he read. Then he sat back in his chair, his fingers drumming on the desk.

"So here's the thing. Your policy doesn't have coverage for a woodstove."

"But it's the same policy my dad had. On the same house and I never used the stove."

"I realize that, but for all practical purposes, you taking it out makes it a new policy. We don't grandfather in clauses in insurance policies. They are based on each person as an individual. Your father may have had a woodstove in his policy on the house, but you don't."

A shiver of dread trickled down her spine. "I was told I could take over my father's policy."

Carl slowly shook his head, trying to look sympathetic but not hitting the mark. "Whoever told you that was wrong. You are a new and unproven client—it would be a new policy. They would have given it to you to read over if you had questions."

Tabitha remembered now. The lady who had sold it to her had given her exactly that opportunity, but Tabitha hadn't wanted to sit in her office, struggling to decipher the words of an insurance document in front of a lady who had already treated her with vague disdain and a measure of impatience. It was difficult enough to work her way through books or newspaper stories, let alone the convoluted legalese of an insurance policy.

"I'd asked questions about it," she said. "Lots of questions. But how...? Why didn't...? Why wasn't I told about the stove? Whoever drew it up should have known what my dad's policy covered. Why didn't they inform me about the woodstove? I would have removed it." She was growing more frantic, more angry, more frustrated and, as a result, more shrill. She clamped her lips together as she caught Carl's expression.

"I'm sorry. We'll have to see what the adjuster says, of course, but I have to warn you—it doesn't look good."

Don't cry. Don't give him the satisfaction.

Oh, Lord. Why all this too?

Had she done something horribly wrong somewhere? Messed up so badly that she was being punished?

I should have read the policy. I should have checked it over.

Trouble was, she couldn't.

Another reminder of who she was and what she couldn't do.

Illiterate, dyslexic Tabitha.

Behind that came an even more insidious thought.

She was glad Morgan was gone so she didn't have to face him with yet another failure in her life.

Morgan hit a button on the screen on his truck's dashboard, ending the phone call he had tried to make to Tabitha. Again.

Nathan was sleeping in the backseat of the truck, his head lolling sideways despite the pillow Donna had provided for the trip back to Cedar Ridge.

The visit with Donna had gone well. She was so excited to see her grandson but, to Morgan's surprise, Nathan had acted shy around her. Morgan had felt bad for Donna, but what had shocked him even more was how Nathan had clung to his hand.

In spite of the small breakthrough he'd experienced with Nathan, however, the entire time he was gone, his thoughts were tied up with Tabitha.

In spite of a number of calls from him to her, she had neither answered nor called him back. He was trying not to panic. Too easily came the memory of the last time she had walked out on him. How she had shut him out and he hadn't heard from her again.

Please, Lord, get her to answer my calls, he prayed.

His mother had always told him when he prayed to be specific. Well, he was being specific now.

An hour later, he pulled into his own driveway, parked the truck and dragged his hands over his weary face. His ears were ringing from the steady engine noise and his head ached.

Nathan still slept while Morgan took their suitcases into the house. When he came back, he unbuckled his son and smoothed his hair back from his face. Nathan's lips twitched, and when he opened his eyes and looked at Morgan, he smiled.

Morgan's heart clenched at the sight, and as he lifted the still-sleepy boy out of his booster seat, Nathan wrapped his arms around Morgan's neck, laying his head on his shoulder.

Morgan laid his head against his son's, a deep, abiding love seeping through his soul as he held his boy tight. He carried him up the stairs into the house, his booted feet echoing in the silence. He brought him upstairs and laid him on the bed, tugging off the boy's boots. Nathan murmured a protest, and then his eyes opened and he smiled at Morgan.

"Are we home?"

"Yes. We are."

Nathan looked around. "Where's Tabitha?"

He was surprised that his son expected Tabitha to be here.

"She's not here."

"But she doesn't have a house anymore. Because it burned down. She should stay here."

At one time Morgan had allowed himself the dream that this might be what happened, but that was not how things seemed to be playing out.

"She has a sister, Leanne. She's staying at her place."

Nathan didn't seem satisfied by that answer. "Can we go see her?"

"Not tonight," Morgan said, not sure when that might happen given Tabitha's lack of contact with him.

"Tomorrow?"

"We'll see."

Nathan seemed satisfied with that and allowed Morgan to change him into his pajamas. He snuggled down in his bed and smiled as Morgan settled on the edge of his bed to say good-night.

"I'm glad we could see Gramma," he said.

"I'm glad too." Morgan brushed the boy's hair away from his face again, just because it gave him a chance to touch his son, to connect with him.

"But I like being home." Then Nathan looked around his room. "Can I hang up my posters tomorrow?"

"Of course you can," he said, smiling so hard it almost hurt. "We'll put them up first thing in the morning."

"Gramma never let me hang up my pictures. She always said I would have to take them down again. But she told me that I was staying here. Forever. And that you would take care of me." Nathan's eyes seemed to bore into Morgan's. "You will, won't you?"

"I will. Forever and ever." Then Morgan took another risk, bent over and kissed his son's forehead. "I love you, Nathan."

Nathan grinned, then pulled the blanket up around his neck and curled up on his side. "I love you too."

Morgan thought his heart would burst with joy. Though he had been extremely reluctant to visit Donna, something good had come from the visit after all.

He gave Nathan another kiss and said his prayers with him. He didn't want to leave but his cell phone started buzzing.

He felt a jolt of anticipation. Tabitha?

He pulled the phone out of his pocket as he left the room, leaving the door open and the hallway light on exactly the way Nathan liked it.

But his heart dropped as he saw the number on the screen.

Not Tabitha.

His brother, Cord. Probably calling to make sure he made it home okay. Morgan was tired and didn't feel like talking to anyone, so he slipped the still-ringing phone back in his pocket and made his way downstairs. He sank into his chair and dropped his head on the back, staring up at the ceiling.

So, now what?

He felt as if his life had been thrown off course the past few days. The plans he had dared make for a future with Tabitha seemed even further from becoming reality than ever.

And if Tabitha wasn't answering his calls, he doubted she would be coming to take care of Nathan.

Chapter Fifteen

"What are you doing?"

Leanne walked into the spare bedroom and sat down on the chair tucked into the corner.

Tabitha shoved the few clothes her sister had given her into her backpack and zipped it shut, trying not to wince at how little space the few earthly possessions she had took up.

"I need to get away. Just leave for a few days."

"Where?"

"I'm heading up to Sundre. I have an old college friend there." Tabitha slung her backpack over her shoulder and gave her sister a wan smile. "I'll be back in a couple of days."

Leanne held her gaze, her expression serious.

"Have you talked to Morgan?"

"I phoned Ella and told her that I need to get away. She offered to take care of Nathan."

"That's not what I asked." Leanne blew out a sigh and got up. Tabitha tensed herself for the mini-lecture she guessed was coming. She so didn't want to talk about Morgan. Didn't want to think about the failure her life had become, yet again.

"He's been trying to get hold of you. I think you should at least let him know you're okay."

"Well, I'm *not* okay." Tabitha lifted her head, chin up, gaze holding Leanne's. "I've got no way to pay back his father. I couldn't even take the time to read my insurance policy because it was too much work and as a result I messed up. I'm a—"

"Don't you dare say it." Leanne held up a finger in warning like she would to her toddler son. "You did what you were supposed to do. Your insurance adviser should have done exactly that. Advised. It wasn't your fault."

"Well, you can say that all you want, but at the end of the day I still don't have a house to sell."

"You have the land. It's got to be worth something."

Tabitha shrugged. "Not as much as the house." She blew out a sigh, wishing her sister would let her go. "Anyhow, I need to get away and clear my head."

"I wish you would let me help," Leanne said.

As soon as Leanne had found out about their father's debt, she had tried to give Tabitha money as well, but Tabitha had refused. Though Leanne worked on her father-in-law's ranch, George only paid her enough for her day-to-day expenses. Tabitha knew Leanne didn't have much extra money. Besides, if she did have extra, Tabitha preferred that her sister set it aside for her son.

"I'll figure something out," Tabitha said with a weary smile.

"You'll call me, though?" Leanne asked.

"Of course I will."

"And Morgan?"

Tabitha answered that with a shrug. She wasn't ready to face him yet. Didn't know if she ever would be.

I can't avoid him forever and I still have an obligation to Nathan.

The thought of leaving him, abandoning him, bothered her more than she wanted to think about. But seeing Nathan meant seeing Morgan, and there was no way she could face him right now.

"I'll call you when I get to Sundre," Tabitha said, giving her sister a quick hug. "Give Austin a kiss for me too."

Leanne returned her hug, then held her by the shoulders, looking like she wanted to say more, but then she shook her head. "I will. Drive safe and call me when you get there."

Tabitha nodded. Then, before she could chicken out, she left. As she got in her truck and drove away, she tamped down her second thoughts. What she didn't tell her sister was that she wasn't going to Sundre only for a break.

She was going for a job interview, and if she got it she was leaving Cedar Ridge and all the bad memories behind her. Starting fresh in a new place as she had hoped. She would sell the acreage and give what she could to Boyce and not come back.

Her sister's question about Morgan rang through her head. Leanne seemed to expect that she would simply call up Morgan and carry on. But she knew that wasn't happening. She was too ashamed.

It was the For Sale sign that finally did it.

All week Morgan had been waiting to hear from Tabitha. Dr. Waters was grumbling about her taking time off. He would have more things to grumble about if things went the way Morgan hoped.

Nathan had been upset as well, and there were times that he wasn't sure which betrayal bothered him more. Her betrayal to his son or to him.

Morgan had thought that something was happening between him and Tabitha. Some relationship that meant that she would turn to him if she needed help, but clearly he had read it all wrong.

Nathan was at his father's place, so when he was done working, he drove to Leanne's. He needed some answers.

Tabitha's sister was working in the garden when he pulled in.

He got out of the truck, then hesitated, feeling a sudden attack of nerves. Did he truly want to hear what she might have to say? What if Leanne told him that Tabitha was never coming back?

Please, Lord, show me what to do, he prayed. *Help me to say the right words. Ask the right questions.*

Leanne's little boy, Austin, was waving a stick around, chasing butterflies. Leanne was bent over a row of beans, weeding them, humming to herself. Okay. This was good. Tabitha's sister was in a good mood.

Morgan sent up another prayer, straightened his shoulders and marched toward the garden.

Austin was the first to see him. He stopped, then ran to his mother, crying.

Excellent start, Morgan thought, stopping where he was, concerned he would make the poor kid even more afraid.

Leanne caught him just as she looked over her shoulder. She lifted Austin into her arms, then stood.

"Hey, Morgan."

Morgan drew in a long, slow breath, then walked toward her. "Hey, Leanne. I'm hoping you can help me."

Leanne squinted against the sun, her expression unreadable. "Let's sit over there," she said, pointing her chin in the direction of the patio and the wicker furniture parked in the shade of a large second-story deck.

Leanne set Austin down by a box of toys and he immediately began rummaging through it.

"I imagine you're here to ask me about Tabitha," Leanne said as she sat down.

Morgan decided to go directly to the point. "I noticed there's a For Sale sign on the property."

"Yes. I tried to talk her out of it. Tried to tell her to work with the insurance company and rebuild but—" Leanne stopped there, cutting her gaze over to Austin.

"But what?" Morgan sensed there was more going on.

"Not my story to tell."

"Well, don't try to tell me to call Tabitha to find out because she's not returning my calls."

"Still?"

Morgan nodded. Leanne sighed.

"What's going on, Leanne?" he pressed. "Please tell me."

Leanne looked as if she still wasn't sure what to say.

"I care about your sister. I really do. She means as much to me as my son does. I know when I first moved back here I wasn't the kindest to her, but I had my reasons."

"It was because she broke up with you."

"Yes, and did what she's doing right now. Retreating and shutting me out. She didn't tell me why she left then and she won't tell me now."

Leanne folded her arms over her chest, looking out over the backyard, a wistful expression on her face. "I'm sure that was a hard time for you."

"Hard? I had bought an engagement ring."

"I know. Tabitha told me. It broke her heart to walk away from you."

"I don't want to go back over the past," Morgan grumbled. "That's finished. I need to deal with the present."

"Have you ever thought the past and present might be connected?"

"What do you mean?"

"When Tabitha left you the first time, did you ever wonder why she made such a huge change?" Leanne said. "I mean, one minute you guys were planning a future together. The next, she'd left town."

"She told me that I'd meant nothing to her. That she'd been leading me on." He couldn't keep the bitter tone out of his voice.

"And you believed her?"

"I tried to challenge her about it but she got angry and started yelling at me, told me that I was a fool to think that I meant anything to her. Then she left and I heard nothing from her. The next time I see her she almost runs over my kid."

"I heard that Nathan came out of nowhere," Leanne said, a slightly annoyed tone in her voice. "It wasn't her fault."

Morgan smiled at her dogged defense of Tabitha.

"At any rate, it'd been a long time of nothing," Morgan said, returning to the topic at hand. "And it looks like she's descending into the same pattern and I don't know what to do."

A moment of silence fell over the conversation. Then Austin fell and started crying. Leanne hurried over to pick him up, then brought him back, holding him close. She kissed his head and sat down, still cuddling him.

The sight made Morgan feel despondent.

"He's a lucky boy," Morgan said.

"In one way, yes. In another, no."

"What do you mean?"

"He doesn't know his father."

"Of course. I'm sorry."

"But he has me. And a mother will do whatever she needs to do to take care of her child. Just like your mother did."

Her words caught his attention. "What do you mean? What did my mother do?"

Leanne held his gaze another beat. Then when Austin wiggled off her lap, she leaned back in her chair, crossed her arms over her chest and stared over the backyard. "Ask Tabitha."

"And how am I supposed to do that?"

"Go. Find her. Ask her. You let her go once without challenging her. Without trying to find out why she did what she did." Leanne reached up and toyed with a strand of her hair, twirling it around her finger. "Sometimes a girl likes to know that you're willing to go the extra mile. To fight for her. Take a risk." Then she looked over at him. "In spite of how you see it, I don't think you did that the first time."

Morgan could only stare at her.

"You don't know what she said to me. You can't understand how humiliating it was for me."

Leanne snorted. "Don't talk to a Rennie about being humiliated. If you care about her like you claim you do, you'll know what to do." She got up and picked up her son. "Now if you'll excuse me, I have a garden to weed."

Morgan got up as she left, more puzzled than ever. He still couldn't figure it all out, but there was one thing he did know. Leanne was right. He needed to forget about himself. His pride and his hurt feelings.

He needed to fight for the girl he cared about. He had let her walk away from him once before without chasing after her. He wasn't going to let it happen again.

Chapter Sixteen

Tabitha dropped her backpack on the bed of the motel and pressed the heels of her hand to her face. Another round of interviews in yet another town and still no job. She had come to Sundre with such high hopes but her spotty résumé was no help.

She sat down on the bed and flicked through her cell phone. Thankfully Morgan had stopped texting her and leaving messages. She didn't listen to any of them. She was afraid they would make her cry, and she was tired of crying and feeling weak.

She closed her eyes, the headache hovering behind her eyes threatening to explode.

I've been through worse, she reminded herself, remembering other motels, waiting with Leanne for her father, wondering when he would show up.

Her thoughts shifted to Nathan, and she felt another clench of dismay.

Probably just as well she left, she told herself. *Morgan is his father and that's all he needs.*

She took a breath, then pulled out her Bible and

opened it to a passage she'd been reading last night, the same one the pastor had preached on a few weeks ago.

"Are not five sparrows sold for two pennies? Yet not one of them is forgotten by God. Indeed, the very hairs of your head are all numbered. Don't be afraid—you are worth more than many sparrows."

Each time she read this she was reminded of her worth. Self-worth had been something she'd struggled with so much of her life. Even now, in spite of what she read, it still was difficult to accept her true value.

Her rumbling stomach reminded her it was time to eat. Though she had told her sister she was staying at her friend's, it hadn't worked out, so Tabitha opted instead to stay at a motel, renting a kitchenette to save a few dollars.

She put her Bible down and got up to make something when a knock on the door stopped her in her tracks.

Who would be coming here? Her friend was working. No one else in Sundre knew she was here.

Then her heart jumped. Maybe it was one of the employers where she had dropped off a résumé. Come to give her a job?

Even as she hurried to the door, her practical self told her not to be silly, but she couldn't stop a sense of expectation.

Then she opened the door and the expectation turned to utter shock.

Morgan stood in the doorway, his cowboy hat in his hand, his expression guarded and weary. His eyes sought her out, an almost hungry look in them that set her heart racing.

"What…? How…?"

"Leanne" was his concise reply.

"I asked her to not tell you."

"Why not?"

She wasn't sure what to say.

"Aren't you going to invite me in?" he asked.

Tabitha looked over her shoulder at the cramped motel room, the dinginess of it hitting her suddenly.

"No."

"I need to talk to you. Can we find another place?"

She hesitated, not sure she wanted to talk to Morgan yet or what to make of his presence here. She had thought of him so much, and seeing him now, his hair pressed down from his cowboy hat, the stubble shading his jaw giving him a weary and vulnerable look, she would have a hard time saying no.

"I'm not leaving until we talk, Tabitha. Until you explain to me why you left. *Both times.*"

He emphasized the last two words, which sounded ominous to her.

Confusion and fear warred with a surprising happiness at seeing him again.

"I'm not letting you walk away again without the truth," Morgan said.

She sighed as she heard the resolve in his voice.

"Okay. I'll get my key," she said, stepping into the motel room and closing the door on him. She stood in the middle of the room, her heart pounding in her chest.

Help me, Lord was all she could say as she pulled the key to her room out of her backpack and shoved it into her pocket. She stepped outside, then turned to face Morgan and his questions. But before she would answer any of his, she had her own.

"How's Nathan?"

"He's good. Asking after you."

She fought down a sense of disappointment in herself.

"And Stormy?"

"Not asking after you."

She almost smiled at that. "Why are you here?"

"I told you. I need answers."

That didn't sound very romantic. But she supposed he had a point.

"We have to walk this way," she said, walking past the motel and heading toward downtown. "The path cuts off past the real-estate office."

"Speaking of real estate, I noticed your place is for sale."

Tabitha nodded, shoving her hands in her pockets, wishing she could act as casual as he seemed to be.

"So you're not rebuilding?"

A sudden flash of shame pierced her again as she thought of why that wouldn't happen. "No. I'm not. Don't have the energy."

She hurried down the sidewalk as if she was outrunning the memories, suddenly angry with him for making her go back to that humiliating moment in the insurance office.

"But you can hire someone to do it. The insurance would pay for it."

"Yeah, well, that's where things fall apart. I can't get the insurance company to pay for it because apparently they won't cover me because I had a woodstove in the house and I didn't know that."

"What? Why didn't you know that?"

"Because I didn't read the policy. And you know

why I didn't." She kept looking ahead, not wanting to see his face.

"The agent didn't read it to you?"

Tabitha walked past the office to a path leading to a trail along the river. "I was too ashamed to ask for her help," she murmured. "I assumed I was getting the same policy my dad had."

Morgan said nothing, and she was thankful. She didn't want to be faced, once again, with her short-comings.

You are worth more than many sparrows.

The words resonated through her, and once again, she clung to them.

"So what does this mean?" Morgan asked.

Tabitha clenched her fists, fighting down the shame as her feet beat out a steady rhythm on the packed path. They were walking past trees now. The air was cool on her heated face. "If I can't rebuild the house, then all I have left is the land to sell. Which means less money to pay your father back."

"Is that why you stayed away from me? Because you can't pay my dad as much money as you hoped?"

He caught her by the arm and turned her toward him. She wanted to resist but was tired of fighting.

"Yes."

"I told you—it doesn't matter to him."

"Well, it does to me."

"And the first time you broke up with me? Why did you run away then?"

"I don't think we need to talk about that," she said.

"I think we do. Because when you didn't answer my phone calls the past few days, I thought it was a re-peat of the first time. I was scared that you had decided you didn't want me. Again. I want to make a life with you but I can't keep thinking you're going to leave me whenever things get tough. So this time I'm not letting you walk away without telling me everything. I want to trust you but you need to show me I can. So, why did you leave me the first time?"

She held his gaze, still weighing. Still measuring.

"Why?" he insisted.

"I didn't want to tell you because I know how much you loved your mother and—"

"My mother? What does she have to do with it?" His defensiveness was almost her undoing.

In that moment, however, she knew she had to fight for him. For them. She had given in too easily before. He had come all the way here needing answers.

They came to a bench overlooking the river and she sat down, looking at the flowing water, letting it soothe her as she thought of what to tell him.

"After I quit school, your mother came to visit me to talk about me and you. Unfortunately she came to my dad's place. My place," she amended, mentally slipping back to that horrible time in her life. She faltered, but then pushed on, struggling to find the right words. "I had just come back from working with the horses and was dirty and grimy, and your mother, as she always did, looked so elegant. She told me we needed to talk about our relationship, yours and mine."

"My mother came to visit you?"

"Yes. She did."

She hesitated again, those humiliating words coming back. Haunting her.

Out of the corner of her eye she could see him watching her, eyes narrowed.

"What did she tell you?"

"She told me she had one message to deliver and one only. She wanted me to end our relationship. Somehow she had heard that you wanted to marry me and not go to veterinary school. She said she wasn't letting that happen."

"How did she hope to stop that?"

"By convincing me to break up with you. She said you were smart and had a bright future ahead of you. Then she reminded me that if I loved you, I wouldn't allow you to make that sacrifice. Her coup de grâce was when she told me that I wasn't worthy of you."

"And you believed her?"

She sighed. "Of course I did. I had quit school and was already struggling with a sense of self-worth. I knew what you were giving up to marry me and was feeling guilty over that. I still saw myself as the dumb girl. The one who wasn't good enough for a man like you. A man who had a bright future."

She could see Morgan's struggle to reconcile what she was saying with what he knew about his mother. Once again self-doubt assailed her.

"I know it's hard to believe this about your mother but it's what happened. I know you won't believe me." She was about to get up when she felt Morgan's hand on her arm, pulling her back. Once again he turned her to face him, his hand gently urging her to look at him.

"No. I want to believe you."

"Only want to?"

Morgan pulled in a long breath. "Hey, you toss this out at me and I'm supposed to just take it without questions?"

She wasn't sure what to think.

"Give me some credit here," he said, his voice holding a hint of pain. "This is new to me. I have to think about this. Let it sink in."

"Well, I have thought about it enough."

She got up and started walking away. She had finally told him the truth. Now it was up to him.

Morgan watched her go, struggling with what she had just told him. His mother? Chasing Tabitha away? Making her feel like she wasn't important?

And what am I doing now, just sitting here?

Morgan pushed aside his own doubts and ran after her. Like Leanne had told him to.

"Tabitha, wait," he said, catching her by the arm. Turning her to face him. "I'm sorry. I... I believe you."

Tabitha held his gaze as if testing his sincerity.

"I do. I know you don't lie. Why would you?"

"I know you cared about your mother—"

"Of course I did. She was my mother." He released a slow, melancholy smile. "But I also knew my mother wasn't crazy about you. She told me many times I should end our relationship. I never told you that because I thought she would come around and see you the way I saw you. I had no idea she had come to you directly. She never said anything to me. In fact, when I told her you had left, she said it was for the best. That if you couldn't stick with me, then maybe I was better off without you. I sensed she was wrong but I was too afraid to stand up to her. So I went along with what she said. That was wrong of me. I should have run after you. Taken that risk you said I was afraid to take."

Tabitha just looked at him, her arm tense beneath his

hand. Then she seemed to relax as his hand slipped to her shoulder, caressing it lightly.

"I couldn't tell you because I didn't want to come between you and your mother," she said. "Particularly when I thought she was right."

Morgan's eyes narrowed as a flash of anger surged through him. "You are an amazing person who has had a lot to deal with in her life. And I'm sorry for what my mother put you through. Put *us* through. But she was very, very wrong." He fought down a sense of loss and frustration with his mother. He tried to figure out what to do with the information Tabitha had just given him. "I wish you would have told me."

"How?"

Her simple question underlined the reality of his relationship with his mother. He thought back to what his father said. How his mother had spoiled him and Amber.

"Your mother was a teacher and I was a high school dropout," she continued. "Like I said, I thought she was right."

"And like *I* said, she wasn't."

"I know that now, but at the time I had many reasons to believe her."

"Do you now?"

She was quiet a moment, then slowly shook her head. "No. I know that God values me and that my worth is not in the stuff I have. I'll still struggle with it, but I hope I'm in a better place."

"With me too?"

"Especially with you."

"We've lost so many years…" His voice trailed off as sorrow replaced his anger.

Tabitha squeezed his hands, smiling at him. "But we're here now and, I'd like to think, stronger for what we've had to deal with. I know I've had to learn a few lessons. In realizing that God values me above many things, and that I only need His approval. Not your mother's. Not the community's."

He watched her, pride and admiration replacing the hollow anger he felt.

"I'm sorry I let you go back then," he said, his thumb stroking over her cheek. "I'm sorry I let you go without a fight. Yeah, it's hard to hear what you said about my mother, but in a way, it makes everything easier to understand."

She held his gaze, her eyes growing soft.

"I'm sorry" was all she said.

"You have nothing to apologize for. Nothing. You've been amazing through all this. A true example of strength and integrity that I, among many people, can learn from."

He leaned in and kissed her. Then he drew away from her, resting his forehead against hers.

"Tabitha, I'm never letting you get away from me again. I love you. Even more than I did when I wanted to marry you the first time."

She gave him a tremulous smile, then brushed a kiss over his lips. "I love you too."

"I'd like to try again," he said, digging into the pocket of his jeans and pulling out the same ring he had bought her all those years ago.

"Tabitha Rennie, will you marry me?"

Tabitha covered her mouth with her hands, her eyes shining. Then she threw her arms around him and hugged him tight. "Yes. I will. Of course I will."

She pulled back and he took her hand, slipping the ring on her finger, the diamond winking in the sunlight like a promise. He laughed. "It doesn't seem as big as I thought. It's the same one I had bought when I didn't make as much money—"

"It's perfect," she said, cutting him off. Then giving him another kiss. "Absolutely perfect." She held her hand up to look at it again.

Morgan felt as if he'd been running a marathon and could finally rest. He sat back on the bench and pulled her close, tucking her head under his chin. "I guess this is where we get to make plans."

Tabitha was quiet and Morgan felt a niggle of unease at her silence.

"Of course, we can wait—"

"No. I'm sorry. Plans are good," she said, fingering the button on his shirt. "It's just that I had such different ones. I'm not sure what to do about them now."

"You're thinking of your land."

She nodded, silent again.

Morgan drew in a slow breath, knowing that in spite of what he knew his father would say, Tabitha needed to finish this last piece of business.

"At any rate, we need to go tell my father and Nathan our good news. So when we do that, we can talk about the land and your debt. And assure Nathan that you aren't going to be out of his life." He hesitated to say the words but he knew that was how Tabitha saw it.

"Sure. Let's do that."

Frustration dampened the beauty of a moment so long in coming. But he also realized that if they dealt with this final issue, they could look to a future without shadows.

Chapter Seventeen

"Last chance," Morgan said. "You sure you want to do this now?"

Morgan turned to Tabitha, his arm resting on the steering wheel of his truck. They were parked in front of Boyce's house on a tree-lined street in Cedar Ridge. Morgan had called ahead and explained to Boyce that they would be coming and to please keep Nathan occupied. They needed to talk.

Boyce was curious but, thankfully, said nothing, only that he'd put on a television show for Nathan to watch so they could talk in peace.

Tabitha bit her lip, glancing from the diamond ring on her finger to the concern etched on Morgan's face.

She would have preferred to wait and enjoy the reality of her and Morgan, finally together.

But she also knew that, until she talked to Boyce, this would hang over their future.

"I'm sure."

"Okay. Let's do this."

They got out and walked hand in hand up the sidewalk to the house.

But then Morgan's father was at the door, holding it open, smiling as he looked from one to the other. "Come in," he said, stepping aside, his grin growing as he caught a glimpse of Tabitha's left hand. "I'm guessing you two have something good to tell me. Nathan is upstairs. He's watching television in my room. He doesn't know you're here. If he did, he wouldn't leave you alone, and I thought we might like some privacy."

That set Tabitha back. Clearly he knew exactly what they were here for.

They stepped into the house and Boyce limped ahead of them, leading them through the narrow hallway into the kitchen at the back. "I'll make some coffee."

"Don't bother, Dad," Morgan said. "We just want to talk with you."

"And talking is done best over a cup of coffee." Boyce shot Tabitha a smile. "You should know that, Tabitha. All those old guys yapping in the corner of the café in the morning when you used to work there."

Tabitha's smile felt forced as she settled into the old wooden chair at the small table. She sent up a prayer for strength, courage and hope.

A few awkward moments later, Boyce set down mugs in front of each of them and poured the coffee. Then he sat down himself, grinning. "So? What do you need to talk about?"

"I think you know that I've asked Tabitha to marry me and she's accepted," Morgan put in.

Boyce grinned. "I guessed that when I saw that ring on Tabitha's finger. Congratulations." He got up and gave Morgan a hug, then pulled Tabitha to her feet and held her close. "I'm so happy. Welcome to the family, my dear girl. I don't know if I should congratulate you or feel sorry for you."

Tabitha returned his hug, allowing herself a flicker of joy. It had been a long time since she'd received a hug from someone other than Morgan. "I'll take the congratulations but not the sympathy. I love your son. He's an amazing person."

Boyce patted Morgan on the shoulder. "I'd have to agree with you."

"But there's something else I need to talk to you about," Tabitha said, slowly sitting down, staying on the edge of her chair, her heart beginning a slow, heavy pounding. Morgan found her hand under the table and squeezed it, encouraging her. "And that's why we're here."

"You come to ask who's paying for the wedding? Well, that would be me, of course," Boyce said, grinning as he sat down as well. He took a sip of his coffee, looking from Morgan to Tabitha.

"No. Not that, though it does have to do with money." Tabitha bit her lip, hesitating, but then plunged on, needing to get this out of the way. "It has to do with the money my father stole from you."

Morgan's hand tightened and she shot him a grateful look, so thankful he was here beside her.

Boyce looked thoughtful as he turned his mug in circles, his silence making Tabitha even more on edge.

"Now, honey," he said slowly, drawing out his words. "I don't think you need to worry about that—"

"I know my father pulled a fast one when he shifted the title of my house—my former house—to me," she amended. "But I had every intention of making it right. That's why I was working so hard to fix it up. So that

I could make it worth more money. I wanted to sell it and pay you back. Pay off the debt my father owed."

Boyce's smile grew gentle and he leaned across the table. "Give me your hand, Tabitha. The one with that ring my son gave you."

Curious, Tabitha did as he asked. Boyce took hers in his rough, scarred and gnarled hands, his touch gentle as he touched the ring she wore. "See this ring? It means that you're going to marry my son. In my eyes, you saying yes makes you family. And family doesn't owe family money, so it all balances out."

His words almost made her cry.

"But my father isn't family—"

"And he's gone, God rest his soul. I don't know why he did what he did, but you shouldn't take that on," Boyce said, his eyes narrowing and his voice growing harsher. "You aren't your father and you aren't responsible for his wrongdoing."

"But it was so much money—"

"No. It was *only* money." Boyce leveled her a stern look. "Nothing more. Money isn't as important as people. That's something my daddy drilled into me and, I'm hoping, I instilled into my family." His expression grew softer and he was smiling again. "Like I said, it was only money. I got through it and so did everyone else. You're not responsible for what your father did."

Tabitha could only stare at him as his words registered.

"I know I love you and I know that God loves you," he continued. "That makes you valuable and that's all that matters. You also need to know that we all have bigger and more important debts that can't be paid. None of us righteous and none of us can stand before God with what we owe Him. He covered our debt. Covered yours. And that's a far more important debt than the one you seem to think you owe me. You are your own person, Tabitha Rennie. And you shouldn't let other people's mistakes or decisions determine how you see yourself. If God values you enough to send His son to save you, then you need to see your own value as well."

His words struck a chord. The same one she'd been hearing whenever she thought of the passage that stayed with her.

You are worth more than many sparrows.

But before she could react, Boyce slapped his hands on the table as if ending that particular line of thought. "And now, the only other financial thing we're going to talk about is what you were proposing to me, Morgan."

Tabitha struggled to wrap her head around what he was saying.

"Proposing? Other than marriage?" Tabitha asked, confused.

"I didn't have a chance to tell you, what with the proposal and all and hoping you would accept and then you wanting to clear things up with my dad," Morgan said, sounding breathless. "But I have a plan for that land of yours, if you're willing."

Tabitha shot Morgan a puzzled look. "What's that?"

"Well, I think it would be a great place for a new veterinary clinic. Your property is close enough to town and big enough that we could set up some pens and corrals and such."

"Wait, what? A vet clinic? What are you talking about?" She was struggling to keep up.

Morgan tucked a strand of hair behind her ear as he spoke. "I have this vet degree and the guy I'm working for doesn't give me enough hours and I know this amazing girl who has an equine health degree and acres of undeveloped land close to town that would be a perfect place for a clinic."

"A vet clinic? On my place?"

Morgan smiled. "I know it's all a bit much. I've only been here a few weeks but I can tell that things aren't going to get better with Dr. Waters. I had someone give me a pep talk recently on taking risks and I think I'm willing to do it. If I can advertise that I have an equine specialist who also trains horses, I would do that much better."

Tabitha shook her head, as if to process all this information.

"You should have waited to tell her like I told you to," Boyce said. "Now you're just confusing her."

"You're right. I'm jumping way ahead." Morgan brushed a light kiss over her forehead. "I'm excited to think about a future together." He pulled back and gave Tabitha a smile. "For now, why don't we focus on what we're telling Nathan."

"Tell him the straight-up facts," Boyce put in. "And from what I've seen of the boy, I think he'll be tickled pink."

Then he turned to Tabitha. "I'm so glad you and Morgan found each other again. I'm so glad you made it back here to Cedar Ridge and our family. You're family now."

Tabitha looked from Boyce to Morgan, the reality of what he said settling in. She was going to be part of a family.

She turned to Morgan. "Thank you for coming after me," she said.

"It took me a few years, but I can be taught." Then

he kissed her again and got up from the table. "And now I'm going to get my son."

He left and Tabitha, still dazed, could only stare at Boyce, still trying to absorb everything that had happened, still not sure where to put it all.

"I'm happy for you," Boyce said, gifting her with a wide, cheerful grin. "I've always liked you and was sad when Morgan and you broke it off." He grew serious, frowning a little as he looked at his mug. "I know that my wife got between you two," he said, his voice growing quiet. "And I'm sorry for that."

"No, please… I don't want you to think—"

"I loved my wife but I also knew about her dreams for Morgan. They were good dreams but I also think she should have given you two a chance to plan your own life. There are many times I wish I had intervened. Said something to you, but you left and I didn't have a chance. I'm sorry for that."

His apology humbled her. "You have nothing to be sorry for," she said.

"And neither do you."

His words reinforced what he had said earlier and she slowly realized the truth of what he was saying.

Then a pair of footsteps came thundering down the stairs and Nathan burst into the room.

"Tabitha! You're here." He stopped in front of her, and then he frowned.

"Why did you leave?" His voice held an accusing tone that Tabitha knew she deserved.

"I had some things to sort out. I'm sorry," she said, hoping, praying he would forgive her. "But I'm back now."

Nathan walked over to Morgan, catching him by the

hand, still frowning at her. The sight of him turning to his father warmed her heart even as his frown hurt her.

How would this little boy react to their news? Sure, he liked her, but that was as someone training his mother's horse. He had just got used to the idea that Morgan was in his life as his father. How would he react to her being his mother?

"Nathan, Tabitha and I have something to share with you," Morgan said, sitting down and taking Nathan's hand as if to prepare him. "I want you to know that I love Tabitha very much. And because we love each other, we want to get married."

Nathan frowned at that, glancing from Morgan to Tabitha. His confusion only increased Tabitha's apprehension.

"So does that mean you will be living in our house?" he asked, still sounding hesitant.

"After your father and I get married," Tabitha said, folding her hands on her lap, shooting Morgan a concerned look. He just smiled, then reached over, resting his hand on her shoulder.

Nathan seemed to consider this. Then a slow smile crept over his face. "So you'll be able to work with Stormy all the time then," he said.

"Tabitha will have work to do as well," Morgan said. "She'll be working with me when I start the new clinic."

"But when she lives with us, she can help teach me to ride after supper." Nathan's smile grew and Tabitha's worry shifted to a curious humor.

"I guess I could," she said.

"So does that mean you'll be my mommy?"

"It means I'll be helping to take care of you," Tabitha said, gently easing him into this new idea.

Nathan's grin grew and, to Tabitha's surprise, he threw his arms around her neck, giving her an awkward hug. Then he drew back and his expression grew serious. "I will still miss my other mommy," he said.

"Of course," Tabitha said, her hand tightening on his. "She'll always be your mommy. But I'm hoping that you will like having me around too."

"I really like you," he said, as if amazed she even questioned this. "We'll have fun together. We can ride horses and you can help Morgan…my dad make supper and you can tuck me in at night." He nodded with each statement as if underlining the reality of it. "It's all good."

Tabitha grinned at his succinct summary of the situation.

"I think it is too," she said, looking over his head at Morgan.

He returned her smile, then pulled closer, making the circle smaller, closer.

"I hope that we can be a blessing to each other," he said, his gaze holding hers, his love shining out of his eyes.

"I hope so too," she said.

Then, to her surprise, Morgan brushed a gentle kiss over her forehead. It was a whisper of his lips over her skin but it warmed her to her very soul.

"Well, this has been a long time coming," Boyce announced, getting up from his chair. "I can't wait to tell the crew at the Brand and Grill."

Morgan shot him a frown. "Maybe wait until we get a chance to tell a few people ourselves," he said.

"I guess so," Boyce said, pushing out a disappointed sigh. "Anyhow, you let me know when I can pass on the news."

"We need to talk to Ella and Cord, which is where we are going next," Morgan said, getting up and pulling Tabitha to her feet. "Then find a way to let Amber know, wherever she is."

"I can't wait to go to Uncle Cord and Aunt Ella's place to tell Paul and Suzy," Nathan said, pulling away from them. "They will be so jealous that Tabitha is going to be my mommy." In his excitement he ran out of the house, slamming the door behind him.

"I better follow that boy," Boyce said, heading out the door of the kitchen that led outside.

Morgan chuckled as he pulled Tabitha close. "You don't mind telling the rest of my family right away?"

Tabitha shook her head. "I like the sound of that."

"What?"

"Family," Tabitha said, leaning into his hug.

"For better or worse, you're a part of all of this now." Morgan glanced at Tabitha, sharing a grin.

"Here's your last chance to change your mind," he said.

"Not a chance, Morgan Walsh. I let you go too easily the first time. There's no way I'm changing my mind now."

"You know I love you, Tabitha Rennie."

"I do. And I'm so thankful. And you know I love you."

"No doubts there."

She stood on tiptoe and brushed a kiss over his lips. "That's good. We've had enough of those in our past."

"So, let's go and face the future."

Tabitha slipped her arm around his waist and together they walked out the door to do exactly that.

* * * * *

THE TEXAN'S TWINS

Jolene Navarro

This book is dedicated to the tribe of women
I am blessed to call my aunts: Kathy, Dollye,
Nellie, Molly, Jan, Melody, and in memory of Trish.
Thank you for being role models and inspiration
throughout my entire life.

I can't go without acknowledging the people who
have made the dream of being a writer my real life.

The brainteam: Alexandra Sokoloff's 2016 group at
West Texas Writer's Academy. Also Sasha, Storm
and Damon. And a special thanks to Jeannie Lyons
for all her help. And Matt Sherley for insight into
the background information of Reid's arrest.

To my agent, Pam Hopkins, for believing in me
even when I completely doubt myself.

To my editor, Emily Rodmell.
Thank you for working so hard to make my stories
the best they can be.

He will turn again, he will have compassion upon us;
he will subdue our iniquities; and thou wilt cast
all their sins into the depths of the sea.
—*Micah* 7:19

Chapter One

The numbers blurred on the computer screen as the reality of Danica's financial situation became clear. The bank statement bore the proof that her dream of a thriving animal sanctuary was morphing into a nightmare. She rubbed her eyes and opened the grant proposal file.

Linda Edward had trusted her to take care of the fur babies. Danica's father thought it was a waste of time and money, but it wasn't only her dream in jeopardy. The animals depended on the facility. There were a couple of big cats and a crippled bear that had nowhere else to go.

She leaned back and sighed. Was she fighting so hard just to prove her father wrong? He had always been right before. Glancing above her desk, she took the time to count her blessings.

Most days, the montage of family pictures and her daughters' artwork inspired her. Including one photo with her and her mother bottle-feeding an injured fawn. It had been taken the week before her mother's accident. Danica had been the same age her twins were now when she lost her mother.

Her sisters reassured her their mom would be one hundred percent on board with the sanctuary. Nikki, her oldest sister, told her to ignore her father's grumbling. It was just his way of dealing with anxiety. With her history, he had a good reason to worry.

Scanning the happy memories and big life events, she realized one was missing. The only photo from her wedding. It was hidden away in her room, deep in her closet. She'd thought about burning it, but one day her twins might have questions.

Her daughters. Her fingertips brushed the rhinestone clusters along the edge of the frame the girls had made. They had their father's beautiful eyes. As much as Reid's abandonment had almost destroyed her, he'd also given her the greatest gift. Her five-year-old twins inspired her to be a fighter.

Leaning back, she pulled a folder from the cabinet behind her. Enough musing—she had a future to figure out. The past was the past.

Danica needed a plan to save the animals. Otherwise, the wildlife rescue would be forced to close its doors, and she'd lose the land. The spiral of death swirled on the outdated computer. Waiting, she swiveled the old office chair to the right. The large window faced the east.

From here, she could see a couple of ponies playing with a miniature donkey. They'd been rescued from a roadside carnival, and now the trio romped in the sun.

Finally, the file opened. Before she started, a vehicle crunched the gravel in the front drive. Praying it was the exciting news James had hinted about at church on Sunday, she made her way to the door. As the local parole officer, he often sent her workers that needed community hours. Free labor was always a win.

The old unmarked Uvalde County car came to a stop at her door. Hope surged through her veins. James Bolton was also on her board, and he knew she needed someone who could manage the unique diet plans and daily health issues of multiple species, along with transportation. It was hard to find trained and experienced people who were willing to work for free. If he had a parolee with that background, it would be a perfect fit for what she needed to complete the application.

Standing next to the patrol car, James waved. "Hey, beautiful. I come bearing gifts. You can take me to the movies to show your gratitude." He wiggled his dark blond eyebrows.

She shook her head and grinned. The county officer was always flirting with her, but she never took him seriously. "James Bolton, you'd hate the movie I'd make you see." She glanced to the passenger's side of the car. He went around to open the back door, but the man stayed inside. With the partition between the seats, she couldn't make out much.

If he was a vet tech, she might run and hug him. On the edge of the step, she turned to James. "Please tell me your latest ward is certified in animal husbandry?"

"Yes, ma'am."

Everything inside her wanted to dance and sing. She lifted her face to the sun. *Thank You, God.*

A hand appeared on the top of the door, and in slow motion the man straightened. His head stayed down, the cowboy hat blocking his face. He was over six feet tall and well built. Younger than she'd expected. He didn't move. She hoped he was all right.

The man just stood there for a while. He removed

his cowboy hat and slowly raised his head. His eyes reached hers.

A rush of ice froze her blood in its place. There was no way. She could not be seeing the person she thought she was seeing. It didn't make sense. Rubbing her eyes, she looked again. His dark skin highlighted startling gray-green eyes that stared straight at her. The exact same eyes as her daughters'.

"Danica, this is my latest parolee, Reid McAllister. He comes with exceptional references and the experience you need. Reid, this is…"

James kept talking, but he no longer existed in her world. Reid McAllister stood in front of her. The man who had vowed to love her forever, before she knew how short forever was.

After a six-year vanishing act, her husband, the father of her twins, stood at the steps of her sanctuary.

Her heart stopped, and her knees went numb. To remain standing, she wrapped her fingers around the post. Her girls!

In a panic, her gaze darted around the area. The girls weren't here. They were safe with her sister. Forcing her attention back to James, she took a deep breath and tried to gain control of her brain.

That was a problem she always had around Reid. Crazy sounded fun and reasonable. But the impulsive, reckless girl she'd been was gone now. She needed sensible, rational thoughts.

No one knew she was foolish enough to elope and marry a man her father didn't even like, except the man standing in front of her. A parolee.

Reid in prison? She was going to lose her lunch.

Strong fingers gripped her elbow. Blinking, she

focused on her friend. He was safe. James stepped closer. "Do you need to sit down? Are you sick? What's wrong?"

He led her to the large wooden bench by the front door. Looking over the uniformed shoulder, she found Reid. At some point, he had moved closer to her and now stood at the bottom of the steps, hands in his pockets.

His expression was as hard as the cold stone of the Texas Hill Country. This man wasn't her Reid.

Her Reid had always had a smile and a spark in his eyes for her. The gray-green of his irises struck her, but they looked flat and cold now. His black hair was cropped close to his skull. What had he done to end up in prison, and why hadn't he told her?

She rubbed her head. "It hurts."

"I'm going to get you some water and aspirin. Don't move." James disappeared through the front door.

Reid was as still as a snake trying to hide in the tall grass. He just stood there and stared at her, his full lips in a small snarl. Acting like a rescue animal that didn't trust anyone, even the ones trying to help. He had no right to be mad at her. She was the injured party here.

"Are you dating him?" Each word tight and low.

Anger jolted through her. Standing, she took a step forward, then stopped. "Six years without a word and... that's not any of your business."

There was a slight shift in his expression, but then the I-couldn't-care-less face was back in place. He shrugged. "Are we still married?"

"What?" Lowering her head into her hands, she dropped back onto the bench. She just couldn't process this. "I got one call from you, telling me our marriage was a mistake. That was it. No way to get ahold of you to make sure you were all right. You were just gone. I thought you had gone back to New Orleans."

Through a haze of confusion, she studied his face. His throat tightened, but there was no other change in his expression. "You show up at my door, asking me if we're still married. You can't be real."

She'd thought a new parolee had been an answer to a prayer. Was this some horrible joke?

Reid looked down the drive that had brought him here. "Baby, as soon as he comes back, I'll tell him I can't do it. He can take me back to the ranch."

"Which ranch?" Sweat slipped down her spine, causing her to shiver. His voice made her want to cry for everything he had taken from her. Baby. She used to love the way he called her baby with that accent.

That voice carried her back to the days she loved just sitting and listening to him talk. He had been twelve when Katrina sent his family to Houston. The rhythm and sounds of New Orleans still rolled off each syllable. She shook her head. It didn't change what he did. "Reid, I don't understand. Why are you here?"

"I took a job at Hausman Ranch. I'm a wrangler." The door opened, and Reid retreated. She needed to talk to him, to find out where he'd been. Why had he left her? Prison. Why had Reid been in prison? Questions bombarded her brain faster than she could process them.

Her nails cut into her palm. If she didn't know yesterday, she didn't need to know today. He was her past and needed to stay that way.

James sat next to her. "Here, take this."

She took the painkiller he offered and the mason jar of ice water. Long slow drinks of the cool water soothed her burning throat. She needed time. Her brain was overloaded. "Thank you." She cupped the large-mouth jar in both hands and studied the ice before risking a glance in Reid's direction.

He stood with his hands braced on the top of the car, head down. "Officer Bolton, can you take me back? She doesn't want a convict working at her place."

James shook his head. "I bring her parolees all the time." With narrowed eyes, James faced her again. "Plus, she needs someone with your skills. Danica, are you sure you're okay? Do you want me to call Jackie or your dad?"

"No!" Taking a deep breath, she willed her blood pressure to slow down. "I'm fine. I've been sitting all day working on the paperwork for the application. I didn't eat lunch. I must have gotten up too fast. Just dizzy."

James didn't look like he believed her. With one hand on her shoulder, he leaned closer. "Are you sure? You need to take better care of yourself."

She managed a smile. "Yes, I'm sure."

Reid turned. Leaving his profile for her to study. There was a harder edge to his jaw than she remembered. A scar that hadn't been there before cut next to his ear. Her stupid heart missed a beat. No, no, no.

With his back now leaning on the patrol car, he stared out across the five-hundred-acre sanctuary. He crossed his arms, causing his shirt to pull tight over his broad shoulders. He'd filled out, gotten stronger. *He's been in prison.*

"Reid was a pre-vet student from your old stomping ground over at A&M. In prison, there was a rodeo program, and he worked with large animals. He was able to finish an associate's degree in animal husbandry. You need him to get the funding, right?" James turned to Reid. "She's in a rough place, and the sanctuary needs the global certification to qualify for a grant that will give her the funds needed to keep the place running."

His gaze found her. "So, you're the veterinarian?" A line formed between Reid's eyes as he spoke.

"I didn't finish college. I had to come home my junior year." Let him think about that.

James kept talking as he stood. "No, she's not the vet. Dr. Ortiz out of Uvalde serves as the vet. I sit on the Hill Country Wildlife Rescue Board. When I got your paperwork, it was a true gift from God. Thought I'd surprise her and get to play the hero. You know, save the day, keep the sanctuary open and all that." He laughed. "Actually get a date."

"James." She was not in the mood to deal with his jokes.

Reid's head jerked around, his sharp gaze penetrating. "Without my help, you might have to shut down?"

She hated to admit it, but yes. She needed Reid McAllister. Well, the animals needed him. She didn't want anything to do with him. With a nod, she got to her feet. "Yes." She had to wonder at God's timing.

Bobby, the groundskeeper, came from behind the building. Even though he was pushing seventy, his tall frame moved with well-earned confidence. He outworked any of the younger guys she had on the property. The sun weathered his face, digging deep creases into his skin. With his steel gray mustache, Danica liked to think of him as her own Sam Elliott.

The officer greeted him and shook his hand. "Reid, this is Robert Campbell. He lives here on the grounds and takes care of everything. Reid here has a degree in animal husbandry."

Bobby stepped forward and offered his hand. "You're one of Jimmy's parolees?"

Reid gave a stiff nod as he shook the older man's hand. "Yes, sir."

"What were you in for?" Bobby kept Reid's hand firmly in his. They stood eye to eye, both over six feet with the muscular frames of hardworking men.

"Transporting drugs across state lines." His stance and gaze stayed steady as he met Bobby's question head-on.

She pressed her hands against her rapid heartbeat. She needed to calm down. "Did you do it?" Her voice struggled to climb out of her throat. She couldn't imagine her Reid doing anything like that. Maybe he'd been framed.

He pulled his hand from Bobby's and shrugged. "When someone offers you a couple thousand dollars to drive a car from one state to another, you know. Even if you don't ask and they don't tell. But I thought a shortcut to money was worth the risk."

"Sounds like there was a girl you wanted to impress." Bobby adjusted his cowboy hat. "It's always about a girl. I had a little run-in with the law myself when I was younger. It didn't pay off." He glanced at his watch. "Well, I got animals waiting for me." He nodded at Danica. "Remember, I'm just one click away if you need anything." Turning back to Reid, he pointed to his walkie-talkie. "I always have this, so if she needs me, I'm there. Nice meeting you." With the last word, he left.

James shifted his attention to Danica. "Are you feeling better? I could bring Reid back tomorrow."

If she wanted a fighting chance to keep the sanctuary running, she didn't have a choice. "I'm good. Whatever it was, I'm over it."

She was over loving her husband, too, so why did he have to show up now and throw her heart into an undertow? Pulling her denim jacket tighter over her chest, Danica peeked at Reid from the corner of her vision. She was stronger than some leftover love that had dug into the bottom of her heart. "I could take you on a tour if you still want to do your community service here."

He nodded. Grim would have been a happy description compared to the hard set of his jaw and eyes.

She was going to have to keep him away from her daughters and her family. What would he do if he found out he was a father? Would he even care?

Reid fell in behind Danica. Somehow, she was more beautiful than the last time he'd seen her. Of course, he hadn't known it would be the last time.

Easy money was never really easy. Reid had known better, but he'd thought a few days to make enough money to impress her father would set them on the right path. The few days had turned into six years, and he was pretty sure her family hated him now more than back then.

It was not the path God intended. But being young and impatient, he hadn't had enough faith to wait. Now the best thing that had ever happened to him was out of his reach.

Officer Bolton took a call and moved away from them. Danica stopped and glanced back at the officer.

Being this close to her was dangerous for his sanity. The sun was high over the hills, and a soft breeze played with her red curls, picking up golden highlights. A random strand crossed her face, and she tucked it away only to have it fall loose again.

Her hair always fascinated him. He'd called it red. She'd told him it was strawberry blond. From that day on, he'd loved strawberries.

She wore it shorter now. In college, it hung below her waist. Fisting his hands, Reid stuffed them in his back pockets to keep from touching her.

This was not how he'd imagined their first meeting, and he had spent hours daydreaming about it. Then again, prison wasn't in his plan on the day he had promised to love her forever.

She cut a hard glare at him. Caught staring, he suddenly found his worn boots fascinating. He had no right to be thinking of her or looking at her.

From the corner of his eye, he glanced at the porch. She scanned the area with short jerky movements. Taking a step closer to him, she twisted and lowered her head, trying to make eye contact with him. He gave in and stared right at her.

The connection didn't last long. Danica quickly looked away. "You've been in prison? I don't understand. Why are you here now? After all this time?" She bit her lip and straightened. Back stiff and arms crossed, she looked off to the surrounding hills.

Reid had always loved the way she showed her emotions around him, not afraid or ashamed. But now he could see her fighting back the tears, fighting to be stoic with each blink. Her bottom lip disappeared between her teeth. Instinct told him to hold her, to reassure her.

Stalling for time, he cleared his throat and prayed for the right words. Fully aware there weren't any. "Baby,

I know sorry is not good enough for what I did to you, but it's all I have."

No explanation was good enough. He shrugged. "I didn't mean to show up on your doorstep unannounced this way. I didn't know he was bringing me to you." His throat was still dry, but he had so many words he needed to say to her. "He just told me a wildlife rescue program needed a vet tech."

When his mentor had showed him a list of jobs needing his skills, he couldn't believe there was a ranch close to her hometown. Wanting to see her so badly, he thought maybe it was God giving him an opportunity to make it right. Now he realized it could have been his pride. "If me being here is a mistake, let me know and I'll leave."

An annoyed sound came from her beautiful lips. "What did you hope to achieve? I've moved on. You told me you had decided to go home. That our marriage was a mistake and you wouldn't be back. One phone call and you left me without a way to get in touch. You just left." Her breathing was short and hard.

The numbness that encased his heart a couple of years ago slipped a bit, and he stood before her with fresh wounds. He rubbed his face and focused on the hills. He didn't have the strength to be near her and not want to be in her life. She had been his until he'd destroyed their future. He knew right then that without her forgiveness, he was still in prison.

"Danica, our marriage was a mistake. My family tradition is failure, prison and violence. I thought I had escaped, but it followed me. I'm not asking to be part of your life, but I'm here with the skills you need. Let me help until you get someone else." He clenched his jaw and looked over her shoulder at the building behind her. Chipped paint revealed years of neglect.

His own father had destroyed his beautiful Creole mother. Now the promises he'd made Danica lay shattered on the ground. To keep his hands out of trouble, he stuffed them in his pockets. His gaze was not as easy to control. Tall and lean, she was so much stronger than his mother.

At least he hadn't brought children into this mess.

Without a word, she stared at him. Guilt and shame were heavy burdens to carry. Lowering his head, he took deep breaths. In prison, he'd learned really quickly to avoid eye contact, and it was hard to change the habit.

Officer Bolton joined them. "Call just came across the radio. During a drug bust on the edge of the county, they got a surprise in the basement. They found a caged bear and an old black jaguar. The cat has a bad leg. There was talk of putting the animals down. I told them I was with you, and we could transport the animals here. I already called Dr. Ortiz to meet us there." He smiled at Reid. "Initiation by fire. It looks like you're jumping into the deep end today."

Reid looked at his wife. No, he couldn't think of her in those terms. It was too dangerous to get wrapped up in what could have been. Her hard glare felt like heat burning his skin, starting at his neck and traveling down.

Bolton slapped him on the back, causing him to jerk around. The officer laughed. "You go in the truck with Danica. She'll update you. I'll wait for you to gather your things, and you can follow me." With a big smile, he headed to his patrol car. "Welcome to the world of rescue."

"Come on, Mr. McAllister." She didn't wait for him. "I need to get the supplies. Have you moved large sedated animals before?"

He followed. "A few times, Mrs. McAllister."

She stopped in front of him, and he bumped into her back. His hands went to her arms to prevent her from falling forward. He shouldn't have been so close. In that instant, he reacted as if she was still his. He closed his eyes and inhaled her scent, savoring the shape of her arms under his hands.

With a twist, she was out of his reach. Her breathing made her shoulders rise and fall in quick succession. "I never changed my name. I'm a Bergmann, and we don't forget. And we sure don't forgive easily. So, you will call me Ms. Bergmann. No one knows I married you, and it will stay that way."

With the precision of a general, she turned and marched to the small house. He followed. He had a feeling he would follow her to his death if she let him.

Sometimes when something was broken, fixing it wasn't an option. The best a person could do was throw it away and move on. *God, is this where You wanted me, or am I being a stubborn fool?*

Chapter Two

The patrol car slowed down in what looked to be the middle of nowhere, surrounded by nothing. Perfect place for activities that needed to be hidden from the law. Except they found this one.

"Is it safe for you to be out here?" He didn't like the idea of her being around these kinds of lowlifes, the kind that made up his family.

With a quick glare, she gave him his answer loud and clear. It left a bitter burn in his gut to see the hostility coming from eyes that used to look on him with love.

They followed the county car down a narrow, over-grown dirt road. It was another five or six miles deep into the wooded ranch before they came up to a fortress-like structure. Who would want a home that looked like a prison on the outside?

Once through the gate, a building that looked more like a Malibu beach house appeared before them. Several different types of law enforcement were coming in and out of the house. Boxes and computers were being loaded into vans.

Cold sweat broke out over Reid's entire body, and his

skin shrunk around his bones. Three breaths in and one long exhale helped a little. They were not here for him. They weren't taking him back to the small windowless concrete cell. He was free and not doing anything that would put him back there.

"Reid? Are you okay?" Hearing her voice calmed him better than all his coping techniques and self-induced pep talks.

Trying to give her a reassuring smile, he nodded. "Just a few too many uniforms with weapons for my peace of mind."

Officer Bolton tapped her window and waited for her to roll it down. "Dr. Ortiz is right behind us. I'll find out the location of the animals so you can park the trailer close."

She opened the door. "I'll come with you. I have a couple of questions before we enter the area with the jaguar and bear." Over her shoulder, she talked to Reid. "Wait here. When I get the information, can you move the trailer up to the area we'll be exiting with the animals?"

With a nod, he got out of the truck and moved to the driver's side. A few of the officers glanced at him. He kept his head down and counted his breaths.

The ex-con label would be attached to him until the day he died and beyond. He gritted his teeth. It would be part of his life forever now, so he'd better get used to it.

Nothing new. Every male in his family carried the stigma. Being the only one to finish high school hadn't saved him from his family tradition. He popped his knuckles. Could they tell by looking at him?

Before he hid inside the cab, a large white truck with several compartments in the back pulled up next to him. A tall Hispanic woman stepped out. She came straight to Reid with an inviting grin and her hand out. Reid had to wonder if she bleached her teeth or if they were naturally so white and perfect.

"Hi, I'm Sandra Ortiz. I'm Danica's on-call veterinarian. Since I've never met you, I'm hoping she finally found a vet tech with an animal husbandry degree."

"Reid McAllister. Yes, I'm her new vet tech. For now."

The woman's smile went bigger as they shook hands. "Good, good. I told her not to worry. God would provide."

Reid wasn't sure if it was God or his selfish desire, but he didn't say anything.

"Hey, Sandy." Danica returned and gave the other woman a quick hug. "Seems we have a full-grown male jaguar and a very young bear cub in the basement."

With quick, efficient motions, the vet started pulling equipment from the back of her truck. "Congratulations on the new vet tech. I'll call Gloria and let her know to close the search."

"Oh, no. Don't do that. Reid is one of James's parolees. He's here temporarily, so the faster I can get someone in full-time the better."

Reid saw it. The friendliness turned to suspicion the second the doctor learned she was talking with a convicted criminal. He needed to get used to it.

Every time he started over, people would know, and he'd be an ex-con for the rest of his life. An ex-con without a home or family.

Danica loaded the rifle with the dart Dr. Ortiz had prepared, taking careful aim at the black jaguar as it paced and growled in the small enclosure. There were white patches of hair sprinkled over his coat, indications of old wounds and injuries.

They would have to move fast once she shot him. Anger welled up at the humans who had caged this beautiful wild animal and removed his front claws. His fangs were coated with gold, and a gaudy diamond collar was too snug around his neck. One of his hind legs was not bearing weight.

They'd already removed the young bear cub. She was small enough for Reid to carry her to the large crate secured in the trailer. He now hung back from the other men. Backed into a dark corner, much like the young bear they'd found huddled in her cage.

"Is she going to shoot the cat through the bars of the cage?" She couldn't see who Reid asked, but her husband's low voice caressed her skin.

It had taken her almost two years to get him out of her mind. She stopped missing him four years ago, but it seemed as if parts of her heart had already forgotten she didn't love him anymore.

She sighed. "Some of us are working over here if you don't mind. The big guy is already scared, and I want to make him as comfortable as possible." Bringing the rifle back to her shoulder, she cast the big cat in her sight. As soon as she pulled the trigger, the jaguar snapped at the spot she hit on his rump. It didn't take him long to go down.

"We need to move fast."

Reid didn't hesitate a minute. He attacked each of the steps like a pro. Dr. Ortiz was working right alongside him as he finished securing a cloth over the animal's eyes to keep the cat calm when he woke. With James and a couple other men, they lifted the cat onto a long board and carried him out.

The entire time, Reid talked in a quiet voice to the animal while they moved him. The same voice that calmed her when she was upset or stressed.

First thing in the morning, she would start calling her contacts and get the application to the National Wildlife Federation turned in ASAP. She needed to get Reid out of her life, the sooner, the better.

With the animals secured, Reid disappeared inside the truck as she went to touch base with the lead officer.

Unfortunately, he was waiting for her with three more crates. The day was not quite over. She would be leaving with more than the two in the trailer. "The animals are secured. The basement is all yours. What do you have there?"

"Goats. Six kids. We crated them so you could load them quickly." He smiled as if they were a gift.

James came up behind her and touched her arm. "I'll help you with these. I know time is sensitive." He picked up the one closest to him, and the two goats inside started bleating.

Reid joined them. "Is everything okay?" He kept his gaze on her, ignoring the FBI agent.

"Seems as if we have a few more additions to our family. Baby goats." She looked from the FBI agent Reid was avoiding to the crated goats. "Reid, place them in the bed of the truck. There are bungees in the back seat."

With a quick nod, he went to work.

A short time later she drove over the hills, back to her struggling sanctuary, with six baby goats, a black bear cub, an old jaguar and one secret husband in tow.

How had this become her life?

God, I'm working on turning this worry over to You,
but right now I'm feeling a bit overwhelmed. Lord,
please show me what to do!

"Did you say something?" Reid kept looking over
his shoulder, to the cargo they were hauling.

She didn't think she said anything out loud. Great.
Now she was mumbling to herself. "Just having a conversation with God. The babies are safe. No one will get out."

"What about the jaguar? The tranquilizer will wear
off soon." He looked back again, his brow furrowed.

"Reid, this isn't my first rodeo. I know what I'm
doing. We might have to sedate the big guy again before we can unload him. I've gotten good at working
with wild animals, and I know how unpredictable they
can be. I promise I've got this under control."

"The bear looks too young to be away from her
mother. Will you have to hand-raise her?"

"Yes, but we'll keep hands off as much as possible.
She'll be assigned a number. Once she's old enough,
we'll either release her into the wild or the bear section
on the ranch. You were great, by the way. Some people
have a hard time working with the big animals, even
when they're out."

"I learned to work fast while staying calm. It's the
best way to survive when you have a two-thousand-
pound bull that needs medical attention. I've never been
this close to a big cat. He's stunning."

"He's a beauty." This didn't seem real. She was sitting with the man she married six years ago, talking
as if he hadn't walked out on her and their daughters.
She glanced at him. He was checking the trailer again.
"Why did you move close to my hometown? Did you
know I was living here?"

"You were always close to your family, and I couldn't imagine you being away from your twin sister for too long. When we talked about the future, it involved Clear Water and your family. So even if you hadn't moved back home, I knew you would be around. I meant it when I said I hadn't planned on blindsiding you like this." He turned to face her. His gray-green eyes scanned her face before coming back to meet her gaze.

With a sharp breath, she turned her focus on the rural highway. Just because Reid's eyes still did things to her insides didn't mean it was wise to trust him. That was more evidence that she needed to be wary and keep her distance.

"But why even come back to the Hill Country? Why not New Orleans or Houston? Don't you have family in both of those places?" It would have been so much better if he stayed away. She had gotten good at the out-of-sight-out-of-mind game she played with herself.

"None that I want to claim. There's nothing in Houston or New Orleans for me other than trouble. While in prison, I met Ray Martinez. His church had a prison ministry and organized Bible studies. He changed my life. Well, God used him to change me."

Her jaw started to hurt, making her take a deep breath to relax. The resentment burning in her gut would turn toxic if she allowed it to fester. "I tried to get you to church the whole time we were dating. You were always too busy." Sarcasm might not be the best option, but it made her feel better. "So, you found God in prison, and now you want to right all your wrongs?"

"It's not that easy."

He was fortunate she didn't throw things at him. Hand over hand, she turned off the highway onto the farm-to-market road that led to the sanctuary. Silence lingered, and she let it hang between them. She needed to focus on the hurt and abused animals and her daughters. She had to figure out what would be best for them.

Pulling up to the large gate, she rolled down her window. The Texas heat hit her. It felt good in contrast with the coldness of the cab. Leaning out the window, she punched in the code for the gate. The gate paused halfway. She hit the box, and it started moving again. She needed someone to look at the motor. Maybe her baby sister would do it for free.

Dr. Ortiz followed along with Reid's parole officer. Her long-lost husband had a parole officer. There was no reason for him to know about the twins, and her innocent girls didn't have to find out their father was a convict.

Once parked, they all got out and sedated the cat again. As a team, they moved fast to get the cat in an exam room so Sandy could check him. There was an old break in his hind leg that they wouldn't be able to correct. Bruises and small cuts covered his body. While the vet and Danica tended to the big guy, Reid stayed at the jaguar's head the whole time, keeping him calm and watching for signs of stress.

Removing the gold caps from the deadly fangs, Sandy shook her head. "I just don't understand people. Taking a beautiful animal and turning him into a freak show for their warped entertainment."

Lowering the table, they slid him into an enormous wooden crate. As Danica closed the door, the cat lashed out and caught the edge of Reid's hand with its teeth.

Once Danica secured the latch, she grabbed his hand. Without asking, she pulled him to the sink. "I don't think it needs stitches." She glanced at Dr. Ortiz. "What do you think?"

Reid tensed under her touch as they crowded around his minuscule injury. She glanced up and found him staring off at the crated cat. "Are you okay?"

He jerked his chin. "I've had much worse."

Sandy went to the cabinets and came back with ointments and bandages. "It's not deep. I think you'll just need to keep it clean and bandaged for a few days."

"After checking the cub, we'll need to fill out an incident report." Danica kept her head down.

Both women worked on his hand. At one point, he tried to pull back. His free hand rubbed his forehead. "It was my fault. You don't need to write him up. He was scared, and we all have the instinct to protect ourselves."

He didn't flinch once while they worked on the cut. "The cat's not going to get in trouble." She carefully added the small metal clip to hold the wrap in place. "But I do have to write up the incident. Not following the rules is what gets us in trouble. Hiding the truth doesn't help anyone." Her voice grew a little stronger than it needed to be.

Sandy gave Reid a hard look. "We can't put the refuge at risk because of a simple documentation you don't want to take the time to fill out."

Reid rolled his neck and looked down, a frown on his face. This wasn't Sandy's fight, so Danica wasn't sure what happened to the vet's usual friendly manner. Possibly she was having a tough day. Danica could relate to that. Instead of wasting time trying to figure out other people's problems, she went to the baby bear.

The small black bear looked healthy, except for being a little underweight and hungry. Sandy filled out the health form. "He'll need to be hand-fed for now."

The little bear seemed to have bonded with Reid, wanting to cling to him. Danica went into the kitchen area to fix her a bottle. Sandy followed her.

"I need to go. I'll take the new guy with me and drop him off wherever he belongs. Or I could take him to Bobby."

"He's fine. It's been a while since we had a baby of this type, so I need Reid to help prep the enclosure."

"I don't think that's wise. I'd stay, but I need to finish my rounds. He's not staying here, is he?" Disgust dripped from each word.

Danica stopped mixing the formula and looked at Sandy. "No, he has a job as a wrangler at the Hausman ranch. What's wrong with you? We use parolees all the time."

"All the others stayed with Bobby to get their hours. Are you so naive that you don't worry about being alone with an ex-con? Worse, as a vet tech he has access to everything in the office and will be spending most of his time with you. Alone. You just met him today. Do you even know what he did?" Her friend and vet looked more vexed than she had ever seen. She stood with her arms crossed.

"James Bolton is his parole officer. He wouldn't bring a dangerous convict out here. The charge was transporting drugs."

Sandy's eyes went wide. "You have a drug dealer in here. Do you realize some of the drugs kept here have high street value?"

Danica tried to stop the eye roll, but she wasn't sure she was entirely successful. Sandy didn't know how well she knew Reid. "I'm not stupid enough to trust him. Yes, he's an ex-con, and yes, I have everything of value locked away. I need his expertise to get my paperwork finished and filed. As soon as you find me a vet tech with the right degree, he's gone." Thrusting her hip out, she pointed to her walkie-talkie. "Bobby is one click away."

Reid cleared his throat from the doorway. The cub curled in his arms, lying against his chest, sound asleep. Her traitorous heart thought of him holding their daughters. Heat caused her skin to burn. "Reid—"

"A girl named Sarah is here. She said to let you know she's feeding the orphaned bats." His eyes looked more gray than green before he returned to the other room.

Sandy stepped in front of Danica as she started following Reid. "Now, don't go feeling sorry for him. He's a criminal. You know I've always been uncomfortable with having the parolees out here."

The need to apologize ate at her. "He's a human who is trying to do the right thing."

"You've known him one day. That man is not one of your rescue projects. He's a grown adult that knows right from wrong, and he chose wrong."

"You don't know him."

"Neither do you. Unfortunately, I do know men like him. He'll get what he wants and leave you smashed and bleeding. When he's taken everything he needs, he'll walk out without a backward glance." Sandy reached out and took the bottle from her. "Trust me. I know what I'm talking about. I'll get this to Sarah. When I leave, I'll take the cub with me."

Danica took the bottle back. "Thank you for the warning, but I've got this. You can go. I'll have Bobby take Reid back to the Hausman Ranch. By the way, he has a name. Reid. And just like my animals, he deserves to be treated with respect. Okay?"

She sighed. "You sure you got this?"

"Yes." She laid her hand on Sandy's arm. "Thank you for caring, but I know what I'm doing."

With a grunt, Sandy shook her head. "Those words almost guarantee impending doom."

Going into the other room, they found Reid in the rocking chair. The cub was still asleep curled up in his arms. Danica grabbed the long leather gloves and prepared to feed the new baby. Sandy glared at Reid. "I'll be back out tomorrow to do a follow-up. Will you be back?"

He nodded. "I have the early shift at the ranch, so I'll be here at two o'clock."

The vet turned to Danica. "I'll be here at two. We can evaluate if the big guy is ready for release and do a follow-up with the little one." With one last hostile stare at Reid, Sandy left.

Danica sighed and reached for the bear. The smell of the formula in the bottle had her awake and making noises. She couldn't help but laugh at her antics. "Poor baby is hungry."

A loud rumble came from Reid's stomach. She raised a brow. "Are you needing to be fed, too? When did you eat last?"

His golden tan skin flushed a bit. He shook his head and kept his eyes focused on the bear.

"Reid. When did you eat last?"

He shrugged. "We had an early breakfast at the ranch."

Knowing ranch life, that would have been before sunup. "It's after four! Why didn't you say something?" The bear finished the last of the mixture.

"Sorry. Making my own decisions still feels odd. After six years, I got used to others telling me what to do and when to do it. Some habits are hard to shake."

That made her heart break a little. She remembered

the carefree young man who loved being outdoors, riding bulls, drawing and poetry. She fell so hard in love with him. But like Sandy said, she didn't know this Reid.

She wanted to know why he did it. Why Reid gave up on them so quickly. If they had worked hard, they could have made it. He hadn't had enough faith in them.

"I have some sandwich stuff in the refrigerator."

The bear moved and crawled up his leg, trying to get under his shirt. "Are you going to give her a new name? Her collar said Slasher." He gently pulled her out and hugged the bear close. "I don't like that name."

"With the intent to keep them wild, we have a policy not to humanize them. She'll be assigned a number for her file, but no name. You shouldn't hold her so much."

"Babies need to be held. So she'll get a number? Will she spend the night in the crate?"

Taking the cub out of his arms, she put her back into the wooden structure. They placed blankets and a floppy stuffed bear for her to cuddle. "After I feed you, we can clean and prep a large enclosure we made a couple of years ago for two orphaned bears. She'll live there until we can release her in the bear habitat. If we do this right, she could be a candidate for release into the wild. We don't want her to rely on humans too much."

With the baby tucked away, she went to the central building. One of the volunteer college students was doing homework while covering their twenty-four-hour hotline. "Hi, Diego. This is Reid McAllister. He's our new vet tech." The men shook hands. "Is Sarah still here?"

"She was bathing the bats a minute ago."

She introduced Reid to Sarah and the orphaned bats, then headed to the kitchen. Digging in the refrigerator she found enough supplies to make two sandwiches. They finished their meal in silence.

There were a hundred ways to start a conversation with her secret husband, but she needed to keep it professional until he left for good. With empty plates in the sink, they went outside. They got in her favorite ATV, a double-seated four-wheeler that looked like a golf cart on steroids. The large enclosure was deep in the ranch.

"What happened?" Reid pointed to the old homestead as they passed it, a ranch house built in 1918.

"When Linda, the owner, was moved to full-time care, the house caught fire. It was small, and it just took out the back room, but it did enough damage that it would take lots of money to restore it. It had been her plan that the caretaker of the sanctuary would live there."

"Aren't you the caretaker?" His gaze moved from the turn-of-the-century old rock home to her.

She blinked. Another dream put aside. She had planned to move out of her father's house with the girls, but for now, she was grateful they had a safe place to live. "Yeah, but all the available funds have gone into the direct care of the animals." She sighed. "I always wanted to. Maybe someday." But at this rate, she doubted it. When did faith turn into stubbornness? Would she even be able to tell the difference?

As the enclosure came into view, Bobby waved. He had already started pulling the old bedding out. She parked and got off the cart with Reid to join Bobby. With the three of them working, it didn't take long to get the chain-fence enclosure ready for the newest baby on the ranch. Reid stood in the center after they finished, sweating. He had dragged a large tree branch that was knocked down in the last storm. "Where do you want this?"

"We can tie it to the corner post and the stand. It will give her something natural to climb on and sleep in if she wants. From here, she can also get in the hammock, too."

A small book fell from Reid's pocket when he bent over to grab at the tree again. Without thinking, she reached down, and they bumped heads. "Sorry." She picked up the leather book. It was a Bible. "You carry a Bible with you now?"

He took it and grunted.

She looked down and noticed a couple of yellow ribbons had slipped from his pocket, as well. "Oh, Reid."

In college, he'd told her the story behind them. She had cried for the little boy that thought his father would come back home if he tied the yellow ribbons outside. He had heard the song "Tie a Yellow Ribbon Around the Old Oak Tree" and truly believed it.

It took her back to her childhood, when she desperately wanted her mother to come home, but she was dead. At five, she hadn't understood.

"You still have those?"

"They're just bookmarks." He stuffed them back into the Bible. "They don't mean anything."

"Reid, that's not—" Her phone vibrated. She glanced at the screen.

Oh, no. It was later than she'd thought. Turning away from Reid and Bobby, Danica spoke with her father. "Sorry, Daddy. We had some emergency arrivals, and I lost track of time."

Along with a long-lost husband showing up on her doorstep. With a quick glance over her shoulder, she found Bobby showing Reid some of the things they made for the bears.

Her father was talking, and she needed to focus.

"Yes, let them know I have a great story to tell when I get home. I'll be there in the next hour... No, don't— Hey, girls." She moved farther away and lowered her voice. "That's right. I promise to tell you everything... Yes, I'll take pictures... Okay. Love you more."

Bobby looked at her with one brow raised. "Everything good?"

"Yes." She put her phone away. "I just forgot to tell Daddy we had new arrivals. He expected me home a couple of hours ago."

"Did you tell the g—"

She cut the facility manager off before he could mention her twins. "I think it's time to call it a night. Reid, I can drive you to the ranch."

"That's nonsense." Bobby's gruff voice told her what he thought of her being alone with Reid. Why did everyone in her life act as if she had no survival instincts? It was getting old.

He rubbed his mustache and adjusted his hat. "I'll take him, and I can pick him up tomorrow."

Reid looked at her like he wanted to say something. He probably had plans to talk more about their little problem when they were alone. Maybe it would be better for Bobby to take him, because she couldn't handle more alone time with her husband.

Sandy was right about him breaking her heart. What the other woman didn't know was that it was already too late. Her heart was left in bloody pieces six years ago. Her daughters were the one thing that forced her to pull herself up and move on with life. Now it was up to her to protect their innocent hearts.

Chapter Three

"How long have you been out?" Bobby turned down the backcountry road that would take them to Danica. Hopefully, the second day of his return would fare better than the first.

"Not long." He didn't want to talk. He'd rather torment himself with thoughts of his wife.

"How long do you plan to stick around?"

"As long as Dani needs me." He groaned and laid his head back. He had let her nickname slip past his lips.

"I think it would be best if you referred to her as Ms. Bergmann." They hit a pothole on Reid's side of the truck. Without his seat belt, he would have hit his head.

"Yes, sir." He didn't want to hear another warning to stay away.

The old cowboy found a couple more potholes to hit. They finally made it to the gate. Reid knew he had some new bruises. Bobby winked at him.

As they pulled in behind the old bunkhouse, Danica and Dr. Ortiz were waiting for them. He greeted the doctor as he got out of the truck. A few others joined them. "Reid, this is Stephanie Lee, Linda Edward's niece. She's on the board. She has been an advocate for the dream her aunt had for the ranch. Stephanie, this is Reid McAllister. He saved the day with his degree in animal husbandry. Best of all, he has experience with big animals and wild horses."

"Welcome aboard." In high heels and with perfect hair, she looked more prepared for a day in the courtroom than one spent hanging out with wild animals. Her red lips stretched into a tight smile as she looked him up and down.

Reid tried not to be oversensitive and stood still. He learned fast to always appear confident, even when he didn't feel that way. She reminded him of the court-appointed lawyer who threw him to the wolves and walked away without a care.

Stephanie was a trusted member of Danica's circle, and he wasn't. So he smiled and offered his hand. Yeah, she wasn't happy about touching him.

Danica, who had been speaking with Dr. Ortiz, waved them over. "Dr. Ortiz examined our new cat. The jaguar is in general good health, but the back leg is permanently damaged. We'll release him into the north cat area." She looked at Dr. Ortiz, then at Reid. "Are we ready to move him?"

The wheeled crate was four feet tall and six feet long. Reid could hear the black cat pacing. Working as a team, they loaded him into the back of a trailer and slowly drove out to the cat area in the far back part of the ranch. It took some maneuvering, but they got the crate placed inside a double-fenced area that was free of trees.

By the time they rolled the crate up against the second gate, the sun was high, and the Texas heat had stopped being friendly. Danica had everyone clear the area and stand outside the enclosure. She and Reid were the only people inside, ready to let the cat into his new home. Dr. Ortiz stood next to the tall fence with a tranquilizer if they needed it.

Danica jumped on top of the crate. She looked like an Amazon queen, surveying her land. She was born to do this. Twisting around, she looked at Reid. "I'm going to lift the front panel. He'll either dart out and run, or hide in there. We'll have to wait for him to enter his new world." Easing down, she laid her body flat on the top of the crate and peered into the openings. In a low, soothing voice, she started talking to the animal.

"What do you need me to do?" Reid kept his voice steady and calm as he checked on the black jaguar from the side panel.

"Stay to the back of the crate until he moves out the front. As soon as he leaves, I need you to slide and secure the gate so he can't come back into this area. I'll roll it out of the way."

She sprang to her feet. "By nature, they want to avoid humans, so he should run for the trees. Okay, here we go." Giving Reid a nod, she got in position.

Poised for action, he kept his full attention on her. It would be safer for her on the outside fence area with the others, but he knew better than to suggest it.

Danica pulled the panel up. Nothing happened. Reid pressed his face against the top slot to see inside. The cat had his nose in the air and took one cautious step toward the opening. Then he stopped and just stared out.

Slowly slipping down to the ground, Danica stood next to him. He was tall, and her lips were close to his ear when she leaned in. "All he's known is captivity, his whole life. The open space probably scares him."

"Freedom can be overwhelming." He had only been locked up six years and was surprised how hard it was to adjust. Facing freedom after a whole life of being in a cage had to be paralyzing.

She nodded. With the palm of her hand, she wiped at her face. Reid pretended not to notice. Her warrior face was back, as she focused on the jaguar.

The cat eased closer to the opening and once again sat and put his nose in the air. He turned around and went to the back of his shelter again.

"No. Go. Run," Danica whispered. "There are rocky cliffs and trees for you to climb and explore. You're safe here."

The cat paced again and stopped at the door. His ears twitched. Reid stopped breathing for a few seconds as he waited for the cat to claim his freedom.

Danica slid her hand into his. Reid heard her praying under her breath. She was so focused on the jag he doubted she even noticed. He resisted the urge to squeeze, hoping she would stay. If this caged and abused wild animal could make it, maybe he had a chance, too.

It took almost an hour for the cat to get his whole body out of the crate. Suddenly he stood straight. With a flip of his tail, he lifted his head high, and his nostrils flared. He looked over his shoulder, then back again. With a lunge, he ran for the tree line.

Danica pulled the crate back. "Lock the gate."

He had gotten so caught up holding her hand and watching the cat, he almost forgot his job. The small group behind them started applauding. The black cat reappeared and darted across the open grass, running straight back into the fence. Panting, he stopped and went flat. Danica held her hand up, and everyone went silent.

Reid hated seeing the big cat in distress. "Should we let him back in the crate? He doesn't feel safe in the open space."

With narrowed eyes, she kept her focus on the cat. "He's okay. Let's give him a bit more time." The animal's golden eyes scanned the land. Lying flat on his stomach, he crept back to the tree line.

One swish of his tail and he turned back to the trees. One leap and he climbed onto the low branch of a giant oak. Danica looked at him with a huge smile. "I think he's going to adjust fast." Hands on the crate, she unlocked the brakes and started rolling it toward the volunteers. They rushed forward to help her.

"That was so exciting, Ms. Bergmann. Will he be able to find the water and his food?"

"I think so. We'll keep an eye on him to make sure he does. The more he does on his own, the better." Danica gave the small crew directions. Dr. Ortiz hugged her, then got in her fancy vet truck and left.

Reid stood back. They all laughed and talked about the excitement of setting the cat free. Everyone had a job and knew what to do. A touch on his left shoulder caused him to spin with his fists up for a split second before he saw it was Danica. "Sorry." He stuffed his hands in his back pockets. "I didn't know you were behind me." He hated the pity that clouded her eyes.

"I didn't even think about how—"

"I'm fine. What do you need me to do?" Relaxing his jaw, he focused on his breathing. Once back to normal, he looked down at the beautiful woman who had looked at him with love a lifetime ago. The tender gaze was gone—now it shifted from suspicion to pity. She had a don't-get-close look he'd never seen before.

Even though he was free now, he felt as if he'd suffered a lifetime conviction. Ray said it was a self-induced sentence, which God had released him from. Now that he had his physical freedom, all the guilt and stress were back. He didn't feel free anymore.

"Reid?" Her bright green eyes searched his face. He forced himself to be still, to meet her gaze. She gave him a sad smile and nodded as if they had agreed to something he wasn't aware of. "Are you ready to move the baby cub to the enclosure? I don't want a crowd for that."

Right now, he would love to get away from this group of young, energetic college students. It seemed a lifetime ago that he had been a part of that life. If he heard the words *awesome* or *amazing* one more time, he was going to beat his head against the side of the truck.

Then there was Bobby. The old man eyed Reid with a warning whenever he got a chance. "Is there anything else needed done here?"

"Are you sure you're okay?" Her forehead wrinkled with worry, and it was his fault.

With a nod, he gave her the lopsided grin she'd always loved. "Yes. Ready for the next adventure."

She waved to the others. "We're heading back to introduce the cub to her new home. Y'all take the truck. Sarah, do you have the phone today?"

"Yes, ma'am. Can we come watch?"

"I want to keep the environment calm and quiet when we make the transition. I need y'all to finish here and do the usual rounds. We'll take the four-wheeler back to headquarters." Without waiting for him, she jumped on the long leather seat of the ATV. Hands on the handlebars, she leaned forward, making room for him behind her. If he got on that thing, he would have to touch her. Not good.

"Baby, I'll walk."

"What? It'll take you an hour to get back." She started the engine. "Do you want to drive? Is that the problem? I don't remember you being so macho."

Okay, he was making a bigger deal out of this than it needed to be. Swinging a leg over, he slid as far back on the seat as possible. Trying to settle in behind Danica, he found there wasn't much room to avoid her. Her hair was in a tight braid, but a few curls had managed to escape. He could get lost in her hair. Looking to the sky, he kept his focus on the clouds above. His hands gripped the bars next to his legs. A rock in the road caused the four-wheeler to tilt to the side.

Without thought, his fingers immediately circled her waist to steady them both. Muscles briefly contracted as he remembered how perfectly she fit in his hands. Those hands needed to be somewhere else.

One quick movement and he had a tight grip on the bars again. Those were the kind of memories that would get him in trouble and just cause him more pain. He needed to block all of them.

How could he do that? He remembered everything about her, and he would until the day his heart stopped beating. He imagined it was possible that even beyond this life, he would remember her. Not that it would do him any good. He was dancing in the middle of a stampede and would be going down soon.

This quick ride turned into a torture trip. Next time,

he would walk. *God, I need strength only You can give. I have vowed to do the right thing, but I'm not sure I'm strong enough.*

Parking the four-wheeler by the back door, Danica jumped off as fast as she turned the key to shut down the engine. She needed to get away from Reid.

Driving with him so close, it took her back to the early days of their marriage. Their very short marriage, because he didn't have enough faith to believe God would take care of them.

"I need to check something up front. Go ahead and get the cub ready."

Not waiting for his response, she moved to the front porch. She had to get herself under control. Emotions and feelings had gotten her in trouble in college. Now she was a grown woman with two innocent baby girls relying on her. Their future was at stake. *God, I need You to lead me this time.*

It didn't matter how Reid McAllister made her feel. Her heart was off-limits, and she needed to use her brain. Coming around the corner, she stopped midstep. No, no, no.

"Momma!"

"Momma, we came to see the baby bear."

The girls charged at her. "We want to see the bats. Can we see the bats? Are they sleeping like little bur-ritos?"

There was no pause between the girls. They had a habit of talking with their words flowing from one sis-ter to the next.

Her gaze darted behind her. Reid had gone into the building. With her heart in her throat, she stared at her twin sister. "Jackie, what are you doing here? I told the girls I would bring them later tonight."

Jackie narrowed her gaze. "What's going on?"

With another quick glance to the house, she took a deep breath. Maybe she could get them out of here without him seeing the girls. She bit her lip.

"Momma, please."

Or before her sister saw him. This was crazy. Smiling for the girls, she took a deep breath. No time to drown in her own mess.

Balancing on her heels, she squatted and hugged each girl. "I need you to go home with your aunt." She pushed the loose curls out of their faces, their red hair and gray-green eyes in contrast to their light golden skin.

They were a perfect mix of her and Reid. "You can't be here right now. I promise I'll bring you back, and you can help me feed the baby bats tonight." She usually only allowed the girls to watch the bats. At this point, she was willing to use anything to get them back in the big green family Suburban her father still owned. Standing, she placed a hand on each of the girls' shoulders and started herding them back to the SUV.

Jackie was frowning at her. "They both got a hundred on their spelling tests, so I thought this—"

"It's fine. I just need you to take them home. I still have a lot to do today.

A door behind her opened. Her sister gasped. Dread froze the rapid flow of her blood. Fear held her in place. Her two worlds were about to collide. "Please, get the twins to the car and leave." *Please, please, please don't let him notice the girls.*

"Jackie?" His deep voice vibrated down her spine.

"Reid?" Jackie's screech was more like nails on a chalkboard. Eyes wide, she looked at Danica. "Is that Reid McAllister?"

The girls turned to see the newcomer. "Hi!" They tended to talk in unison when they were excited. "I'm Susan Bergmann this is my sister—"

"Elizabeth Bergmann. Everyone calls us Suzie and Lizzy. We're twins."

Focusing on her daughters, she kept her back to Reid. Maybe he'd assume they were Jackie's if he didn't look too close.

Lizzy gently pressed her fingertips on Danica's face and pulled her attention away from Jackie. "Momma, please let us just see the bats. We won't touch them."

She groaned and closed her eyes.

"Or even make a noise. We promise to be real quiet." On her other side, Suzie wrapped herself around Danica's arm.

"Yes, we'll be good." They both looked past her and smiled at Reid. "Have you seen the bats?" Suzie faced him.

"We were here when they came to the sanctuary." Excitement bubbled from each of Lizzy's words.

"They were the size of our thumbs." Both girls held up their thumbs and giggled.

Danica's lungs burned. She took in a deep breath. She needed to breathe. Passing out was not an option. On second thought, it would be a great distraction and buy her some time.

She finally turned to face Reid. His gaze was on the girls, darting back and forth between her wiggling, joy-filled babies. Lizzy had grabbed her hand. "Momma, please just one peek."

Tearing her gaze away from the shock on Reid's face, she looked down. "Sweetheart, we have some real important things going on right now. I need you to go home with Aunt Jackie. I'll bring you back tonight for the late-night feeding."

Jackie stepped forward and took the girls by the hand. "Come on, sugars. The sooner your mom gets her work done, the faster she'll come get you." She glanced at Reid, then back to Danica. "Are you okay? Do I need to call anyone?"

"No. Really, I'm good. Reid is here to help." Crossing her arms, she swallowed back any tears that would expose the desperation she was trying to hide. "Call me once you're in the car if you want, and I'll let you know when to expect me."

Her sister hesitated. "Bobby's here?"

"Yes, along with Stephanie and a couple of interns. We just released the cat, lots of people are here. I'm good."

Watching her daughters leave with her sister, her gut burned. Maybe he'd go away if she ignored him. She felt him move next to her. His breathing was hard enough to brush her unprotected neck. Closing her eyes, she prayed, with every bit of energy in her body. If she could, she would drop to her knees.

She did not want to deal with this.

"I'm a father? Why didn't—"

She turned on him, her fingertip against his chest. "You, Reid McAllister, are not a father. You made me a mother, then you left. That does not make you a father. Don't you dare try to act like the victim here." Heat ran through her limbs.

Devastation flared in his eyes. Years ago, he shared

dreams of forging a family with her, the type of family he had only seen on television. Reid had talked about being the kind of father he'd wanted to be, a good father. He'd wanted to do things differently than his parents.

At the time, she was foolish enough to believe him.

Danica stared him down, the gray in his eyes glossed over until only a dark green burned. So let him get angry. She didn't care. Her rage heaved and pulled against the shackles she'd locked it under years ago.

Her finger thrust against his rock-hard chest. "I waited for you." Her voice shook. She squared her shoulders. "When I took the first pregnancy test, I was alone. I've been alone every step of the way, except for my family. My girls are Bergmanns, and that's all they know. You showing up on my doorstep does not change the fact they don't have a father. They never did, and they're fine, better than fine. They have my father. The kind of man I want them to know."

Mouth open, he didn't say a word. Deep in the back of his throat, his voice emerged. "They're mine."

"No. You gave up that right when you decided it was easier just to vanish than tell me what was happening. I'm not talking to you about them." Unable to deal with his self-inflicted wounds any longer, she marched past him and into the office. Slamming the door felt better than it should.

She didn't have time for this drama or his wounded pride. "He should have thought of that before he drove a suspicious car across state lines."

"Who are you talking to?"

Stephanie's voice caused her to jump. She forced a laugh. "Just myself." She looked around. "Where is everyone? What are you doing in my office?"

"Oh, they're putting everything away, and Sarah is checking on the bats. I wanted to get the updates on the paperwork." She leaned her perfectly dressed hip on the corner of the worn, outdated desk. "How are we looking financially?"

Danica moved past her and bit down on the inside of her cheek. This was not what she wanted to deal with right now. "We have a board meeting soon. I'll be able to give a full report then."

"I spoke with Dorothy. As your friends and board members, we're worried. Do we have enough money to hire a vet tech?" Stephanie started looking through some photos Danica had taken for the grant. "He's a convicted criminal. Is it smart to have him around so many drugs and exotic animals?"

"He needs community hours, and we need him for the grant. James trusts him. Sorry I don't have time to go deeper, but I have lots of work that still needs to be done before the end of the day."

Her temper was on the edge of exploding, but it wasn't Stephanie's fault. Plus, she really couldn't afford to be rude to her. Not only was she Linda's only living relative, but she stood by her side as a major advocate for the sanctuary.

"I'm sorry. I know your aunt's dream for this place is as important to you as it is to me. But right now, I don't have time, I promise I have a report, and I will answer all of your questions then." She took a breath. "Thank you for helping today. I know you also have a busy schedule with your law firm."

"Danica, are we going to move the cub?" Reid stood at her door. He wasn't looking at her, though. He seemed to be staring at Stephanie.

"Seems the felon needs you. Shouldn't leave him unattended for long. I have to go anyway. I'll see you at the board meeting." She ignored Reid as she went out the other door.

Danica swallowed, or tried to anyway. The ball of fear and worry hung in her dry throat. She shouldn't have rushed Stephanie out. Maybe she could call Bobby, so someone would be between her and Reid.

"I'll be with the cub." Not giving her a chance to reply, Reid turned on his booted heel and left.

Bracing her hands on the edge of the desk, she hung her head. "God, please give me the wisdom to handle this the best way for the girls." Her wounded heart wanted to lash out at him and make him pay, but that wouldn't help anyone. As good as it would feel to scream and throw breakables against his head, she knew it would just destroy her in the long haul. More guilt was the last thing she needed right now.

With a deep breath, she turned to face the door leading to Reid and the baby bear. There was no reason for her to feel guilty. For six years, she'd stayed strong. God had been preparing her for this day. Danica swallowed any emotions that might give him an opening to her heart and stepped into the room with her husband.

Chapter Four

Reid held the bottle as the baby bear clung to him. He took a deep breath, pushing his lungs past their comfort zone. Releasing all the tension, he counted to five. Held it. Again.

It wasn't working.

No matter how he tried to center his breathing, the word *daughters* bounced around in his head. The double image of the most beautiful sight he'd ever seen ricocheted in his thoughts.

Two curly-red-haired girls. He had two daughters with the same color of eyes as his mother. Two daughters who were already five years old. Five years he could never get back. Anger threatened to abolish all his good intentions.

Danica was right. He'd walked out on her when she needed him most. He'd ruined his own life. A life that not only shined with Danica as his wife but two precious girls who…

His family had ridiculed him for trying to make a better life, for reaching over his head for things that belonged to other people. Not him.

The night he was arrested they had been proven right. There was no escaping his family blood.

But daughters? What did he do with that information? Even after seeing them, he still couldn't believe it. He wanted to yell and hit something.

He stroked the bear's fur and looked down, into her trusting eyes. Centering his thoughts and turning to God was what he needed to do now.

As much as he wanted to blame Danica, he couldn't. The mistake was his, and now he had a great deal to prove to her.

The rocking chair creaked as it rolled back and forth. Reid leaned his head back. The peeling paint on the old wood panel revealed decades of colors just painted on top of each other. It needed to be sanded and repainted. No one had ever taken the time to do the job right. Layers of paint had been slapped onto each other, covering the old stains.

If she had the supplies to make repairs, he could work on restoring the old wood. Words were not going to regain the trust he'd lost. It was going to take a lot of work and time to show her he could be counted on.

His mother had put her husband above her children. Each time his father got out of prison, his mother took him back, no questions asked. A corner of his lip twitched as he looked down at the bear. "Danica made it clear I wasn't getting anywhere near her babies. I think she might be the definition of mama bear."

"Are you talking to the bear?" Not making eye contact, Danica marched across the room. She gave no indication she had actually heard what he said,

"No one else will talk to me."

A snort came from her as she pulled bottles and assorted supplies out of the cabinets. "When you finish with the feeding, we'll move her out to the enclosure." With jerky fast motions, she stuffed them in the bag. "I'll wait in the Jeep that's parked out back." Without a glance at him, she flung the bag over her back and left.

Standing, he cleared his thoughts and prepared himself for her proximity again. He didn't want to put the bear back in the traveling crate, so he carried her out the door.

With the bear sleeping like a baby in his arms, he joined a silent Danica and carefully closed the door. Slowly, she maneuvered the Jeep over uneven roads. By the time she put the vehicle in Park, the sun was low on the horizon. In the far side of the sky, a large moon was already making its climb.

Taking a moment to collect his thoughts, Reid sat in the Jeep. The moon was one of many little things he'd taken for granted before he was locked up. In his arms, the sleeping cub made a few grunting noises. He wondered how his babies slept. Did they snore? Did they wake up all through the night or sleep without a care in the world?

Monumental everyday life moments he'd lost forever.

The gate to the closed-in area was wide-open. Reid got out of the Jeep and walked into the bear's new home, closing the gate behind him. It was a hundred times larger than the cage in the basement. Even bigger than his cell.

Danica stopped in front of the Jeep and went through her bag. "It won't take long to get her settled. Then I'll have Bobby take you home." Busy movements took her around the enclosure and into a shed that was a few feet away. Finally, she stilled and stood a distance from the fence as if afraid of him.

A pressure tightened in the center of his chest. He pushed past it and cleared his throat. "We need to talk."

Danica had all the power here, and she knew it. His heart twisted. She made it clear she was going to ignore him as she checked the bag again.

"I'm not asking you to tell them I'm their father." He needed to find a way to explain his intentions. *God, help me.* This was tough. The desire to run and hide pulled on every nerve. But he needed to take a stand and face what he feared. "I want to know them. An opportunity to show you I can be trusted. I want a chance to—"

"No!"

He pressed his lips tight. She was the mother of his children. The kind of mother who would protect her children from the corruption in the world, even if that included him.

Danica was so much stronger than his mother.

"Danica. I know I messed up." He moved to the hammock, planning to place the small cub into the cocoon. It was easier to talk to her if he didn't make eye contact. "I took something precious, and I crushed it." The bear's eyes went half-mast. He made sure to relax his hold and regulate his breathing. "But I've seen our girls. I can't undo that." Steel chains seized his lungs, and his eyes burned. "Tell me what you want, and I'll do it. Just let me see them. They don't have to know who I am. I understand you're protecting them. I..." He couldn't even express how much that meant to him.

"Because of you, I'm stronger than I ever thought I could be. You leaving forced me to be independent and focus on what matters. I didn't have the luxury to fall apart." She crossed her arms as if a chill had swept through her.

The hills to the west received her full attention. "The pain you caused? It hurt beyond what I thought possible to survive. I lost my mother, my grandparents. My oldest sister had left us, and then you, but when I found out about my babies…"

With a tight fist, she tapped her heart. "I had to turn all that pain into faith and love. You broke me, but when I pulled everything back together, I found a woman who can stand on her own. I don't need anyone."

Anger and pride stiffening her spine, Danica looked him straight in the eye. The green irises burned bright, but not with the love he'd remembered for the last six years.

"I can't have you in my life. My daughters don't need a man who will walk out on them without warning. I don't trust you."

The desire to hold Danica, to comfort her, shredded him. He had done this to her. "Danica. I'm sorry."

"You need to let her go. The longer she stays around humans, the harder it will be for her to adjust." She moved back to the Jeep.

"If I had to do it over again, I'd call you and tell you everything. If I got to do it over, I'd never take the job." He eased the baby into the hammock and studied the rescued animal as she settled. "When is their birthday? Tell me that at least."

Hunger for any information about them clawed at his gut. A long heavy pause lingered. Not able to take the silence any longer, he turned. She wasn't even looking at him. She placed her hands on the hood of the white Jeep, gazing out at the surrounding hills.

"Are they in school?" The burn of venom crawled up from the back of his throat. Six years of memories lost. "Danica, they're my daughters. I have some rights. Is my name on their birth certificates?"

Fire flared in her eyes as she grew taller and marched

to the chain-link fence that separated them. A hostile finger pointed at him. "You don't have any rights when it comes to my girls." Her breaths came in quick pants.

A few steps and he stood before her. He gripped the interlocking chains. The edge cut into his skin. "I don't want to fight you, but I can't act as if I don't know that I have children. You know I vowed to be a present father. I have to be a better father than mine."

"Then you should have stayed out of prison I guess." The starch left her spine. Pulling her jacket tight around her, she looked away.

The dying sunlight seemed to set her hair on fire. The shades of golden red radiated warmth. She turned, heading to the Jeep. Reid panicked.

The bear habitat closed in on him. He rattled the fence. "Danica! Don't leave me!"

"I'll call Bobby and tell him to take you home." She disappeared on the other side of the Jeep.

In his fear, Reid had forgotten he could unlock the gate and walk out. He flipped the latch and followed her. "We have to talk about this."

She kept walking, but it didn't take many steps for him to catch up with her.

Danica held her phone up. Reid assumed she was looking for a signal. Moving to the other side of the road, she paused again. "I'm not even thinking." The walkie-talkie was pulled off her hip. "Bobby, meet us by the bear enclosure. Reid is ready to leave."

"Be there in ten."

He had ten minutes to find out something, anything about his girls. "What do they know about me?"

She climbed into the Jeep, slamming the door. That

was it. Danica was going to leave him out here without even the smallest fact about his daughters.

He rushed to open the passenger door. "I just want to know their birthday. Can I have that much?"

Hands on the wheel, jaw clenched, she turned and glared at him. "They were born February 14. Your very last Valentine's gift to me. Now shut the door."

She turned the key. "Bobby's on his way. He'll pick you up tomorrow, too. You'll work with him. I would appreciate it if you stayed away from me. It's the least you can do."

Shifting gears, she barely gave him time to shut the door and move back. She hit the gas, throwing pebbles and dirt into the air. A few might have pelted him, but he didn't notice.

He watched her drive away as he stood alone on a dark country road like an idiot. For most people, February 14 was Valentine's Day. But it was so much more for them.

When he finally worked up the nerve to ask her out as kids in school, Valentine's Day. Their first kiss, Valentine's Day. One year later, she'd lifted him out of darkness when she whispered she loved him. On Valentine's Day, their junior year, he'd asked if she'd be his and spend the rest of her life as his wife.

Despite her family's protests, she'd trusted him. She'd run away from everything she'd known to marry him in Vegas.

Now, he felt lost, trying to process the fact that one year after promising to love and cherish her, Danica had given birth to their babies. Alone.

Happy Valentine's Day.

The hole in his heart grew bigger. At this rate, the regrets of his life would fill all of Texas.

Chapter Five

"I can't believe he has the nerve to show up here." Jackie scooted closer to her on the pew. As always, they sat on the third bench. Her family never sat anywhere else, ever. Even on the rare occasion they were late, the pews were left open for them.

No need to look over her shoulder to see who her twin was horrified to see. Sweat beaded under her shirt. She resisted the urge to fan herself. What was he doing here?

"He's walking down the center aisle. Wait. He stopped. He's looking around." Jackie spoke the play-by-play through clenched teeth.

Danica stopped breathing for a moment. She frantically searched the sanctuary. The girls had left for children's church. Her father! Where was her father?

"Who's here?" Sammi sat on the opposite side. Her little sister didn't know what was going on. She twisted around.

Danica put her hand on her sister's leg. "Don't look back there."

Sammi gasped. "Is that—"

"Hush!" Head down, Danica relaxed her hands.

Her oldest sister, Nikki, moved into the pew in front of them with her husband, Adrian. With a narrowed gaze, her brother-in-law stared at them. "What's wrong?"

Sammi put her hand on the back of the board in front of her and leaned forward. "I might be imaging things, but I think that's Reid McAllister." She turned to Danica. "That's him, right? Did you know he was in town?"

Nikki's gaze darted between them and Reid in the back of the church. Confusion seeped into her older sister's expression. "The father of the twins?" Nikki hadn't been around when Reid came home with her from college, so she didn't understand the history like her other sisters did.

As one, her family turned around. Her stupid heart missed a beat when she saw him standing alone. He had the look of a trapped animal, not knowing whether to run or fight. He had his black cowboy hat in front of him, the brim crushed in his grip.

On the other side of her, Jackie lowered her head and leaned in closer. "Not only is he here in town, but he's working at Danica's animal rescue place."

"What!" Sammi's eyes went wide. People started staring at them.

Stiff, Danica faced forward. "Shh." This conversation needed to end.

Adrian shifted to get a better look at them and the back of the church. "Wait. The twins' father is in town working for you, and you haven't told anyone?" He looked back at Danica. "Is he here to cause trouble for the girls?"

Danica closed her eyes to stop the urge to seek Reid out. "No."

"He didn't even know about the girls until I messed up and took them out to the ranch without talking to Danica. He saw them."

Adrian now looked as confused as Nikki, and a little angry. "You never told him you were pregnant?"

Jackie gave him a hard look and put her hand on Danica's shoulder. "He left her before she even knew. He just showed up and told her he's been in prison."

"What!" Sammi sat straight up.

"Shh." This time, they all shushed her. People filing into the church looked over at them.

Her family looked at her with different levels of shock, except for Jackie.

Her twin had gone back to glaring at Reid. Danica wanted to hide under the pew. "Can we not talk about this right now? The girls don't know, and I would prefer it if no one else knew until I figure out what to do."

"What about Daddy? He's going to have a fit if he sees Reid. That man doesn't have any right to be here. He needs to leave now." Jackie shot a hot glare to the back.

"You can't kick him out of a church. This is God's house. He has every right to be here." Danica didn't want to have any soft feelings for him, but if he really found God in prison, it wasn't for her to judge where he worshipped.

Two of her sisters were about to give their opinion when Mia, Adrian's daughter, joined them. She hugged her father's neck.

Danica touched Mia's arm. "Hey, sweetheart. Do me a big favor and find the twins. Just take them straight to children's church. Okay? After service, we'll all go to The Drug Store for lunch."

Mia stood and looked at them. Flipping her braid back over her shoulder, she nodded. "Sure. Is everything okay?"

Adrian smiled and nodded. "Yeah. We just need to make sure the girls stay out of the sanctuary right now. I'll explain later."

With a quick kiss, she was gone.

Gripping her Bible, Danica kept her head down. "There's no way to keep Daddy out of here." She was going to be sick.

"This is ridiculous." Jackie put a hand on Danica's knee. "I'm going to tell him to move on down the road. There are like eight churches in this tiny town. He can go find God in one of those."

"Please don't. A scene at church is the last thing I need."

Jackie shook her head. "And you think when Daddy walks in here and sees him, there's not going to be fireworks?"

Nikki stood. "I'm going to talk to our church visitor and make sure he understands what's what." Without waiting for permission, she stood and marched straight down the aisle. Her military training radiated from every movement.

Adrian got up to follow. "Don't worry, I'll make sure she behaves." He patted Danica's hand, which now had a death grip on the back of the pew.

She forced herself to relax. If she didn't turn it into a big deal, then no one would even notice.

The youngest Bergmann sister sat back and crossed her arms. "Were you even going to tell me?"

Danica focused on the painting behind the baptismal.

The mural of a tranquil Frio River stared back at her, painted by her grandmother five decades ago. Gram was gone now, but the love she had for her family and community lingered. What would she tell her to do?

Sammi turned again to watch the drama unfold behind them. She pressed her shoulder against Danica's as she whispered, "Pastor Levi is taking Reid to meet Lorrie Ann and Maggie."

Danica tried to tilt her head enough so she could see without being noticed. Nikki and Adrian arrived just as Reid shook hands with the pastor's wife and her aunt.

Maybe she should leave. The urge to run and hide battled with her need to stay and make sure her sisters didn't cause more problems. Her two worlds were colliding, and there was nothing she could do to stop the explosion. The best she could pray for was the least amount of damage, mainly to her daughters.

The pressure pushed against her temples. Not able to take it anymore, she stood. She needed to find her father before he joined the fun.

In the back room, she found her father with Sonia. Again. Her dad was spending a great deal of time with Lorrie Ann's mother.

When had her father start helping the choir get ready for worship?

"Daddy, I'm going to help with the children's church today." It wasn't unusual for her to volunteer, so her father didn't give her a second glance.

"Okay, sweetheart." He gave her a quick smile before going back to his task.

Sonia placed a hand on her father's arm and frowned at her. "Are you all right, Danica?" The woman was giving off a girlfriend vibe her sisters talked about, but she didn't have the time or energy to worry about her father's love life.

Straightening her back, she gave her a big smile. "It's all great."

Her father looked up, his gaze darting between the women. "Is there a problem?"

"No, Daddy. I'll see you after the service."

Once outside, she rested against the stone wall. Fresh air was good. She would need to let her father know Reid was in the area. This would be easier if Reid just stayed on the ranch.

Oh, no. The Hausman ranch brought the steers in for the 4-H play-day each weekend. Her girls ran the barrels and poles. Her father had just gotten them a new horse to run. He was never going to miss this local event. What if Reid showed up, too?

"Danica?"

The rich, smooth drawl washed over her. His voice always melted her. Dropping her head, she closed her eyes. At least her father wouldn't see him if Reid was out here instead of inside the church.

"What are you doing here, Reid?" She opened her eyes and shifted her weight as her heels started sinking into the soft ground.

He looked good. His jawline smooth from a fresh shave, his jeans crisp and clean. A buttoned-up shirt starched under his black vest. Even his boots were free of dirt and grime. He didn't fit her image of a man who'd served time in prison.

As the bell started ringing, his gaze went from the town's main street to the church tower. After a long heavy pause, he took a breath but still didn't make eye contact. "I'm not following you. John Levi is one of the pastors with the prison ministry network. When he heard I was in the area, he came to visit and invited me to attend. I didn't know your family was here."

"Now you know."

He finally looked at her. The heat and accusation in his gray eyes forced her to look away. She had no reason to feel guilty.

"I can't sleep. Questions keep bouncing around in my head since I saw them. How were they as babies? When did they learn to walk? What were their first words? Who would it hurt for me to see them?" He stepped closer. "I also try and imagine you waddling in the last months, not able to get up. Did you have morning sickness the whole nine months?"

"Eight. It was eight months. They were early. I had to go home before they were released. Leaving the hospital without them was one of the worst days of my life."

He reached for her. His fingers brushing her shoulder before she stepped away.

"Don't. Touch. Me."

Thrusting his hands into his pockets, Reid put distance between them.

Breathing became easier, but each inhale brought a scent of fresh, clean soap. Danica wanted to lean into his neck and breathe deep. She pressed her back against the rough rock. It anchored her and kept her from doing something stupid. "It would be best if you left."

"I don't know if I can."

"There's nothing you can do." She glanced at him, then quickly looked away. The warm gray in his eyes mirrored the pain in her heart.

"Pastor Levi gave me a personal invitation to attend this church. The church where you and the girls worship. Don't you think God had something to do with that? Maybe I'm not supposed to walk away."

Blood slammed into her heart. "No. No, God has nothing to do with this." She needed him to go. The emotional roller coaster was wearing her down. She needed to get off. She didn't have time for this drama. To many people and animals were counting on her. The sanctuary needed her to stay focused. "Stay away from town. I'll get a restraining order."

With a couple of steps, he stood in front of her, forcing her to make eye contact. "Danica, calm down. I'm not going to hurt you or the girls." He rolled his shoulders. With his head back, he closed his eyes. "I just want... I'm not sure what I want, but I'll play by your rules. You're in charge. I just want the opportunity to see them. I asked Officer Bolton for the name of a family lawyer in Uvalde."

He brought his chin down, and his gaze penetrated her, holding her in place. "I want to give you the divorce, but I also want to know my rights as their father."

"You told James?" Breaking eye contact, she moved to the left. She started pacing, crushing acorns with each step.

"No. I just asked about a family lawyer."

She opened her mouth to speak a couple of times, but words became elusive. Feet planted, she forced herself to stop and look at him. "A divorce would be good. I also—"

The door in the hallway connected to the Sunday school classes opened. Amy, one of the children's church volunteers, poked her head out. "There you are. I'm glad I saw you out here. Suzie is sick."

"What's wrong? Where is she?" Danica rushed to Amy.

"In the bathroom with Mrs. Trees. She was singing, then suddenly she got sick."

"Where's Liz?" Danica followed Amy, then realized Reid was right on her heels. With a glare, she tried to tell him to back off, but he didn't seem to notice.

"Lizzy is in the craft room and happy as a lark. Do you want me to get her?"

"No. I'll take Suzie home. Will you tell my dad? Oh, wait. We came with him today…"

"I'll drive you home." Reid stood right behind her.

Her initial protest dropped away when she saw Suzie, flushed and sweaty.

Mrs. Trees held her, stroking her hair back. "Poor pumpkin. It just hit her so fast."

Danica took the youngest twin. Amy smiled. "I'll go tell your dad. Mr.…." She looked at Reid with a smile and raised an eyebrow.

He held out his hand. "Rei—"

Danica cut him off. "Tell Daddy that one of the guys from the wildlife sanctuary is taking us home." The girl nodded. "Thank you, Amy. You, too, Mrs. Trees."

"No worries. Hope she feels well soon."

Reid held the door open. "I'm parked behind this building. Do you want me to carry her?"

"Mommy, my tummy hurts."

She kissed Suzie's forehead. Heat radiated from her skin. "No, I have her. I'll just follow you. Honey, how are you feeling? Mr. McAllister is going to drive us home. Okay?"

Wrapping one arm around Danica's neck, her daughter rubbed her eyes and peeked at the man walking next to them.

Once they reached the ranch truck, she settled Suzie in the back and climbed in next to her. The diesel roared to life. Reid carefully made his way out of the church parking lot and onto the main road. How had she ended up in a truck with her husband?

Reid kept glancing at his passengers in the back seat. Danica gave him the directions to her home. One of his daughters was close to him. He wanted to talk to her, but…

He gripped the steering wheel and made sure to stay on the smoothest part of the country road. This opportunity might not happen again.

Checking on them in the rearview mirror, he saw Suzie's head in her mother's lap, Danica's long graceful fingers stroking her dark red curls.

"You sure have beautiful hair. Red is my favorite color."

"Thank you. My mommy and aunt Jackie have red hair, too, but theirs is lighter."

"My father had red hair the same as yours."

"Reid." Her voice drew deep with a warning.

"But you're—"

"Suzie!" Danica cut her off.

He pressed on. "My mother was Creole from New Orleans. My father was a redheaded Scotsman. Had the temper to go with it. You and your mom seem to be all sweet and not much spice."

She giggled. His heart melted. "My mom can get real mad, but not much. She gets mad when people hurt her animals."

"I imagine she'd get angry if someone hurt you, too."

Her little face was serious as she nodded. "On the bus, a boy put Lizzy's Hula-Hoop around her neck and left a bruise. When we got off the bus, Momma saw it right away and wanted to know who did it. She was so mad she chased down the bus and made it stop and charged inside. She made Shane apologize and got him suspended from school, and he still can't ride the bus. Boy, she was mad."

"Is Lizzy okay?" He met her eyes in the mirror. With a nod, she looked back down at the sick child leaning on her.

The gate to her family house appeared. As he eased down the drive to the two-story farmhouse, he had a strong sense of coming home, but it wasn't his home. He would never be part of this family. Knowing his girls had this, strong roots buried in love and faith, somewhat eased the pain. If he did nothing else right, at least his children had a mother who loved them and protected them from the ugliness of the world.

Reid parked and got out as Suzie started groaning again. "Momma, my tummy hurts real bad."

"Shh, it's okay, sweetheart. We're home." A gagging sound was the only warning before Suzie lost the rest of her stomach.

Reid opened the passenger door and released Suzie's seat belt. "I've got her. There's a blanket in the front you can use to wipe off. If you can unlock the door, I'll take her to the bathroom. You can change."

"Mommy, I'm sorry." Her daughter started sobbing.

"Shh." Reid gently moved her away from the mess. "Moms are…um, waterproof. We'll just take her out back and wash her off." He lifted the five-year-old as if she weighed nothing. And he didn't even hesitate over the mess. "Thankfully, most landed on the truck floor, so we're all good."

With the blanket, she cleaned it off. "Reid, go to the side door. It's open."

With their daughter pulled up against his chest, he turned to the left with a scowl. "Does it stay unlocked with you and the girls inside, too?"

She tried not to be insulted by the tone of his voice. "It's Clear Water. Nothing ever happens here."

That wasn't completely true. The father of her children was in her house, helping her with a sick child. She had a feeling there would be no going back from here.

Leaning down while keeping Suzie close, he pushed open the kitchen door. Their daughter had her arms wrapped around his neck as he walked into her home.

Pulling her jacket off, Danica threw it over the bench. Her shoes were next. It would be easier to throw the whole outfit away.

Her shoulders had a new weight on them, and it had nothing to do with a sick daughter. Her phone vibrated in the jacket pocket. Careful not to touch anything gross, she checked the number. It seemed all her sisters suddenly needed to talk to her.

Tossing the phone on the table, she headed to the washroom. She had a load of clean clothes in the dryer. "Take her to her room. It's the third door on the right from the stairs. I'll be right there."

She hurried into clean clothes and left everything on the floor. She'd get it later.

Rushing up the stairs, she froze at the girls' bedroom door. The man she had given everything to in another lifetime sat on the edge of the narrow pink bed covered with stuffed animals. Curled up with her head resting on his thigh, Suzie was asleep. She was already cleaned up and settled.

He was staring at their daughter. Raising his head, he

looked at Danica. Awe and terror seemed to be swirling in those moss green eyes.

Clearing his throat, his focus returned to the sleeping child. "She got her favorite nightgown, and I got a washcloth from the bathroom." Running the cloth across her forehead with one hand, Reid rested the other on her shoulder. "She's so small."

She needed to get him out of here before her heart completely melted or her family showed up. "Thank you. I've got it now. I'm sorry about the truck. I can—"

"Don't worry about it. It's made for handling mud, and anything else you get from working on a ranch with animals. Are you all right?"

She chuckled, remembering his words. "Yeah. You know us moms. Wash-and-wear." Moving to the bed, she took the washcloth from him. "You need to go. I have a feeling the family will be here soon, and it'll be easier if you're not here."

"Right." Keeping his gaze on Suzie, he gently lifted her head and put her back on her pillow. "She seems better. Just tired now." He looked up at her. "Are you taking her to the doctor?"

"If she is still sick tomorrow, I will." She eased onto the bed, taking the place where he had been sitting. "Bye, Reid."

He nodded. "If she needs anything else, you'll let me know?"

"My dad and sisters will be here soon. We've got this covered."

He took his hat off and backed out of the girls' room. His gaze lingered on the walls. Walls covered with posters of horses, family pictures and…

Oh, no. The painting. She could tell the minute Reid saw it.

"Danica. That's the drawing I did for you." It was a whimsical ink drawing of a garden with baby animals having a tea party under giant sunflowers. Washes of color danced across the picture. He had made the frame from scraps of old wood that he'd found in one of their barns.

It had been his Valentine's gift to her the day he asked her to marry him. He'd told her they would create their own world. She gritted her teeth.

"Reid. It doesn't mean anything. I never told them who painted it. I always loved your art, and it's perfect for the girls' room." She brushed back her daughter's hair. "You need to go."

He turned at the door and paused, hand on the frame. "The Hausmans said they're providing steers for the county play-day next weekend. Do the girls ride there?"

"They run the barrels and poles." She needed to stop talking. "If you see us there, you can say hi." Her sisters were going to kill her. Now she had to warn her father. "I'll tell Daddy you're in town." She looked down to make sure Suzie was still asleep. "I want to make it clear, this is not me giving you permission to tell them who you are. You said you just wanted to see them. That's all this is."

"I get it. Thank you." With a nod, he left.

She went back to tending to their daughter. Her daughter. He would be gone as soon as she had a new vet tech. The idea of him leaving should not make her sad.

Gritting her teeth, she reminded herself why loving him again was a mistake. She had already grieved the lost dreams of them growing old together, raising their family. Enough time was wasted over Reid McAllister. She couldn't afford to give him any more of her.

Chapter Six

"Daddy, please. Don't cause any trouble." Danica gripped the railing on the stock trailer and peered through the bars at her father. He eased the big palomino gelding out the back.

"I'm not the one you need to worry about." He glanced around the area behind the arena. "Where are the girls?"

"They went to the concession stand with Nikki and Mia."

"You think that's wise? What if he sees them and does something?"

"Like what?" Hands on her hips, she stared at him. "He's not going to do anything other than say hi. We have an agreement."

"I suppose you trust him? Just like the last time." He looped the lead rope and checked the saddle. "I think we should get the girls and go home."

She tried to imagine how he would react if she told him that they were married. A shudder skipped up and down her spine. No way did she want to face that disappointment. Okay, it was official. She was a coward.

"No. They wouldn't understand, and they would be dev-astated. They don't know who he is other than he works with me at the sanctuary."

He shook his head as he went back into the trailer to get the pony, Cinnamon. "You and your lost causes. I don't understand." He stopped and looked at her through the slots. "Most kidnappings are done by a biological parent."

She closed her eyes and took a deep breath. "Daddy, he's not going to kidnap them."

"He's already been in prison once. What's going to stop him from taking them and skipping town?"

"I think he's trying to make things right. He wants to see them. That's all. They are his daughters." Her stomach plunged downward. They were his daughters, and nothing would change that.

"You don't think it's a bit strange that of all the places he could have moved to, he ended up in your backyard? Working on your sanctuary."

"He thinks God put him here." She didn't know what to believe.

Her father snorted. "God has nothing to do with him."

"Daddy, you don't know that."

"I know he hurt my little girl. He walked out on you. And if he tries anything with my granddaughters..."

Placing a hand on his shoulder, she tried to think of words that would make him understand the position she was in. "Daddy, he's the reason you have these grand-daughters. They are as much his as they are mine." When did she get in the business of defending Reid?

"He's already working his way back into your life.

I'm not going to pick up the pieces again. If he says more than hi to the twins, I'm calling James."

"I can give you his number if you need it." Reid stood at the edge of the old green Suburban, a bottle of Big Red soda in his hand. "My parole officer is here tonight, so if you feel the need to talk to him about me, go ahead."

Her father didn't say a word, but if looks could kill, she'd be writing Reid's obituary. She stepped between the men. "Hi, Reid."

"I saw the girls at the concession stand. Figured you'd want to be around when I talked to them." He turned to her father, head down. With a deep breath, he stood straighter and looked her father in the eye. "Mr. Bergmann, I know you have every reason to hate me and rightly so, but I want you to know that I'm not here to hurt Danica or the girls in any way. I do have amends to make, and I hope you believe me when I say that I am truly sorry."

"It's God's place to forgive you, not mine. And keep those sunglasses on. Otherwise, people will start asking questions about your eye color." With the lead in hand, her father took the pony to the other side of the trailer.

"Reid, I'm sorry."

"Don't be. He's right." He turned his face to the opposite side of the arena. "I saw them with Frito pies and Big Red."

She checked Jingle's hooves. "Big Red is their favorite. We don't have soda in the house, so it's a special treat once a week." Moving to the gelding's mane, she started braiding it. His neck was chest level to her.

After a moment of silence, she stopped and looked at him over the pony. She probably shouldn't tell him this, but her mouth opened and… "Every time they get one, I think about you and your obsession with the drink. Strange, the things they inherit."

"Do they like school?"

"They're only in kindergarten. But they love school. They ask tons of questions and enjoy talking and being around people. Animals, too. They're obsessed with animals, all kinds, even insects. The other day they found a spider in the house. Sammi was going to kill it, but they made my dad catch it and release it outside."

He smiled at her, and his eyes sparkled. That's the expression she lost her heart to, the same expression she had seen in her daughters. Turning away from him, she tried to think of something else to say.

The girls were dangerous to talk about. They were her weak spot. "How's your mother doing? It had to be hard on her when you went to prison." She needed to remind them both why he didn't know his children. It was the consequence of his mistakes, his choices.

He'd always been worried about his mom, but Danica never got to meet her. She never thought about her as her children's grandmother. She hadn't even thought about his side of the family at all.

His hands in his pockets, Reid's gaze locked on to some far-off place. Someplace she couldn't see. "Reid?"

"Mom died my second year in." His jaw popped.

The world went quiet as she focused on him. She stepped around the horse she had put between them, wanting to be closer. Wanting to wrap him in her arms. "Reid…" She stepped forward.

Reid looked at Danica as she moved toward him, but the sound of sweet giggles stole his attention away. The twins, his daughters, were running toward him. One of them had on a pink cowboy hat with matching boots and a glittering shirt. The other one wore a black hat to go with her dark purple bandana. They had cheesy Frito pies in hand, and their aunt Jackie carried a couple bottles of the cold drink he loved.

"Mr. Reid!"

"Hello."

The girls greeted him with a smile. Standing behind them, Jackie glared. Her thoughts on him being here had been made perfectly clear.

A huge silver dually with a matching horse trailer pulled up behind them. With the engine cut off, Nikki jumped down from the passenger side, followed by her stepdaughter, Mia. The frown on her face made it clear he was not welcomed. "Oh, look, the whole family is here."

Danica put her hand on Suzie's shoulder. "Nikki."

With a shake of her head, the oldest Bergmann sister scanned the area. "Where's Sammi?"

Mr. Bergmann came from the other side of the trailer and shook Adrian's hand. "Her horse was hyped up, so she's running off his energy in the arena. Need any help unloading?"

Suzie shoved the last spoonful of chili into her mouth. "Can I go? I want to warm up Sunny."

Lizzy shook her head. "Nothing is going to make him go faster."

Suzie started arguing.

"Girls, stop it." Jackie held up the bottles. "Do you want the rest of your soda?"

"Can you put it in the ice chest, please?" Suzie glared at her sister. "I want to save it for later."

She moved to the palomino tied at the end of the trailer. Standing next to the big gelding, his daughter looked so small. Reid laid a hand on the thick neck. "This is your horse?"

Suzie nodded. "I wanted a faster horse, but Grandpa says I have to wait until I'm double digits. That's a long time. Momma, can I ride now?"

"Be careful and stay on the railing."

She unfastened the reins and looked at him. "Can you help me mount? I just need you to cup your hands so I can reach the stirrup."

He steadied his breath. It didn't mean anything. He was just the closest to Suzie and her horse.

Lizzy sat on the side step of the trailer, her Frito pie in her lap and her Big Red next to her. "If you rode a smaller horse, you could mount yourself."

"I don't want a baby's horse."

"Jingles is not for babies. He runs. He runs faster than Sunny. All he does is trot."

"Yeah, but Jingles's legs are so short he has a slower time."

"Girls, stop it, or we can load the horses up and go home."

"Yes, ma'am," both girls mumbled.

Reid smiled as Suzie put her pink-booted foot in his cupped hands. With ease, she leaped into the saddle and adjusted the reins as she slipped the tip of her toes into the stirrups, heels down. She sat well in the saddle.

"Mr. Reid, do you ride?"

"I do. I rope, and I've been known to ride a bull or two."

Danica smiled. "The first time I saw him, he was riding a bull."

Lizzy's eyes went wide. "The first time? Where was that?"

Reid looked at Danica, wondering if she'd meant to say something about their past. By the stiffness in her shoulders and slight panic and regret in her gaze, he assumed not.

Mr. Bergmann reappeared then, his long strides bringing him next to Lizzy. Quickly, he lifted her up over his head, causing her to giggle. He pressed his nose to hers. "Are we going to ride today or just sit around and talk?" The girls forgot their questions and cheered. Back on the ground, Lizzy mounted the shorter horse.

Suzie pulled back on her reins and moved the big gelding away from the trailer. "I'm going to be out there before you."

"Girls, it's not a race." They ignored their mother.

With a kick to her horse, Suzie moved out into a trot. Her red hair bounced around her shoulders. "I'm going to beat you!" she yelled at her sister as Lizzy mounted her pony.

Danica stood with her hands on her hips. "Careful, girls, or the horses are going back into the trailer."

Mia moved her horse past them. "I'll watch them."

Mr. Bergmann followed the three girls to the arena.

Danica turned away from Reid. "I can't believe I said that. Why did I tell them I knew you before? Where was my brain?" She slammed a few straps of leather into a bag.

Danica frantically moved around, stuffing things in a large black bag. She was mad at herself. Off to the side, Reid looked like he wanted to say something.

Jackie acted first, slamming the lid to the big silver

ice chest. Standing, she crossed her arms and glared at Reid. "Since they were born, everyone makes comments about their eye color. Even to this day, when I take them somewhere, it is the first thing people see. If you're serious about respecting Danica, and not forcing the issue, then you need to stay out of town and away from people that know the girls."

Danica's face tightened. She shut the back door of the Suburban and just stood there, looking at nothing. "Maybe it would be easier if I just told the girls."

"No." Reid and Jackie stared at each other, startled to find themselves in agreement.

He cleared his throat. "They would want to know where I've been. I can't lie to them. I can't tell them the truth, either."

"So it's about you being embarrassed." Jackie leaned back against the trailer. "What about you just disappearing again? You've been here for a little over two weeks. Danica's a grown woman and can make her own mistakes, but my nieces have big hearts. They haven't learned to protect them yet. I'm not going to let you crush them just so you can play daddy for a little bit."

"Enough." Danica pushed her way between Reid and her sister. "I agree. The girls aren't ready." Her gaze jumped between the two of them. "For all the reasons you stated, and more. Jackie, I love you, but this isn't your fight."

"You're thinking of taking him back, aren't you? How can you still love him? After everything he did?"

"I don't love him." On the edge of yelling, she closed her eyes and swallowed.

She didn't love him anymore. He knew that, but it still hurt to hear the words.

"This isn't about me. I have to figure out what is best for Suzie and Lizzy. If you'll excuse me, I'm here to watch my daughters ride." Green eyes stared him down. "You have steers to take care of."

She hoped the message was clear. *Don't join the family.* He gave her a quick nod. "I'll see you Monday at the sanctuary."

Danica took her sister's hand and headed to the arena.

After a few riders, the announcer called Suzie as the next rider. Reid went to the railing and pulled himself up to get a better look. He scanned the stands. Right up front, Danica sat with her father and two of her sisters. They were laughing about something.

Ready to take pictures, Mr. Bergmann had a camera with a monster zoom lens. Reid wished he had something to take a picture with, but his phone was so basic it wouldn't be able to take one from this far.

Adrian joined him. They stood there in silence, but for some reason, he didn't feel as alone as he had before. The big gelding moved to the gate. With a kick, Suzie leaned forward and urged her horse to move through the clover pattern.

He had to smile. The big animal flicked his ears back and forth but never went past a trot.

Adrian laughed. "That girl would give anything for a faster horse. They're having a hard time keeping her on that pace. She wants speed."

"What about Lizzy?"

"Oh, she's the slow, steady one. She's happy with the pony. I don't see her advancing to the upper-level rodeos. She's just here for the Frito pie and Big Red."

"Hey, Reid!" James hollered.

He jumped at his parole officer's voice. For a moment, he panicked wondering what he'd done wrong. "Have you seen Danica? We have a problem. It seems a few of the big cats got through the fencing on the west side and were seen stalking goats."

"There's no way they got out."

"All I know is we got a few angry ranchers at the sanctuary, demanding something be done. Or they're going to start taking care of the situation themselves."

He glanced across the arena and found Danica looking at him. She turned away when they made eye contact. "I'll go get her. Let me tell Philip I'm leaving, and make sure he can get the steers back to the Hausman ranch without me."

"I can help him if he needs it," Adrian offered. "She'll need backup with those ranchers. They've been looking for ways to shut her down from day one."

Reid nodded and made his way to Danica. Taking the stairs two at a time, he ignored Jackie's hard glare at the landing and went straight to Danica. "Hey. There's trouble at the sanctuary."

Chapter Seven

Parking behind Stephanie's Mercedes, Danica got out of her vehicle and slammed the door behind her, striding toward the oncoming storm.

Reid followed her. On the porch, a group of men in cowboy hats, starched jeans and worn boots gathered around Officer Bolton and the lawyer.

A barrel-chested rancher, Walter Riggs, stepped away from the group when he saw them. "You promised us they wouldn't be a threat to our herds."

Marching up the steps, Danica faced him directly. "Y'all are a bigger threat to my old crippled cats than they are to your stock."

That was the wrong thing to say. A flurry of angry words flew through the air.

Reid took a step forward but stopped right behind her left shoulder. "Yelling at her won't fix the problem."

She'd lost her composure for a moment. That couldn't happen again. They were threatening her animals, and she needed to keep a level head in order to protect them. Reid stared straight at the lead cowboy.

Reid stood tall but relaxed. "We'll collect the cats,

fix the fences and put procedures in place to make sure this doesn't happen again." He glanced down at Danica.

She nodded, grateful he had a cool head. With the aviators on, he was an imposing figure.

His finger brushed her back, but he quickly retreated and crossed his arms over his chest.

With a clear focus, she took control of the conversation. "It's our priority to discover how this happened, and make sure it doesn't happen again. For the safety of your livestock, and of the rescue animals on the premises."

Walter closed the space between them. With his hands on his hips, he lifted his chin in a challenge. "Who are you?"

"I'm her vet tech, and I just got out of prison, so I don't scare easily."

Her father's friend took a step back. He glanced to the deputy, then back to Reid. "Is that a threat?"

"No, sir. Just letting you know you can't come here expecting to bully Ms. Bergmann. Her family wouldn't appreciate it."

"Reid." Her hand touched his arm. The warmth seeped through the cotton material of his shirt, so she pulled her hand away quickly. "Reid, as he said, is my vet tech. He's worked with large animals before. We will have the cats back on the property before nightfall."

Another long, lanky rancher spoke up. "We don't have a problem with you or your animals if they stay on your place. Danica, you promised these cats wouldn't be a threat to our livestock. Now they are running wild over the countryside. I have my boys out looking for them. We're going to get them off our ranch one way or another." He shot a nervous glance at Reid. "If you get them first, that's fine, but I'm not sure this is the place for this kind of rescue facility. It's surrounded by working ranches."

James stepped up. "Now, there's no reason for threats, Henry."

Stephanie straightened her jacket. "We have every legal right to be here. If you have any complaints, make them formal. Showing up at the sanctuary as a mob is not acceptable." She glanced at her phone. "I've got an appointment, but if you need anything else, you know how to contact me."

"Thank you, Stephanie." Danica turned to Reid. "I'm going to move the car. Can you gather the supplies we need for retrieval, and bring the truck and stock trailer around?"

Without taking his eyes off the small group of men, he nodded. She didn't want to think how easy it was to trust him, especially in a tense situation like this. No, for now, she needed to focus on the real problem. She needed to get her cats home.

"The crippled jaguar is close to the fence line, hiding under a cedar. He's acting like he wants back in the sanctuary. I've got a small team here, including James." Bobby's thick drawl came over the radio. Reid looked over at Danica as she listened in.

"We have the small female. Reid and I are taking her back, and we'll put her in the clinic for tonight. Did James get pictures of the fences?"

"Yes, ma'am. Looks like someone cut the fence, then chased the cats out."

"Can you make the opening bigger, then try to herd

the jag in that direction? If we can get him back without tranquilizing him that would be great."

"With the volunteers, we can also secure the fence in no time. We'll have it back right as rain before the sun sets."

"Thank you, Bobby."

"Sure thing." The line went dead.

Slamming a fist against the steering wheel, Danica's delicate jaw looked hard as steel. "This was done on purpose. Who would want to close us down so bad?"

"You'll need to make a list and turn it over to the sheriff. Hopefully, they'll take it seriously and investigate."

With a rigid jerk of her chin, she stayed focused on the road in front of her. They sat in silence until she parked behind the clinic. Even then, she only gave short, direct instructions to help her with the animal.

Checking the cat, they placed her in a holding crate. Danica briskly put things away, her movements stiff. She started wiping down an area she'd already hit twice before.

He moved behind her, and gently placed his hands on her upper arms to hold her still. "It's going to be okay." He pressed his face into her hair. For a moment, everything was right with the world. She was in his arms, her warmth and scent surrounding him.

She relaxed against him. The citrus smell of her shampoo flirted with his senses. Just as quickly, she braced her hand on the counter and stiffened. "Reid, you don't know that."

Turning to face him, she tried to put distance between them. If she wanted space, she wasn't getting it. He had her trapped against the counter. She needed to listen to him. "Dani girl, it's going to be okay."

With a grumble, she ducked under his arm and started to rearrange containers. "Go see Bobby."

"Baby. You're upset. I know I'm part of the problem, but you've been so strong for so long." Standing next to her, he placed a hand over hers to ease the nervous moments. "If you're mad, get mad. I can take it, then you can go back to being strong."

Suddenly she was in his arms, her fist hitting his chest, her face on his shoulder. Feet planted, he took the hits with his arms around her.

"I'm tired of being the strong one. I'm tired of being responsible for everyone and everything else! You left me. You left me to take care of everyone and I…" With a sob, she collapsed against him.

Digging his fingers into her hair, he held her close as tears saturated his shirt. His own might have joined hers. "I'm sorry. I'm so sorry." He repeated the useless phrase over and over against the soft skin of her ear.

Taking two hard gasping breaths, she lifted her head. Her green eyes were bright with tears. "Why? Why did you throw us away for a quick score?"

A question that had tormented him for the last few years. There was never an answer good enough. "I lacked faith."

His thumb traced her bottom lip. He became fixated as memories of their first kiss rose to the forefront. She had been so sweet and tender on that cold February day. She was stronger now.

Dropping his hands, he leaned in closer. Closer to the dream that had sustained him for the last six years. Closer to the peace she always gave him.

Soft as he remembered, her lips gave way under his.

He went deeper. His hand cupped her jaw as he explored and rediscovered the wonder of Danica, his wife.

One step closer. He had waited for this for a lifetime. Time stood still as he claimed what had once been his.

Danica pushed on his chest. "No." One step and she was beyond his reach again.

Yanked out of his dreams, he faced the cold, hard reality of his choices. He let her go.

Moving to the other side of the room, the heated glare she shot at him made her mood clear. With the medical table between them, she brought her breathing back under control. "No. Not now. Not ever again." Spinning around, she rubbed her face. "I had my meltdown. You need to go now. Bobby will be back soon, and he can take you to the ranch."

"Danica, I'm sorry." He had to find a way to reach her.

"Yeah, I heard you the first few hundred times. I forgive you. We're done." Dry-faced, she stiffened her spine and looked at him straight in the face. "I know you're invited to our church. If you do attend, please don't talk to the girls or me. I recommend that you stay away from everyone in my family."

"If I were a better man, I would without question. But I can't ignore the part of me that wants to fight for my family. For my rights as a father."

The color drained from her face. "Please don't. You've hurt us enough. The best thing would be for you to go. Leave before the girls learn who you are and what you've done."

"Would that be so bad?"

"I would rather they not learn that their father transported drugs. That he comes from a line of people who took the easy path to prison. You're not the kind of man I want in their lives."

Every doubt he had walloped him in the face. He grabbed the edge of the counter for support. His girls would be ashamed of him. Just as their mother was. He was the son of Calvin McAllister, and he was drenched in the sins of his father. His insides hollowed out, not an ounce of blood or a twitch of muscle was evident. It was gone. Ray had promised him God's forgiveness if he asked for it. Forgiveness from Danica was not so easy. "I don't even deserve it."

Eyes narrowed, she glared at him. "What are you talking about?"

"Forgiveness. I know it doesn't erase my mistakes." His jaw hurt. "I don't deserve you or the girls. Knowing I haven't earned the right to have you in my life doesn't stop the wanting. I want to be in the girls' lives in some sort of way."

A few labeled containers seemed to be out of place as she turned her back to him and rearranged them again.

He straightened. "I'll check the cub." He glanced at the large crate that held the still-sleeping female cat. "Do you need help releasing her?"

He waited at the door for her to say something. What he wanted, he wasn't sure, but he didn't want to leave her this way. Her back stayed rigid, and her usually graceful moments were stiff. She dropped a canister of swabs, and they scattered across the cold tiled floor.

He rushed to help her.

"Reid, just go. I can—"

"Momma!"

"Momma, can we see the baby bats?"

Her head dropped, but only for a brief second. Steel in her eyes, she glared at him. "Go."

"Mr. McAllister!"

"Call me Reid." He smiled at them as he went down to their eye level. "Mr. McAllister makes me look around for my father."

The twins giggled. Their aunt Jackie walked up behind them, placing her hands on their shoulders. She encircled them and pulled them back a little.

"Mr. Reid, have you seen the baby bats?"

He rotated to face them. "Yep. Yesterday I fed them and gave them their bath."

They clapped and jumped. "We got to watch Momma bathe them, but we're not allowed to play with them. They like us, though."

"They're the cutest things ever!" They both turned to their mom. Identical moss gray eyes, full of wonder and all the good things in life, took his breath away. He never knew such beautiful parts of him could ever exist on God's earth.

"Can we see the baby bats now? We won't touch them."

"No, sweethearts. They need to be free of human contact as much as possible."

Their sweet faces fell, and he wanted their smiles back. "I took a little video of them yesterday." He pulled his phone from his back pocket. "Do you want to see it?"

"Yes!" The girls echoed in stereo as they ran to him.

"Girls!" Their mother and aunt had the same stereo effect. He couldn't help but smile.

"Reid." Danica joined them, putting both of her hands on Suzie. "You can't—"

"It's just a video."

"We want to see it," the girls said in unison.

He hit Play and held his phone out so the girls could see the small screen. They stood in awe, giggling and squealing each time the bats moved. He forced a smile. The longing to pull them close and take in everything about them dumbfounded him. It hurt deep in his gut.

"Okay, girls." Danica's tone remained firm, the voice of a protective mother. "That's enough. I need to feed the cub. Want to go with me?"

"But we want to watch it again!"

"No, we need to let Mr. McAllister get back to work." Jumping, they went to her. It didn't take long to lose their attention. "Come on. We need to get the formula." She took their hands in each of hers.

For a moment, he imagined them parenting together. She would be fussing at him for never telling the girls no. "I can text the video to you."

The girls cheered. Jackie rolled her eyes. "Send it to me. Danica has a lousy phone. You know, since she has to support her family on her own."

"Jackie!"

Ignoring her sister, Jackie gave him her number. "Come on, girls. Let's go."

Lizzy started following, but stopped and looked back at him. "Are you coming with us?"

His heart skipped. Danica started to speak only to be cut off by Jackie as she stepped in between them. "No, he has to stay here." Her glare made it clear he wasn't welcome.

Stepping to the side, Danica looked at him, her eyes a bit softer, but not much. "Mr. McAllister has work to do here."

He stood and put the phone back in his pocket. He had Jackie's number, not that it would do him any good, but it was a connection to his girls that he didn't have before.

Pausing at the door, Danica sent the girls ahead with Jackie. He held his breath, waiting to hear her voice. Anything to keep her in his physical world.

"Don't forget to record your time so I can sign it. It's due to Officer Bolton Monday, right?"

"Yes, ma'am." He stuffed his hands in his pockets.

With a nod, she left and jogged to catch up with Jackie and the twins. He moved to the door. A hollow feeling settled inside him as he watched his family walk away.

Once they were out of sight, he went to the supply room at the back of the building. His thoughts kept returning to the girls' faces as they watched his video. They had looked at him with such excitement and love.

In their life, they hadn't been taught to be wary and skeptical of strangers. They had a protected life. To them, the world was a good and safe place.

What would happen if they found out he was their father? He broke out into a cold sweat.

Stopping at the orphaned bats' station, he checked on them. Each was wrapped tightly in a little bright-colored towel. They were surprisingly cute. Big eyes and ears, tiny little noses, and completely dependent on the kindness of the humans in charge of them.

One of the little guys yawned and blinked at him a couple of times before snuggling back against his brother bat. Reid took out his phone and snapped a few pictures. The girls would love it.

With Jackie's number already memorized, he sent

the pictures to her and hoped she would share them with Suzie and Lizzy.

Scanning the room, he noticed so many things. Old and broken-down. A forgotten forge. He figured most would find it a lost cause, but he saw potential. If he knew Danica, she thought the same thing.

A thought occurred to him, and he got an idea. The genuine smile felt good on his face. Doing a quick search on the internet through his phone, he smiled again. Live camera feed.

The girls might not be able to spend as much time with the baby bats as they wanted, but this way they could keep an eye on them and watch all the activities that helped the bats grow stronger.

Looking at his phone again, he reckoned he had enough time to plan another project that he'd been considering since the first time he drove the property with Danica.

Chapter Eight

Danica restocked the butterscotch candy on the counter. The free sweet was a tradition going back to when the first Bergmanns ran the lumberyard.

Growing up, she'd felt trapped by the old limestone walls. The fact her family had owned the building since the founding of Clear Water hadn't meant anything to her then. Now it gave her comfort and a place for her daughters to belong.

Even the family squabbles gave her a sense of comfort. At this moment, Jackie and her father were in the loft, debating a new arrangement of the store.

She chuckled at the predictability of her family.

The bell chimed, and she looked up to greet the customer. Her smile slipped.

Reid. If she didn't know better, she'd think he was tormenting her. All day she had fought to keep him out of her thoughts. She wasn't winning the battle.

He stood at the door, not moving forward.

Danica braced her hands on the edge of the counter. She was glad to have something between them. "What are you doing here, Reid?"

With a frown, he looked mad at her. "What are you doing here? Don't you work at the sanctuary during the day?"

"Not on Tuesdays and Wednesdays. I cover the—" Why was she explaining herself to him? "It's a family business. Family has to work it."

"Do the girls spend time here?" He walked over to a poster and looked at the illustrations of the building from the day it was opened over one hundred years ago. Another picture was from two years ago, when it was added to the list of Texas Historical Buildings.

He bent to get a closer look. "There're the girls." With just the tip of his fingers, he touched the glass. "They've grown since this was taken. Do you have more pictures of them?"

"Why are you in the store?" Leaving the safety of the counter, she headed to the nail and screw aisle. She'd been sorting inventory when Jake came in for his supplies. "Did the ranch send you? They usually call in their orders ahead of time." It would be easier to talk to him if she was busy. Someone had mixed the nails. Her father would have a fit if he saw the mess.

"No. I came to talk to Adrian. I was told he'd be working here today. Upstairs."

"Oh." Why did it matter that he hadn't come seeking her? "Yeah, he's with Nikki. I think they're taping and floating the new drywall. What do you need to talk to him for?"

"About a job." Head tilted back, Reid looked at the decorative tin that covered the tall ceiling.

"Already tired of wrangling for the Hausmans?" Okay, that sounded snarky. Without turning, she glanced at him from the corner of her eye.

Reid shook his head and crammed his hands deep into the front pockets of his jacket. Now he studied the old wooden floor. His profile was hard and impressive, even with uncertainty etched in every line.

"I like working with the horses. With you looking for a new vet tech, I thought I'd line up more work. Pastor Levi said Adrian might have something for me. I like staying busy. Keeps me out of trouble."

"It won't be that easy. My brother-in-law is one of the hardest-working guys I know. He has a strong sense of commitment and loyalty. He doesn't like working with people who might just up and leave, abandoning a project."

"Ouch." No emotion went along with the word. His gaze stayed on the back of the store.

"Sorry. I just don't—"

"Baby, it's okay. Don't worry about it." At the counter, he picked up a flyer announcing the fund-raiser for the sanctuary.

She knew he used the term of endearment without thinking, but it still did things to her.

"Rodeo Bonanza? The guys were talking about this. You know I rode in prison. They held a first-class show." He looked at her with the smile of old on his face. "I was riding the first time we met. Right after being introduced to you, I was so distracted the bull tossed me at the gate."

She couldn't help but laugh at the memory. "You're still blaming that bad ride on me?" Walking to the end of the aisle, Danica crossed her arms and leaned on the endcap.

"You were the best thing that ever—"

"Mr. McAllister." Her father stomped down the stairs. "Can I help you?"

Glancing up, she found her sister on the edge of the railing, staring down at them from the loft. Her father directed a frown at Reid before he turned and made eye contact with Danica. Her twin shook her head as if disappointed.

Now what had she done? She scowled back and shrugged. As an adult woman, if she wanted to talk to the father of her children, it was not the place of her twin to judge.

"Sir, I came looking for Adrian. I was told he—"

"He's upstairs." Standing next to Danica now, her father waved to the stairs. "It's that way. Turn to the left. You can't miss him."

"Thank you, sir." With a respectful nod, Reid slowly took the stairs. Passing through the office loft, he greeted Jackie. She didn't say anything, but her gaze stayed on him as if waiting for a rattlesnake to strike.

Reid was a proud man. To keep smiling at their obvious hostility had to be a difficult hit to his pride.

The first time Danica brought him home to meet her father, it had not gone well. Despite his promise not to cause problems, the twenty-year-old Reid had not been able to ignore any slight that he saw as an insult to his manhood.

It had been a week of the two men arguing and stomping around each other like two bulls in a small pen. She had been so stressed, trying to keep the peace between them. By the end of the visit, she'd just wanted to get back to school.

Back to just the two of them. With Danica, Reid had been such a different person. When it had just been the two of them, she'd never seen the angry young man her father and sisters had.

That should have been a warning sign, but the haze of love had been too thick for her to pay attention. The bitter truth was her father had been right.

"Danica!" Her father said it as if he'd already called her a few times.

"Sorry, Daddy. Did you need something?" She went back to organizing and counting nails.

"Do you still love him?" The deep lines of his face were not from smiling.

"Daddy." Head down, she recounted the box.

In silence, he stared at her for a bit.

She gave up on her task and looked at him with her hands on her hips. "No."

He raised one eyebrow.

Taking a deep breath, she stood still despite the urge to fidget with her shirt. It was not a lie. It wasn't. *Please, God, don't let it be a lie.*

"She's lying!" Jackie yelled from the loft, arms crossed.

"Am not." Great. They had dissolved into five-year-olds. All she needed to do was stomp her foot.

"Whatever, but lying to yourself is not going to help anyone." Jackie turned and disappeared into the office. Fine, she'd let her sister have the last word this time.

Her father moved closer. "Be careful. You have the girls. Don't make the mistake I did. Being with the wrong person is not worth it. God has someone for you. A Godly man who will love you and the girls the way you deserve."

Since her jaw was locked, she just nodded. Reid might be as selfish as Sheila, Sammi's mother, but

Danica was afraid it was already too late for her heart.
Maybe she had never actually stopped loving Reid.
She'd just buried it, waiting for him to come back.

"I promise, Daddy, my girls will always come first."
They would not experience the pain that had left her
heart a scarred, bloody mess. Her mom's death, her oldest sister's departure, running away, her stepmother not
loving them enough to stay. And Reid.

But being tired of trying to stay strong was not an
excuse. Danica could overcome any weakness that encouraged her to accept Reid as her one and only love.
He'd already demonstrated he couldn't be trusted.

Just because he hadn't started an argument with her
father or sister this one time didn't prove anything. Second chances were God's business, not hers.

Anger sat in his gut like embers. He needed to release the pent-up tension. There was nothing for him to
prove. He hated the anger his father had planted in him.

It was up to him to not give in to it. Something physical always helped. Back at the ranch, the guys had a
punching bag set up in one of the barns. He pressed his
right thumb into his left palm.

"Reid?" Nikki stood in the doorway of the front
room.

Remodeling a house was hard work, but it would
keep him focused. Physical work, that's what he needed.
He liked having a mission.

"Hi, Nikki." The oldest Bergmann had different coloring but still looked just like the twins. They seemed
a lot like their father at first, but they looked more like
their mother from the old photos Danica had shown

him once. If he remembered correctly, they were about the same age now as their mother was when she died.

Adrian came up behind Nikki, resting a hand on her shoulder. "Hey, Reid. What's up?"

"Bobby's been doing little things around the house on the sanctuary, the one that has fire damage. At the rate it's going, it will take years. I told him that I could add it to my volunteer hours and we could get it done faster. I thought you might help me figure out some of the details. But I don't want Danica and the girls to know just yet, or her father. She might not accept my help."

Nikki blinked. "Wow. That's a great idea actually, but she said she might lose the land if they have to close the sanctuary."

"She only has to keep it running a couple more years. Do you think she is going to let anything close her down? Look at all she's done. She's willing to work with me to keep it open."

He took a deep breath and slowed his pounding heart. "Nothing is going to stop her, and if she lives there that's even better. With all her focus on the animals, what Danica always wanted has been lost with everything else she does for other people around here."

At least the couple wasn't staring at him with open hostility. They were easier to talk to than the rest of the Bergmann family. It was all the encouragement he needed. "On the first day, I saw the house, and she told me how she had planned to live there but didn't have the time or the resources to fix it."

Crossing the room, Adrian stopped in front of him. He was shorter than Reid, but he was solid and didn't look like a man you could push around. "Why are you doing this? What are you expecting in return?"

"I'm not playing a game. It is what it is. Danica wants to live in that house, and I want to give it to her. So, when she tells me it's time for me to move on, I can leave knowing they have a home of their own." He took a breath. This part was tougher. "I hope that her family, who happen to own a lumberyard, would help me make her dream come true."

Nikki joined her husband. Her stance was just as fierce. "No strings?" Her eyes narrowed.

"None."

Adrian crossed his arms. "What's your long-term plan?"

The Bergmanns were a family. A real family. The kind that supported each other no matter what. They were the only family his daughters would know, and he could sleep well knowing they were loved. Even if he couldn't be the one to love them.

He had done better than his father already. Now his only job was not to mess it up.

"I don't have long-term plans right now. I'm learning to live one day at a time. I start each morning with God, and try to keep Him in everything I do throughout the day."

Each word was painful. It went against Reid's instincts to talk about his personal business, but he needed someone in Danica's family to not see a total loser when they looked at him.

Adrian nodded. "We all make mistakes. How we get back on the right path is what matters. We don't know each other, but this is my family too now. Do you want to be a part of the girls' lives?"

He wanted to yell yes, but his father's words dragged across his brain like the jagged edge of a cut fence. There was no escaping who he was. His father's son. He clenched his fist. He wanted to be better, but could he be? Was it possible?

"Man, think about it carefully, because it's a serious commitment. Once they know you and love you, there is no going back without damaging them."

Nikki slugged him in the arm. "Adrian. Simmer. Mr. Never Missteps here tends to be a bit overprotective of the girls in his life. Between the two of us, I'm the one that made the huge mistakes. So I want to help you, but you need to understand that if you hurt my sister or my nieces, I will hunt you down, and I have the skills to do it."

"She does." Adrian slipped his arm around her waist. They made a solid wall. "So, what's the plan?"

"When it comes to telling the girls, I'll let Danica decide. Other than that, I want to do as much as I can while I'm here. I want to make the ranch house livable."

They nodded in unison. Adrian spoke. "So, how can we help with the Home for Danica Project?"

Reid smiled. "I've done construction and know my way around a basic job, but I thought you could look at the house and see if I'm missing any serious problems. I thought your dad might provide supplies. I'll pay, but I don't think he'd sell to me. Plus, I wasn't sure if he would fight the idea of her and the girls moving out."

"Let me see when I'm available." Adrian pulled out his phone and flipped through it. "Looks like the end of this week works."

Nikki smiled. "I'll take them to Kerrville for dinner. Let me take care of Daddy. I don't know why we haven't thought of this before now. She loves that place. It seems a bit obvious she should move into the house."

"Knowing her, she didn't want to bother anyone. It was a small fire, so hopefully, the structure is solid and not compromised."

"It's not going to take her long to figure out what's going on."

"I know, but I think once the plan is in motion, and the repairs are started, she'll be fine."

"This is a good thing you're doing." Nikki was the first Bergmann to look at him with something other than disdain. Of course, she hadn't been there the first time around.

Adrian held his hand out. At first, Reid didn't realize the man wanted to shake. He was an idiot, reaching forward to grasp Adrian's palm. His grip was firm.

The song "Wish Upon a Star" started playing from Adrian's pocket. Nikki laughed. "You need to get your daughter a new horse, or you're going to have to live with girly ringtones. She's ready for a faster horse." She turned to Reid. "That's his daughter's way of letting him know she is not happy about his decision."

"No. I'm not giving in to ringtone blackmail." Shaking his head, he walked out of the room as he answered his phone.

With nothing else to say, Reid dipped his head. "Thank you, Nikki. I'll talk to you later." He turned to leave.

"Wait." She lowered her voice. "Can I have a minute?"

Outside the oversize windows, clouds shrouded the sun, casting a darkness over the room. He knew better than to assume he could walk away without taking a hit. Planting a smile on his face, he turned back to her and waited. He would smile and stay calm, no matter what she thought he needed to know.

"You're not the first to walk out on her. There is a long line of people she loved and trusted that disappeared on her. Including me. So be patient. She's strong and independent, but more important, I'm afraid she's not going to let anyone close to the real her. You must know for sure if you're in this for keeps. Because you'll have to cross the Grand Canyon without a safety net to reach her."

"How do I make this right for both of us? My family history doesn't offer me a great deal of hope. I want…" His hands were cold. "I don't know if I can do what I want to do. I want to be a good family man and father, but what if it's not in my DNA? I have a screwed-up past. What I did to Danica is just part of it."

"God is in your DNA. With Him, your past does not have to be your future. I know that firsthand. I'm not a counselor like Adrian or any kind of spiritual leader, but I know God gave me a new beginning. I ran for about ten years. God brought me back here. To my family. To Adrian. To a community that I thought would reject me when they learned what I had done."

"I don't even know how to be part of a normal family."

She laughed, "There's no such thing as normal. On the surface, it looks all-American, but hang around, and you'll find out all our sordid secrets." She looked over her shoulder. "Except for Adrian."

"Don't listen to her." The male voice carried through the rooms. An edge of laughter floated right behind it. "I have issues, too. Just ask my daughter's mother."

"We're not talking to you," she yelled back so Adrian could hear, a smile on her face as she shook her head. "The point is all of us have messed up. Including my father, so don't let him fool you."

"If someone like me came around one of my daughters, I'd chase him off, too. Undoubtedly in a violent matter. Then I'd definitely be on the run."

"You're leaving? Where are you going?" Danica was on the stairs, concern and maybe even a little panic in her expression. "Reid, don't do anything to get yourself in more trouble. They'd throw you back in prison! I'm not taking my girls to visit you in jail."

Nikki chuckled. "That's what happens when you jump into a conversation midstream."

"I thought you wanted me to leave." Hope was a deadly thing.

She stood at the top of the stairs as if she might take off running.

He slowly moved toward her, but not so close that she'd bolt. "Are you thinking of letting me see the girls?" Words were hard to get past his dry throat.

"You've already met the girls. But that's not the point. Who were you going to chase in a violent manner?"

Nikki chuckled. "I'll let you handle this one, big guy. I'm sure Adrian needs my help with something."

Danica cut across the room to an old pine table. She wouldn't look at him as she ran her fingertips across the worn surface. "This belonged to my great-grandparents." She looked around the room. "This was the family living quarters in the early days."

"You didn't answer my question. Are you thinking of introducing me to our daughters?"

She crossed her arms. "And you didn't tell me who you wanted to fight. You know you're going to have to let insults slide, right? I noticed you're better at holding your temper than you were when I brought you home last time. So don't let anyone control your emotions. It's not worth it."

"Yes, ma'am." Hip on the table's edge, he crossed his arms and smiled at her. Just being in the same room with her was a gift. "We were talking about fathers and daughters. I told her if some punk like me showed any interest in one of my girls, I'd hit him. I didn't see it the first time we came to visit, but I have a much deeper appreciation for your father. He was right. You shouldn't have trusted me."

"If you stick around, the girls will have no chance of dating. Between you, my father and Adrian, no boy would be brave enough."

The need to be near her beat down his resistance. Not able to take the distance any longer, he worked his way around the table, until he stood next to her. Her fresh, sweet scent invaded him, reassured him.

He placed his hand where hers had just traced the wood pattern. It was still warm from her touch. Head down, he watched her hands. "Danica, I want to stay for the long haul. I do. I already missed six years. Years I'll never get back. Please, let me be here for the next fifteen." He swallowed and hoped she didn't hear the catch in his throat.

For what felt like an eternity, they stood in silence. Reid feared to take a breath.

Soft bells chimed from her pocket. Taking out her phone, she swiped the screen. "I need to go pick up the girls from school. One day a week, they get to go out and help feed the animals." Flipping her braid over her shoulder, she looked out the window. "Do you want to go with me? I could use the help. As a friend."

His heart slammed hard against his chest. "Yes. Thank you. I came into town with Wade, but I'll let him know I don't need a ride back to the ranch."

"Okay."

She already looked like she was regretting the invitation. Reid followed her down the steps. "I appreciate this. I know it's big for you to trust me this way." He struggled with ways to assure her. "I promise I won't say or do anything without your approval."

"I'm counting on that." Back on the store level, she retrieved her bag from under the counter. "Daddy, we're getting the girls and heading to the sanctuary."

Her father blocked the narrow hall that led to the back door. "We? He's not going with you."

Reid tried to stay calm, but as always, Mr. Bergmann brushed against his brittle ego. He closed his eyelids and breathed before opening them and meeting the man's gaze. Facing the grandfather of his daughters, Reid prayed for wisdom. He needed to earn this man's favor. So far, he hadn't done a thing to deserve that honor. His short fuse was his problem, not her father's.

Making sure to keep a glare from forming on his face, he waited for Danica. No big deal. He could do this. He forced his fists to relax, right along with his jaw.

Chapter Nine

Danica blew out some hot air, puffing her cheeks. Her father wasn't even looking at her. He was too busy staring down Reid at the back of the store. "Yes, Daddy. Reid is going with me to the sanctuary."

He crossed his long arms. His jaw twitched. "It's Tuesday."

God, please save me from the overprotective people in my life. "Yes, it is. Tomorrow is Wednesday."

"You don't need to get smart with me, girl."

Keys in hand, she walked toward Reid. "You didn't raise me to be stupid, Daddy."

Her father reached for her arm, stopping her. "The girls go with you on Tuesday. You're taking him to pick up the girls? Are you sure that's wise?"

She sighed and resisted the eye roll. Really, she was too old. "Daddy, please don't start." She looked around the store to make sure it was clear of any other ears. "He is their father, whether you like it or not."

"I don't like it. Don't go getting weak on me. It's not just you that he'll hurt this time." He grunted. "I feel like I'm repeating myself too much."

She glanced at Reid. He stood relaxed and calm. Not like he had just been insulted by her father. Wanting to encourage him, she smiled. If she still knew him, this was hard on his pride.

She hugged her father, then stepped around him. "Come on, Reid. Let's go."

"If you don't want to listen to me, maybe you want to live somewhere else."

This time she couldn't stop her eyes going skyward. Reid looked worried. "He doesn't mean it."

"Danica! Don't go rolling your eyes at me. You're too old for that!"

She went back to her father. "I love you, but please don't treat me like I'm five." With a quick kiss on his cheek, she turned to leave. "Bye, Daddy. I'll see you for dinner tonight."

"You're not bringing him into my house."

With a sigh, she took Reid by the arm. "Do not engage. Just walk. I need to get my own place." She mumbled it under her breath, but she must have spoken louder than she thought.

"In good time, baby." Reid winked, his expression relaxed despite her father's surliness.

Her lungs threatened to stop working. This was the playful Reid she had fallen in love with. He held her car door open. The now-familiar seriousness quickly replaced his mischievous smile. "You sure about this? I don't want to cause more problems."

"Daddy will be okay." She paused before getting into the car. Straightening, she looked into his eyes. They were grayer today. "But no, I'm not sure. The last time I was sure about something, I ended up alone and pregnant." He had to know this was not easy for her.

"Danica…"

"Let's go before I change my mind."

It didn't take long to get the girls. Excited to see Reid, they chattered from the back seat the whole ride.

She slowed the car down.

"Momma! Why are you taking us home?"

"There's something I need to get at the house before we head out to the refuge."

Reassured, they went back to asking Reid a million questions and telling him all about their day at school.

They were so engaged in their rapid-fire conversation, no one asked her what was in the bag she put in the back. She wasn't even sure if she was going to give it to Reid. Maybe her father was right, and she was weak. Her resolution to keep Reid at a safe distance was already eroding.

Reid laughed as the girls told him who got in trouble at school, and who had the best lunches. As they pulled into the gates of the sanctuary, the girls started talking about the cub and the baby bats.

"Can we feed them, Momma?"

"Please. Can we help give them their baths?" As usual, the girls spoke at once.

"Girls, if you're very quiet, you can watch, but we don't want them getting used to a bunch of people." Danica parked and cut the engine before hopping out of the car with the rest of her crew. "They're wild animals, and we need them to go back into the wild."

The twins ran around to join her as she walked up to the building. "I want to live with the wild animals," Suzie said, and Lizzy nodded in agreement. They turned to Reid. "When we grow up, we are going to live with a wild animal and do research and make a TV show."

"We're going to be famous. The Wild Bergmann Sisters." They giggled. "We've designed the set and everything."

"You'll have to show me." Reid looked at her with that mischievous grin. "I have a surprise."

That expression used to make her giddy. Now it caused her stomach to drop, and not in a pleasant way. "Reid, what have you done?"

"Come on, and I'll show you." Reid moved past and held the door open for them. "I did it a couple of days ago, and you didn't even notice."

"What is it! What is it!" The girls jumped and danced inside in search of this big surprise Reid had supposedly prepared.

He walked farther into the room and picked up the old laptop to flip it open. With a few strokes of the keyboard, he turned the screen around for the girls to see. In unison, they leaned forward and then gasped as one.

"What is it?" Danica peered over the girls' shoulders.

"Look, they're wiggling." Suzie pointed to the bats on the screen.

"Oh." Her orphaned bats were on the laptop, streaming from a live feed. "Looks like it's feeding time. They're getting hungry." She went to the other room, scanning the area. High on the shelf was a small camera.

"Now you can watch them whenever you want without bothering them. Your mom can even log on with her phone, or on your computer at home. You can even go back a couple of days and watch what you missed."

"This is the most awesome thing ever!" Lizzy rushed at Reid and wrapped her arms around him. Suzie followed.

"Thank you, Mr. Reid. Thank you." And just as quickly, they went back to intently staring at the screen.

Danica shook her head. "You always loved surprises. But now I'm afraid the girls aren't going to get anything done at the house." Prepared to turn and scowl at him, she had to pause at the look of wonder on his face. He was more into this than the girls, and they bounced with excitement.

His eyes glistened. He wiped at them with the back of his hand.

His jaw flexed, and then he gave her a thoughtful smile. "I'm sorry. I was going to show it to you first, but today took an unexpected turn for me. I thought it would be fun to surprise you all. Do you want me to take it down?"

"No!" Suzie's eyes teared up, making the gray shimmer. They looked so much like Reid's. She was losing her children to him. Was he doing this on purpose?

"No." Liz, the calmer one, took Danica's hand and squeezed it. "Please, Momma, we'll listen to you. We'll do our chores."

"It can stay, but we're going to make some rules for when and how long. Okay?"

"Yes, yes! This is the greatest!" Suzie jumped and returned to the screen. "Look, the little one is licking the one next to him." Their laughter was magical. Even on her worst days, it was the one thing that could soothe her.

Liz gave Reid another hug. "We love it. Thank you!"

Head to head, they stared at the screen. "Girls, you stay here while I feed and bathe them, okay?"

"Okay, Momma." They answered in unison as usual.

Reid stood. "I'll go feed the cub."

They all went about their chores. After a while, she

gathered the girls and went to the front porch. Using the walkie-talkie, she called Reid for his location.

"Back at the bear enclosure. Are you ready to go?" His voice was low.

"Girls, do you want to see the cub before we leave?" She smiled as they danced and clapped. It was a ridiculous question. She spoke into the walkie-talkie. "We'll come join you, then leave from there."

"Do we get to ride the Mule?" Another of their favorite activities, riding the all-terrain vehicle.

"Sure. Climb on." With the girls buckled into the back seat, they took off. Over the last hill, the enclosure became visible. Slowing down, she parked the vehicle off at a distance, so as not to bother the cub too much. "Remember, girls, stay quiet."

"Yes, ma'am." They all climbed off, as quietly as possible.

When they reached to the fence, the girls wrapped their fingers between the chain links. "Oh, Mr. Reid, the baby bear thinks you're her daddy."

The bear had gotten bigger but still loved cuddling against Reid's chest. She was holding her bottle as he rocked her.

Suzie looked at her mom. "Do bears stay with their dads?"

"No, bears are raised by their mothers."

"Just like us, but this bear has Reid."

All of a sudden, their innocent words clawed into her heart. She made the mistake of glancing at Reid. Would she ever stop losing her breath when he looked back at her? Her heart started racing. The girls never talked about their lack of a father. It was just the way of life for them.

"I'm not her father. Just a caregiver, until she can be on her own."

"Isn't that what a father does?" her older daughter asked.

"How much longer will she need you to take care of her?" Her sister didn't want to be left out of the conversation.

"Your mom is the one who mainly takes care of her, and gave her a safe place to grow up. She just likes it when I get to feed her." Bottle empty, he sat her on the thick branch that stretched across the pen. He ducked under it and came to the gate, exiting the enclosure. The cub rolled down to the ground, then clambered to the top of the little cave like structure. From there, she crossed to the smaller branch. Running, as if being chased, she leaped into the small water tank.

The girls laughed at the cub's antics. "She's so funny."

They asked another hundred questions while they watched the baby bear scurry around. The bear even ambled to the fence and stuck her nose through. The girls giggled with delight.

The light softened as the sun started slipping behind the western hills. "Girls, we need to go. We have to take Reid to his ranch before we go home."

"Can he come have dinner with us?"

"No, not tonight."

"Maybe another night?" The twins pouted, pleading with their eyes.

She looked at Reid over the heads of their daughters. The loneliness and yearning in his eyes hurt her heart. "Maybe."

"Yay!" They raced to the four-wheeler Reid had come on.

"Can I ride with Mr. Reid?" Suzie asked.

"No! I want to!" Lizzy frowned at her sister.

"Neither of you are going with him. There aren't any seat belts on his four-wheeler."

"Oh, Mom. He'll drive slow, right?" Lizzy looked at him.

Danica raised one eyebrow and put her hands on her hips. "I don't think he does anything slow."

He swung the girls up and planted them on the big Mule's back seat. "I think your mom means business."

The girls grumbled. "She always means business."

"Because she loves you. Do you know how blessed you are to have such a great mom? Not everyone gets a mom likes yours."

Liz nodded. "Our friend Celeste, her mother's dead. Travis, a boy in our class, his mom yells at everyone."

Suzie leaned forward. "She's crazy. Once the police had to come get her at school."

"Girls, stop. That's gossip. It's not nice to talk about people. If you're worried about your friend, we need to tell someone."

"It's not gossip. We saw it. Everyone knows." Suzie looked at her mother. "That's not gossip."

With a frown, Lizzy nodded. "It happened at school. Poor Travis. His dad, Mr. Monardo, was arrested. He's in jail." She looked at her sister. "Maybe that part is gossip."

They started talking about what gossip meant. "Girls, that's enough. When it is other people's business, it's gossip. Unless there are ways we can help them, we shouldn't be talking about them." She'd heard the same gossip in town, but she didn't know Travis's family. Talking about them behind their back made her uncomfortable.

She made a note to ask Pastor Levi.

"Travis Monardo?" The girls nodded at Reid's question. "There's a man in my group by that name."

"Group?"

Oh, no. She needed to derail this conversation. "We should head home before it gets too dark. Come on, let's go."

Instead of going to his four-wheeler, Reid went down to sit on his heels and look the girls in the eye. "I'm in a group that studies the Bible with Pastor Levi. We have all been in prison."

Both girls' eyes went wide. "You? You were in jail?"

"What for?"

"Suzie, that's not a polite question." Danica put on her seat belt. This was becoming dangerous territory.

"It's okay." He smiled at the girls. "I had a problem, and instead of waiting for God's time, I tried to take a shortcut to make money. I broke the law. I served my time, and I'm working hard to make better choices."

Liz touched his face. "Opa says if you turn your problems over to God, He'll forgive and get you back on the right path."

"Your opa is a very smart man."

Suzie reached for his hand. "He also says it's easier to stay on the right path and not get lost than having to find your way back."

"Easier to stay out of trouble than to get out of trouble." Lizzy lowered her voice and gained a bit of a German accent, sounding just like her grandfather.

He laughed. "Now, those are some words of wisdom I hope you try to follow. It's true. So stay out of trouble."

"Are you still in trouble?" Lizzy tilted her head.

"I'm working to prove I can be trusted. It's a long road, but I'm on it."

"We trust you." Both girls nodded.

His arms went around the girls. "Thank you. That means a lot to me."

Danica couldn't take it anymore. Gripping the steering wheel with one hand, she cleared her throat and blinked the tears away. With her other hand, she started the engine. She needed to put distance between them.

Suzie and Lizzy gave their trust without ever having had it betrayed. Her job was to make sure they got through their childhood without any scars on their sweet hearts.

"Look, if we stay any longer, the sun will be in bed before we get home. Opa will worry about us."

He nodded and turned away, heading back to his four-wheeler.

As fast as she could, Danica drove the girls back to the main sanctuary house and loaded them into the Suburban. Reid pulled up behind them and shut off the four-wheeler before climbing into the passenger seat of the SUV. He seemed to have read her mood and let the girls talk about a project they were doing at school.

It didn't take too long before they were pulling through the ornate entrance of the Hausman ranch. Past the main house and elaborate stables, she stopped in front of a row of old cabins. Cowboys hung out on the porches

"Which one do you live in?"

"The last one." He pointed.

"It's like a little town for cowboys." Suzie sounded way too excited about the idea of cowboys.

"That reminds me, I won't be out at the reserve at all on Saturday. We have some big corporate event, and they need all hands on deck. We have to make sure that none of the city folks injure themselves as we drive the cattle from the west pasture to the back five hundred."

"Sounds fun?" Sounded like something he would hate.

"Yeah, horses and animals I can handle all day. People? Not my thing. I'd rather be hanging out with bats and bears, but we'll get it done. Thanks for the ride. Bye, girls."

"Bye, Mr. Reid. Thank you for the bat cam."

"You're welcome." Out of the car, he turned and leaned in, grinning at the girls. "Don't make your mother get mad at me because you aren't doing your chores."

"We promise."

If she was going to show him the photos, she had to do it now. Would it send the wrong message? The door started closing. "Oh, Reid. Wait! I have something for you. It's in the back."

Hopping out of the Suburban, she ran to the back. Some of the cowboys hollered out a greeting. She waved in a hurry. A few joked about Reid's date bringing him home, the others mentioned the cute chaperones in the back seat.

He shook his head, shutting the passenger's door. "Sorry about that."

"Don't worry about it. Remember, I grew up here at the lumberyard. I know how cowboys can be." She opened the back door and pulled out the large bag by its handles.

A line was being crossed that she couldn't undo as she passed on her memories of the last six years.

"What's this?" Taking it in both hands, he opened it and looked down. Just as quick, his gaze shot back up. "Is this what I think it is?"

Biting at her lips, she nodded. "It's the scrapbooks I started with my first doctor appointment. The first sonogram when we saw two heartbeats." She had to stop talking, because she couldn't cry here. Not with all the cowboys watching.

"Hey, Reid. She giving you enough food to share?"

What had she been thinking? This was not the place to give these to him.

She kept her gaze down, focused on his hands. There was no way she could look at his face. "There's one book for each year. It goes up to their first day of kinder." Pulling away, she crossed her arms and looked off toward the lights of the main house.

The only thing saving her dignity was the dark. The lights from the porches didn't reach them.

Danica sighed, relaxing. "There's a flash drive with movies of them rolling, crawling, walking. It's gone by so fast. You can keep the flash drive, but I need the scrapbooks back."

"Of course." His voice was rough and low.

She wasn't daring enough to hug him, let alone look at him. If she touched him now, she might never let go. He reached up to touch her face, and she stepped back. "Well, I have to go. The girls are waiting."

"All right." Good-natured ribbing and jokes were thrown his way as Reid followed her to the driver's side and shut the door. She didn't look his way, making sure to keep her gaze straight ahead.

Why did it feel like she just gave him her heart again? She didn't. They were just pictures of her daughters. His daughters. That was all. He was their father.

It didn't mean she was going to fall in love with him again. She couldn't. Once someone left her that was it. They never came back.

He was sure the guys called out to him, making stupid jokes, but the blood pounding in his ears was all he heard. In his hands, he held the lives of his daughters.

Danica had given him all their milestones and everyday wonders. Hoping he looked casual, Reid made his way to his room after watching the Suburban drive off. The front steps seemed so far away. The porch was longer than it was this morning. The door wouldn't open. His roommates had locked the door? No one ever locked anything around here. It usually drove him crazy, but of course, they'd locked it this one time when all he wanted was to go inside and be alone with his new gift. He resisted the urge to beat his fist against at the door.

While fumbling for the keys, his breathing became hard. He needed to get into his room and devour each picture, each snippet of life he'd missed while locked away.

The door finally opened. Now to get to his room.

The fourteen-by-fifteen space was bigger than his cell, yet he felt suffocated. With slow, steady movements, he sat the bag on the empty nightstand between his bed and an old ranch chair.

He went back and closed the door. Something he

hadn't done since the day he first sat his duffel bag on the bed.

It wasn't rational, but every nerve in his body rebelled at the thought of being locked inside again. The idea that he could get up and walk out anytime still felt raw. Too unreal.

Yet this moment with his girls was his alone. He didn't want anyone interrupting. They'd respect a closed door.

Taking a deep breath, he sat down and peered into the bag. There were five binders, each one with a date written in fancy lettering. He pulled out the oldest one. Susan Marie Bergmann and Elizabeth Ann Bergmann were inscribed on the cover.

His fingertips hovered over the names of his daughters. Would they ever know his name? Would they be ashamed to be a McAllister?

The spine creaked as he opened the book. Page by page, he watched Danica's belly grow to the point it looked impossible. Her sisters Jackie and Samantha were in many of the pictures. From baby showers to the trip to the hospital.

Then the girls, both in pink. One wore stripes, and the other was dressed in polka dots. So tiny. Time ceased to exist as he stared at them. How could the girls he knew have started out so small?

He tried to imagine holding them. They would have fit in the palm of his hand. His lungs burned. Everything he missed, and there was no one to blame but himself. One stupid shortcut and he'd lost all of this.

He quickly wiped away moisture that gathered in the corner of his eyes. By the end of the first book, the girls were standing. Laying that one on the bed, he picked up the next one.

With snaggletoothed grins, they were proudly walking. Their hair was finally growing. They wore their red curls in funny little pigtails on the top of their heads.

At this point, they had started feeding themselves, and not effectively. There looked to be more tomato sauce and noodles on them than on their plates. More than ever now, he wanted to make that house ready for them. Even if he never got to live in it with them, his love would be embedded within the walls.

The last book was incomplete. Blank pages waiting to be filled with new memories. He wanted to be on those pages. Laying his palm flat against the empty pages, he prayed. He slipped from the chair and fell to his knees, head bowed.

He prayed for his girls. All three of them. He prayed for their protection. And he prayed for peace.

Chapter Ten

The sun was just waking up. Reid had his favorite cold drink, and the day ahead looked good. For two weeks, he and Bobby had secretly been working inside the house. Today was going to be big. They wouldn't be able to hide the secret project any longer. Philip and Wade, the two cowboys he lived with, rode shotgun on the way to do some major work on the house. It humbled him the way the other cowboys stepped in and helped whenever he needed. No questions asked. They were also doing it for her.

Philip had gone to school with Danica. Wade knew her from the church. So, of course, they were more than happy to help. "Thank you, guys, for volunteering. With extra hands, we can make a huge dent in restoring the house."

"Glad to help. Didn't have anything else to do today." Philip took a slow sip of his coffee from the biggest insulated metal cup he'd ever seen.

Wade yawned. "Tearing down walls sounds more fun than burning cactus."

"There's a bunch, so it's cacti," Philip informed him.

"No. It's not a Latin word. It's German." Wade went on to explain the difference.

Reid chuckled. They would argue over anything and loved every minute. Despite that, he hoped they would get everything done today. Jackie had taken Danica and the girls into San Antonio. Adrian had gathered up some volunteers from the church, but there was still so much to get finished.

He took another long drink of Big Red. He needed to calm down. It was all going to work out. By the end of the day, when she saw the house, it would be too late for her to tell them to stop.

That was the plan anyway. Would Danica get mad at him, or smile at him like she used to back when his life was good? When they were dating, he'd lived to surprise her, and she'd loved it. Her laughter and her smile had made him believe anything was possible, that he could outrun his father's legacy.

"Yo, McAllister," Philip hollered at him.

He glanced in the rearview mirror. "Sorry. I didn't hear you." Lost in thought, he'd missed the conclusion of the debate.

"Who else is going to be there?" Wade asked.

"Not sure. Nikki, Adrian and George will be there for sure. He said some others would be coming, too."

Pulling up to the ranch road, he stopped for a truck to pass. On the door was the Dumann Lumber logo. It was pulling a flatbed loaded with lumber and panels. In the back of the truck, there were large boxes that looked like appliances. Nikki must have gotten her father to help on the project because Reid certainly didn't have enough money for all those supplies. His heart pounded.

Following the truck through the gate, he hit the brake

hard out of shock. There weren't just a few cars, but a full parking lot. A horn honked behind him. He was blocking the road. Refocusing, he drove forward and found an empty spot in the back next to the old pecan tree.

Wade whistled. "Looks like I wasn't the only one avoiding pasture work."

Philip laughed as he got out of the front seat. He stood at the hood of the truck. "I remember this place. I used to make money mowing the old lady Edward's lawn. She always paid me extra."

Mr. Bergmann stepped out of the truck with Nikki and Samantha. Joaquin was with them, too. He started untying the lumber in the flatbed. "Where do we unload?"

Nikki started directing people. With her in charge, no one had a chance to stand still and be useless. She put everyone to work. Reid found Adrian and got the update on all the people. Apparently, more were arriving.

In work overalls and a beat-up baseball cap, Samantha stomped over to them. "I need something to do that's dangerous."

Reid looked to Adrian to handle this problem. He didn't even know where to begin.

Adrian grinned. "What did he say you can't do?"

"Apparently, I'm too weak to unload the manly lumber. I grew up in a lumberyard!" She threw her hands in the air. "Do I look too fragile to handle hard work?" She put her hands on her hips. "And don't try to humor me. I'm a grown woman who knows what I'm capable of doing."

"What about the roof? Not only is it hard work, but

he'll see you up there working, and you won't have to say a word."

"Yes." She hugged his neck. "You're the best brother-in-law." She turned. "Oh, Reid. Well, you're not my brother-in-law, you're the girls' father but… I mean I like you, too, I just…"

"Get out of here before you embarrass yourself even more." Adrian pointed to the west toward his twin brother. "George is in charge of all things roofing."

"Sorry. Everyone knows I have no social skills." She stomped away, her long braid swinging. Turning, she walked backward. "Make sure to tell my sister I fixed that lame gate motor for her."

Reid nodded at her, then looked at Adrian. "Mr. Bergmann limits the kind of work she does?" That surprised him. "All the girls seem to know their way around the lumberyard."

"No. It's not her dad." The laugh lines around his eyes went deeper. "Joaquin teases her, and she takes the bait every time. Between you and me, they would be much happier if they'd just admit they liked each other. It's like they're still in fourth grade."

Not knowing how to respond to that, Reid shrugged. "Adrian, this is so much more than I expected. Where did all these people come from?"

"Most of them from the church. The sanctuary also has quite a few friends. Plus, Damien's family has been a cornerstone of this community. Getting the opportunity to give back to them is rare, and people want to help."

The sheriff's patrol car pulled into the drive. Reid scanned the area. Had he done something wrong? He planted his feet, crushing the urge to run.

"You've met Jake Torres, right?" Adrian waved to

the lawman. "He used to do construction and help renovate several houses in the county."

There was no way Reid would ever feel comfortable around anyone in a uniform. As a kid, he was taught they were out to get him. Then they did get him. Now after serving time? They made his skin feel too tight. With an easy smile on his face, Adrian greeted Sheriff Torres, then turned to Reid.

Every breath was focused with intention. Reid made sure to relax his tense muscles before shaking hands.

"I hear you need an electrician?"

Adrian answered first. "The damage doesn't look too extensive. The plan is to get the appliances installed before Danica shows up later today. Mr. Bergmann has all the needed supplies. Reid, will you show him the way? I'll check the lumber for rebuilding the back porch."

From there, the day went fast. Sounds of hammers, drills and laughter filled the air. He helped replace windows and doors. People came and went all day long.

Every few hours someone showed up with food. It was the most amazing thing he'd ever seen. At times, it felt as if he was invisible, watching all the activity from the outside. Everyone knew everyone else's name. It was one big messy family.

New counters went into the kitchen as he stepped back to look at the work. Someone he didn't know offered him and everyone else in the room a drink. "They look great with the cabinets. Danica is going to love this."

Reid took a drink. There were too many people. Needing some fresh air, and silence, he walked to the big pecan tree at the back of the yard.

The need to pray was overwhelming. He didn't belong here, not with all these good, hardworking people. Why were they so friendly? By now, they must know he'd been in prison.

Yanking the aviators off his face, Reid braced his hands on the hood of the truck and bowed his head. He let the words flow as he gave the Lord thanks. He turned his fears and insecurities over to God. Ray had told him forgiveness was his when he asked, but he didn't know how that was possible. His mistakes felt like grooves in his hide that he'd never be able to sand down.

Boots crunched the grass behind him. Fists clenched, he turned. Danica's father frowned at him. His father-in-law. The grandfather of his children. He lowered his hand, flexing his fingers. "Sorry."

The man who probably hated him more than anyone else, and with good reason, stood before him.

"You okay?" The subtle edge of the old German accent was proof of his connection to this community. The Bergmanns had roots that ran deep. They couldn't be more different as people.

Mr. Bergmann stared at him, waiting for a response. Reid's lack of words made for an awkward moment. "Yeah." He had a hard time meeting the man's narrowed gaze. "All the people coming and going is a bit unsettling. I just needed a moment alone."

"I'm not big on crowds, either." Crossing his arms, he looked back to the house for a moment. Another awkward silence lingered between them.

Reid figured it was better than saying something stupid. So he let it drag out.

Clearing his throat, the older man studied Reid for a bit. "All this—" he jabbed his thumb over his shoulder "—it's a good thing you're doing, but I want to make it clear, I'm not going to forgive you. Don't ever expect me to welcome you into my family. You did enough damage to last a lifetime."

Not his family. Acid burned in the pit of his gut. "I know." They were in good hands. "Thank you."

His thick eyebrows shot up. "Thank you?" Hard eyes narrowed again. "For what?"

"For protecting my girls when I walked out on them. For being there for them and loving them. I…" He had no idea how to articulate what he was feeling. "Ray told me there are times in our lives we don't even know what prayer we need. So, we trust God has us. We praise him for it all. Good and bad. Even our unspoken prayer will be answered." Reid took a deep breath. "I don't know if this makes sense, but Danica was always in my prayers. I made a mistake, but she paid the price for my sin. I don't want to imagine what would have happened to her and the girls if you hadn't taken care of her the way I should have done."

"She's my daughter." His jaw tightened. "The best a father can hope for is that his children find happiness. When they don't, I hope they can come to me." The older man looked down. "I'm not always easy, but I love them." The eyes that looked so much like Danica's stared hard at him again. "I'll protect them with everything I have. It seems at times I have to protect them from themselves. Danica has worked hard to take her life back and to become a great mother. I'm not allowing you to pull her or my granddaughters down into your muck again."

He knew it was all truth, but it was always hard to deal with rejection. "I promised her I would be leaving as soon as she found a vet tech to replace me. I'll stay on the Hausman ranch, and out of her life. It's the least I can do. And I understand where you're coming from. If some man treated Suzie or Lizzy the way I treated Danica, well, I'd probably be in jail again. So, thank you."

Someone laughed in the background. He turned to watch the commotion. People were still so busy working to make this shell of a house into a home.

Reid smiled. "Your granddaughters don't know how cruel the world can be, and that's because of you. At their age, I knew how to call 911 when my mother took too many pills and how to ice her lip from the hit she took from her latest boyfriend. I learned to hide the guns and grocery money when my older brothers stopped by the house. Children should never have to grow up that way, acting like the adult. Thankfully, the girls won't have to develop those survival skills. So yeah, thank you."

The look of contempt on Mr. Bergmann's face shifted. Reid rolled his shoulders. He didn't need anyone's pity. His life was just what it was—his life. Like thousands of other kids'. But not his girls, because they had Danica and this man scowling at him.

Reid gestured to the house. "Looks like they're unloading the appliances. That's my cue to get back to work." He nodded at Danica's father and left to join the others once again. No more moping.

In the house, all evidence of the fire was erased. It was coming along great. His throat tightened.

"The floors look great." Vickie, the sheriff's wife, stood on the counter, hanging some fancy curtains over the window. "I can't believe how much work was finished without her knowing."

Philip laughed. "Reid hasn't slept in two weeks. I'm surprised no one called to report suspicious activity."

"Oh, I thought it was Bobby and Adrian."

Reid shifted on his feet. He didn't want people to know how much he had put into this project. They might start asking questions.

Sheriff Torres walked up to him and patted his back. "They did. The first time I showed up, I thought he was going to run." He looked up at his wife and frowned. "You shouldn't be up there."

She rolled her eyes. "It's way too early for you to get this bossy. This is my third pregnancy. I think I know what I can handle."

Jake moved closer, glaring at her. "Well, it's my first, so you'll just have to deal with it. Let me help you down."

"As soon as I'm finished you can carry me off caveman style, but not until then. Help the guys get the refrigerator hooked up."

Shaking his head, the sheriff grinned at him. "Pregnant women are hard to deal with."

Reid nodded like he knew anything about it. Had Danica climbed up on high places? Had anyone helped her down?

With help, they slid the big black appliance into its new home. Sheriff Torres went to his wife and with one gentle motion had her safely standing on the ground. A quick kiss was added to the movement, making Reid feel a little guilty for being in the room with them.

Philip's smirk didn't help. Then the room went silent. The hairs on the back of his neck itched. His back was to the door. Slowly, he turned and came eye to eye with Danica.

She scanned the area. Confusion, awe and shock tumbled across her face. Her attention shifted to him. Everything and everyone blurred on the edges of his brain. He could see her beautiful mind working, but he couldn't tell if it was good or bad.

"Surprise?" He straightened and took the gloves off.

"You did this?" She didn't move, just stood there staring at him, her fingers clenched around the leather strap of her bag. The large open kitchen got smaller as the number of people doubled.

Samantha rushed in from the front door and threw herself at Danica. "Isn't this amazing? Surprise!" She laughed and held her sister at arm's length.

Envy crept into his blood. He wanted to hug his wife and stand next to her with pride.

The youngest Bergmann entwined her arm through her sister's. "Let me show you what we've done. Everyone's been working since sunup. There is even a new roof."

With Samantha dragging her sister through the room, people started laughing and smiling. Shouts of thanks went back and forth. Everyone crowded the house to talk to her, to show her what part they had in the make-over.

The open door was calling to him. Easing his way outside, he tried to fade into the background. Air was hard to find.

"Mr. Reid!"

As one, the twins greeted him with arms wide-open. He went down on his haunches so he could return the hugs. For a moment, he held them tighter than necessary. He knew they greeted everyone in their world with such enthusiasm, but for this moment he imagined it was just for him. For this moment, he pretended they were a family, all of them together at their home.

Jackie walked up behind them. She was looking at the house. "Wow. There are people everywhere, and the house actually looks livable."

He stood. "It's almost there. Another week and it'll be ready."

"Ready for what?" The girls looked up. Their gazes darted between him and their aunt.

Reid placed his hands on top of their little heads. "We're fixin' the house for you and your mom to live in."

"Really?"

"We'll live with the animals?" They both clapped. Both of them took one of his hands and pulled him to the house. "Is Momma already inside?"

Lizzy suddenly stilled. The whole group stopped with her as she stared at her sister. "Wait. We'll still be in the same room, right? Do we have to sleep alone now?"

Jackie rubbed her red curls. "You get to share a room as long as you'd like."

The girls let go of him and ran ahead.

"Did you and Danica share a room?" he asked Jackie. Her glare sliced him, making it clear she didn't want to talk to him about her sister.

After a moment, she shook her head. "We did until my father remarried. Shelia believed we needed to learn to be apart and made us move into separate rooms, but she found out we were slipping into Nikki's room and all sleeping together. She told us we weren't dogs. The next night, she started locking our doors."

Her jaw flexed, making her look just like her father.

"Wanting to be as close as possible, we slept on the floor against the door that separated our new rooms. We could always see a bit of each other through the gap under the door. It was enough."

Gleams of tears hugged her lashes. With an even harder glare, she turned on him. "I'm not going to let anyone hurt her ever again." Without giving him an opportunity to say a word, she stomped off after the girls.

There were two Bergmanns that would never accept him. How would it feel to have family that loved him as much as they loved Danica?

The thought of a tiny Danica locked away from her sisters, alone and curled up on the floor, tore at his heart. He pictured her against the door, wanting out and not being able to get to the sisters she loved so much. Her support system. He was glad this Sheila woman was gone from their lives.

Hands in his pocket, he made his way to the house. It was probably time to go back inside, but all the people put him on edge.

"Reid?"

He lifted his head and stopped walking. Danica stood on the top step. Arms crossed, she frowned at him. What had he done now?

"Are you going to be antisocial for the rest of the day?" Hopping down the few short steps, she strode toward him as if she had a mission. "You did this?"

Pointing to all the vehicles, he avoided her eyes. "There are beaucoup people here putting this all together."

"Stop it." She wrapped her fingers around his hand and lowered it. "Adrian told me you went to him and asked for help to get this…" Her lips tightened, and she blinked a few times. Taking a deep breath, she released his hand and crossed her arms over her chest.

The warmth was gone. Danica took a step back and looked at the house. "You asked for help to get this done before you had to leave. You even asked my father for help."

"Everyone loves you. You never let anyone help. I thought Adrian should take the lead. Then no one would wonder why the ex-con was building a home for the hometown sweetheart." Anger bubbled up. He loved her but had to act like she didn't matter to him. "I asked what it would take. Next thing I know, it seems like the whole town decided to do some sort of old-fashioned barn raising."

"Thank you." Pulling her sweater closer around her, she chewed on her top lip. He shrugged. The silence grew heavy. She scanned the yard. "The girls have already picked out a room."

"Do they want pink and green like their other room?" He needed to start moving, so he headed to the porch. "I'm going to start painting the bedrooms and living room. Thought you'd want to pick out the colors since you own a lumberyard."

She grinned and followed him. "Jackie is the color expert."

On the porch, he paused. "Yeah, your sister already gave me the list of colors, but I thought you might want to choose the colors you wanted. I know you're twins, but you seem so different to me."

"Really?" She stopped and turned to face him, leaning against the closed door. "Most people still can't tell us apart. I'll have whole conversations with people before I realize they think I'm Jackie."

"That's crazy."

"Reid, thank you." She reached out and put her hand on his forearm. The heat seeped right through his cotton shirt. "This is the most thoughtful thing anyone has ever done for me."

Hope was deadly. The higher it lifted his heart, the harder the fall would be when this was over. But if these moments were all he got, then it was worth it. His blood pounded in his ears as he leaned forward. His hands went to her arms.

The door behind her opened. Reid's hold tightened to stop her from falling backward. Her father loomed behind her, glowering at him. Knowing she was sound on her feet, he let go and stepped back.

What had he been thinking? He was an idiot.

Mr. Bergmann stepped to the side, and Danica slipped past him. He shifted slightly, blocking Reid's entry. "I thought I made myself clear earlier."

"Yes, sir. We were talking paint colors when you opened the door." Every instinct told him to look down, avoid confrontation. But the need to be seen as a man overrode his survival instincts. For an eternity, they stood in the silent standoff. "I understand I'm unworthy of her. My father made that clear."

Mr. Bergmann's eyes narrowed.

"If you want me to leave now, I'll have to collect Philip and Wade." He wanted to stay and watch her move through the house he was making for her, but if it was going to cause a scene, he'd leave.

"That's a good idea. It's getting late. And the fewer people that see you around the girls, the better."

The anger that lived in his gut flared again. He wasn't sure if it was aimed at the man who was keeping him from his family or at himself. Taking a deep breath, he turned it over to God.

It was the only thing that ever worked. It still burned, but the rage was low and controllable now.

Finally, the older man moved to the side. He nodded and went inside. Walking through the kitchen, he smiled at the people. Philip and Wade were working in the master bath.

"Hey, guys, you ready to leave?"

James looked at his watch. "We still got a couple of hours of daylight."

"Mr. Reid, have you seen our room?" Suzie's mop of red curly hair popped out from the doorway across from the master room.

"Is this the one you picked?" He stepped inside. It was the room with the large window seat. He had already pictured the girls in this room. There would be enough space for two beds, dressers, dolls and dancing. Or whatever it was little girls spent their time doing.

Sheriff Torres held Lizzy. Danica and Vickie sat in the window seat looking at something in Vickie's lap.

"They're picking out material." Suzie ran back and crawled next to her mother.

Lizzy looked at the man holding her. "Thank you for your help. I better get over there, or Suzie will pick out crazy things."

Laughing, the sheriff bent down and let her go. He looked back at Reid, studying his face. "You have some unusual eye color there. Is it gray? Green?"

Reid touched his cheek, only just realizing he'd left his sunglasses outside on the hood of the truck. He'd gotten so distracted by prayer and Mr. Bergmann that he'd forgotten to put the aviators back on. And leave it to the lawman to be the first to notice. Panic settled in deep, tightening his chest. "Just an eye color. Nothing special."

"Right." The sheriff was shorter than Reid, but he didn't lack power. Feet planted, he crossed his arms and stared at him. The authority of a man who knew he was on the right side of God. "I guess if Danica wanted us to know, she'd say something."

Cold sweat broke out over Reid's entire body. Ignoring the comment, he made his way to the window. "Danica, I'm leaving. Got to get back to the ranch."

She stood. "I just got here." Disappointment pulled at her mouth. That's what he saw anyway. The expectation that he could have more would destroy him faster than anything that had happened to him in prison.

He wanted to tell her how much he missed her, how much he loved her. How she filled his thoughts and dreams every single day and night.

"I'm scheduled to be here tomorrow." That was safe and not so lame. His feet refused to turn. Like an idiot, he just stood there and waited for something that wasn't going to happen.

"I'm going now… Bye."

She tilted her head as if he was a puzzle with pieces missing. "Bye."

With a nod, Reid left. He walked out before he did something stupid. Maybe he needed to call Ray and get the prayer warrior on his side. It was a dangerous slope he was slipping down. Wanting more than what he deserved had gotten him in trouble too many times in the past. Homes and nice families were not for men like him.

Chapter Eleven

A week had passed since the surprise, and Danica was still floored. She paused before stepping into the room that would soon be for Suzie and Lizzy. Steadying her breath, she leaned against the doorframe and watched Reid carefully place the white trim along the edge of the ceiling. He reached up from the top of the ladder. One of her favorite songs came over the radio, and he started singing and swaying to the beat.

She smiled. They had spent so much time dancing in his small apartment. Being poor students, they hadn't had the money to go anywhere, but that had never stopped them from having fun.

Straightening, she shook her head. Memories were dangerous. All the pain was filtered out. Why was she so weak when it came to Reid?

He had painted varying stripes of pink against the soft white walls. A pretty green wainscoting surrounded the room. The time and detail he put in showed a man who cared.

This was all done without any promises from her. She hesitated to get his attention. After all these weeks, she'd gotten used to him being around. Now it was over, and she didn't like the heaviness that sat on her shoulders. What would happen if he wanted to stay? If they told the girls who he was?

She closed her eyes. The board meeting hadn't gone well last night. Her phone vibrated, and the slight noise brought Reid's head around.

"Danica." He smiled.

She looked down at her phone. Jackie had texted her.

Are you in the house with Reid?

After a pause, another text came through, and her notification went off again.

Please tell me you're not alone with him.

She didn't want to deal with her sister, the board or Reid. Running away and hiding sounded good, but she had to be an adult.

Her phone went off again.

You're not responding. You're with him, aren't you?

Jackie hadn't even given her time to respond.

Don't do anything stupid. I'm on my way.

"Your phone is doing a great deal of talking." He turned so that he sat astride the top of the four-foot ladder. One gorgeous eyebrow went up. "Are you going to answer?"

"It's Jackie." Treating her like a child. She slipped the

phone into her back pocket, but the notification buzzing kept up a steady pace.

"You're not talking to your sister?"

"She's a few minutes older and seems to think that means she can lecture me like a child."

"It's about me, then. What did I do now?"

"Apparently, you exist."

"I don't think there's a way for me to fix that problem. Sorry." His lopsided grin slipped into place.

The phone went off again. She could not stop the eye roll this time.

He chuckled and leaned forward over the top of the ladder. "Maybe you should answer? Just a suggestion."

"If I ignore it, she'll give up."

"Or rush here to save you from the ex-con. How did the board meeting go last night? Anything new with the sheriff's investigation?"

"Nothing new in the investigation. They're interviewing some of the local ranchers who filed a complaint about the animals." She tried to think of a way to talk about the other complaints without hurting him. Sighing, she walked into the room. "Some board members have concerns with a convicted criminal working unsupervised. There's some talk that the problems began when you started working here."

His face went into the stone mode. Not even a single flex in the hard jaw. Those moss gray eyes turned cold. "What do you think about that?"

"It's ridiculous. I was tempted to tell them we were married, but that would only make matters worse. I just want to get that grant. Then I'll have the financial backing to fix everything else."

"You'll get it. But I think the sheriff might suspect the girls are mine."

A headache ruptured in her head. This was getting too complicated. She had stalled enough. "There's a reason I'm here. We found a volunteer for the vet tech job." There, she'd said it. The words burned her throat, but she kept her smile in place. Arms crossed, she looked everywhere but at him. They had agreed to this plan, to replace him as soon as possible. To get him out of her life.

"So, this is it. You don't need me anymore." Swinging his leg over the ladder, he jumped down. The sun from the tall window haloed him. "There's still some things I need to do to finish the house. And outside. I haven't even started in the yard yet. I want to fix the fence, and redo that fancy little gate."

"I grew up in the lumberyard. I think I can handle it. Plus, I have my dad, Adrian, my sisters, Bobby, Joaquin, James—"

"I get it."

Pulling her bottom lip in between her teeth, Danica thought about how calm her life was before Reid showed up in her office without warning. Now she lived in a constant state of turmoil.

He tossed the hammer into his toolbox. From across the room, the heat of his now-gray eyes froze her in place.

Breaking the hold, she focused on the renewed wood floor, all evidence of fire and water damage erased. The old carpet and musty smell were gone. Adrian told her the carpet had protected the old floors.

The smell of a freshly peeled orange filled the room now. And paint. "I need to get area rugs." Her brain wanted to focus on something mundane. "The trim looks good. I like the way it repeats the trim on the wainscoting." Now she needed to find a way to fill the room.

"Danica. I can help with the furniture."

"No. I'm good." The skin pieces of an orange curled in a meticulous pile next to an empty soda bottle on a small table. Was that all he had for lunch? When he left here, who was going to make sure he ate?

Ignoring Reid, she went to the table and gathered the trash. That was an easy problem to fix. Reid? She had no idea what to do with him.

"Danica. Let me stay and help." He now stood behind her, just a feather's width away.

If she leaned back, she would feel his heartbeat.

His hand lightly touched her upper arm. His breath was soft across the back of her neck. "We can tell everyone the truth. I have the job at the ranch. I don't have to officially work here if it's going to cause a problem, but I can help in other ways."

The trash can was by the door. It wasn't that difficult to walk across the room. Just a few steps. Before she found the strength to walk away, Reid lowered his head. She could smell the oranges on his breath. He tilted his head and pushed a few loose strands of her hair back.

Was he going to kiss her? She stood still, not breathing. Waiting.

His lips were next to her ear, but he didn't touch her.

"I need to know how to make this right." His hands gently cupped her elbows. From there, they slipped down to her palms. Long fingers weaved between hers. "I don't know where to start, but the thought of leaving and never seeing…" His hands tightened around hers.

"I want to help fill the pages of those photo albums. Whatever it takes to earn that privilege, please let me."

"Reid—" Her phone vibrated, and didn't stop. Someone was calling her. With one hand, she balanced the orange peels, or tried to anyway. A few pieces fell to the ground. With her free hand, she lifted the phone to her ear as she took a step forward, away from his warmth.

Staying close to her, he picked up the fallen scraps and the ones still in her hands to dump them in the trash.

She was so distracted by him, she didn't understand a word Jackie said. "What?"

"You didn't return my text. What's going on?"

"It's fine. I told Reid about the replacement. He's leaving." She made the mistake of looking at him. Leaning against the doorframe, blocking her way out. He crossed his arms, and a grim expression set hard on his face.

"I'm on my way," Jackie practically yelled at her through the phone.

"Jackie, cut the drama. Really, you're overreacting. We were talking about the—"

Reid rushed past her to the window. Looking out, he muttered something about someone being out there. She couldn't understand. Just as fast, without explanation, he ran out the door.

"Danica! What is going on?" Jackie demanded her attention.

"Sorry. I have to go." Not bothering to listen to her sister, she ended the call and went looking for Reid. Instead, Bobby's truck cut in front of her. Everyone in her world was going crazy.

Engine still running, Bobby rolled down the window. "We got another hole in the fence. I don't think anyone got out this time, but you might want to get the Jeep and check out the north end of the property."

Dread filled her. Last night's board meeting had not gone well, but she'd reassured everyone she had it under control. *Lord, I need some major help here, on all fronts.*

"Have you seen Reid? We were talking, and he just ran out."

"Nope. Just came in to touch base with you and pick up some supplies. I won't be coming into the sanctuary tonight. Someone is sneaking around on our land in the dark, and I'm going to find them. So I'll be out there in the field if you need me."

"Who's doing this?" Hopelessness gripped her heart. She really couldn't do this much longer.

He shook his head and shifted gears. "Don't know. But we'll find them."

She stepped back so he could leave. Scanning the area for any sign of Reid, she made her way to the office. She wondered what could have happened. Had he gotten mad and left? He didn't have a car so he couldn't have gone back to the ranch. An ache in her belly started growing.

God, I need to turn this over to You. I'm stuck in the middle of a mess, and I don't know which way to go. You're my only way out.

Maybe if she'd trusted God more, she wouldn't be in this mess to begin with. *Forgive me. Guide me.* She wrapped her fingers around the braided leather bracelet on her left wrist. The charms she collected over time. Her favorite was the one her twin gave her when she first returned home, broken, pregnant and alone. John 16:33.

These things I have spoken to you, so that in Me you may have peace. In the world you have tribulation, but take courage; I have overcome the world.

A tiny laugh escaped her. The answer was always with her. Why did she ignore it until she became desperate?

As she started around the corner of the office, a horn blared from the road. A heavy sigh deflated her shoulders. Jackie had arrived. Great. More drama.

You have overcome the world, Lord. Please let me remember.

Dust flying, the green Suburban came to a stop at the front steps. Jackie had barely put it in Park before Sammi jumped out.

"Really, you brought reinforcements? You think Reid is that dangerous, or I'm that weak?"

Without permission, Sammi hugged her. "I came for you. Jackie's always telling me what to do, too, so I thought you'd need backup."

Jackie shook her head as she joined them. "She thinks you'll do the smart thing. She didn't know about the dark place you went to last time he left."

"Maybe he's not leaving this time?" Sammi stood next to her and glared at Jackie.

"How did you become a hopeless romantic? Where did the optimism come from? It's unsettling."

Danica shook her head and started for the other side of the office. "Listen, I don't have time for personal issues right now. Bobby found another hole in the fence. Besides, Reid took off. I don't even know where he went."

Wrapping an arm around her waist, Sammi walked alongside her. "We'll go with you."

Jackie followed. "Another pair of eyes couldn't hurt. Do you know who's doing this?"

Danica sighed. "No, but Sheriff Torres is asking around."

"I hope he questions Reid. You do realize that it all started when he showed up."

"Ugh." Danica rolled her eyes but refused even to look at Jackie. "He has nothing to do with this."

"How do you know? It's a perfect setup for him to do an inside job."

Turning, she headed to the Jeep. "I don't have time for your crazy conspiracy theories. You watch too much TV. It rots the brain."

Sammi laughed. "It's been proven."

The bottom of Danica's stomach dropped. All four tires on the Jeep were flat. "That's not possible."

"They've been slashed." Jackie moved over to the four-wheelers. "These, too, and the trailer." Her sister looked at her. "Someone wanted to make sure you didn't get to the fences."

Sammi went down to look at them. "I could change them, but I'd need tires. Do you have more than the one spare?"

All three sisters jumped when they heard a door slam. Reid rushed around the corner. He paused when he saw them, a short knife in his hands.

Jackie crossed her arms and glared at Reid. "Returning to the scene of the crime?"

That's all he needed right now, another hostile Bergmann. Reid sighed and tucked the knife back into the holder on his belt and focused on Danica. "Someone in a black hoodie was sneaking around the offices earlier."

He glanced at the vehicles. Too late to do any good, and he didn't even find the person he'd been hunting. He looked at Jackie. "You think I did this?"

She shrugged. "Who else?"

"Whoever wants to make Danica look bad." Sammi stood next to Danica, her arm around her.

Reid nodded. "Someone doesn't want her to get the grant. How close are you to getting the final word?"

The shrug was to give an I'm-not-worried vibe, but the concern in her eyes betrayed her. She was worried.

"They said the paperwork was in order. In a couple of weeks, they'll come for a visit." She scanned the vandalized property. "This is not good. I don't have the money to replace all these tires. I need to call Jake and let him know we've had more problems."

Reid checked the spare. "They didn't hit this one." He turned to Danica. She was on the phone with the sheriff, so he spun to face Sammi. The little sister seemed to be more welcoming at least. "Was Bobby here? Does he know about the tires? I know the ranch where I work keeps extra. Does she have some here?"

"I don't think so. Danica said Bobby was out checking fences, and she was going to join him. There are more holes."

Lifting his hat, he raked his fingers through his hair. "I don't like this." A few strides around the Jeep to check it all out didn't give him any answers. There was no evidence screaming out the guilty person's name. "They didn't want us to get to the fences."

Jackie crossed her arms. "You disappear, then show up with a knife."

"I know I haven't done anything to prove you can

trust me, but I'm here for one reason. To make things right. This is Danica's dream. I won't let anyone hurt it."

Danica joined them. "Jake will be here soon. He said not to touch anything."

He wanted to hold her but now wasn't the time. "I'll call Philip at the ranch. Maybe they can bring a couple of horses. We can ride the fences in the old-fashioned way."

Not looking at him, she nodded. "Okay. Thanks. I'm going inside to contact Bobby on the radio."

Catching up with her, he touched her elbow. "You know I didn't have anything to do with this, right? Jackie's way off base."

"I don't know what to think, other than someone wants me to fail." She took one step away from him, and he let her go. There wasn't anything else he could say.

Danica stopped and turned. "For what it's worth, I do believe you. I just don't have the energy to deal with anything else right now." She walked into the old bunkhouse, the screen door softly shutting behind her.

Reid pulled out his phone and started sending some text messages to the guys back at the ranch. There had to be something he could do to help. Hopefully, he had cavalry in his back pocket.

A black Mercedes pulled into the drive. Stephanie, the lawyer in high heels, got out and walked toward him. "I heard on the scanner that there's been trouble out here again." Even though she was much shorter, she managed to look down her nose at him. "What do you know about it?"

Danica opened the door and stepped onto the porch. "Hi, Steph. I didn't expect to see you out here today."

"I'm worried that you've gotten in over your head.

Have you thought about looking for alternatives for the animals? You don't want to be rushed if you have to close."

"We are not closing."

"I heard the big cats got out again." She made her way up the steps and put an arm around Danica to comfort her.

Reid wasn't buying it. "None of the animals have gotten out. Bobby found the holes in time, and I've got guys coming from the ranch with horses so we can check the rest of the fences."

Jackie and Sammi joined them. The glare he usually received was being shot at the lawyer now. Good, Jackie wasn't happy with her, either. "Danica has it under control. We don't need to be talking about shutting the place down. The sheriff will find out who's sabotaging the sanctuary, and she'll be back in business."

"Oh, I'm sure she'll be able to do it. I'm just worried about the stress and legal issues she is dealing with."

Reid lifted his head. "Legal issues?"

Danica stepped back, her forehead wrinkled. "What legal issues? Why didn't you say anything at the board meeting last night?"

"In a way, I did. I brought up the concern of having an ex-con working here. The neighboring ranchers are unhappy. With the lack of security and high rate of accidents, there are rumors of lawsuits." She sighed and put her hand on Danica's shoulder. "There's nothing concrete yet, so I didn't bring it up at the meeting, but I'm worried about you and what might happen."

Reid joined them on the porch. "I think a doomsday scenario is a little premature. The grant is looking good.

Next week is the fund-raiser. I'm sure that will help."
He looked at Danica. "You've got this."

He hated the doubt that clouded her eyes. Rumblings
from the gate caused them all to turn. Two heavy-duty
trucks were pulling in long gooseneck trailers, followed
by another truck. Cowboys and horses from the Hausman ranch had arrived. More than he'd expected, and
far more quickly than he'd hoped.

Nose in the air, the lawyer crossed her arms. "Who's
that?"

Hopping down the steps, Reid turned back and
grinned. "The cavalry."

Samantha let out a holler and ran up next to him. Her
arm locked around his. She leaned in and whispered
low. "You just might be hero material yet."

She ran ahead and greeted the men getting out of the
trucks. The trailer came loaded with saddled horses,
ready to ride. He glanced back at Danica. She smiled
at him, then called out from the porch, "I'll get a few
radios for them so they can connect with Bobby."

He grinned and turned back to greet the crowd of
cowboys here to help, just because he'd asked. His chest
swelled with humble gratitude. If only he could be that
for Danica. He'd give anything to be her hero again, but
time was running out.

Chapter Twelve

The church was quiet as Reid walked into the empty worship area. A week had passed since the last incident at the ranch, and no new information had surfaced. He couldn't help but notice some people were looking at him with suspicion. He wasn't sure if it was just who he was or if they thought he had something to do with the recent trouble at the wildlife refuge.

His boots didn't make a sound on the dark red carpet as he walked to the front of the church. At the steps, he fell to his knees. From his worn denim jacket, he pulled out the beat-up leather Bible. In his rough, calloused hands, it was small, but the words had changed his life.

During the second year of his sentence, Ray had invited him to a small group Bible study. He hadn't been interested, but it had been something to do, so he'd gone.

For the first time, he heard that God loved him, that he was worthy of that love. Not because of what he'd done, but because he was a child of God. Lost, but still wanted.

Grace was his, but now he struggled with his pride

again. How did he differentiate God's plan from his desires?

Old yellow ribbons marked the verses he tried to live by in his new life. Philippians 3:13–14: *Brothers, I do not consider myself yet to have taken hold of it. But one thing I do: forgetting what is behind and straining toward what is ahead, I press on toward the goal to win the prize for which God has called me heavenward in Christ Jesus.*

It was easier to let go of the past in prison when he couldn't see the consequences of his choices firsthand. He'd hurt Danica, and his daughters had been raised without a father.

He flipped to his second yellow ribbon. Revelation could be a dark and difficult book, but it had called to him. He touched the 2:10 verse. *Do not be afraid of what you are about to suffer. I tell you, the devil will put some of you in prison to test you, and you will suffer persecution for ten days. Be faithful, even to the point of death, and I will give you life as your victor's crown.*

Lowering his head, Reid prayed. He opened his heart and his mind to the word of God. It all seemed so murky. All he wanted was a clear path. Lifting his head, he studied the stained glass designs above the large painting behind the baptismal. The lamb lay at the base of the cross. A dove flew overhead.

"Lord, I come to You not knowing what to do. You know my heart. I love Danica and our daughters, but is leaving them the tribulation I have to walk through? Or do I stay and fight for them? I won't be welcomed by her family or the community. Is this my test? What is Your will?"

In the stillness, he waited, but nothing came. Silence echoed in his head. He bent forward, pressing his forearms against the polished wood that made the upper-level floor.

"Reid?" Pastor Levi stood behind the grand piano. "My secretary said you were looking for me. Do you still want to talk?"

"I don't mean to bother you." Checking the time, he sighed. "I just needed to talk to someone to get my head on straight before I saw Danica and the whole town at the rodeo tonight."

"It's no bother." Pastor Levi sat on the edge of the piano bench and leaned forward, resting his elbows on his knees. "What can I help you with?"

Reid licked his dry lips. How did he explain without telling him everything? "Will this be confidential, just between you and me?"

"If that's what you need. As long as it's not unlawful." He gave him a half smile like maybe he was joking, but maybe not.

"No, I'm not planning on breaking the law. That didn't work out so well for me last time." He shifted so he sat on the top step and looked at the side windows with all the colored glass. It was easier than looking straight at the pastor. "Danica and I eloped in college before I was locked up. We're married."

"Okay. So the girls are yours?"

"Yes," Claiming them made his heart burst with pride. To get to say they were his made him choke on unfamiliar emotions. He pressed his forehead hard into his palms. It also felt like he was betraying Danica. "She didn't want anyone to know. Even her family isn't aware we're married. They know the twins are mine, but that doesn't do much to endear me to them. She's embarrassed that she married me."

"That's got to be tough. What are you struggling with tonight?"

"She wants me to leave. I didn't know about the girls before I got here. I just wanted to make amends, apologize and move on, but she's still my wife. We have daughters. I want to respect her wishes, but I can't just walk out on them again. I don't know what to do. I want to submit to God's will, but it's hard to know what His will is. I keep waiting for His voice to tell me what to do, but I get nothing. Is there something wrong with me?"

"A burning bush would be nice, but it's not always that clear or easy. Sometimes we just don't see it. I do know that God's voice won't come in anger, fear, or doubt." He pointed to the opened Bible. "What are you reading?"

"Revelation 2:10."

He nodded. "That's a good one. I see why you're reading it. What does it mean to you?"

"Not living in fear. That's what got me in trouble the first time. I feared not having enough money. I feared that she would stop loving me. I didn't understand how she could love someone like me to begin with. So I reminded myself that choices made out of fear only lead to regret." A peace settled over him. "I have to take the fear out of the equation." He looked at the pastor. "That's easier said than done."

"Yeah. Living in fear can be a survival technique. So, ignoring that fear seems counterintuitive." Pastor Levi sat up and turned to face the piano. "Do you mind if I play? It helps me focus and think."

"No. I've always loved music. I tried learning to play,

but I couldn't get past a few chords." The piano strings hummed a soft sweet tune, helping Reid relax.

"In your verse." The pastor kept his eyes on the keys and his fingers. The music filled the room. "It talks about prison. What do you think about that?"

"Prison is where I found God. In a way, it was so much easier there. I had a clear path. Now that I'm free, I thought I'd be happy. But I'm in a different kind of prison now. I'm more trapped than ever."

"What has you trapped?"

"This guilt. I abandoned Danica when she needed me most. How can I even ask for forgiveness? She made it clear from day one not to expect anything from her, and I don't blame her, but I want to be a father to my girls. The Bible talks about the sins of the father. I thought I could be better, I tried. None of the men in my family ever graduated high school. I wanted to break those chains, but I panicked and tried for the easy money, not only destroying my future but letting down Danica and leaving my girls without a father. Just like my dad."

"One mistake doesn't have to shape your whole future. You can make the decision that your past will not become your future. Of course, the one thing you can't control is Danica. It's up to her if you get to be back in her life." He stopped playing and turned to Reid. "It takes time to rebuild trust. Once it's been destroyed, it won't be easily given again. What are the alternatives? What about you staying close and being part of her life indirectly?"

"That's what I've offered, but I don't know if I can watch the girls without being their father. Or maybe that's the trial I have to walk through. Plus, I don't know how much longer we can really keep pretending they aren't mine. We have the same eyes, and I think the sheriff has noticed. He probably thinks I'm a dead-beat dad."

"Living with secrets is never healthy." The pastor picked up the beat, then let it fade away into a slow melody. "The longer you don't tell the truth, the harder it gets. Is there a reason she doesn't want anyone to know?"

"Fear? I don't know other than she didn't believe I would stick around long."

"You've been here for a few months now. Any plans to leave?"

"No. I'd like to make it my home if she'd let me."

"Have you told her that?"

"I figured she knew that by now."

"You want her to just know your intentions? It helps if we talk to people, and don't assume they know. It creates a lot of problems. Believe me, I know that first-hand."

"Tonight, after the rodeo, I need to make time to have a heart-to-heart. What if she doesn't want me here?"

"You're not who you used to be. You're redeemed, and you need to let her know what your wants and fears are. If the girls are important to you, you need to let her know you are willing to do whatever it takes to be their father. She might need more than words. The past can be hard to overcome."

"Yes, but it's worth fighting the fight. If this is what I have to do, then I can be a patient man. I hope she hears me."

The pastor stood from the bench and joined him on the steps. "You want to pray before you leave?"

"Yeah, I'd like that. I feel like my whole life is riding on this one conversation."

"It's not. Just take a deep breath, and have faith."

Reid laughed. "Isn't there a warning about praying for patience?"

Pastor Levi put his hand on Reid's shoulder. "Yes, sir. Let's pray."

They bowed their heads, and Reid let the words of the pastor's prayer wash over him. It was cleansing.

Now to face Danica and the whole town. Would he ever get to stand with his family in public? He couldn't help but feel tonight his life was going to take a new direction, hopefully one that involved Danica and their daughters.

The dust and sounds of a rodeo created a familiar chaos that Danica usually loved, but tonight Reid was riding a bull. If he showed up. She scanned the grounds for Reid. He was always early to anything he went to, even back in college. Maybe he'd changed his mind and wasn't coming. Her breath caught in her throat.

Maybe he had finally decided to leave. He wasn't happy when she told him about the new vet tech. The thought that he would leave for good hit her hard. She wasn't sure how she felt about it, but it wasn't good.

Everyone eventually left anyway, so she didn't know why she was so surprised. Some of the cowboys waved as they walked past her. She made sure to smile, but inside she wanted to curl up under her covers and hide. He must have left.

She'd almost told the girls who he was, but now they didn't have to know that their father walked out on them again. Why had she expected anything different?

"Because you're a pathetic dreamer who never learns your lesson." She pulled herself up on the railing. She needed to find something to distract herself with or she was going to cry.

"I don't know what lesson you're working on, but you've never come close to being pathetic."

She jumped at the sound of Reid's voice. His hands went to her waist to steady her. She glared over her shoulder.

He laughed. "Didn't mean to scare you. Dani girl, you're one of the smartest people I know. If there's something you need to learn, I have no doubt you'll master it."

"You're late." Danger lurked in those gray twinkling eyes, so she turned to break the line connecting them. Staring straight ahead, she really couldn't say what she was looking at. He was just inches away.

"Watching for me were you, baby?" He stepped up to the railing next to her and leaned over, resting his chin on his forearms. He watched the same arena she did.

"No. They're pulling the bulls soon. If you're late, you'd forfeit your ride and entry fee."

"Yeah, I remember how it works. Looks like a great turnout."

"People around here are good at supporting the local nonprofits. It's not just us, but the volunteer fire department and the youth center."

"The funds should help hold you over until you get the grant."

"I hope so, as long as we don't suffer any more problems. I'm sick to my stomach at the idea that someone wants us to fail."

"It doesn't make sense. The ranchers are more of the

straightforward type. What happens to the property if the sanctuary fails?"

"If I have to close the doors in the next couple of years, it reverts back to Linda's estate, but the only family left is Stephanie."

"Really?" He turned his full attention on her. "How much is the land worth? You don't think that would be motive enough, do you?"

"No. She doesn't want the ranch, so I'm hoping to work out a deal with her if it comes down to that. So don't go there. She's been my strongest advocate since Linda's death. I don't know what I would have done without her advice and support."

"She's made it clear she doesn't like—" He tucked his head. "You're right. I don't know her enough to make judgments. I just don't think this is the ranchers' style of fighting."

"Which takes us right back where we started. With nothing."

"Tonight, I want some time to talk to you. Just the two of us. No interruptions."

Her stomach dipped. "Is everything all right?" The announcer called the bull riders to the back gate. "You better go. We'll talk tonight. I'll have Jackie take the girls home."

He nodded as he hopped from the railing. Pausing, he stared at her. For a moment, she thought he might move in for a kiss. It seemed too natural. Swallowing, she hooked one arm over the rail. "Be safe. Don't wrap your hand in. You don't do that anymore, do you?"

"No, ma'am. I'll be ready to jump clear when I'm done."

"You're getting too old for this, you know. A father

has to make sure he's whole and healthy for his children's sake. You need to start thinking about that kind of thing."

His grin grew wider as if she'd given him a gift he'd always wanted.

"Duly noted. So, let's say this is my last ride." He took a step closer. "I have no problem walking away from the bulls if I'm walking to you and the girls."

She wasn't sure how it happened, but the world shifted, and she leaned forward to touch her lips to his. Just for a moment. Then she remembered where she was and pulled back, glancing around. What had she just done?

Hands in his pockets, he stepped back. "Don't panic. I don't think anyone saw you kiss the convict."

The hurt in his eyes tore at her heart. "Reid."

"No worries. I've got to go. But before I forget, I have your keys. The Jeep was blocking a gate, so I moved it for the guys. You shouldn't leave them in an unlocked car."

"I should lock them in the car?" She smiled at his eye roll. "I trust everyone around here. These are hometown people."

"You never really know what hidden agendas they might have." He pulled the keys out of his pocket and looked at the preschool pictures she had on the chain.

She held out her hand, but he slipped them back into his jeans.

"I think I'll keep them for now. After the rodeo, we can drive somewhere to talk."

All she could manage was a nod. Their relationship would take another turn tonight; she could feel it. For good or bad, they would have to make a decision about the future. Her stomach was in a knot. What direction were they going? She hated the unknown.

She watched him until he was out of eyesight. Then she climbed up as high as she could on the railing, scanning the back of the gates to try and find him. What did he want to talk about?

"I'm thinking you two have more of a past than you let on."

"Jake!" One hand went to her chest. "You startled me. Sorry, I mean Sheriff Torres."

"Stop that. You've known me too long to not call me Jake. Are the girls running tonight?"

"No, I don't think they're old enough yet for the type of speed that will be needed for this event."

He nodded and adjusted his tan cowboy hat. "So, I've been digging around and found your latest volunteer was in the same program at A&M the exact same time you were. On the rodeo team, too. He went to prison about the time you came home pregnant."

"What does this have to do with the investigation?"

"I need all the facts to make sure I have everything I need to put the puzzle together. Everyone always comments on the unusual eye color of the twins." He stopped talking and just stared at her.

Scanning the arena, she found the girls with Jackie and her dad in the stands. "It's a personal issue that we're working out. I'd rather do it without any drama. He has nothing to do with the accidents."

"A couple of the board members disagree. They think the problems started when he showed up, and your judgment is impaired when it comes to him."

"What? That's ridiculous. He stayed so we could

get the certification." She took a deep breath. "He has nothing to do with the problems."

"There's also some concern that you're desperate and willing to make some questionable decisions."

"I'm sorry, Sheriff Torres, but this is sounding like you're questioning me in the investigation."

"Just a friendly chat, trying to get the whole picture."

"If you have any more questions, please make it official. Maybe I should talk to my lawyer."

"If that's what you feel you need to do."

"Thank you for being here tonight. I'm going to find my girls to watch the rest of the rodeo. Good night."

"'Night, Danica."

She was well aware that he was watching her walk away. She wanted to run and find Reid. People were talking about them. Already questioning his relationship with the girls. She should have been better prepared.

But what was she doing? Kissing him. Ugh. She hit the side of her head. Stupid.

"Momma! Did you see Mia's run!" Lizzy jumped with excitement.

"It was awesome. Please let me ride next year!" Suzie wasn't going to give up her desire to ride at a higher level.

"Look what Aunt Jackie did." Glad Lizzy was changing the subject, Danica let her girls pull her forward to Jackie and her father. They were her world and everything she did would affect them.

"She has the camera Mr. Reid put on the baby bats!"

"Look!" Suzie held Jackie's phone up.

Right now, she needed to be with the girls. They deserved all her attention. Jackie looked at her with a question in her eyes. Taking a deep breath, she smiled, shook her head and looked at the phone screen. The time with her family was the most important.

"I see Mr. Reid!" Suzie stood and waved. "Mr. Reid!"

Not to be outdone Lizzy joined her sister and yelled his name, too.

"Girls, sit down." Leaning in, she kept her voice low. Glancing up, she saw Reid waving back, a big grin on his face. Her heart skipped a beat. He walked along the catwalk behind the chutes. Lean muscles moved over his frame as fluidly as the river moved over the rocks, smooth and easy. Back in college, she'd had a hard time keeping her gaze away from him. Now he was even more interesting. Not the boy anymore, but a man.

Jackie looped her arm around Danica's. "One thing I can say for sure, you picked one good-looking man."

"He has a good heart, too. If you take the time to get to know him. He had a hard life."

"Don't blame me. He's the one that left you. Got stuck in prison. And he didn't even bother to tell you." She pressed her head to Danica's. "Don't get blinded by those beautiful eyes of his. You deserve someone that will be by your side and stay there no matter what. No one is going to hurt my little sister again."

"You're only older by five minutes," Danica said out of habit. Reid was good-looking, but it was so much more than his charm that captured her heart. "What if he's changed? Do you believe in redemption and second chances?"

"Not if my sister and nieces are the ones who were hurt."

"Hey, guys. Sammi's running next." Nikki slid into the bench seat behind them. Adrian was holding her hand.

Her father patted Adrian on the back. "Mia had a good run."

With a father's pride, he nodded. "Yeah, it was her best time. Don't think it will keep her in the top five, but each run has gotten faster."

"Did you hear which bull Reid pulled?" Danica couldn't even pretend not to care. Adrian laughed. "He pulled Mr. Darcy."

Her forehead wrinkled. "The bull's name is Mr. Darcy? That doesn't sound very tough."

"No, and the bull must be mad about it. He wants to charge every cowboy he sees. I don't think anyone has stayed on him for a full eight yet. He's a tough one."

All the color must have left her face, because Nikki elbowed her husband.

"Oh, sorry. Reid seems to be the type to handle himself well."

When they were younger, she loved watching him ride. The adrenaline was a rush, and to think he was hers was exciting. Now all she saw were the ways he could get hurt or killed. Those bulls were two thousand pounds of muscles, hooves and horns.

"He'll be fine." Adrian smiled and tried to reassure her again.

Her father pointed to the gate. "Samantha's about to run."

The girls started cheering. "Go, Aunt Sammi!"

Sammi and her roan mare charged into the arena, cutting so close to the first barrel it wobbled, but it ultimately stayed in place. Finishing all three barrels, she lay over her horse's neck and sprinted home. The announcer called her time. It was the best of the night They all stood and cheered.

A truck drove out into the arena and hauled the barrels away, clearing the deep sand for the last event. The bull riding. Danica's stomach clinched. She wasn't sure she could even watch.

Her family kept up a constant stream of conversation, and she let them distract her. She loved them for it. Then it was Reid's turn. The girls got excited seeing him climb into the chute as they got the bull ready.

Eight seconds. That was all, then it would be over. Knots pulled her insides tight, twisting beyond her stomach and squeezing her heart. It was easier to look elsewhere. That's when she noticed a couple of unfamiliar cars pull into the area behind the gates.

Men in suits got out, and Sheriff Torres walked over to them. Shaking hands, they talked.

A whole new fear took all the energy out of her muscles, and a nauseating numbness took over. Was Reid in trouble? It couldn't be him. He hadn't done anything.

James joined them. A sweat broke out over her entire body, despite the breeze. His parole officer was involved?

James had other jobs in the county so it might have nothing to do with Reid. It was just a coincidence they were all together where Reid was about to ride.

She glanced over at him. He nodded with his arm high in the air. She wanted to yell at him. To warn him. About what, she wasn't sure.

The gate swung open. The bull came out spinning. The crowd went crazy as the big animal changed directions, but Reid moved with him. Leaning back, then coming forward, his movements rolled with the bull. The horns thrust at the air as the bull kicked and twisted. Eight seconds had never lasted so long.

At one point, she stood but didn't remember moving. The twins were jumping up and down. Finally, the buzzer went off, but the ride wasn't over. He still had to dismount and clear the arena without getting gored or stepped on. The rodeo clowns moved in to distract the dangerous animal as Reid jumped from his back. He was thrown with such force that he landed on his knees in the deep sand.

Danica gripped Adrian's arm as Mr. Darcy lowered his head and ran at Reid.

The shorter clown darted between them and waved a flag. Another came up behind to get the bull's attention. Reid was on his feet and ran for the railing closest to him. Which was where she and her family sat. With a jump, he climbed up and waved his hat to let the crowd know he was good. Just a few feet from them, he tossed the girls his hat, a huge grin on his face.

Adrian whistled. "That was a great ride. It has to be in the nineties."

Reid jumped from the rail and thanked the cowboys as the bull now went calmly into the back gate. The girls fought over who got to wear the hat. All Danica wanted to do was grab him and make sure he was whole and healthy. She didn't trust that smile. He was good at hiding bruises. Once he even walked off with a smile with a busted rib.

She leaned in to tell Jackie she was going to check on him. With a small eye roll, her sister nodded. At least they had gotten past lecturing. Halfway down the steps, law officers met her. Jake and James looked grim.

She didn't recognize the other men with them. This couldn't be good. "James. Jake." She nodded at them, then glanced at the men with them. "Is there a problem?"

One of the men handed her a sheet of paper. "Do you recognize the narcotics listed here?"

Nodding, she looked up at the men. "Sure. These are some of the drugs we keep on the sanctuary."

"Do you currently have any in your possession, or do you know of any missing in your inventory?"

"No. Why would I—"

James moved closer to her. "There's been an anonymous report—"

The tall stranger with dark aviators stepped forward. "Officer, we'll take care of this. Mrs. Bergmann, we need to check a Jeep that belongs to the Hill Country Wildlife Rescue."

"The Jeep is here, but I don't understand." She looked at Torres. "Is this about our conversation earlier?"

"What's going on?" Reid came up behind her. His hand rested on her lower back.

The simple touch calmed her. "They want to check the Jeep."

He looked at the sheriff. "Do you have a warrant?"

"We were hoping she would make this easy and work with us."

Reid started to say something else, but she placed a hand on his arm. "It's fine." She moved around the men and marched in the direction of her car. They all turned and followed her. She stopped when she realized it wasn't where she'd left it.

Her heart froze. Reid had moved the Jeep. She didn't know where it was parked now. She looked at him. A nasty feeling paralyzed her. The last thing he needed was to be involved in any type of investigation with drugs.

Jake walked up next to her. "What's wrong?"

"Um. Forgot where I parked." Not wanting to say anything else, she glanced at Reid.

"Oh, I moved it." He dug into his pocket. "Here are the keys."

"Do you have access to all company vehicles?" one of the suits asked.

James cleared his throat. "Let's just go to the car. We'll ask the questions that need to be answered then."

The small group followed Reid to the back of the dirt parking lot, weaving through the maze of trucks and trailers. When they reached the Jeep, one of the unknown law officers asked them to unlock the car. As soon as the click was heard, they started searching. Even though she knew there was nothing for them to find, fear gripped her.

"Mr. Reid!" Suzie yelled as she and Lizzy ran toward them, followed by the rest of Danica's family.

Chapter Thirteen

Reid was having a hard time breathing. He was surrounded by law officers searching Danica's car, and now her family ran to them. Suzie had his black cowboy hat on. The smile on her face became his whole world for a moment.

He went down, and she ran to him. "I get to wear your hat first, then Lizzy gets it. Opa said we have to give it back to you, though."

"I gave it to y'all. If you want it, you get to keep it."

"Thank you." She hugged him.

"Now you have to promise to share it."

Lizzy was right next to her. "It's my turn to wear it."

"Girls, not now. I'll hold it if you start fighting."

"Yes, ma'am," they said in stereo. Lizzy leaned in and whispered something to her sister, and the hat was handed over.

Mr. Bergmann frowned at the sheriff. "Why are there men searching my daughter's car." He glanced at Reid like it was somehow his fault.

"Something to do with the drugs that are kept at the wildlife refuge."

Deep lines creased her father's forehead. "Drugs?"

Jackie approached the sheriff. "Jake, this is ridiculous. You know Danica. She wouldn't do anything illegal."

Reid's instinct was to run, but there wasn't a reason. Everything he did when he returned was to stay out of trouble. But they had the power to take away his freedom, his life. His father's shadow was long and dark.

James shook his head. "Not our call, but we'll have it cleared up soon."

The men turned, one holding up baggies full of drugs that had been locked in the medicine cabinet at the sanctuary yesterday. The other man pulled out a bank bag. It was the one from the concession stand. Cash was stuffed inside.

Reid couldn't breathe. This had to be a nightmare.

"Mrs. Bergmann, do you recognize these?"

"Of course. It's a drug we use on our big animals. We keep them locked up, so I don't know why they are in the trunk of my car. That money isn't mine. I don't keep money in my trunk."

"And these. Are you claiming you have no knowledge of these, either?" With a horse blanket pulled back, there seemed to be hundreds of small baggies of white powder.

His knees turned to mush.

Danica looked confused. "What is that?"

Without a doubt, Reid knew that they were in trouble. Someone was about to be arrested, and they were not looking at him. The tall officer took Danica by the arm. Handcuffs out, he started reciting the Miranda rights.

"No!" He couldn't let them put those on her. He

stepped between them, blocking her from the man's touch. "It's mine. She doesn't even know what that is."

"Reid?" She twisted around to look at him. "What's going on?"

The sheriff was called over the radio on the man's shoulder. He stepped away, and everyone turned to stare at Reid. "Who are you?" the one with the aviators asked.

James sighed. "He's my parolee. Reid McAllister."

"What was he in for?"

"Drug trafficking."

"And you had full access to this car?"

"I had the keys. I was the last one to drive it." There was no way he was going to let them put Danica in handcuffs.

James nodded, his expression grim. "He's the vet tech at the sanctuary. He has full access to the drugs."

The disappointment in his parole officer's eyes was hard to take. Unable to make eye contact with anyone, Reid kept his focus on the distant hills. He was commanded to turn around and put his hands flat on the car. He locked his jaw to keep the bile down as they searched him.

"What are you doing?" Danica's voice was unusually high. "Reid hasn't done anything wrong. He has nothing to do with this."

He cut a hard glare right at her. "Take the girls and leave." He couldn't even glance at the girls who were so happy to see him just a minute ago.

"What's wrong? What's happening?" The girls' voices mingled. He squeezed his eyes shut. Blocking out the world, he closed down all emotions and thoughts. What had he just done?

"Jackie. Sammi. Take the girls." Mr. Bergmann's voice was firm but edged with anger.

Reid dared to glance over his shoulder. Sammi was holding Lizzy, and Jackie had Suzie as they rushed from the scene. Away from him.

They pulled his arms behind him, locking them down tighter than was probably necessary. Danica still stood next to him. He couldn't look at her. "Go, Danica."

"Reid, no. You didn't do this. Tell them you didn't do this."

He growled. Why was she so stubborn? "Go!" He lowered his voice. "I don't want you here."

She touched James's arm. "He didn't do this. I don't know who did this, but it wasn't Reid."

"This doesn't look good, Danica. I suggest you leave with your father. The car will be compounded for evidence."

"Reid?" Her voice broke.

He couldn't afford to look at her.

This was it. It was over. He had hoped he could be a new man in Christ, but handcuffs were back, and this time he hadn't even done anything wrong.

"Daddy, do something." Danica wasn't leaving.

He hated the desperation he heard in her voice. Arms locked in place behind him, Reid stared at the horizon over the top of the Jeep. The tall officer listed his rights, but he'd heard it all before.

Danica shot forward. "No! He didn't do this. He's just—"

"Danica." Reid's voice was sharper and angrier than he'd intended, but they would arrest her if they thought she was going to cause problems. "Stop it. Go with your father. The girls need you."

Her father grabbed her arm and started pulling her away. She called out to him. "Don't say anything. Do you hear me, Reid McAllister? Don't speak another word. I'll get a lawyer. We'll figure this out."

They pushed him forward, back to their car. "Leave," he growled through locked jaws.

Her father finally got her out of the way. Good. Making this walk alone was better. It was.

People gawked. Speculated. Whispered. The grounds seemed unnaturally quiet. How did he think he could belong with the respectable people of this community? Head down, he was tucked into the back seat. The door slammed.

He stared straight ahead. If he made eye contact with anyone here that he had come to think of as a friend, he'd lose it.

A black void crept into the edges of his vision. Drugs. He'd admitted to stealing and transporting drugs. Prison again. And this time, they wouldn't let him out. He'd be locked away forever. It was over. *God, I don't understand. I just don't understand.*

The handcuffs cut into his wrists as he instinctively strained against them. For the first time in his messed-up adult life, he wanted to yell and sob. Head down, he stayed silent.

Chapter Fourteen

Danica and her dad caught up to Jackie as she got done settling the girls into the back seat of the Suburban. "Daddy, we have to get him out. He didn't do it."

Her father shut the car door and glared at her. "How do you know? He's been in prison for transporting drugs before. He's from the streets. This is what I was worried about when you brought him home six years ago."

"He hadn't done anything six years ago until he wanted to make enough money to impress you. But we aren't talking about six years ago. Today they came to arrest me. They came for me! Someone claimed that I was stealing drugs and selling them from the trunk of my car. When he saw them, Reid came over to help me. If it were his stuff, he would have taken off. He didn't know it was there any more than I did."

He turned on her, his face hard and unforgiving. "So why did he claim it was his?"

She hadn't seen him this angry in a long time. "To protect me. He didn't do this. I just know it."

Jackie came around from the other side and put her arm around Danica. "I'm not a fan of his, but even I can tell he did this for her. He didn't want her to get arrested, so he said it was his. Words mean nothing, but his actions today showed me his character." Pressing her forehead to Danica's, Jackie's eyes glistened with moisture. "Daddy, don't you see? He sacrificed his freedom, to take her place."

"Then who did it?" Now her father just looked confused.

"I don't know. Someone that had access to the sanctuary and wants it to fail." It had to be someone she knew, and that was just too hard to imagine. "They set me up to get arrested. Whoever is damaging the fences did this. They're sabotaging any chance of us getting the certification and the grant."

Her father looked over her shoulder. "He took your place?"

"Yes. Reid allowed them to put him in cuffs to protect me. I can't let him go it alone. I need bail, and a lawyer I can trust."

"We can help with bail." Nikki walked up with Adrian.

He nodded. "Whatever you need, we're here."

"Thank you!" She hugged each of them, holding them tight.

"What about Stephanie?" Her father crossed his arms. "Can she help?"

"She's on the board, and I can't go there for help with personal issues. Plus, Reid doesn't trust her." She pressed her palm against her stomach. Who could she trust? Her world was upside down. "I'm not sure I do, either. I'm not allowing Reid to fight this alone. I'll get him out."

Her family deserved the whole truth. Secrets had to end. "There is something that I never told you." She glanced at the girls tucked safely in the back seat. The rest of her family stared at her, waiting. "In college... during Spring Break, Reid and I eloped. We're married."

Her father turned and hit the hood of the car. "I told him no!"

"We shouldn't have kept it a secret, but I wouldn't change anything." She glanced at the girls, now wide-eyed and looking more worried than before. "He's made mistakes, but he didn't do this. I can't let him take the fall for something he didn't do."

Jackie nodded and put her hand on her father's arm. "Right now, we need to stay focused on the main problem. We'll start with bail."

"I'll cover bail." Her father turned when he spoke, startling everyone into silence. He approached Danica and cupped her cheek. "What did I do to make my girls think they had to hide so much from me?"

She shook her head, eyes burning. "I didn't want to hurt or disappoint you. When he left, I was too embarrassed to tell anyone." She glanced at her sister. For the first time ever, she couldn't tell what Jackie was thinking.

Her father grunted. "There's a lot to talk about, but right now we need to get the girls home. I'll call Sonia. I'm sure she'll watch them so we can get him out."

"We're coming, too." Nikki looked at Adrian.

He nodded. "I'll take Mia home to George. We'll get Sammi and her horse, and be right behind you."

"Then let's meet at the house and make a plan. Does anyone know how much bail will be?"

"I'll call James." Danica held her phone up to her ear as they all climbed into the Suburban. She had told her family the truth, and they were still there. In the back seat, the twins were unusually quiet. Leaving a message for James, she turned to them. "Are you okay?"

They nodded, talking around each other at the same time. "Momma, why did they take Mr. Reid away? Did he do something to get in trouble again? Is Opa mad at us for being nice to him?"

Her whole world shrank, crushing her beneath a sudden pressure. She glanced at her father, his jaw clenching. She could barely speak, her voice shaky. "No, sweetheart. Of course not." She looked them both in the eye. "Reid isn't in trouble. It's just a mistake, and we are going to straighten it out."

Her father put the monster in Drive and weaved through the parking lot, people staring. She wasn't going to hide her husband any longer.

They were about to pull out of the fairgrounds when Cody Baxter, the foreman of the Hausman ranch, stopped them. She rolled down her window. "Do you need something, Cody?"

"One of my wranglers was just escorted out in handcuffs. You know what's going on?"

"He didn't do anything wrong. We're going now to bail him out and get this fixed."

He adjusted his hat. "Let me know what we can do to help. Wouldn't be the first good cowboy working for me that had a mix-up with the law."

"Thank you. I'm sure he'll be back to work as soon as we get him out." They nodded at each other, and he walked away.

Now she needed to tell the girls, but maybe that was something they'd do together. She just needed to get him out first.

* * *

Reid wasn't sure he heard correctly when they told him he'd made bail. "You have the wrong guy. I'm Reid McAllister."

They looked at him as if he was a little off, but ignored him and went through the process. He was being released. It didn't make any sense. Who would do that for him?

There hadn't been anyone to call. Maybe the guys he worked with at the ranch? Cowboys could be a close group, but he hadn't been there long enough to gain bail money loyalty.

Did he even have a job anymore? Employers definitely frown on drug dealers who steal money from a fund-raiser. That was just about the lowest.

There was Danica. She hadn't turned away from him at the time of the arrest, but she didn't have that kind of money or collateral to make bail. If she even would.

He swallowed back emotion, remembering how she'd argued with the police. No one had ever fought for him before.

Last time he'd been arrested, he just stayed in jail. When he got out, Ray was going to pick him up, but his wife had gone into early labor. So he couldn't blame the guy for that one. Being alone was nothing new.

That night he had walked past huge signs on the road, warning drivers they were close to a prison and shouldn't pick up hitchhikers. He hadn't really minded walking the miles to the bus stop that took him to Kerrville, though. For the first time in six years, there hadn't been a fence or someone telling him where to go.

Tonight, however, there were no buses. Maybe he

could call Pastor Levi, but it was too late. He glanced at his watch. Or too early.

Man, if he didn't have a job, he didn't have a place to live. He needed to let James know he was out at least. Opening the heavy door at the end of the hall, he looked up from the dull, worn tiles and froze.

Danica walked toward him, then paused. The ugly green chairs were filled with people he recognized. They all stood, surrounding her like a small army of family and friends.

They were smart enough to not allow her to come alone.

He glanced behind him. Maybe it was safer back there with the bars between him and her support team. Like an idiot, he didn't move. Not knowing what to do, he rammed his fists into the pockets of his Levi's jacket. Why was she here?

He must have stood there too long, because she started moving toward him again. Taking a step back, he glanced over her shoulder at the grim faces behind her. They couldn't be happy she was here. "What are you doing, Danica? Where are the girls?"

"They're at the house with Sonia. We're here to take you home, and make sure you never come back. Why would you let them arrest you?" Her eyes cut all the way to his core, down to the soft spots he hid from the world. How did he explain to her that she was purity and innocence to him? She needed to be protected at all costs. "I couldn't let them put you in handcuffs. I'd do anything to keep you safe." The ugliness of his world couldn't touch her. It was bad enough he was in her life.

Mr. Bergmann walked up to him and held out his

hand. Confused, Reid took it. The grip was firm. "Thank you, son."

Staring down at their hands, Reid couldn't quite get his thoughts lined up. *Son.* This couldn't be real.

Jackie stood on the other side of Danica. Clearing her throat, she crossed her arms and narrowed her eyes. "Someone wants the sanctuary to implode, and they set her up. You took the fall for her. For now, you're family. We need to get this figured out. So, what do we do now?"

Danica put her hand on his shoulder and looked into his eyes as if checking to see if he had a concussion. "I'm sure you need to eat." She looked at her crew. "We can go to that twenty-four-hour pancake place. There, we can make a game plan." Coming back to him, she paused. "Is that okay?"

The word *family* had stopped all brain function between his ears. He scanned the group. Nikki, Adrian, and Sammi, even Jackie and Mr. Bergmann were all here for him. Joaquin gave him a nod.

Not once in his life could he recall people being there for him. If he tried to utter a word, he might actually cry. He blinked and focused on Danica. Somehow, he managed a nod.

As the Bergmann herd turned and headed through the door, James greeted them. Reid's instinct was to run. He was out. Fresh air hit him as his boots stepped onto the sidewalk. Every fiber of his being rebelled at the thought of going back inside.

Breathe in, five...four...three...two...one. Breathe out.

James smiled. "Oh, good. You have a ride." He chuckled as he patted Adrian's shoulder. "More than one from the looks of it." He walked up to Reid and held out his hand. "Danica is convinced you had nothing to do with this and were just keeping her out of jail." He held his hand a little tighter when they shook and locked him in with eye contact. Then he nodded and backed up. "If you need anything, call me. Anytime."

Danica hugged him. "We will. Thank you, James."

He gave her a lopsided grin. "You should have told me I was asking a married woman out. I would have given up a lot sooner." With a tap to his cowboy hat, he left.

Married? They knew? They piled into the giant green Suburban. Danica opened the front passenger door for him. "Go ahead and ride up here with Daddy. I know how you feel about small spaces."

"They know we're married?"

"No more secrets. The girls are the only ones who don't know, but right now, we need to figure a way to keep you out of jail. We'll talk to them later. Go on, get in before Sammi calls shotgun."

"Okay. Later." The idea that she not only knew about his problem with crowded seating but that she also cared just about undid him. He didn't deserve her. It had to be some fluke that she'd agreed to marry him six years ago, and now they were in the same place again.

What's the plan, God? Because I'm in way over my head. I have nothing left. Maybe this was where God wanted him. Paul had done ministry from prison. It wasn't the life he wanted, but he feared it was the life God intended for him.

Driving down the old highway, Mr. Bergmann glanced over at him. "You haven't said a word. What are you thinking?"

Reid didn't want to even try to put his thoughts into words, but Mr. Bergmann had offered a truce and deserved his respect. "I've heard people say God doesn't give us more than we can handle." Facing forward, he watched the lines on the highway. "But I think we get more than we can handle all the time. The trick is learning to trust God for strength and—"

He had to swallow. A hard knot clogged his throat. He wasn't saying it right. "I need to learn to let others help me. It's hard to let people see you when you're—" he looked out the side window "—not in a place of strength. I don't deserve your help."

"My daughter thinks you do. You protected her." He reached up, pulled an index card from his visor and handed it to Reid. "With all the girls in my house, I started using my car for prayer time years ago. I keep a couple of verses here. It seems appropriate for both of us to remember."

Written across the top in pencil was the verse 2 Corinthians 12:10. The last line went straight to his heart. *For Christ; for whenever I am infirm, then I am powerful.*

He looked at the man sitting next to him. The man who'd raised the woman Reid loved. "Raising four daughters alone had to take a great deal of faith and strength."

Gray eyebrows went up as he looked in the rearview mirror. Women's voices talked over each other, filling the vehicle. He shook his head. "I should have used more faith. I built walls and tried to control things I couldn't control. I made huge mistakes, and my girls paid the price."

Danica leaned across the bench seat in front of her.
"Daddy, what are y'all talking about?"

"Daughters." Mr. Bergmann winked into the rear-view mirror.

She rolled her eyes. After Mr. Bergmann had parked
in front of the old corner drive, everyone climbed out.
Thankfully, the restaurant was empty. They scooted
into a large round corner booth, and orders were soon
placed.

The sisters spoke all at once. Reid couldn't keep up
with the threads of conversations. They only paused
when the drinks were sat on the table.

Adrian interjected, and they all went quiet. "None
of that will matter if we don't find out who actually set
Danica up. Who knew where all the drugs were kept
and was also at the rodeo? They took that money out
of the concession stand."

Silence settled over the group as they all turned in-
ward. Reid hated his gut instinct. Danica wasn't going
to like it. "I think we need to look at the lawyer, Stephanie. She has the most to gain if the sanctuary is closed."

Danica shook her head. "She doesn't want the land.
But it doesn't matter. She wasn't at the rodeo."

Adrian frowned. "Yes, she was. I had spoken to her
right before I left to join y'all in the stands. She told me
she was worried the committee was wasting money by
giving some of the earnings to Danica's rescue efforts.
I thought she was just being a lawyer and looking at
the negatives."

Playing with her straw, Danica kept her head down.
"I don't want to believe it, but even if it were true, how
would we even prove it?"

Everyone stopped talking as the smiling waitress

loaded their table with pancakes, bacon, eggs and hash browns. Joaquin was the first to grumble something. "If only we had enough money for a security system at the sanctuary. We'd be able to catch whoever stole those drugs."

Reid cut into the tall stack of syrup-drenched pancakes, then froze. "The bats!"

Everyone looked at him as if he'd lost the last bit of his brain, but Danica sat straight up, her eyes wide. "The camera you installed. You can see the locked cabinets."

"There should be a seventy-four-hour backup. We need to get to the hard drive."

Jackie pulled her phone out. "I'll call Vickie and see where Jake is. He can get the recordings and give it to the right people."

Samantha stood and waved down the waitress. "We need to-go boxes."

"I'll take care of the check." Mr. Bergmann moved to the register by the front door. "Tell Jake we'll be there in under an hour."

The trip was a blur. They all ate on the way, talking over each other. The Styrofoam box in his lap was empty, but he didn't remember eating a bite.

Jake's car, his parole officer's car and one he didn't recognize were parked in front of the bunkhouse.

Everyone climbed out and headed inside, but he found his body didn't want to move. Was it really going to be this easy? Nothing in his life ever worked out the way he wanted. His door opened.

Danica stood there. "What's wrong?" She took a step closer and placed her hand on his arm. "They aren't here to arrest you. We're going to find out who did this and the right person will go to jail."

"Why did you do this? Bailing me out. Trying to find out who really did it." Could she love him again?

"Because you didn't do this. I couldn't stand by and just let it happen. It's wrong, and it's my fault. They were after me, not you." She moved back, giving him room to get out.

Samantha stuck her head out of the door. "Are y'all coming? They're downloading the recordings."

When they finally walked in, the sheriff was on the phone. Two suits were at the computer. James came over and shook his hand. "There's been developments in the case."

His nerves knotted. Developments were never good when it came to him.

Danica stepped forward. "That was fast."

"It seems the stash found in your Jeep was connected to another case that is connected to Stephanie. A couple of people also called the sheriff's office today." He looked at Danica. "They didn't realize it until later, but they captured some photos with Stephanie around your car. One actually has her opening the back and putting a bag in it." He gave Reid a lopsided grin. "Seems everyone wants to make sure we know you're innocent, even though you confessed." He slapped Reid on the shoulder.

"So, you know he didn't do it?" Her gaze darted to her father, then back to James. "Once she's seen stealing the drugs, he'll be cleared, and everything will be dropped, right?"

"Basically, yeah."

"We got her," one of the suits called out. "We have to take this computer as evidence."

The sheriff joined them. "We have a warrant for her home and office already."

James reached over to place a hand on Danica's shoulder. "Sorry about Steph. I know you counted her as a friend. I didn't see this one coming, either. It's been a crazy day. Why don't y'all clear out and go home? Bobby's here. We'll make sure everything is locked up."

"Good idea." Mr. Bergmann pulled Danica into a hug before turning to leave.

Reid's feet didn't move. He was missing something. "It's over? I can go?"

"You're no longer a suspect. You're still on probation, so don't go all crazy on me, but yes, go home. Get back to work." He left to join the other officers.

Adrian slapped him on the back. "Congratulations. Seems kind of anticlimactic, but that's for the best."

Reid couldn't clear his head. Danica grabbed his arm and pulled him outside. He felt stuck in slow motion. They all climbed back into the Suburban like it was the end of a regular day on the ranch. He wasn't going to prison. He was still free.

The Bergmann sisters started talking at once again as they drove away. Mr. Bergmann eventually pulled into the drive of the family home. The family poured out of the Suburban, everyone except Danica. "Daddy, I'll take Reid home." She crawled out of the back seat. "Reid. You stay right there. I'm going to check on the girls, then I'll be back."

So, he wasn't invited inside. Mr. Bergmann didn't move from his seat, but Reid couldn't take his eyes off Danica as she walked away. The way she moved in the faint light of the early morning seared into his brain. The days were closing in on him. Soon, he would be back to only having memories of her.

At the side door, Danica stopped and looked back at the car. Was she going to invite him in to see the girls? He stopped breathing. His hand on the door handle, ready to open it with one word from her.

She started back to them. "Daddy? What are you doing?"

"You go on. Get inside. It's time Reid and I had a talk." He had rolled down his window.

"Daddy?" There was a warning at the edge of her voice.

"Go on in, Danica."

Reid wasn't sure he wanted a heart-to-heart with Danica's father, but he was right. It was past time.

Standing with hands on her hips, she looked like a warrior. With a shake of her head, she turned and disappeared inside the house.

"Everything worked out tonight, but it doesn't erase the last six years. What exactly are your plans?" The older man kept a tight grip on the steering wheel. His hard jaw popped as if each word he spoke painfully slipped through.

"First, you have to know I'm not the man I used to be. I think Danica saw the potential all those years ago, but I let her down." He took a deep breath. *Lord, give me the words.* "I know it sounds cheesy, but in some ways, prison was the best thing that ever happened to me. Through Ray and his ministry, I truly found the Lord."

"So, Danica should forget and forgive. You want her to take you back?"

Acid burned his gut. "No. But I did want to tell her face-to-face that I was wrong. I hadn't planned on working for her. I had no idea we had children. That sort of changed things for me. I know I don't deserve it, but I want to be their father, even if she no longer wants to be my wife."

With a nod, Mr. Bergmann finally turned to him. Eyes that looked so much like Danica's glared at him. "I haven't always been the best father, but I love my daughters. Anyone that hurts them is not welcome in my home."

"Yes, sir. I—"

"I'm not finished. Six years ago, she brought you home. I basically shut you out for no other reason than I didn't like your background."

"I under—" A sharp glare told Reid to stop talking.

"I was wrong then. I've prayed a great deal about my role as a father this last year. If I had been... I don't know, more open, it would have allowed both of you to talk to me. Better decisions could have been made. All I'm saying now is that I am here for my daughter. If she wants a divorce, then I will help her with that. If she wants you in her life, I will be here to support her and my granddaughters. If you stay, I do pray you are the man of God you claim to be. Their welfare is the most important thing to me. I will always be close. Do you understand?"

"Yes, sir."

"Now, what are your plans with my daughter and granddaughters?"

"I love them. I want a second chance, but that depends on Danica."

Thunder rumbled over the hills, and Mr. Bergmann looked out the open window. "Looks like we might get a morning storm. Those are rare."

Reid frowned. Was there a hidden message, or were they finished? Texans loved talking weather when they had nothing else to say.

Danica darted out of the house and approached, opening the driver's door. "Everything good?"

They both nodded but didn't say anything.

"Okay." She grinned. "Were any real words spoken, or was it just glares and grunts? Seems to be a language you both know."

Her father slipped out of the car and kissed her forehead. "Don't be such a smart-mouth."

She patted his cheek. "Better than being a dumb one. Since I seem to be without a car for now, can we take the green monster?"

"She's all yours." With a nod to Reid, he turned and left.

As the soft rain started tapping the top of the car, Danica climbed in and backed down the long drive. On the road, she glanced at him. "So, what did y'all talk about?"

He shrugged. "Daughters."

"Again?" She laughed. "That must be a loaded topic."

He sat back and enjoyed the sound of her joy. He closed his eyes, trying to memorize it for the days ahead. They settled into silence as the wipers created a rhythm with the rain that fell harder. They needed to talk about the future. He couldn't hang on the edge, not knowing, any longer.

"Reid."

"Danica."

Speaking at the same time, they now slipped back into silence.

He rubbed his forehead. "Sorry. You first."

"I was just going to thank you. You shouldn't have said anything. They didn't even consider you."

"The thought of handcuffs on your skin or the girls seeing you being arrested was… I couldn't let that happen." He shoved his hands in the pockets of his denim jacket. Anything to stop from reaching for her. The need to touch her consumed him at times. "Danica, I need you to make a decision about my role in the girls' lives. I don't think we can keep it from them much longer."

"I know. But I'm... There has been so much..."

He wanted to drop to his knees and beg her to let him stay, but this needed to be her decision. Calming his nerves, he gripped the Bible tucked into the inside of his jacket.

He took it out and opened the small book, pulling at the faded yellow ribbons. "I can't live on the edge anymore." He laid the strips of cloth on the console between them. "I told you about the song 'Tie a Yellow Ribbon Around the Old Oak Tree,' remember?"

"I do."

"I understand if you don't want me to be part of your life. The girls are thriving without me as their father." Fear of rejection was just his pride talking, not God. He had to put it aside. "I want you to know that I'll always love you. Doesn't matter if I'm in Clear Water or on the other side of the world, my heart will always be with you." Looking down, he ran his thumb over the worn silk ribbons. "I've written my number on these, so if the girls ever want to call me, I'll be there for them."

He swallowed back the acid that burned in the pit of his belly. "I need to know if I'm welcomed, so tie one to the gate if I can come home to you. If I don't see one, I'll keep driving." He kept his gaze down, not wanting to see her reaction. "No awkward goodbye."

"What if I need that awkward goodbye?"

"You mean for closure?" He was sick to his stomach. "Just call me anytime. I'll meet you wherever you want."

Silence filled the space. He wanted to press her, to hear her say she didn't need the ribbons. That he was welcomed. But she stared down the road, and he didn't ask.

Driving through the ranch, she stopped in front of his little bunkhouse. His roommates were sitting on the porch, watching the rain and drinking coffee. They stood and waved, stupid grins stretched across their faces.

"They actually look happy to see me."

"Why wouldn't they?"

He looked at her. "Most people don't like having a housemate that just got out of prison."

"I've found that cowboys for the most part are a pretty loyal group. Once they count you as a friend nothing is going to change that. Plus, they know you didn't steal the drugs from the sanctuary. The foreman even offered to help. He told me to make sure you got back to work as soon as possible."

He looked out the window at Philip and Wade. "They're smiling like idiots."

"They probably know we're married. I'm not keeping it a secret any longer."

His focus jerked back to her. "Everyone knows? Not just your family? What if we get divorced?"

"Then we get divorced. I'm done with secrets." She shrugged as if holding his whole world in her hands was no big deal. To be fair, she didn't know he was giving her full control. He wanted her to come to him because she wanted to, not out of guilt or obligation.

Reluctantly, he went for the door handle. Words swirled in his brain, but he didn't know which ones to use, or how to put them together.

He wanted to be her hero. But he was a McAllister. Not hero material. "I better be going. The sun will be up soon, and we need to be out feeding."

He wanted to hit his head against the window. He was so lame.

"You need to get some sleep."

He grinned. "Don't think a night in jail is a good excuse to miss work."

"You're too hard on yourself." She glanced at the ribbons in her hand as if they held some great knowledge. Looking up, her eyes pulled him back from the opened door.

He had to say something, or he'd regret it forever. "I'll never be the man you deserve, but no one will ever love you more than I do. No matter what you decide, you will always have my heart."

Without waiting, he turned and launched himself out of the Suburban. In a couple of long strides, he was on the porch. He didn't look back until he heard the big green monster crush the gravel under its tires. Once it was safe, he turned to watch his Dani girl leave.

She paused at the first gate. His phone vibrated.

"Oh, he's already getting a honey-do list." Philip and Wade laughed like they had made the funniest joke, instead of some old lame one.

Thinking the text was from his parole officer, he looked down. It was from her.

His gaze darted to the back of her car. The brake lights turned off, and she vanished into the early-morning rain.

His heart raced as he touched her name. Her text read, Read Jeremiah 31:3 out loud three times. He frowned and pulled out the Bible tucked in his jacket.

"So, are we going to be breaking in a new wrangler, or is everything good?"

Unable to really focus on Wade's voice, he shook his head to process what they had asked him.

"I think he needs coffee." Philip smirked.

He wanted privacy to read the passage she'd sent

him. "It's all good. They found the person responsible." He didn't want to be standing here, talking about nothing. "I'm going to get some coffee."

They both laughed. He didn't care. As soon as he stepped into the small living space, he opened his Bible to Jeremiah. "'Yes, I have loved you with an everlasting love. Therefore, with loving kindness, I have drawn you.'"

He read it out loud again. With one hand, he poured a cup of coffee. Spilling some, he brought his hand to his mouth and licked it off. Sipping the black liquid, he read the verse again.

Something shifted inside him as he repeated the words. God made him and loved him with an everlasting love. He sat in a chair at the old table. No matter what, God loved him.

Despite what his father or mother had done, even despite what he'd done, God wanted him in all his wretchedness and sin. Vile and disgusting, he still had a Father who was willing to wash the filth off him with His own two hands. Reid was only lost, not forgotten. He buried his face in his hands. He fought back the emotions that overwhelmed his body, but he knew without a doubt that God loved him.

Later today, he would find out once and for all if he still had Danica's love, as well.

Danica picked up one of the ribbons and rubbed her thumb over it. At their daughters' age, Reid had already been left alone in the world.

He didn't know it, but what he was asking for was a family. A home to call his own. A place to belong.

Tears fell. She needed to make a decision, and she might not be able to trust her heart.

Dear God, I love him so much. I want to give him that home and family. But is this Your plan for me? Has it always been Your plan for us, or am I trying to control things again?

Sitting in the driveway, she pressed her head against the steering wheel and prayed. The screen door opened and Jackie stepped out into the rain. Nikki followed her. Her twin walked to the car with a pink-and-white umbrella. Nikki just pulled her jacket over her head and ran for the Suburban. The wind pushed rain in when they climbed into the back seat.

Jackie shook out the umbrella and tucked it under her feet. "I can't believe you chose today to sit out in the car."

"Um… I didn't ask you to join me, and I thought you would both have gone to your own homes by now."

"After everything that happened today? You're joking, right?" Jackie, her straightforward no-emotions-needed sister, had tears in her eyes. "You're married, and you never said anything." She blinked and bit her lips, as if that would stop any unpleasant reaction. "I thought we told each other everything."

All the sisters went quiet, one of the few times in their lives when they had nothing immediate to say.

"I'm sorry." Danica reached out and took her sister's hand. "I was so embarrassed. It was impulsive. When we went back to school, I was so mad at everyone for not giving Reid a chance, then I thought I'd find a way to tell you over the summer. But…well, you know what happened next. He disappeared on me. I was humiliated and ashamed. Instead of trusting you or God, I hid."

Nikki leaned forward. "I wish I had been here for you. Maybe if I had been honest about my pregnancy, instead of hiding, you would have felt safe enough to tell us everything."

Jackie put her hand on top of Danica's and Nikki's. "No more secrets. Agreed? We are a solid wall of love."

"Agreed," they all said in unison.

The screen door opened and Sammi stuck her head out.

Jackie sighed. "Looks like little sister found us."

"Were we hiding from her?" Nikki opened her door and waved her over.

"No, I just think of her as the little sister. We really need to start inviting her to these meetings."

Climbing into the front seat, Sammi shook the water off. "I've given up waiting for an invitation." Her tone brisk, she looked at her older sisters. "So, have we decided what Danica is going to do about her husband?"

Jackie and Nikki giggled like girls. Then Nikki rubbed Sammi's arm. "First, we're glad you joined us. Second, that's what we're trying to find out."

They all looked at her. Her sisters. Her best friends.

She shrugged. "I don't know. I loved him so much, but that doesn't mean Reid should be in my life. Six years ago, one impulsive act set all this in motion. I don't know if I can trust my own judgment."

Nikki sat back. "I can understand that. I was so afraid of my love for Adrian, I almost lost him."

Jackie grunted, sounding just like their dad. The other sisters grinned as they looked at each other. "What?"

"You sound just like dad when he doesn't want to talk about something." Danica winked at her.

Sammi nodded. "Yeah. Like Sonia. I know they're dating, but he won't admit it."

Jackie threw a hand in the air. "Don't get me started on that relationship." She sighed. "But going back to

Nikki and Adrian. You can't compare the two men. Adrian was born with an oversize dose of responsibility. He's a solid guy that would never run. Reid is more like Nikki. Adrian loved her, despite her being a flight risk."

"Thanks." Nikki glared.

"Well, it's true. I'm just saying, people can change. A flight risk can settle down." She smiled at Nikki.

Sammi nodded. "Reid has worked so hard since he's been here. I like him. Plus, if you have a parent who wants to be part of their children's lives, you should let them. It's the right thing to do."

Danica's heart broke a little for her baby sister. Her mother had left before Sammi even started school. Then she would return for short periods, playing hide-and-seek in her only child's life. Most of the time it was hiding. "You're right."

"You love him?" Sammi whispered the words.

"Yes. It's hard to believe, but I do now more than I did six years ago."

Nikki leaned closer and reached for her hand. "He seems to love you."

"He says he does." She picked up the ribbons and told them the story of him waiting for his own father to come get him. "Tonight, he said he would stay away if that's what I wanted." She bit her bottom lip to regain some sort of control. "Then he told me his heart would always be mine. No matter what happened between us, he would always love me."

Tears spilled over. She loved him so much, and no one else made her feel as loved as he did.

Jackie put her hand over Danica's. "Do you have any doubt where you belong?"

She shook her head.

Sammi's hand went over Jackie's. "So, you already know what you want."

Nikki joined in. "How can we help?"

Chapter Fifteen

The old ranch truck moved about ten miles under the speed limit as Reid hugged the edge of the curves, driving up and down the hills. The hills that he hoped took him home. Had he made a mistake giving Danica the ultimatum? Tapping the brakes, he slowed the truck again and pulled to the uneven shoulder.

The Bible Ray had given him in prison lay on the empty seat next to him. He wrapped his fingers around the warm leather.

"God, we know I'm not worthy of her, but I can't imagine a life without her. Please hold me as I drive past her place. Let me honor my promise to her to keep going if that's what she wants."

Fear made him sick to his stomach. He promised her that he'd keep driving if she didn't want him. He'd never call or visit again. He'd make it as if he'd never existed if that was what she thought she and the girls needed.

Now, as he sat on the side of the road, he had to find the strength to walk away from the only life he'd dreamed of since meeting her.

The hope of Danica would be lost to him forever. To

never see her or his daughters again, to not exist in their world, it would be the most painful life.

Cold sweat sent chills along his neck and down his spine. The sun sat right on top of the hills and slowly climbed into the sky. He lowered his head and prayed. He prayed with every ounce of his being. If he could have laid out flat on the road and turned everything over to God, he would have.

He'd stalled long enough. It was time to rip the bandage from the wound.

Hand over hand, he turned the truck back onto the old ranch road. A big green Suburban came at him. The driver honked, and an SUV full of females waved. It was the Bergmann clan. He glanced at the rearview mirror once they passed. Had Danica been in there? Where were his twins?

Was that his answer from Danica? He swallowed. Had they taken her away in case he didn't keep driving? Taken her away from him?

His knuckles turned white, strangling the steering wheel. But when he saw the first yellow ribbon, his boot slipped off the gas. Pressure built in his chest. A few posts down, another yellow ribbon was tangled in the barbed wire, fluttering in the breeze left behind by the storm.

The big heavy tires dropped another ten miles per hour. Crawling along the road to the sanctuary's entryway, Reid stared down the long line of cedar fencing. Yellow bows were wrapped around each rough gray post in the sunshine. At the stone-and-iron gate, huge yellow streamers intertwined with the arch of letters that spelled out the original ranch name.

He stopped the beat-up, worn-out truck as the dented grill crossed the cattle guard. The scene in front of him became watery as his eyes stung. She wanted him. She wanted them to be a family.

Voices from the past, his father, his brothers, his prison guards, commanded him to leave. They told him he wasn't good enough. He wasn't made for this life. He didn't have the right to be part of a good family. He would never be the man they needed.

Heavy chains encased his rib cage, pulling tighter until his breath gave up the fight to get to the surface. He inched down the drive. God's voice was stronger than all the other voices combined.

He passed the old bunkhouse where he had first seen her. Where the baby bats slept.

The yellow ribbons led him down a path to the old ranch house he'd helped restore. His dream stood on the porch. His vision blurred. Blinking, he needed to make sure what he saw was real.

Danica's hair was pulled back in a yellow headband. Her curls brushed her bare shoulders. The yellow sundress fluttered at her knees.

The twins jumped in place and waved. Smiling at him, as if excited he had arrived from a long journey home. Wide yellow sashes were boldly tied around their middles over soft purple dresses.

The pressure from the chains pulled tighter. Reid's hand went to the gears, and he put the truck in Park. Ice crawled along his veins, freezing his muscles. Was he dreaming? Danica turned to the girls and spoke with them. His gaze stayed glued to her as she slowly moved down the steps and started walking toward him. Was it a trick? Was she still mad at him, and this was her revenge?

"Reid?" She paused halfway down the drive. "Are you okay?"

Cutting the engine, he sat in complete silence. The voices from his past faded. He took one deep breath and tore away the chains that held him in place. God was on his side and would not allow his past to hold him prisoner any longer. Opening the truck door, he watched as she took another step toward him.

Each step that brought her closer was cautious. She tilted her head. "Reid?"

His gut tightened. Was she really trusting him with her heart? With their daughters?

Boots to the ground, he stood next to the truck. The giant pecan tree that shaded the house was covered with long yellow ribbons dancing in the breeze. Even the porch was covered in yellow. Then he realized he'd painted her home a soft yellow with white trim. He had been asking her to invite him in from the very beginning.

She stood halfway down the drive, concern in her eyes. A golden-red curl crossed her face. With a graceful movement, her long fingers pushed it back, getting it under control.

He took a deep breath. "Are you sure?"

He moved one foot forward, then the ice returned. If she changed her mind, he'd shatter. "Danica, if I go up those steps and walk over that threshold, there will be no going back. I'm never leaving."

A soft smile and a gentle love filled her face. "I'm counting on that."

The last of the chains shattered. He charged forward until she was in his arms. He lifted her up, loving the feel of her as she wrapped her arms around him. She fit against him in the most perfect way. "I'm staying with you forever until God takes me away." Her hands moved up his arms to his face. Soft hands cupped his rough jawline. Now he wished he had taken the time to clean up. "I'm sorry. I should have shaved before I came over."

Leaning closer, she looked straight into his eyes. "You're perfect the way you are." Her lashes lowered, and she pressed her lips against his.

His body melted into her warmth. He was hers. He had always been hers, but now she claimed him. Setting her down and cupping her hands, he pulled back an inch. "I never imagined someone like you could love me."

"Momma!"

"Can we come off the porch now?"

He stepped back. "Do they know?"

She grinned at him. "Maybe. I asked if they thought you'd be a good father for them."

His heart launched out of his rib cage. Swallowing it back down, he glanced over her shoulder to the porch. "What did they say?" The gravel in his throat made it hard to get the words out.

She laughed. "They said they'd been praying that you'd be their father." She took his hand and pulled him toward their girls. "Come on. Let's introduce you to your daughters."

His fingers squeezed hers. His boots hit the steps with a solid thump. They rushed him, their small bodies almost knocking him backward.

Love was a powerful thing. Tangible in his arms. *Thank You, God.*

He closed his eyes and used all his senses to absorb this perfect moment. Danica's hand pressed against his back. The girls' arms tightened around him as they hugged him close.

He was home.

Epilogue

Reid stood on the top step of the restored ranch house. It was finally happening. The old pecan tree shaded the guests sitting on the front yard. The sun was shining, and the air was crisp. A perfect February day in Texas.

Hanging from the tree, long yellow-and-white ribbons danced in the wind with tiny paper hearts tied to the ends. Large white spheres that radiated with light were scattered among the hearts and lined the porch.

They were all waiting. Over three hundred people stared at him, but he didn't notice.

Pastor Levi leaned over. "You need to breathe. You don't want to steal her moment by passing out. I've seen it happen."

As best man, Adrian was on his left. "They aren't even late yet. So, relax. I guarantee you, they aren't letting you get away this time."

On the lower steps, Bobby and Philip chuckled. Reid pulled at his collar. He had never worn a tie in his life.

Derrick, one of the teens from church, sat on the far end of the porch and strummed on a guitar. Then the music changed. Lifting his head, Reid stopped breathing.

They were here. A small herd of women gathered at the new archway that stood at the front of the yard. Samantha opened the wooden gate and marched toward them with the biggest grin on her face. For the first time since he'd known her, she was wearing a dress. They'd joked with her about being one of the grooms- men instead just so she could wear jeans. She did win the battle over shoes, proudly striding forward in her cowboy boots. As she moved to the side, she winked at him. Next was Nikki, followed by Jackie.

His daughters danced through the gate next, waving to people as they threw yellow petals on the ground. When they saw him, they yelled and ran to him. Going down, he opened his arms and pulled them close.

Jackie tried to get their attention. There was some soft laughter from the yard. He was sure they'd broken protocol. But he didn't care. Today, they would become an official family in front of God, the Bergmanns and the whole community of Clear Water.

"We're all getting married today, Daddy."

"Do you like our dresses? Momma said they were a birthday surprise."

"You're beautiful." To be honest, if asked, he prob- ably couldn't tell anyone what they were wearing, but it didn't matter. His daughters loved him.

Little white flowers were pinned in their red curls. "Happy Birthday," he whispered as he kissed each of them on their forehead before sending them over to their aunts.

He couldn't imagine a better way to celebrate this day than showing them how much he loved their mother. The music changed again. Under the wooden arch, standing on this side of the gate, was his bride. His. Bride.

The world disappeared and he lost contact with his own body. Danica was stunning. Tall and elegant, she seemed to be floating toward him. Her hair was pulled up with those same little white flowers, and a yellow ribbon. Long curls fell down her graceful neck.

The February breeze played with her hair. She looked straight at him. A secret smile curved her lips. She was his. And in front of all these people, he would get to stand next to her in holy union. This amazing woman was his. Even more stunning? He was hers.

He clenched his fists and took a deep breath. His dream was within reach. If he went down the two steps, he could hold her and make sure this was real, but he waited. She finally reached him and stopped.

"Who gives this woman to this man?"

"I do, her father. And in memory of her mother." *Aww*'s could be heard throughout the yard.

"Us too! Us too!" The twins jumped up and down, causing light laughter. The last of their flowers were scattered.

This was happening. He glanced at Mr. Bergmann. The older man nodded and laid Danica's hand in Reid's palm, stepping back.

Jackie moved forward to take the bouquet. She narrowed her eyes at him. "Cowboy, don't embarrass yourself in front of the whole town." Her voice was hoarse like she'd been crying.

Oh, man, his eyes were leaking. He gritted his teeth and took Danica's hands in both of his. She anchored him. He focused on their point of contact. Her hands were so much smaller than his, but they were strong hands, graceful and pale with light freckles scattered over her skin.

Pastor Levi cleared his throat. "We have gathered here today to celebrate and renew the vows of a marriage that took place six years ago. Today, before God and family, Reid McAllister and Danica Bergmann McAllister..."

McAllister. Danica had taken his name. He didn't hear anything else the pastor said. At that moment, his world was made up of one woman. His bride. His wife. The mother of his children. His Dani girl.

God had given him gifts greater than anything he could have ever imagined for himself.

Adrian nudged him, and he realized they were exchanging rings. His hand shook as he slipped the simple gold band on her finger. She recited her vows and placed a ring on his.

Claiming him in front of the respectable people of Clear Water, and God.

"You may now—"

Just like his daughters, he couldn't hold back any longer, he needed her in his arms. He grabbed Danica, lifting her off the ground.

Before the pastor could get the whole sentence out, he was kissing her. Laughing, she threw her arms around him and kissed him back.

The girls joined them, hugging their legs. He picked Lizzy up and settled her on his left hip, gripping Danica's hand in his right one. Suzie held her mother's hand as they walked back to the archway as a family. His family.

Lizzy kissed him on the cheek, her arms around his neck. "This is the best birthday party ever!"

He had to laugh, then saw years of extravagant birth-day parties ahead of them. Danica leaned in closer to him. "We might have set the expectations a little too high."

He didn't care. Whatever kept his girls happy.

"Happy Valentine's Day to my one true love," she said. "You've always had my heart. I'm so glad you brought it home."

"You are my home, Dani girl. My bride, Mrs. McAllister. My name never sounded so good."

Home. She was his home. A special place God had made just for him.

The twins ran ahead to join the bridal party.

The yellow ribbons danced around them. He leaned in close to her ear. "You are my heartbeat, baby. Never forget that."

Her fingers cupped her jaw. "I never did, Reid." With a soft touch of her lips to his, she whispered, "Welcome home, love. Welcome home."

* * * * *

WE HOPE YOU ENJOYED
THIS BOOK FROM

LOVE INSPIRED
INSPIRATIONAL ROMANCE

Uplifting stories of faith, forgiveness and hope.

Fall in love with stories where faith helps
guide you through life's challenges, and discover
the promise of a new beginning.

6 NEW BOOKS AVAILABLE EVERY MONTH!

SPECIAL EXCERPT FROM

Love Inspired

Could this bad-boy newcomer spell trouble for an Amish spinster...or be the answer to her prayers?

Read on for a sneak preview of
An Unlikely Amish Match,
the next book in Vannetta Chapman's miniseries
Indiana Amish Brides.

The sun was low in the western sky by the time Micah Fisher hitched a ride to the edge of town. The driver let him out at a dirt road that led to several Amish farms. He'd never been to visit his grandparents in Indiana before. They always came to Maine. But he had no trouble finding their place.

As he drew close to the lane that led to the farmhouse, he noticed a young woman standing by the mailbox. A little girl was holding her hand and another was hopping up and down. They were all staring at him.

"Howdy," he said.

The woman only nodded, but the two girls whispered, "Hello."

"Can we help you?" the woman asked. "Are you...lost?"

"*Nein.* At least I don't think I am."

"You must be if you're here. This is the end of the road."

Micah pointed to the farm next door. "Abigail and John Fisher live there?"

"They do."

"Then I'm not lost." He snatched off his baseball cap, rubbed the top of his head and then yanked the cap back on.

Micah stepped forward and held out his hand. "I'm Micah—Micah Fisher. Pleased to meet you."

"You're not *Englisch*?"

"Of course I'm not."

"So you're Amish?" She stared pointedly at his clothing—tennis shoes, blue jeans, T-shirt and baseball cap. Pretty much what he wore every day.

"I'm as Plain and simple as they come."

"I somehow doubt that."

"Since we're going to be neighbors, I suppose I should know your name."

"Neighbors?"

"*Ja.* I've come to live with my *daddi* and *mammi*—at least for a few months. My parents think it will straighten me out." He peered down the lane. "I thought the bishop lived next door."

"He does."

"Oh. You're the bishop's *doschder*?"

"We all are," the little girl with freckles cried. "I'm Sharon and that's Shiloh and that is Susannah."

"Nice to meet you, Sharon and Shiloh and Susannah."

Sharon lost interest and squatted to pick up some of the rocks. Shiloh hid behind her *schweschder*'s skirt, and Susannah scowled at him.

"I knew the bishop lived next door, but no one told me he had such pretty *doschdern*."

Susannah's eyes widened even more, but it was Shiloh who said, "He just called you pretty."

"Actually I called you all pretty."

Shiloh ducked back behind Susannah.

Susannah narrowed her eyes as if she was squinting into the sun, only she wasn't. "Do you talk to every girl you meet that way?"

"Not all of them—no."

Don't miss
An Unlikely Amish Match *by Vannetta Chapman,*
available February 2020 wherever
Love Inspired® books and ebooks are sold.

LoveInspired.com